Dorothy on the Rocks

H Aria

Dorothy on the Rocks

a novel by

BARBARA SUTER

ALGONQUIN BOOKS OF CHAPEL HILL   2008

Published by
Algonquin Books of Chapel Hill
Post Office Box 2225
Chapel Hill, North Carolina 27515-2225

a division of
Workman Publishing
225 Varick Street
New York, New York 10014

This is a work of fiction. While, as in all fiction, the literary perceptions and insights are based on experience, all names, characters, places, and incidents either are products of the author's imagination or are used fictitiously.

Library of Congress Cataloging-in-Publication Data
Suter, Barbara.
    Dorothy on the rocks: a novel / by Barbara Suter. — 1st ed.
      p. cm.
    1. Middle-aged women — Fiction.   2. Actress — Fiction.   3. Women
alcoholics — Fiction.   4. Baum, L. Frank (Lyman Frank), 1856 – 1919 —
Dramatic production — Fiction.   I. Title.
    PS3619.U875D67 2008
    813'.6 — dc22   2008008621

10 9 8 7 6 5 4 3 2 1
First Edition

In Memory
Jeffrey Roy

"They carried the sleeping girl to a pretty spot beside the river, far enough from the poppy field to prevent her breathing any more of the poison of the flowers . . ."

—L. Frank Baum, THE WIZARD OF OZ

1

The phone rings once, twice. I open my eyes. Morning sun slaps me full in the face. Damn. I pull the sheet over my head and the answering machine picks up.

"Hi, honey," a familiar voice says, "we're on the corner at Broadway and Ninety-sixth, waiting for you. Hope you're on the way." I sit up and squint at the clock. My left eye twitches and my head begins to throb. Shit. The voice belongs to Dee-Honey Vanderbilt. She produces the Little Britches Children's Theater. She's over eighty years old and although no one knows for sure, rumor has it she served with Florence Nightingale in the Crimean War.

"Maggie, dear, are you there?"

I reach for the phone.

"Hi, Dee, what's up?" I say.

"We're waiting for you. We have a *Wizard* in Connecticut. Did you forget? I'm sure you confirmed with me."

"Oh no, what time is it?" I ask.

"It's eight o'clock. We're waiting for you."

"Uh, I was sick. I was going to call you—food poisoning—had some bad tuna," I say, lying neatly through my teeth. Truth is I had totally (and perhaps wishfully) forgotten I am supposed to play Dorothy this morning.

"Do you think you can be here in ten minutes? We want to miss the traffic."

"I don't know, Dee. My stomach is still queasy."

"We'll get you some Pepto-Bismol. Fix you right up. The kids love you as Dorothy, Mags honey, and we can't disappoint them. We'll drive down to Eighty-seventh. Meet you right on your corner." Then she hangs up. Damn and double damn. My cat, Bixby, peers up from his nest at the foot of the bed. He gives me a knowing look.

I definitely need coffee. As I throw my feet over the side of the bed I hear someone in the bathroom and then a flush. My God. Someone has broken into my apartment and is using the toilet! Seconds later a tall handsome young man walks into my bedroom.

"Mornin', Maggie Mae," the handsome young man says with a grin.

My head starts to pound louder than the tympani section in the second act of *Das Rheingold*—the result of shock smacking butt up against big hangover. I force a smile because by now I'm pretty sure he's not a burglar. Mr. Handsome is barefoot, bare-chested, and holding a pair of Nikes. He sits on the side of the bed and puts on the left shoe then the right. He finds his shirt in a pile of clothes in the center of the floor; I can't help but notice my black lace Victoria's Secret push-up bra in the mix. I pull the bedsheet up to my chin and keep smiling and try to quickly reconstruct the night before. I went to the Angry Squire Bar on Twenty-sixth Street and started off slow with a couple of beers. Then someone played Janis Joplin's "Get It While You Can" on the jukebox, and

I switched to scotch. Apparently I got Mr. Handsome and he got me. Thanks, Janis.

"Mornin' to you too," I say trying to remember his name, but nothing comes to mind. Then, remembering Dee, I say, "I've got to play Dorothy in *The Wizard of Oz* today. I forgot all about it."

"Is that the dog?" he asks, pulling on his shirt

"The dog? No. The dog is Toto. Dorothy is the girl. You know, Judy Garland in the movie?"

"I've never seen it."

"Never seen it?" I ask incredulously. "You've never seen *The Wizard of Oz*? I can't believe there is a person left on the face of the earth that hasn't seen *The Wizard of Oz*."

"Well," he grins, "you're looking at him."

"Where are you from, Mars?" I ask.

"No," he says, buttoning his shirt, "Queens."

"Oh," I say, still smiling.

"Look, I've got to run," Mr. Handsome says. "I have an appointment downtown. It was great meeting you." He leans in and nuzzles my neck.

"You too." I nuzzle him back.

"I'll call you," he says over his shoulder as he makes his exit.

"Sure," I say. And he is gone—out the front door and gone. What was that? I wonder. I shake my head a few times to make sure I'm awake and not dreaming.

The phone rings. It's Dee.

"How's it going? We got the Pepto-Bismol."

"I'm on my way. Can someone get me a coffee at the deli?"

"Okay, but hurry, honey, we're running late and traffic on the Major Deegan is going to be awful this morning. It's already backed up."

"This is a nightmare, Bix," I say to the cat, going to the kitchen and putting out his food. "I hate playing Dorothy. That damn pinafore is too small, the zipper is broken, and gingham makes me look fat." Bixby rubs my leg. He doesn't care if I look fat; he doesn't care about anything as long as I feed him. I get my back-pack, throw in my makeup and my pigtail wig, and shift into high must-get-to-Oz mode.

I emerge from my apartment building to find Dee and the cast waiting on the corner at the end of the block. Randall Kent is leaning against the van, holding a large coffee. He's been out of town for the past few months doing Henry Higgins in *My Fair Lady* at Virginia Stage. He works constantly. He's what they call, in the biz, a triple threat. He sings, he dances, and he acts, all with considerable relish and plenty of ham. His motto: More is better. I met him at a small theater in Wisconsin. I was an ap-prentice and he was the leading man in every show that summer, including playing Tevye in *Fiddler on the Roof* and Don Quixote in *Man of La Mancha*. I called him Mr. Kent, and when I moved to New York, he got me a job with Dee-Honey. That was almost twenty years ago.

"Mags, my dear," Randall declares in his booming actor voice, "how are you?"

"All right," I say. "Good to see you."

Randall hands me the coffee. "For the little princess, from your loyal servant," he says with a bow.

"Thanks, I'll remember this when your clemency hearing comes up," I say.

Dee-Honey sticks her head out the window of the van. "Let's get going. The radio says the traffic's getting heavy."

"And mornin' to you, Dee," I say, taking my first sip of coffee. The caffeine immediately shoots through my system, and the majority of my molecules snap to attention. The rest turn over and go back to sleep.

"And how was the show?" I ask Randall as we climb into the van and get settled.

"Well the show was fabulous," Randall says. "I was telling Dee that the girl playing Eliza was wonderful. She's just out of Juilliard. A lovely voice but needed help with the humor. You've got to find it or it's dull—dull, dull, and duller. And Dylan Ross was playing Pickering. Do you know him, Mags?"

"Doesn't ring a bell." I'm sitting in the backseat next to Pauline Letts, who plays Glenda, the Good Witch of the North, in our little production and also doubles as Auntie Em. She's seventy-three, originally from Georgia, and has been playing the Good Witch for the better part of forty years.

"Pauline, didn't you work with him? At Utah Shakespeare?" Randall asks.

"Oh, yes, he was Polonius when I did Gertrude. Does he still have those nasty dogs? What were they, schnauzers? They were awful. They used to pee in my wig box."

"Maggie, honey, how are you feeling?" Dee chirps from the driver's seat.

"Better, I think," I say.

"What's the matter, Maggie? Late night, dear?" Eddie Houser asks from the far backseat. He plays the flying monkey and doubles as the munchkin. Eddie, now sixty-five, started with the company when his hair was black and his teeth were mostly his own. He is drinking coffee spiked with bourbon out of his Superman thermos.

We all know there is bourbon in the thermos. Dee-Honey doesn't say anything, she just doesn't let him drive anymore.

"Careful when you're spinning on that cellar door. That could really make the old tummy flip," he says with a nasty chuckle.

"Thank goodness you were able to make it, Maggie," Dee says. "I might have had to put a wig on Frank and sent him on."

To Dee, the phrase "the show must go on" isn't just a catchy saying, it's the eleventh commandment, carved in stone and delivered down from the Austrian Alps in *The Sound of Music* by Thespis, the Greek father of actors. Last month I saw her squeeze into the crocodile costume for Peter Pan and crawl on all fours across the stage because Scott Lovelady came down with the flu.

"Anyone have some aspirin?" I ask.

Randall rummages through his bag and hands me an economy size bottle of Tylenol.

"And here's the Pepto-Bismol," he says.

"Thanks," I say, popping two pills and swigging some Bismol.

Dee-Honey does a head count. All the players are present and accounted for, so off we go. I tell myself it's not going to be so bad. The only thing I have to remember as Dorothy is to hang on to the dog and try to get home.

We arrive at the theater ten minutes before curtain. I find Dorothy's costume; white puffy-sleeved blouse, the dreaded blue gingham pinafore, and a white crinoline. I start to squeeze in. The costume is too small and the zipper is still broken from last time I did the part. Pauline is right by my side with a box of safety pins.

"Pull that tummy in, Mags," she says,

NOTE TO SELF . . .

If the costume doesn't fit, suck in your stomach and don't turn sideways.

coaxing the sides together with the help of the pins. The blouse fits, but the pinafore is hopeless.

"Don't turn sideways and you'll be fine," Pauline says as she scurries off, muttering something about false eyelashes. My head pounds in spite of the aspirin, and now random light flickers on the periphery of my vision. I ask Randall about it.

"I don't know," he says, "sounds like the onset of a heart attack or possibly a stroke."

Frank, our trusty stage manager who almost had to double as Dorothy, calls five minutes.

"Feeling all right, Mags?" he asks.

"A little better, and lucky for you I do. Dee said she would have put a wig on you and made you play Dorothy," I say.

"And she would have. Forget that I'm sixty and have a mustache," he says. "Come on, let's do the door thing and make sure it's working."

I follow Frank backstage and we practice spinning the mechanical cellar door, with Frank pulling the cord that turns the wheel and me perched on top. Frank moans and the door turns slightly and Frank moans again.

"Save your energy for the show," I say.

"Sorry, Mags, but have you put on a few pounds?"

"Frank, we've all put on a few pounds."

"Yeah but it's only you I have to spin," Frank grumbles as he totters off to set the rest of the props.

"I heard that," I say.

"Let's do this," Frank announces. "Those kids are getting restless. Places, everybody." The cast assembles in the wings. I find the stuffed dog that plays Toto and stand stage right. The music starts and Randall squeezes my arm.

"Break a leg, kid," he whispers.

The curtain opens. I run onstage clutching the little dog and say, "Oh Toto, Toto, what are we going to do?"

I hear a tiny voice in the first row say, "Mommy, I thought Dorothy was a little girl, not a big lady."

I glare out into the audience. Silence. Followed by more silence. I can't remember the next line. Frank whispers something from the wings but I can't understand him.

Then Dee-Honey comes onstage as Miss Gulch. I squeal and run upstage and hide behind the curtain. Lights flash and Frank makes tornado sounds in the offstage microphone. Randall and Eddie chime in with cow moos and chicken clucks. Pauline darts across stage yelling, "Get those animals in the barn. There's a twister coming." The lights continue to flash. Pauline disappears stage left and the cellar door is pushed on down right.

"Oh Toto, oh Toto," I cry and then climb on the cellar door. Frank pulls the rope. It doesn't budge. "Oh Toto, oh Toto," I cry again. I shake the dog up and down and circle my head as if lashed by the wind. Frank groans as he tries the rope again. I reach over and brace my hands on the floor and try to propel myself around.

"She's too big." It's that kid in the front row again. "She's not a little girl. I want to go home." The child bursts into tears and thankfully the lights go to black. Frank shoves the dead witch's feet onstage, pulls the back curtain across the traveler. I get up off the cellar door. Lights up and Eddie staggers out as the munch-kin, "W-w-wel-l-lcome to Mm-m-un-s-s-ch-kin-n-nland," he slurs as Pauline sweeps onstage as Glenda the Good Witch in her long pink chiffon dress with hoopskirt and sequin trim, her magic wand shimmering with glitter. The kid in the front row stops crying and leans forward, suddenly entranced.

"I'm Glenda, the Good Witch of the North," Pauline says in her honey-buttered southern accent, and in spite of the irony, the show is finally rolling.

When Randall Kent, playing the Wizard, sends me back to Kansas, I start to cry my actress tears, because I don't want to leave the wonderful land of Oz, but the Wizard assures me he can get me back once a year for a visit. Pauline touches me with her wand and the lights flash. I click my heels and twirl round and round and end up on the cellar door again, back home in Kansas—and realize my actress tears are mixed with real tears because back here in this world I can't remember the name of the man I spent the night with, I'm wearing a gingham pinafore that doesn't fit, and I'm being heckled by a six-year-old. Who wouldn't rather stay in Oz?

"Good show," Eddie says as I pass him on my way to the dressing room.

"Got any of your coffee left?" I ask. Eddie pours me a Styrofoam cupful and I down it.

"Oh, and sorry I kicked you during the munchkin dance but I got thrown by that damned heckler in the front row. I could have killed her."

"Forget it," Eddie says, taking a swig from his thermos. "There's always at least one of those when I do *Pinocchio*. Kids have no manners these days. They're all spoiled brats."

I sit at the dressing room table and begin to remove my makeup. Frank switches on the overhead fluorescent lights. I look at myself in the mirror, with my pigtail wig and rouged cheeks, and recoil in horror. I look frighteningly like Bette Davis in *What Ever Happened to Baby Jane?*

"Turn off that overhead light, will you?" I snap to Frank.

"Aren't we sensitive?" Randall says from the other side of the room.

"My vision is weird today, and that fluorescent light makes my eyes flicker," I say defensively.

After we change out of the costumes and pack up the props, we pile into the van and head back to New York. I'm in the front seat between Dee-Honey and Pauline.

"You always make such a lovely Dorothy, dear," Pauline says, and pats my knee. "Just lovely."

"Pauline, you're sweet, but I'm forty-one. I think my Dorothy days are over. Did you hear that girl in the front row?"

"She was a thoughtless urchin. No imagination. Look, Maggie dear, to a seventy-three-year-old, forty-one is still an ingénue, isn't that right Dee-Honey?"

"Oh my yes. You're practically a teenager."

"Teenager," Randall snorts from the backseat. "She's Lady Macbeth if she's a day."

"You hush, Randall," Pauline hisses. " You just hush."

"Thanks," I say to Pauline, then give her a kiss on the cheek. "And I think you're the real reason that Dorothy makes it back home and it's not the nasty old Wizard at all," I say, nodding in Randall's direction. "It's Glenda's good wishes that get her back to Kansas."

"I've always thought that," Pauline says. "When I give her that final blessing with the wand, I envision Dorothy back home safe and sound. I'm glad you feel it."

"I always do," I say.

A few years ago Pauline and I were on tour together in *Freddie and his Magic Flute*. After too many shots of cheap scotch at the motel bar, I confided to her that I was depressed and feeling like nothing in my life had meaning. She took me by the shoulders and said, "Listen to me, Maggie, you have to go on no matter what, because you never know when something wonderful will happen." Then she proceeded to tell me about the time, in a fit of despair, she decided to kill herself. It was a cold December day after Christmas. She opened the window of her apartment — a sixth-floor walk-up on West Forty-fifth Street (where she still lives) — and put on her best black cocktail dress (an Ann Roth design she had worn in a walk-on role with Jon Voight in *Midnight Cowboy*), along with her rhinestone earrings, four-inch stiletto heels, and black elbow-length satin gloves. Her plan was to get a running start and hurl herself out the window, down six stories, and onto the front page of the New York *Daily News*. But just as she was about to get up speed and go, the phone rang. It was a friend, and when she heard his voice she started to cry uncontrollably. The friend (a tall, dark, handsome mystery man is what Pauline leads you to believe) suggested dinner, and since Pauline was already dressed for it, according to legend, they went to the Rainbow Room, then spent the weekend at the Plaza Hotel drinking champagne and eating caviar. That's the official version; unofficially the word is (and Eddie Houser swears to it) Dee-Honey was the one on the other end of the phone who saved Pauline, and then had her admitted to Bellevue for an extended stay.

I look over at Pauline. She is busily crocheting, making hats and scarves for the homeless.

"You remember Mariah Stacky, don't you, Dee?" Pauline says.

"Yes, honey, I do. She went on tour with us to Tennessee with

Pied Piper," Dee says. "She was wonderful as the mayor's wife. Had a lovely soprano. She was the only one that could really hit the F-sharp in the 'Rats, Rats, Rats' number."

"I got a card from her. She's living in Phoenix. For her health, you know. Terrible asthma."

"Really? Is she still married to that fire-eater?" Dee asks. "Remember he worked for Ringling?

"Yes, but he retired. Mariah said they're happy as clams on the half shell."

"Clams on a half shell?" Eddie yelps from the backseat. "That is just like Mariah to think it would be a hoot to be a clam on the half shell."

I lean my head back and close my eyes. Where are those ruby slippers when you really need them?

2

When I get home there is a phone message from Mr. Handsome: "Hey, Maggie Mae, how are you? Sorry I had to take off so early this morning. I had a great time and I want to see you again. How 'bout tonight? You're so great. I mean hot. You know what I mean. Call me. I'm at home and then I'm out, but I'll check my machine or you can call my cell. I'll be free around ten. How was the Dorothy thing? Call me."

I replay the message four times, copying down the phone numbers. Did he mean hot as in exciting, or hot as in hot to touch? I suspect he had mistaken the heat of a pre-premenopausal hot flash for sizzling passion but what the hell. For me it was one of those blurry nights that return in moments of clarity, like freeze-frame pictures. I was sure I remembered that at some point he was wearing a garter belt and I was perched on his lap yelling giddyup. That could explain the bruise I noticed on my left thigh when I was struggling into my Dorothy tights. But what is his name? I can't remember it, or maybe I never knew it. And he didn't leave it in the message.

There is also a call from Charles: "Maggie, darling, where are you? It's Charles. My God, it's so hot and humid I'm sticking to myself. I just got back from Spain. Olé! And I'm dying to tell you all about it. How about dinner tonight? I'm footloose. My treat, darling. Just love to see you. Call me."

Charles is the curator of a small art gallery in Tribeca. His taste is very noveau yet very upscale, meaning he knows what sells for big bucks and doesn't bother with fads. I wish I didn't bother with fads and that I could make big bucks, but my life has been one fad after another. There was the women's lib fad and the rock star fad and the downtown leather fad, the spiritual fad and the soybean diet fad and the Hampton fad, and now the too-much-scotch-not-enough-brain-cells-younger-man fad. And all of them ended up costing me, although what I'm not sure. At dinner that night Charles chats nonstop about Madrid and the matadors and the vino and the art.

"Maggie, dear, you should see my newest find. We agreed on a show at the gallery in the fall. He does acrylics mixed with crushed shells on linen. Amazing textures. And what a colorist! Like O'Keeffe. Pure, vibrant. And yet not overbearing. I think they'll sell like crazy. Very Hampton friendly. You should tell your friend Patty. I think she'd love them. Give me her address and I'll send her an invitation to the opening. You would not believe the place I stayed."

Charles proceeds to wax poetic about the hotel and the gorgeous young man he had met in Santa Pola, a resort town on the coast of Spain that is apparently filled with gay men and nightclubs and nude sunbathing. As he talks my mind drifts off to a freeze-frame from last night. I am sure Mr. Handsome had a tattoo on his shoulder, and I am now trying to get it into focus. I think it was some sort of religious symbol . . . or was it an animal? I'm sure it had several arms and legs, or at least what looked like legs. Maybe it was something Hindu.

"Maggie?" Charles snaps at me.

"Sorry?" I say, coming back to attention.

"Hello, earth to Maggie!" Charles says. "I was talking about my new artist."

"I'm listening, acrylic on linen. I love it. Sounds very Mapplethorpe," I say.

"What do you mean Mapplethorpe? God, Maggie, Mapplethorpe was a photographer. After all these years of my educating you about the art world, I would think you'd at least get the mediums right."

"I can only try," I say. "You have to admit I can pick out a Hockney from a lineup."

"Hockney's easy, dear." Charles smiles at me indulgently.

"Easy for you." I smile back.

"And then in Barcelona," Charles continues, "I met a wonderful glassblower. Amazing vases." He hands me another stack of snapshots.

"He's gorgeous, Mags," Charles says, chewing on his olive. "He told me the secret to good skin is hydration. He drinks two gallons of water a day. Can you imagine?"

"No." I say. "I'd have to wear a catheter just to leave the house."

"I think he must," Charles says. "You know people will do anything these days to look young. Have you heard about sheep fat? If you put it in the blender with some sea salt and cucumbers it makes a wonderful restorative scrub and takes off years."

"Really? I could have used some of that sheep fat this morning. I had to play Dorothy in *The Wizard of Oz*."

"Maggie, you've got to start singing for real again. Get out of that damn pigtail and pinafore and do cabaret. Put on a silky black cocktail dress and sing Cole Porter."

"I can barely get into the pinafore anymore, for Christ's sake. A little girl in the front row heckled me. Called me a *big lady*, which is code for old and fat. And the cellar door wouldn't spin. I practically had to get off and walk to the Land of Oz. I'm not the ingénue I used to be."

"Oh, who is, darling?" Charles says, finishing off his martini. Then he gestures to the waiter for another round for both of us. Charles and I met years ago. He was living with my accompanist at the time, Goodwin Albert DePugh, better known as Goodie, the best piano player to ever come out of Lake Charles, Louisiana. We kicked ass in the East Village clubs doing our Miss Goodie Two Shoes and Maggie the Magnolia act for the extremely hip, the classy cool, and the "true believers," as Goodie liked to call them. We were the "wildly addictive soul sisters with sass and brass," said the *Village Voice*. "Funny and heartbreaking, with harmonies to die for." Goodie was my best friend; I was Ethel to his Lucy, and he was Rhoda to my Mary.

When Goodie started to get sick, we all knew what it was. We knew it was the Big Sick. The Big Sick that no one could get away from in the eighties and early nineties. It was everywhere, and it was so devastating that no one wanted to look—certainly not me.

Sometimes during a rehearsal Goodie would start coughing and couldn't stop, and I would find some speck on the wall or crack in the floor to look at and will myself not to think until the coughing stopped and Goodie took a drink of water and said something about allergies. I would rub his back and try not to think about the Big Sick; I'd tell myself that maybe it was just allergies. After all, the pollen count was high and the ozone layer was disappearing at an alarming rate. Charles got Goodie hooked up to some experimental program. Goodie started having lots of colonics, the theory being you could flush the poison out. Get rid of the fluids—pump in healthy stuff. Purify the body. But nothing worked, and Goodie got thinner and weaker and sicker, and finally it got so bad that there was no place to look and pretend it wasn't happening. Goodie's brother Joe came up from Texas to help out. He was a civil engineer and we hit it off and became a couple, much to Goodie's delight.

"You two were made for each other," he would say with a smile. So Texas Joe and I fell in love while Goodie fell victim to his compromised immune system. By the time the lifesaving "cocktail" came on the scene, he was too far gone. Lousy timing for a guy with rhythm.

Charles and I are having dinner at Ernie's on Broadway. It's a big, airy place with windows that open onto the street. Air-conditioning is pouring out of overhead vents.

"They're cooling the whole damn world; their electric bill must be enormous," Charles notes as he sips his second double martini with two olives, light on the vermouth. He is a slim man with close-cropped hair, a diamond earring, and an assumed patrician air.

"So did you make it back to Kansas?"

"Yeah, but I almost left Toto in Oz. When the lights did their magic flashing thing, I tripped over the Wizard's throne and the stuffed dog went flying. Frank had to throw him back to me from the wings just as Auntie Em ran onstage saying, 'Oh Dorothy, I've been so worried'—well, you know the story."

"I sure do, and all the lines and all the lyrics," he says.

"Gosh, Dee-Honey should have called you this morning."

I glance at my watch. It's nine fifteen. "I have to go to the ladies' room. Will you order me an espresso when the waiter comes back?" I say to Charles.

"Espresso, darling? I take it I'm not your last port of call tonight."

"Hmm, and I doubt that I'm yours."

"Bingo, baby, and a bull's-eye as well."

Charles and I are all that's left of our odd little family. During Goodie's illness, he and Goodie and Goodie's brother, Texas Joe, and I were together almost every night. We had dinner and watched TV and played scrabble and put Goodie to bed and made sure he was medicated and washed and comfortable. In the last months we would eat in his room, where a hospital bed had been installed. Sometimes I would read to him, and then, when he had fallen asleep, I would just sit and watch him breathe. After Goodie died, my affair with Joe came to its logical conclusion: the logic being that he lived in Houston and I lived in New York and neither one of us was willing to change the situation.

I pick up the phone in the ladies' room and dial Mr. Handsome's cell phone number from the scrap of paper I stuffed into my bag. Smart me. Now if I could remember to charge the battery on my cell phone and put it in my purse, I'd almost be living in the twenty-first century. The phone rings and he answers, "Jack here."

Thank God, now I won't have to ask his name, which is the height of rudeness. Or is it? After all I barely know him, except for the lap-riding, giddyup, possibly kinky sex episode.

"Jack. It's me, Maggie," I say.

"Wassup? Where are you? I'm on my way into the city. Let's get together."

"Sure. I'm just finishing dinner. Why don't you meet me at my place around ten thirty?"

"Great. See you then. I'll bring some beer. Rolling Rock, right?"

"Yeah. Till then." I hang up. Wow, he remembered what I drank yet I couldn't remember his name. Obviously he's better at relationships than I am. God is in the details, but then, so is the devil.

I finish my espresso with Charles and walk him to the subway at Seventy-second Street. He's going downtown to dance in some disco with naked waiters and strobe lights. We hug for a moment.

"We are going to go to Saks and buy you a sexy black cocktail dress with sequins. And then I want to hear you sing 'Night and Day' in the key of G."

"Charles, I have plenty of sexy cocktail dresses with sequins," I say.

"Where are they? In cold storage?" Charles asks. "Come on, Maggie dear, it's time to get back in the game."

"And I can't sing anything in the key of G, you know that."

"Well then G-flat," he says.

"That's not funny. You know how singers hate that word *flat*." I hug him again.

"Darling, you never sang flat a day in your life."

"You're too nice."

"I mean it, Maggie Magnolia, it's time," he says, kissing me on the cheek and then hurrying down the subway stairs.

Pesky tears well up in my eyes, and I stand a moment watching as he disappears into the station. Charles is grand in a too grand sort of way, and he's a bit supercilious at times, but deep down in the midnight hour of his being, he is a kind and caring person who believes in his friends, is loyal to a fault, and can take the worst batch of lemons and turn it into the most delicious lemon meringue pie.

With Charles gone, I focus on the rest of my evening, Rolling Rock beer and the Lone Ranger. Giddyup, indeed! I check out the clock over the Apple Bank for Savings on the corner of Seventy-third Street: it's ten o'clock. I hail a cab. There's just time to get home and freshen my makeup and fluff the apartment.

As the taxi hurls its way up Amsterdam Avenue, I think of what Charles said about my doing a cabaret act, and I decide he's right, I need to get back to the music. A few months ago I did a workshop of a new musical about the life of Eleanor Roosevelt, and I liked the accompanist. I'll call him and then I'll call Sidney at Don't Tell Mama, and I'll schedule a show.

The cab stops in front of my building. The meter reads $6.40. I fish around in my belly bag and come up with a ten-dollar bill. "Keep the change," I say, handing it to the driver. I'm a good tipper, mainly because it's easier than doing the math. Dick Andrews, a neighbor, is in front of my building, walking his terrier, Mr. Ed, the talking Westie. Mr. Ed is a great conversationalist. You say something to him, and then he barks back at you in a very credit-able fashion. When Dick and his wife are out of town, I walk Mr. Ed and often fall into deep conversations with him over a beer and doggie treat (for Mr. Ed, of course). He is an engaging little dog with plenty of insight into city life.

"Good evening, Mr. Ed," I say as I bend down and scratch him between his perky ears.

"Arf, ar-arf-arf-arf?" Mr. Ed asks.

"Pretty good and how's by you?" I respond. Mr. Ed sits on his haunches, settling into conversation mode.

"Arf arf ar-ar-arf—ar-ar!"

"No really? You haven't been out since this morning. That is a long time." I scowl up at Dick. "They are mean to you. You have to come visit me next weekend."

"Arf-ar-ar-arf."

"I gotta run, Mr. Ed. Hang tough, little guy." I stand and look at Dick. "Mr. Ed is mad at you."

"I know," Dick says with a perfectly straight face. "You're the first person he's talked to all day."

It's 10:17 by the digital clock on the VCR as I enter my apartment. Damn. I turn on the light in the bathroom. Yikes! The face that stares back at me from the mirror is very ragged. Bixby jumps up on the toilet seat and gazes at me in that punch-drunk way he does when he is rudely awakened from his cat sleep. I get out my economy size jar of Noxzema and lather up. I rinse with very cold water (rumor has it Sharon Stone submerges her face in ice water for a half hour every day—brrrrrr). I quickly apply under eye cover cream, powder, lipstick, and a little mascara. It'll help, but still I'll keep the lights low—that's the ticket. Lighting is everything after forty years of age. I'm sure the person who invented dimmers for home lighting was a woman over forty. And God bless her.

I wish I had time to do one of those facial masks that promises to peel off all the old skin and leave just the brand-new pink undercoat brimming with youth and hope. A new face to greet the faces that you meet. In this case a younger face in the person of Mr. Handsome, or rather Jack, as has now been established.

I lean over and brush my short and sassy blonde, overprocessed hair with its equally overpriced highlights a few times toward the floor in an attempt to stimulate gloss. Blood runs to my head and I momentarily feel dizzy. Oops. Beer and espresso are the worst kind of gasoline, but it's what my engine runs on. Protein, a little voice says. Eat protein. I look in the refrigerator. Skim milk, Dijon mustard, bean sprouts, yogurt, and mozzarella cheese. Cheese is protein, isn't it?

The buzzer rings. Shit, he's here. Forget the protein and put on music. I put on a Billy Joel CD, dim the lights, and suck in my stomach. I turn the knob and open the door and there he is—as tall and handsome as I remember. He's wearing jeans and a black T-shirt and carrying a six-pack of Rolling Rock.

Young man, young man, hit me over the head and drag me anywhere, I think as he places the beer on the table and turns. And before I can say a word, he wraps his arms around me and smothers me in his embrace. Yes, smothers. It's like a scene from a 1940s movie with me being played by Barbara Stanwyck, and Jack, the young man, played by Jack Palance, the Hollywood stud.

I run my hand down his well-shaped gluteus maximus and stumble across a bump, a something or other, a garter belt? He's wearing a garter belt! I knew the one in the freeze-frame memory wasn't mine. So he comes equipped. I don't linger on the telltale bump. I don't want to appear surprised, but I do wonder if he is also wearing hose? Black fishnet perhaps, and who can imagine what else? He is moving his mouth down my neck, headed for my right breast. I moan and press against his privates. Yum. He is hard all right, very hard indeed—unless it's just more equipment. No, this is definitely the real thing. He grabs me under my buttocks, does a quick wrestling maneuver, and just like that we are on the floor, writhing on that cotton throw rug again. Zippers are unzipping, buttons unbuttoning, legs parting, juices flowing. Sex. Sex is happening as it has happened for thousands of years. The double-backed beast, the two-headed monster, the sublime and the ridiculous, but, alas, I am a little too sober to make it to home plate. Damn, I think, as Jack makes his way down, down, down to the part I was told never to touch.

"Don't ever put your hands down there. It's nasty," my mother said as she stood over me, a curious five-year-old playing in the bath. Well fine, I won't; I'll let other people do it. Ha, ha, ha, I laugh to myself. But the thought of my mother and the lack of sufficient alcohol make me sit bolt upright.

"What is it for Christ's sake?" Jack moans, as he rolls off to the side, conking his head on the hardwood floor.

"I have to pee," I say weakly. "Sorry."

"Yeah, sure. You really turn me on."

"Likewise."

I get up and go to the bathroom. My clothes are crooked and tangled; my hair is matted to the back of my head. Recently I had seen a book at Barnes & Noble entitled *The Sadness of Sex*. I sit on the toilet and try to pee, but nothing happens so I turn on the faucet and stare at the wall, humming the opening bars of Cole Porter's "Begin the Beguine."

"Let's take a time-out and have a beer," I say, reentering the room. Jack is still lying faceup on the floor, staring at the ceiling.

"Time-out? We didn't even make it through the first inning."

"I'm thirsty," I say as I twist off the top and hand the beer to Jack. I get another one for myself and sit down on the floor next to him.

"So where did you go so bright and early this morning?" I ask.

"I had to check out some apartments."

"Are you a broker?"

"No, I'm thinking about moving into the city." Jack cracks the knuckles on his left hand.

"Really? Where do you live now?"

"In Queens."

"In an apartment?" I sit cross-legged and balance the beer on the inside of my knee.

"No, I live in a house."

"Wow. That's great. A whole house to yourself, or do you have a housemate?"

"I guess you could call him that. Usually I call him Dad."

I take a moment and adjust my preconceptions.

"You live with your parents?" I ask, trying to keep a straight face and a tone free of judgment, but it's hard. In any other circumstance I would burst out laughing and hit the table a few times. Jack takes a swig of his beer and leans over and runs his hand up my thigh, causing a warm tingle to dance down my spine. Is it really so awful that he lives with his parents? Think of all the money one could save. I do a quick calculation of the amount I could have pocketed if I was still living at home, a small fortune to say the least. What is twenty-some years times twelve months times the average rent? Wow. Of course I knew I'd have ended up locked in some psych ward if I had lived with my parents one second longer than I did, but it's fun to dream.

"So you must be pretty close with your folks?" I ask, studying the curve of his shoulder as he leans closer into me, his eyes focused with intent.

"I don't live with my folks. I live with my dad, and yeah, we get along, and how 'bout we not talk about it right now." His mouth opens on mine. I moan slightly as he pushes me gently down onto the cotton throw rug.

Here we go, I think, here we go again. My hand finds that interesting bump on his thigh.

"Are you wearing a garter belt under these pants?" I ask in a husky tone.

"And nothing else," he replies as his left hand tweaks my nipple. "Ever consider a nipple ring?"

"Nipple ring?" I ask as nonchalantly as I can.

"Yeah, we'll get you one. You'll love it."

Billy Joel is singing "If I Only Had the Words to Tell You." Jack doesn't need any words. His body is communicating just fine.

3

The next morning Jack is gone before eight a.m. Again. He leaves me a note under the hot fudge sundae magnet on the refrigerator: *Last night was awesome. Call you later. You need milk.* There's a five-dollar bill with the note and an empty carton of milk in the sink. I guess the five bucks is for the milk. At least I hope it is and not for . . . No, of course not, nobody is that cheap.

So he left me milk money. That's sweet. I wonder if he leaves his dad money for milk or eggs or whatever he consumes in the morning on the way out of the house they share in Queens. And where, I wonder, is his mother? Is he a product of divorce? Did she abandon him? Is that where I, the older woman, come into the picture? Am I filling some maternal need? Ugh. I look for the slip of paper I jotted his cell phone number on and find it in my bag. I light a cigarette and then punch in the numbers. "Jack here," he answers.

"Maggie here," I respond.

"Wassup, Sweet Pea?" he asks.

The "Sweet Pea" catches me by surprise. Boy, it has been a lifetime since someone called me that, and I'm not sure how I feel about it. Should a woman my age even respond? Wasn't Sweet Pea that strange baby in the Popeye cartoon, the little one with no legs?

"I miss you," Jack continues in his low, sexy voice. "I was thinking about you."

I decide Sweet Pea isn't so bad. In fact, I kind of like it. "I just wondered what happened to you," I say.

"Did you get my note?"

"Yeah, and thanks for the dough. Every bit helps."

"Listen, I drank all the milk. I didn't want you to think I was a freeloader."

"I'm kidding," I say, feeling awkward. "Where are you? What do you do?"

"I'm on the floor at the dealership. I can't talk. I have a client coming in a few minutes."

"What client? What do you deal?"

"Cars. I sell cars."

"Really? I had a car for a while," I say.

"Just for a while?" Jack asks.

"It was a red Gremlin. It drove like a truck. I bought it from my brother for a couple thousand dollars. It was fun for a while, but the alternate side of the street parking finally took its toll."

"So you got rid of it?"

"Yeah, I sold it to my nephew and started spending my mornings at the gym in pursuit of the perfect bicep."

"And what a perfect bicep that is," Jack purrs. "I miss you Maggie Mae. Have a good one."

"Yeah, right, yeah, you too," I say, but he has already rung off. He misses me. Wow. I disconnect on my end and place the phone back in the cradle. He misses me. Maybe it's just a line. But the truth is, I miss him too. Shit. I'll have to ask about the mother some other time.

I glance at the clock. It's ten fifteen. Damn. I have an audition at eleven. I need to jump in the shower and get dressed. Wait a minute. I need to jump in the shower, dry off, then get dressed, and then get my butt out the door and into a cab if I'm going to make it in time. These things usually run behind schedule, in fact 97 percent of the time they do, but that one time they don't, if you, the dime-a-dozen-voice-over talent, aren't there—well, business is supply and demand, and in the world of voice-overs and acting and singing, there is a lot more hungry supply than is ever demanded. So be on time.

At 10:32 I'm walking out the door. The great thing about voice-overs is you don't have to look good. You just have to show up and sound good—makeup and hair is optional, which cuts about forty-five minutes off my prep time.

I get a cab on the corner. "Forty-ninth and Madison," I say as I open my compact and put on some lipstick. "Peter Piper picked a peck of pickled peppers," I quick-speak out loud a few times. "Toy boat, toy boat, toy boat." The cabdriver glances in the rearview mirror. "I'm loosening up my lips," I explain.

"Loose lips sink ships," he cautions.

"I'll remember that." The traffic isn't too bad, and at 10:52 I am pressing the up button for the elevator. The doors open and Sally James steps out.

"Maggie," she exclaims in that overly friendly actressy way she has. "How are you?"

"Great, thanks. Love to chat, but I'm running late." I get onto the elevator.

"Are you here for the voice-over? It's tricky. Bad grammar and the client's a bitch. Good luck," she says, smiling as she waves.

The doors close. *Sally* is the bitch. We are often sent up for the same things, and if she gets there first she likes to warn me about problems, which makes me nervous and I'm sure she knows that. Someone told me she had a master's degree in psychology, with a minor (specialty) in mind-fucking. I put my lips together and blow them out in that horse sound a few times.

"B-b-b-b-b-b-b-b-b-b. B-b-b-b-b-b-b-b-b-b-b-b-b-b."

The man standing next to me winks. "Hi-yo, Silver," he says as he exits on the fifth floor. I reapply my lipstick and get off on twenty-three. I sign in and am handed the copy. It's for a feminine hygiene product. Oh, boy!

> For women on the go in a go-go world.
> Easy, comfortable, worry-free.
> Let's you get on with getting on.
> Now available in scented or unscented.

And to think I began my career in a high school production of Shakespeare's *Romeo and Juliet*. I was seventeen and had long hair and a twenty-three-inch waist. Shakespeare was religion to me. I worshipped it. I memorized long passages and repeated them over and over.

Well, that was then and this is now. I look over the copy sheet in my hand: "Women on the go in a go-go world." I say, changing the emphasis and experimenting with the rhythm. It isn't Shakespeare, but a good voice-over spot can pay the rent for months. My name is called and I go into the casting office. I put the copy on tape. Marge Megin, the casting director, asks me for another run at it with a more upbeat attitude.

"Women on the go in a go-go world," I say euphorically into the microphone. Marge nods and I pick up my shoulder bag and make a quick exit.

Don't linger. That's a rule of thumb in the world of casting calls. Do your thing and leave. The casting people appreciate you for that, and you certainly want them to appreciate you so they call you again and again. It's a matter of the odds when booking voice-overs and commercial spots. The more you're seen for, the better the odds you book. Or in baseball terms — the more at bats the better your chances to hit one out of the park. At least that's the rationale that keeps me going, but lately the going is getting rougher. How many times can a grown woman say "Now available in scented or unscented" with any real conviction?

I walk out onto Madison Avenue and head toward the New World Coffee Shop on Forty-fifth Street. I get out my cell phone and am relieved to see that the battery is charged and ready to go. The cell phone is new for me. I didn't think I was a cell phone type. I preferred being a cell phone resenter. I'd roll my eyes and huff and puff when people used them in my vicinity, even though I knew it would make my life a hundred percent easier. I'm stubborn that way. I put it off until my agent said she would drop me if I didn't get one — and besides, she reminded me, it's a tax deduction. So I converted and got a pay-as-you-go plan, which is why I don't give out my number. I call my home machine to check for messages.

"Hi, honey," Dee-Honey chirps. "I just want to remind you that I have you booked for *Snow White* tomorrow. Call me back as soon as you get this. Thanks, honey. Oh, the show is in Yonkers, so it's a short day."

I call her back and her machine picks up. At the sound of the beep I say, "Dee-Honey, it's Mags, and yes I have *Snow White* in my book. Don't think I always forget shows just because Dorothy slipped my mind the other day. Oh, and please remember, I need the larger costume this time. Thanks."

Janet Newhouse, who also plays the part, is a dainty size four, which is two sizes smaller than me, a robust size eight, and I sure as hell don't want to have to struggle into another damn costume. It's embarrassing. I make a mental note to pick up more pink pretty-girl blush. I'm running low.

In the coffee shop I order a double latte and a blueberry muffin and sit on a stool at the street window. Muffins are really cake — they're the size of a small Bundt cake and packed with sugar, so let's stop pretending and call a cake a cake. I know I should lose ten pounds, but not today. Someone has left the *Daily News* on the counter. I open to the sports page. The Yankees beat the Red Sox three to one. I read down the column. Derek Jeter hit a home run in the fourth and then a sac fly in the sixth and two RBIs. I became a Yankees fan because Goodie was a Yankees fan, though mainly he liked the uniforms, and while Texas Joe was in New York he adopted the Yankees as his team to please Goodie and me. So we watched the games together and talked baseball when it got too hard to talk about anything else. And then the Yankees won the World Series and Goodie rallied for a while and it seemed the cocktail was working, but by the winter Goodie was failing again and failing fast.

I finish my blueberry muffin, aka cake, and decide to walk over

to Don't Tell Mama, my old cabaret hangout, and try to catch
Sidney in his office and book a club date. "Just do it," my Nike
cross trainers sing out as I walk west toward Broadway.

"MAGGIE!" I hear screamed across Sixth Avenue. A large man
with long blond hair is motioning on the other side of the street.
"Stay there! I'll cross over!"

Bob Strong was the production stage manager for a show I did
about ten years ago in Lancaster, Pennsylvania. Every time I run
into him he acts as if it has been years since we've seen each other.
Effusive is the word. He's a dear, but hard to take without a strong
shot of scotch. As he crosses the intersection at a gallop, I exag-
geratedly look at my wristwatch.

"I only have a second, Bob. Got an appointment a few blocks
away." He wraps me in his arms. I stiffen slightly but then relent. I
don't want to be rude, not really. And, of course, you never know
when a production stage manager will have the inside track on a
job. "How are you, Bob-a-lou?"

"I'm fantastic," he says. Bob is always "fantastic." He puts me
at arm's length. "You look tired, Maggie, are you burning the
midnight oil?"

Now, *I* can think I look tired and even *say* I look tired, but
when someone else says I look tired, I get very untired and very
defensive. "I didn't have time to even wash my face this morning
and I just have voice-over things and I feel great actually, in fact,
I'm in the pink. But I've got to run." I kiss him quickly on the
cheek. "How's Piper?" Piper is Bob's teacup poodle.

"Kidney stones."

"Oh, no."

"But he's going to be fine and dandy. So what are you up to?"

"You know, the usual, voice-overs, kiddies' theater? I have a *Snow White* coming up."

"Who do you play? The evil stepmother?"

"No, I'm Snow White," I say. Bob looks at me and then lets out a huge laugh—a guffaw actually.

"What's so funny?"

"Nothing. I was just thinking about you as Snow White. I bet you're great. You must bring quite an edge to the role."

"I do, and I'm damn good. She's not just an ingénue, she's a woman caught in the political machine of autocratic matriarchy. The kids fucking love it."

"Sounds great," Bob says, suppressing another guffaw.

"Catch you later, Bob, got to run," I practically spit at him as I head across the street. A car honks at me. I back up onto the curb.

"Careful, Mags," Bob says. The light turns and I run to the other side. Ogre is what I would cast Bob as. A big, mean, thoughtless ogre. In spite of the ten million plus people in the New York area, it's really a small town and you can never get from one end to the other without running into someone you know.

When I arrive at Don't Tell Mama, three people are sitting at the bar. The place doesn't officially open until four p.m., but a couple of hangers-on are always lounging on the barstools. I ask Freddie, the bartender, if Sidney is in his office.

"Just arrived." He tosses the words in my direction, continuing his housecleaning in preparation for the night ahead. Bars are dreary places in the daytime; they look embarrassed, like a middle-aged woman without makeup caught in bad lighting. God, I know the feeling . . . and the look.

Sidney is sitting at his desk eating a turkey and cheese on rye and sipping a large coffee, light and sweet. I know because I used to bring him one whenever I was doing a show. Sidney is a caffeine freak—I've never seen him without a cup somewhere within reach.

"Maggie, how are you?" he says when I poke my head in the door. "Come on in. Long time no see." He stands and extends his hand.

"I'm okay. How about you?"

"Busy. Always busy."

"That's good, isn't it?"

"You bet. Idle hands are the devil's playground or something to that effect."

"Please don't let me keep you from your lunch." I motion to his sandwich. "I was wondering about booking a couple of dates. I've decided to get back to my old act. Or rather, my new solo act. Anyway, shake my booty again before everything breaks down and my vocal cords retire.

"It's been a while," Sidney says.

"Yeah, but I'm still game and I've still got my money note, as they say in the biz." I know I'm smiling too much. "Look, why don't you finish your lunch and we can talk. I'll be out at the bar."

The phone rings.

"Great," Sidney says, picking up the receiver. "I'll see you in a few."

I order a bottle of Rolling Rock from Freddie. I've run into Sidney off and on over the years, and he always says that when I feel like it I should come in and book some dates.

"Is anybody in the back room?" I ask.

"I don't think so. You can take a look." Freddie is cutting up lemons and limes; a cigarette dangles on his lower lip. Smoking laws don't apply off hours, thank God.

"Thanks." I saunter back through the tables, sipping my beer and humming the first few bars of "Get It While You Can," remembering the other night at the Angry Squire. I hadn't listened to Janis in years. Of course humming a Joplin song is useless—you've got to sing full throttle stoked on about a quart of Southern Comfort.

I pull on the door and enter the cabaret, and the smell of stale cigarettes and Lysol dances up my nostrils. I find my pack of Marlboros and light up. A baby grand piano sits quietly on the stage, waiting for the next ten fingers to bring it to life. A light in the control booth spills onto the tiny stage and the ubiquitous cabaret stool stands off to one corner. I place it next to the piano and sit down. I take a pull on the beer.

The last time I sang with Goodie was in this room. He was still holding his own, but the meds had stopped working and the verdict was in. We did a short show that night. We were the fabulous "soul sisters," with bumps and grinds and a wonderful medley from *Cats* in which I did a number of athletic tambourine solos. About forty people were in the audience, including a large group of Icelandic tourists staying at the Howard Johnson's on Eighth Avenue and, of course, Texas Joe and Charles. For the end of the set we sang "Bridge Over Troubled Waters," which we usually did tongue-in-cheek. Goodie started playing the first few bars. The Icelanders applauded. I decided to skip the patter and just get to it.

"When you're weary, feeling small," I sang. The man sitting at the front table reached out and took his wife's hand. I looked over at Goodie. He was in his usual drag: blonde wig, blue eye shadow, his head thrown back, his eyes closed, the music rolling through his body.

In the last verse our voices locked in a resonant harmony that shimmered in the air. "Sail on silver girl, sail on by."

Being onstage in front of an audience can oddly be the most private place in the world, and that night, at that moment, it was just Goodie and me riding that song like a breakaway freight train taking us on one hell of a ride. At the end Goodie was spent, perspiration running his mascara, making him look raccoonish. I almost laughed, but he caught my eye, and I suddenly knew this was the last time we would sing together. I knew it. The Icelanders started to applaud. Goodie got up from the piano and came to take my hand for the bow. He was very thin, and his fishnet stockings hung loose at his ankles. I hadn't noticed that before. I hadn't noticed because I hadn't wanted to. We looked out at the audience and took our bow. Then I stepped aside and gestured to Goodie, and at that moment the audience stood up and they gave Goodie an ovation. They saw right away what had taken me so long to see, a talented man wasting away in the prime of his life. And they stood for that. They stood to bear witness.

Remembering that last night, I sit down at the piano and rest my hands on the keys, as if on a Ouija board.

"It's been a long time, Goodie, but I still miss you," I whisper. "I hope you are tucked away in some special part of the universe, standing on your hill enjoying the view."

A few weeks before Goodie died he dreamed he was traveling on a bus with his childhood friends and they were going on a picnic. The bus took them to the top of a hill where they spent the day. When the sun started to set, everyone got back on the bus to go home, all except Goodie. He stayed behind because the view from the hill was so magnificent.

I close my eyes and rest my head on the piano. "Hey, Maggie

mine," a voice says, and I raise my eyes. I see a little foot housed in a plastic stiletto heel attached to a shapely leg poking through the slit of a stunning pink evening dress attached to . . . Oh my God . . . I am hallucinating. I blink my eyes and take a deep breath.

"It's me. I'm here, really," the voice says.

"Goodie?" I whisper.

"In the shrunken flesh. I'm back and better than ever!" Goodie throws his arm over his head and does a hubba-hubba dance. Then he sashays up the keyboard in a bump and grind.

"I'm losing my mind," I say. "It's an acid flashback. You always called yourself a fairy, but this is ridiculous."

"No, it's real. Wow, who knew? Who knew heaven was the Barbie department at Toys R Us. I'm living in the dream house. Too much pink but the layout is wonderful."

"What? What are you talking about?" I lean over and put my head between my knees and take deep breaths. I'm afraid I'm going to pass out, or maybe I already have. I'm having a stroke. That's what it is. Lack of blood to the brain. Randall was right about those light flashes. Oh, Jesus, heart attack.

"Maggie Magnolia, sit up and look at me," Goodie says. I raise my eyes and Goodie is hovering at eye level.

"Good God, you have wings!"

"Yes, aren't they great? Gossamer with rhinestones. And this outfit—do you recognize it?"

"No," I say, trying to steady my breath.

"Barbie's prom collection," Goodie says. "I absolutely love the cut."

"So you've been reincarnated as a flying Barbie doll?"

"Well, not right away. I started off with birthday wishes, and, P.S., it really is true about blowing out all the candles, then I apprenticed as the tooth fairy for a while. Not bad, but overrated. When I got a promotion to fairy godmother, I put in a request for you. And when they reviewed your paperwork, they put me on the case."

"And who are *they*?" I ask.

"You never actually see them, so I'm not sure. It's all computerized," Goodie says with a sigh. "The old-timers tell me that being a fairy has lost a lot of its charm, but I don't agree. It doesn't matter how it's all done. What matters is why. And you are why, Mags." Goodie flies closer and whispers in my ear, "They stamped you *urgent*."

"Me? Urgent? I don't know why you say that. I am a-okay."

"More will be revealed, Maggie," says Goodie with a knowing wink.

"More of what?" I ask.

"Maggie," Sidney says, startling me. He is standing a few feet away, coffee cup in hand. "Are you all right?"

"Yeah." I take a drag off my cigarette. I look at Goodie. He is fluffing his wings. Apparently Sidney is not having the same hallucination I am. Great! So I *am* losing my mind.

"How about the twenty-fifth and twenty-sixth of next month? It's a Thursday and Friday at nine. It's a good slot. We get a nice group of tourists. They'll love you."

"Can I get back to you tomorrow?"

"Sure, but no later than that. I've got to book those dates." He turns to leave.

"Thanks, Sidney." I put the stool back where I found it.

Goodie is standing on the piano grinning from ear to ear. "Good girl, Maggie," he chimes. "I can't wait!"

"Why can't Sidney see you?" I ask.

"Because I'm *your* fairy godmother," he says, "and I exist only for you. Isn't that a hoot? Well technically I'm a guardian angel, but I told them you wouldn't believe that—that 'fairy godmother' was more your speed." Goodie jumps onto the keyboard and daintily skips up the scale. "I have to get back to Toys R Us. I'm having dinner with G.I. Joe. Can you believe it? I've had a crush on him since I was eight. Maggie Mine, I'll see you later." And he zooms off leaving behind a jet stream of fairy dust.

I stare after him. Wow. Okay. I'm crazy. I'm seeing things. Maybe it's the beer. No more beer before five. And I must call Charles. And what is being revealed?

At home that evening I leave a message for Charles on his cell. "Call me the minute you can," I say.

Then I dig out the fishing tackle box that I use as a makeup kit and check to make sure I have enough black hair gel for my turn as Snow White tomorrow. I drink only one beer and decide that Goodie was a momentary hallucination caused by returning to Don't Tell Mama. That's all. Some sort of wacky daydream. The phone rings.

"Hi, Maggie, dear. I'm on my way downtown to meet some sexy Spaniards for dinner," he says. "I'll be showing the crushed shells on linen pieces next month."

"Great," I say. "Charles, has anything strange been happening to you? I mean, like seeing things?"

"Life, Mags, I'm seeing life. Sometimes I think for the first time. Like that young man I met in Santa Pola, the glassblower—he's coming for a visit. I want to be the first to introduce him to the New York art world."

"I meant smaller things. Little flying things."

"You mean bugs?" Charles asks. "Call an exterminator."

"No, I thought I saw Goodie today, but much smaller, and dressed in pink."

"I think I see Goodie all the time," Charles says, "but not in pink. I see him in yellow, and he's always off in the distance and I can't quite catch up to him. Once I saw him on top of the Empire State Building."

"Was he flying?" I ask.

"No, kind of perched, but I think his arms were outstretched. I got to run. Call the gallery tomorrow. Ask Tosh for the name of the exterminator we use. They'll take care of anything that is flying."

"Well, I don't want it taken care . . ." I begin, but Charles's phone breaks up. I hear a scrambled goodbye and then nothing. All right. That's it. I'm crazy.

4

*P*ut a little Vaseline on the end of his nose," Dee-Honey says. She is instructing Helen Sanders on what to do about a bad case of fur balls her cat Smiley is suffering from. "Just dab it right on the tip with your finger. That should do the trick."

"Really? I never would have thought of that. Must line the stomach and then the hair doesn't get clogged," Helen says. It's eight a.m. and I'm sitting in the backseat of the van. We're waiting for Gloria, who plays the evil stepmother. She is running late. It's hot. I'm eating a sesame bagel and drinking a coffee that I have to balance on my kneecap, because there is no room to maneuver. Helen Sanders plays Snow White's mother and doubles as the dancing forest nymph. She was a regular on *Days of Our Lives* for about ten years, until a psychopathic cosmetic surgeon killed off her character a few seasons ago. She still works in regional theater, but mostly she's been doing the Little Britches thing. She says it's temporary, but we all know how that goes. Dee-Honey is sitting in the driver's seat, checking her watch and listening to the traffic report on the radio. I sip my coffee and stare straight ahead. I didn't get much sleep last night and it's already feeling like a very long day.

Jack dropped by unexpectedly around eleven o'clock. The nerve, I thought as I buzzed him in. I opened the door and there he was peeking out from behind a dozen yellow roses. A dozen yellow roses—for me. I couldn't even find a vase. I had to put them in the plastic pail I keep in the bathroom for when the ceiling leaks. Jack ordered pizza and we sat on the floor and ate and watched David Letterman and made love and fell asleep. What could be better? Maybe a phone call before the visit, maybe an actual date, maybe the moon on a platter, but then maybe not. Surprises are fun too.

For a change I had to leave first this morning, so I gave him a set of keys. I'll get them back from him tonight. It seemed silly to make him get up and leave an hour before he had to, and I'm pretty sure he's not going to steal my stereo or rifle through my desk drawer and find my safe deposit box key and rob me of the mutual funds I keep tucked away there. After all, he did leave five bucks for milk—I mean the kid's responsible. Although, as I sit listening to Helen recount her latest run-in with her neighbor who plays his music too loud and throws off Smiley's sleep patterns, I can't stop thinking about all those *America's Most Wanted* shows that detail the story of some handsome con man who scams lonely women for everything they have.

Suddenly I feel something moving near my feet. I glance, prepared to scream, and I see Goodie poking his head out of my shoulder bag, which is sitting on the floor. He's wearing a light blue peignoir set.

"Do you like?" he askes, doing a circle turn. "It's from Barbie's trousseau. Look, don't worry about Jack, he's a sweetheart and very cute." Then he winks. I quickly look around, expecting to see everyone staring at me, but no one seems to have noticed. I lean over and close the flap on the bag, shoving Goodie back inside.

"So I said to him," Helen is saying as I tune back into the conversation, "get earphones! And then I turned my back just like I did when I played Nora in *A Doll's House.* You saw that production didn't you, Dee?" Helen and Dee have known each other for years. Helen's first husband worked for Dee for several seasons back in the eighties.

"Oh honey, you were wonderful, very moving," Dee replies.

"Well, remember when I did that final exit, I squared my back and then tossed my head," Helen says demonstrating the move.

"Oh yes, honey, it was very effective," says Dee.

"Well, that's exactly what I did to my neighbor and — here's the best part — when I went back into my apartment, I didn't slam the door; that would be too much. He was waiting for it, expecting it, and I think you must always play against the obvious. It's so important. So I just closed the door gently." Helen nods with satisfaction.

"Oh I'm sure he'll get the message," says Dee-Honey. At that moment, Ron, the charming prince who is riding shotgun, spots our dear evil stepmom making her way across the intersection. Her cell phone is at her ear and she is talking a mile a minute. She is still optimistic enough to think there is a fast lane, and she's determined to stay in it, but the fast lane is relative to the highway you're traveling. If you're doing children's theater, that means the big fast lane has already passed you by, and you're cruising on a two-lane access road. But I say, "Go girl," because you never know when those two lanes might turn back into a four-lane interstate. I guess I can be an optimist too. Truth is, Gloria is ten years younger than I am and should by all rights be playing Snow White. But she's five foot nine in bare feet, which is too tall for an ingénue and much too tall for the costume. Plus she's a tenor.

We pack, or rather fold, Gloria into the car and Dee-Honey guns the engine and off we go—a merry band of players. The show is at the Yonkers Public Library and it's like doing theater in a carpeted recreation room. We set up in the back part of the children's picture book section. I carefully unpack my bag and look for Goodie, but he is nowhere to be found, nor is the peignoir set. I'm beginning to think I might go back to my old therapist if she hadn't moved to Michigan. I'd probably make an appointment right now.

The lights for the show are two fluorescent overheads and a handheld "spotlight," which is a glorified flashlight that Dee-Honey "runs" during the show. Frank, our ever-handy stage manager, has managed to use a few of the set pieces and define the playing area on the red and orange checked part of the carpet. He's a genius at this sort of thing. The audience sits on the lime green section.

This is the lowest rung as far as performance spaces go. Usually we do have a stage and at least one or two lights with colored gels, and if we are really lucky there's a dressing room where we can smoke (if no one catches us) and drink coffee and get zipped into our "drag."

The show goes fine, except when Helen trips over a little foot sticking out from the audience (totally unintentional, I'm sure) while doing her forest nymph *pas d'une,* which she does beautifully in a full body leotard appliquéd in velvet leaf patterns. Granted she was more nymphlike before she put on the extra weight, but she still manages to appear limber and otherworldly. Unfortunately the trip causes her to lose her balance and plunge headfirst into the sea of first graders seated up front, but, thank goodness, no one is seriously injured. Helen finishes the show in spite of a limp, and the kids get a good laugh.

We stop at a McDonald's on our way back to the city. I order a fish sandwich and fries and a vanilla shake. We sit at a big table and gobble down our carbs and grease. I get out my cell and check my messages. I have three, but the main thing is knowing that my home phone is still in working order, meaning that after I left, Jack didn't go wild and pillage and burn the house down. There is even a message from my young prince. "Hey, babe, I love to love you. Talk soon. P.S. I made the bed and turned out the lights and took out the trash." Geez, this guy is the bee's knees or else he has some sort of chemical imbalance.

A hand reaches in front of me. "Do you mind if I have a few of your fries?" Helen asks as she plucks a fistful off my tray. "I've got to ice my ankle the minute I get home. You know ankles can be very tricky," she reaches over for a second handful, "and I got a callback to play the doctor in *Agnes of God*. She's a nervous character, very intense. I've got to lose five pounds before Tuesday. I'm going to do a juice fast starting tomorrow."

I smile my most magnanimous smile, suddenly feeling pounds lighter and years younger myself. It's easy to be magnanimous when I have a young man making my bed and taking out my trash and telling me he loves to love me. It's very easy indeed.

"You can have the rest, Helen, I'm full," I say as I push my tray in her direction, "and I think you'd be wonderful in *Agnes of God*." And then I freeze in horror—Goodie is sitting on Helen's shoulder, munching on a french fry.

"See, Maggie, it feels good to be nice, doesn't it?" he says. I

look at him. I look at Helen. No reaction. Helen grabs another
handful of fries.

"I love the way you're wearing your hair now. It's so much more
flattering," she says. Helen is a kung fu master of the backhanded
compliment. She never gives you an inch without taking two back.

Goodie flutters his wings, swoops down, grabs another fry, and
sails off. Helen finishes the rest and slurps the end of her Coke.

"Let's move out," I hear Frank say, and we all head back to the
parking lot.

"We've got a busy summer, Maggie. We should run through
our schedule soon," Dee-Honey says when she drops me off.

"Give me a call and we'll figure it out," I say as I extract my
makeup kit and bag from under the seat.

"Good, I've got some *Poppers* and some *Wizards* and *Cindys* on
the Cape and something in West Virginia. I'll have to check the
schedule. Oh, and a week at the Westbury Music Fair."

"Hmmm, sounds great, but Dee, isn't there someone else who
can do Dorothy?" I move in close so I can whisper in Dee's ear.
"That stupid little girl heckled me the last time I did it."

"Don't listen to that; those girls are just jealous because you
are so pretty, and besides it takes a mature actress to really understand an ingénue." Dee-Honey waves as she drives off, headed
south on Broadway. *Poppers* is short for *Mr. Popper's Penguins* in
which I play Janie Popper and have a dance solo during the big
finale, "Mr. Popper's Penguins on Parade." And, of course, the
Wizards are the *Wizards* and the *Cindys* are the *Cinderellas,* in
which, thankfully, I play an ugly stepsister and not the pretty
little ingénue, and, since it doesn't look like I'll be doing a season
of Shakespeare at Stratford-upon-Avon this summer, I guess I'll
be on Cape Cod in pigtails and hoopskirts. And Dee's right. You

need some life experience to play an ingénue, at least an ingénue with any depth.

It's just four o'clock when I get home. Close enough to teatime. I pour myself a double scotch on the rocks and decide to tackle my laundry. I empty my hamper out on the floor and separate darks from whites, or rather off-whites, as I have never figured out the Clorox thing so my whites quickly go from sparkling to dingy, but that's okay with me. Perfectionism creates problems in some areas of my life, but laundry is not one of them. I stuff all the darks into the bottom of my laundry bag and the off-whites on top. I stand for a while looking at my bed. Should I strip it or not? I take a sip of scotch and consider the possibility.

It wouldn't be such a big question if my bedroom was large and spacious and my bed sat in the middle of the floor with only the headboard against a wall, but I live in the Big Apple where personalities and ambitions are large but apartments are small. My standard double Mattresses-Are-Us bed is wedged into one end of my tiny boudoir and enclosed by three walls, which makes stripping and remaking a real pain in the ass. But since I've had company for the last few nights, and hope for more, I decide I better go for it. I wrestle my sunshine yellow one-hundred-thread cottons off and shove them into the top of my laundry bag. I grab my detergent, pour some scotch into a to-go coffee cup, and put everything into my shopping cart and head off to the Soap N Suds on Columbus Avenue. When I get there I dump my clothes out of the bag into one of the wheelie laundry baskets and stash my shopping cart under the clothes-folding table. The place is more crowded than I expect and I have to wait for a machine. I sit in a plastic chair, my wheelie basket of dirty clothes at my side, and sip from my coffee cup, which gives me time to think about, or rather gnaw upon, recent events.

I'm a damn good Dorothy, and my Snow White is heartbreaking, particularly in the scene with the woodsman. I think I play that well. Kids are so mean nowadays. Disrespectful. I can' t stand them most of the time. Those little mean faces out there in the dark, judging me. My talent. Who are they anyway? They are a bunch of overprivileged seven- or eight-year-olds without a care in the world. Wait until they are out on their own in the big unforgiving world. I'd like to see that heckler soldiering her way through life. Damn that little shit. She was no Dorothy. She never would have gotten home to Kansas. She would have given up before she even left Munchkinland. I drain the last of my scotch from the cup. A machine opens up and I feed in the requisite quarters and I measure the detergent and pour it into the top compartment.

"Are those your clothes?" the man next to me asks.

"What?" I say.

"In the basket?" He points in front of me, and sure enough my laundry is still in the wheelie basket. I look at him and then at the basket and then at the front window of the machine which is washing away with soap and water but alas no clothes.

"Damn," I say under my breath.

I feel so stupid. I consider telling the guy I'm a city sanitation inspector checking for faulty equipment, but instead I push my basket of clothes to another machine and try not to make eye contact. It's that little girl's fault. Damn her. I check my watch and go next door to the Firehouse Bar and Grill for a beer. I sit at one of the sidewalk tables and smoke a cigarette.

NOTE TO SELF . . .

When someone catches you doing something stupid, say you work for the city.

The sun hits my face, and for a few minutes I let it work its magic — until I remember that the ultraviolet rays can cause all sorts of problems now that the ozone layer is so damaged. And who damaged that ozone layer? Beauticians. Everyone knows it is all that hairspray that did us in, which begs the eternal question: What price beauty?

I get home at six o'clock with my clean laundry. I have a message from Dick Andrews asking me if I'll walk Mr. Ed for him as neither he nor Sandy will be home until late, and a message from my agent about a couple of auditions. I'm starving. I open the refrigerator. There is cold pizza from the night before. I put a piece on a plate and get out a Rolling Rock and sit down at the table. I don't switch on the lights. The summer sun is turning the room a warm pink.

When I was a kid, I spent my summers by the pool at the country club sitting on beach blankets with my friends Ann and Jen. We played crazy eights and ate frozen Milky Ways that we bought at the concession stand. We stayed all afternoon and then rode our bikes home for supper. After dinner I would sometimes go back for a swim with my dad. He always bought a cup of coffee at the concession stand and let me drink half. He swam the length of the pool twice underwater, emerging red-faced and gasping for air. Then he would shake his head to the side and bounce on one foot to get the water out of his ear. We raced across the pool. I swam as fast as I could, and sometimes I would win, but only sometimes.

"Like in life," my dad said. "You don't always win, but you must always try to do your best."

I finish the pizza and decide to tackle the awkward task of putting the clean sheets on my bed. It's awkward because I sort of have to be in the bed to make it, and Bixby likes to pretend the sheets are a fun house that he romps through as I try to smooth and straighten them into position. I get the last corner tucked and then coax Bixby out from the middle of the bed so I can smooth down the quilt. Then I lie down for a moment and close my eyes. I drift off until the phone rings. I let the machine pick up. It's Sidney from Don't Tell Mama wanting to confirm the dates he gave me.

"Sidney, Sidney I'm here," I say grabbing the receiver. "I just walked in the door."

"I'm calling to confirm those dates with you Maggie."

"Right . . . yes."

"The twenty-fifth and twenty-sixth?"

"Yes, of next month, isn't it?"

"Yes, dear," Sidney says with annoyance creeping into his voice.

"Absolutely. It's perfect. Gives me enough time but not too much. In fact I was about to call you," I lie like a rug.

"Good. Got to go. You're in the book. In ink, Maggie."

"Great," I say, but he is already off and running.

My digital clock on the radio next to the bed reads 8:05 in bright red numbers. Good grief, I slept for over an hour. I have to walk Mr. Ed. He will be so upset with me that I'm so late. And then I remember the dream I was having when the phone woke me.

It was my recurring dream. In it I'm getting ready to leave my house, and, when I open the door, I'm looking down into a deep abyss. I can't see the bottom. A rickety bridge spans the chasm, like the ones in the Tarzan movies, vines and a few planks of decaying wood. I grab hold of the vines and start to cross. I'm terrified but I keep moving, and just as I get to the other side I realize there is another bridge, but this one has snakes crawling on it. I gasp and wake up. This is, as I said, a recurring dream. My last therapist, who moved all the way to Michigan to get away from me, told me it meant I was afraid to go out into the world. Well thanks. And to think I paid money for that profound analysis. Yes, I agreed, I see the world as a challenge full of scary things—now tell me something I don't know. Earn those seventy bucks an hour.

I find the keys for the Andrews' apartment. Mr. Ed is right by the door, waiting for relief.

"Where have you been?" he barks at me.

"I'm sorry, Mr. Ed. I fell asleep. Let's go. Where's your leash?"

Mr. Ed jumps up and down, his nose pointing in the direction of the kitchen counter. I grab the leash and off we go at a trot down the four flights of stairs. At the front door I clip on his leash. When we get to the street, Mr. Ed heads for the gutter and gratefully does his business. A smile of relief creeps across his doggie face.

"Let's walk over to the park, little fellow. I could use a heart to heart." It's a warm evening and the sun is going down. Twilight, I think; it is twilight time. A jogger passes us as we enter the park on Eighty-fifth Street. His breathing is labored and steady. He slows down as he approaches us and glances at his watch. He's checking his time, grading his performance, logging his miles. Keeping track. It's important. I keep track of my calories, and I try to exercise three times a week, and I try to keep track of my cigarettes. I pat my pockets and realize I left without them. Just as well. I've got to quit smoking, I remind myself for the millionth time, but the thought of stopping makes me crave one. One cigarette and then I'll quit. And there it is, the whole damn merry-go-round, but my head feels groggy and only nicotine will set it right.

Mr. Ed is happily sniffing everything in sight. He sniffs the ground and the leaves and the flowers and the dirt and the ants and the rocks and the occasional dog that passes and sometimes just the air. He perks his happy ears up and sniffs the breeze as it rushes past his black button nose. I try sniffing the air with my pink button nose but it doesn't make me as happy as it makes Mr. Ed. For dogs, things are simple. I envy that.

We walk over to the Delacorte Theater and sit down on one of the benches. The park is filled with flowering plants and trees. I look out over the Great Lawn where the baseball fields are a warm brick red and the grass is a grass, grass green, as Dylan Thomas might say. "Arf, arf, arf, arf?" Mr. Ed inquires as he hops up on the bench and settles in next to me.

"What's up, you ask? Well, not much," I answer. "I booked a couple of dates at Don't Tell Mama, and I'm seeing this really nice guy, and I feel sad but happy but sad but happy all the time and it's making me crazy. Oh, and I've been hallucinating, or at least I think I'm hallucinating. You haven't seen a little pink or blue fairy flying around, have you?"

"Arrf!" Mr. Ed says, spotting a squirrel next to the sycamore tree behind us. He leaps off the bench and barks like he's possessed. It's hard having an extended conversation with Ed because he is so easily distracted.

"Let's go," I say, pulling at the leash, and he has no choice but to obey. I like that in a companion. We walk around the Great Lawn. At the north end I stop and look south at the skyline. The view is magnificent from here. On a summer weekend it is almost impossible to make it past this part of God's green acre without a couple of tourists asking you to take a picture of them framed by the vista. Mr. Ed spots a Great Dane and tugs at the leash, anxious for a sniff.

On the way back to the apartment my dog companion confesses a rather intense infatuation he had with a very inappropriate Irish setter, or at least that's what I think he says.

He snarls at a poodle as we turn down Columbus Avenue, causing her to yelp and hide behind her owner's legs. He "arfs" with satisfaction and then we ease into a stroll for the rest of the walk home.

I give Mr. Ed some doggie treats and wish him a good evening. He's asleep on the rug by the time I turn out the light. When I get home, my message machine is blinking.

It's Dee-Honey, wanting to set up dates with me for the summer. "So glad you're available, honey," her voice on the machine says.

It's already nine o'clock so I decide to call her tomorrow. I light a much-needed cigarette and get a beer out of the fridge and turn on the radio to the Yankees game. It's the bottom of the seventh inning. They're playing Baltimore and winning, which is not a surprise. I sit in the dark sipping my beer and listening. Derek Jeter hits a home run and the fans yell and the Yankees go ahead four to nothing.

I try to concentrate on the action and not on the fact that I haven't heard from my charming young prince of a fellow who now has a set of my keys and a place at the table of my life. I pick up the phone to make sure it's working. It is.

"Goodie," I say out loud, "are you there? The Yankees are winning. Derek just hit a home run. Remember how you and Joe and I watched the games that summer?" The words catch in my throat. "Goodie, are you there?" I turn down the radio and hold my breath and listen for the flapping of little wings, but there is nothing except the sound of my Big Ben desk clock ticking off the seconds.

5

The next morning I wake up with a start and realize I have fallen asleep on the sofa with the radio on, and now it is seven a.m. and Curtis and Kuby are bantering away about Al Sharpton's latest bid for notoriety. My head is pounding. I take two aspirin and decide to go for a run and start my life over—no more cigarettes, beer, scotch, sugar, younger men, and no more imaginary fairy godmothers. I have a singing gig to prepare for. The thought of it takes my breath away. I light a cigarette and remind myself I have six weeks. Plenty of time.

I splash water on my face and try to get my hair to go in one direction. I make a cup of coffee, smoke another cigarette, then I feed Bixby and leave my apartment. It's not even eight o'clock yet. Amazing! I stop in front of my building and start to stretch out my legs.

Across the street, on the stoop of one of the beautifully-renovated-single-family-million-dollar-plus brownstones, sits a slightly balding, slightly overweight fellow smoking a cigarette and reading a newspaper. This guy spends a lot of time sitting on his front stoop smoking. Obviously he's not allowed to practice his bad habit indoors. He sips his coffee and takes a drag off his cigarette. I'm sure his coffee is not the discount blend I drink but rather a robust, full-bodied import. I feel poverty stricken for a moment and jealous of this man's big brownstone with the chandelier on the first floor and the flagstone patio in back, but then I think, so what? Maybe he does drink a better brand of coffee than I do, and lives in better digs, but nobody is telling me where I can or can't smoke—except the city of New York, but that's beside the point. So there, Mr. Big Bucks! It's horrible, the mean thoughts I construct to bolster my ego so I can get through the day.

I groan as my right hamstring relaxes into the stretch. Big Bucks looks up momentarily from his paper and nods almost imperceptibly. I nod even more imperceptibly and continue stretching. The sky is crystal clear and there is no humidity. A perfect day. I set off at a slow trot and head for the park. I'm more of a runner/walker than a pure runner. My knees have never been the same since I hyperextended the ligaments in a free-fall smash into a fence skiing about fifteen years ago. I stop at the red light on Central Park West and turn on my Walkman, which is clipped to my shorts. Cyndi Lauper fills my ears. "Girls just want to have fun," I sing along with Cyndi as I run/walk down to the boat pond near East Seventy-second Street, and then under the Trefoil Arch heading toward Bethesda Fountain. Adorning the top of the fountain is a bronze angel with extended wings and a long skirt that billows around her legs.

She is the *Angel of the Waters*, commemorating the opening in 1842 of the Croton Aqueduct, which purified the city's water supply. In the Gospel of John, an angel was said to have troubled the pool of Bethesda in Jerusalem and thereby bestowed healing power on its waters. I stop in front of the fountain and catch my breath. I am comforted in the Angel's presence, knowing she is walking this earth, troubling the waters and healing the afflicted. I dip my hands in the fountain, splash the water on my face, and smile up at her. "Let out the bad air and let in the good air," I think as I continue my run/walk up through the Ramble and past Belvedere Castle.

Mr. Big Bucks is not on his stoop when I return. He's no doubt down on Wall Street making gobs of money in that rarified world of high-stakes Monopoly, and good for him, because right now I feel rich too. My body is working in spite of the abuse I heap on it. My skin is clear, my hair still has some natural sheen, and my teeth are all my own. Life is good. Indeed, the waters of Bethesda have worked magic and I don't, at least for the moment, need to find fault with the rest of the world so I can feel better about myself, and that is definitely some kind of miracle.

I open the door to my apartment and find Jack sitting on the sofa reading the paper. I let out a startled yelp. He smiles at me. "Hey, baby, I brought some sticky buns." He gestures to a Hot & Crusty bag on the coffee table. "I would have made some coffee, but I couldn't find the filters."

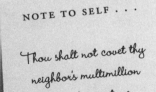

NOTE TO SELF . . .

Thou shalt not covet thy neighbor's multimillion dollar brownstone.

I sit down and try to calm my heart, which is thumping in my chest like the percussion section of a John Philip Sousa marching band.

"Are you okay?" Jack asks.

"Sure, sure," I say, still short of breath. "I'm just not used to walking into my apartment and finding someone here and it caught me by surprise and at first I thought I was going to have a heart attack but I guess not so we won't have to call 911." I take a deep breath.

"Sorry," Jack says.

"It's fine, but I do think I need to sit here quietly for a few minutes and try to slow my heart rate down before it goes into arrhythmia which it has done a few times like when I was on a roller coaster in Sandusky, Ohio, and that's how it feels right now which believe me is scary . . ." I finish with the last bit of oxygen left in my lungs.

"Gosh," Jack says contritely. "I didn't mean to upset you. I thought I'd drop by this morning and have breakfast with you. I'm looking at an apartment in the neighborhood."

He walks over and starts to rub my shoulders. "I know Swedish massage," Jack purrs. "Why don't you lie down on the bed and I can help you to relieve some of that anxiety. It'll feel great." Damn. He is going to get to me again. I'm a sucker for any form of body contact.

"Do you have any oil? Baby oil or something?" Jack asks, heading for the bathroom. Damn and double damn. I am especially a sucker for body contact involving oil.

"Take your clothes off," he says as he enters with a bottle of discount you-know-what.

"Maybe I should jump in the shower," I suggest, suddenly feeling self-conscious about the run/walk sweat I worked up in the summer heat.

"We'll do that later. You smell great," he says straddling me and pulling his shirt over his head. "This is going to be really good, Mags. Trust me. All right. Now close your eyes and breathe. I'll do all the work," Jack coos.

Oh I do like it when someone coos, and I like it especially when someone else does all the work. I moan a little, hum softly, and try to relax.

When I was about five years old, my mother and I tried an experiment we read about in *Highlights* children's magazine. I don't remember the exact directions or all the ingredients, but basically you combined food coloring with salt and other everyday substances, and in a few minutes the raw ingredients were transformed into beautiful crystal sculptures. Jack's alchemy is beginning to transform my raw everyday ingredients into some new configuration, a warmer, softer substance. Or am I just more "me" in the presence of "him"? Or is the mix of exercise endorphins and gentle massage causing me to hallucinate? Whatever it is, it is good. It certainly feels good as I lie on my bow-tie-print quilt with a strong young man straddling my body massaging away the tensions of the world. The massage turns into sex and then into a shower and then into a day. Jack leaves to look at apartments, and I decide it is time to plan my show at Don't Tell Mama. It's time to call Thomas Garrick, the accompanist I like from *Eleanor Roosevelt: The Musical!* He had mentioned that he liked my voice, thought I had a sort of Barbra Streisand quality. So there, it's true, flattery will get you something, maybe not everything, but definitely something.

"Hello, Thomas. It's Maggie Barlow remember me? Aka Barbra Streisand?" I announce into his answering machine. "Anyway, I have a club date in a few weeks and I was wondering if you'd be available to play it. I have all the charts. So it would be a few rehearsals and then two dates the end of next month. The twenty-fifth and twenty-sixth. Give me a call. Thanks."

I open my cupboard. *The* cupboard. The cupboard that stands against the wall in my living room and contains all the "this and that" of my life. This program, that review, this tax return, that playbill, this broken tambourine, that photo album, this sewing kit, and now I look for those charts. Those charts that Goodie had done for me. My music. Our music. We were both eclectic in our taste and had fun putting together odd medleys combining rock and Broadway or blues and standards. Goodie and I worked together on every arrangement so that it sat just right in my voice and expressed just what we wanted. It took a lot of work. We argued, laughed, cried.

I remember standing at the window of his studio one afternoon looking out at the rooftops of West Fifty-fourth Street. "You've helped me to fall in love with music," I said.

Until then music had been a means to an end for me — a way to get noticed, to get a boyfriend, to get a job, to get attention. But Goodie changed that. He made me see that the music wasn't about me. The music was about the music. The second or third session I had with him, after spending half an hour belting out tunes and trying to impress him with my power and my range, he told me to listen while he sat and carefully played the melody line from one of the songs I had been blasting through. He played it slowly, one note at a time, and then he added chords and a harmony and the music began to swell and I heard it.

"That's the song," he said when he finished. "Your voice is just another instrument that serves it. You have to be part of the music and not try to upstage it."

I'd spent most of my life trying to upstage whatever seemed threatening to me. I laughed too loud, drank too much, stayed out too late, all in an attempt to keep "feelings" at bay. Like the pioneers traveling west in wagon trains, I lit bonfires to keep the scary things away from my campgrounds. I didn't like feelings, or maybe more to the point, I didn't know what to do with them. I learned to sing from my mother who sang hymns at the kitchen sink. I can still hear her singing "The Old Rugged Cross" as she carefully dried the cups and plates and knives and forks and put them neatly away. The music seemed to put her in a different place, a place that had nothing to do with two kids and a dog and a mortgage and a Pontiac station wagon, and all the feelings she couldn't deal with—a place where she could be happy with no thought of us and our scrapes and bruises. So I also learned to let the music take me away from my feelings. I wrapped my talent in a flurry of style and attitude and pizzazz and not much else. Until I met Goodie.

I stand looking at the scraps of my life that are wedged into the five wide shelves of my grandmother's cherry wood cupboard. An old eight-by-ten photo lands on the floor as I rummage through the piles of *things:* a coffee tin of miscellaneous buttons, a backgammon set, a Norman Rockwell one-thousand-piece jigsaw puzzle unopened (who has the time?), a flashlight without batteries, three yellow legal pads still in the cellophane, a Xeroxed script of *Little Red Riding Hood,* sides from an under-five on *All My Children,* a half-empty bag of rubber bands. Toward the back on the third shelf I locate the accordion file marked *Goodie/ Charts.* I pull it out, place it in my lap, and untie the string that holds it closed.

Goodie wrote his charts by hand, music calligraphy, beautiful to look at, on ivory medium-stock composing sheets. He wrote in pencil, soft no. 1 lead, sharpened to a fine point in the Panasonic electric pencil sharpener that sat to the left of his piano. Sometimes I stood beside him and consulted. We discussed ideas for the arrangements and agreed on the key and tempo, but really I just watched. I'm a voyeur in that way. I love watching people do things they do well. I love watching painters paint and potters pot and ballplayers play ball. And I loved watching Goodie write music.

"Did you?" Goodie is hovering near the window, decked out today in a long black cocktail dress with gold lamé elbow-length gloves. "Did you love watching me write?"

"Jesus, you scared me," I say. "Goodie, are you real? Or am I hallucinating? Not enough blood to the brain?"

"I'm a figment of your imagination, enjoy it," he replies. "Did you really love watching me write?"

"Yes, I did."

"Well, I loved listening to you sing." Goodie circles the room, then perches on the windowsill. "And it's time now to get out of the Dorothy drag and back on the big-girl stage, Miss Maggie Magnolia."

"Funny, Charles said the same thing," I say.

"Charles and I were often of the same mind," Goodie says. "Especially in matters concerning costumes and cabaret."

"Well, I like that outfit."

"Yes, very Audrey Hepburn don't you think?"

"It's the first scene from *Breakfast at Tiffany's*," I say.

"It is, isn't it?" Goodie giggles and struts back and forth. Then he stops. "Okay, enough about fashion. Now stop looking at that music and start singing it."

"I'll try. It's just that . . ."

"No excuses, love. I won't let you have excuses anymore. Don't you get it, Maggie? It's on loan. Your voice, your talent. All of it. Everything's a rental. So use it up. Wring out every drop before your lease runs out."

"Yikes, Goodie, you've gone New Age on me."

"New Age, darlin'? I've gone completely around the bend. I'm eight inches tall, I'm wearing pink plastic stilettos, and I'm dating G.I. Joe! So listen to me, Mags, dreams really do come true, and now I'm off to a cocktail party. One of the Cabbage Patch dolls is getting engaged to a Power Ranger."

"I thought Cabbage Patch dolls were babies," I say.

"In body only. Those kids are wild. It's quite a scandal and I don't want to miss a moment." Goodie blows me a kiss as he motors out the window and into the daylight.

The phone rings. It's Thomas Garrick, the accompanist. He's available for the club dates. "That's great," I say. "Can we make an appointment for a rehearsal?" We both check our books and agree on two hours day after tomorrow. "Great, I'll see you then," I say and hang up.

"God respects me when I work," an ancient Sanskrit proverb says. "But he loves me when I sing."

And he really loves me when I am gainfully employed and paying my rent and saving for retirement. I look at my appointment book and realize I have an audition in an hour and a half. Enough reflecting. Time to get it up and get it on and get the job. I check my schedule for the next day and am reminded I'm doing the Blue Fairy in *Pinocchio* at Trenton, New Jersey. I make a mental note to make sure I still have some blue glitter eye shadow. Thank God I don't have to squeeze into Dorothy's pinafore again.

The audition is for a national commercial for one of those room deodorizer things that I never use, but I'm an actress and I can be enthusiastic about anything if it pays well.

I pop a stick of gum in my mouth and light a cigarette and start getting ready. The phone rings. It's Texas Joe, Goodie's brother and my old love. We still keep in touch. Maybe Goodie has been visiting him too.

"I've got about ten minutes," I say. "Then I have to scoot to an audition." Joe understands. He's actually a little starstruck by me. That shows what a long way civil engineering is from the performing arts—any closer and he'd know I was light-years from stardom.

"I have another grandchild on the way. Beth is due in December."

"Wow. That makes three, right? Good for you, but I still stay you're too young to be a grandfather."

"Well, I got an early start, I was married at twenty-one," he says.

"That is so scary to me."

"It's scary to me too, now," he says.

"And speaking of all that. How's the love life? Are you still seeing the . . . nurse, is it?"

"Dentist," he says. "And yes we are still seeing each other. She's busy. Lots of teeth down here."

I laugh halfheartedly, take my gum out, and sip the coffee. We talk about the stock market for a few minutes and then about baseball and then about how much we miss each other. It's the same conversation we always have. I tell him about Jack but don't mention his name—or age: "I'm seeing someone. We've had a couple of dates. You know." And then we get into a little of the sex thing. Texas Joe and I had great sex. He wore suits all the time and that really turned me on for some reason. So when we talk, it inevitably gets sexy and I get turned on and Joe's voice gets thick, but today there isn't time.

"I've got to run, Joe. Sorry, but I can't be late. Thanks for calling. I miss you." As I hang up the phone, I know I mean it. I do miss Joe. I hold the phone against my cheek for a moment and then realize I'm sitting stark naked on the toilet seat. I pull on a pair of Jockey-for-Her cotton panties and the rest of my undergear, which is a leopard print bra from Kmart that cost only $6.99. A good cheap fun bra is a real find, and I absolutely recommend Kmart's annual two-for-one sale.

I take time to put on Paul Simon's *Graceland* because it always gets me in the mood for about anything. I approach the mirror. Time to paint the face. At forty-one, I have to say I look pretty good. At least my skin still has a glow and some natural moisture, but time is definitely moving along. My neck is getting that chicken skin thing that my mother always complained about.

"It looks like plucked chicken wattle," she would say as she tweezed her eyebrows in the magnifying mirror held close to her face. I stand now for a moment and review the subtle changes, which are becoming less and less subtle. I pull the neck skin tight by placing my index fingers under my jawbone and moving them back about an inch. And that does it. It is such an easy adjustment it seems it could be accomplished with a desk stapler and a hot glue gun packaged in an over-the-counter kit with some gauze and surgical tape—"A Brand New Face" by Revlon. And Dee-Honey says I'm still pretty. Even that heckler was jealous. I still have it. I go to the kitchen and get a beer. Here's to the eternal ingénue, I toast myself.

I sense something awry down south as I apply some eyeliner. My jockeys feel funny. I scratch a little. I check the clock. Time to get a move on. But there is now a good bit of discomfort. I scratch some more. Something feels sticky. I pull down my panties, but the crotch is stuck. Stuck to what? I think. Stuck to my pubic hair! A wad of sticky gray substance is stuck to my pubic hair! What is this? A fossilized egg that has been trapped in my fallopian tube for twenty years, an early sign of menopause, or possibly the Lindbergh baby?

I pull off the cotton jockeys and realize that the gum I had innocently put in my mouth a half hour ago has somehow ended up in my crotch. I think back over the sequence of events:

1. I put a stick of gum in my mouth.
2. I lit a cigarette.
3. I was getting ready to floss my teeth so
4. I took the gum out of my mouth.
5. The phone rang and
6. I put the gum on the closed toilet seat.
7. I answered the phone and sat down — where?
8. ON THE CLOSED TOILET SEAT!

Now what? I'm dumbfounded for a moment and have no idea what to do. I can't face the emergency room and the rude comments that this situation would elicit. Scissors, I think rather squeamishly. I find a pair and gingerly start to operate. It takes only one snip to realize this is not a good idea. I look in my medicine cabinet and see it. I know it's my best option. Got to do it. I brace myself and reach for the nail polish remover and cotton balls. I swab it on fast. Yowsa! The stingy paint thinner kerosene stuff in the nail polish remover does the job. I jump in the shower lickety-split and the crisis is over. I consider writing the whole experience down and submitting it to Eve Ensler for her show *The Vagina Monologues*.

I get to the audition. I'm out of breath and a little scorched around the

NOTE TO SELF . . .

Keep your gum in your mouth and not in your panties.

privates, but I'm perky and focused and the casting director, Mike Oft, winks as I leave and gives me the high sign. He's a nice guy and I've booked a lot of stuff through him; he always tries to get me the gig. It's nice to have someone on your side. Of course, the final decision isn't his. He's one of many hurdles on the road to production. There is the client, the advertising agency, the casting director, the agent, the receptionist, the guy who delivers the pizza, and, lastly, the talent. Sometimes the client's wife or son or accountant or butcher has a say as well. I did a voice-over for a panty hose brand (I won't name names, but they come in a plastic egg and there is an apostrophe), and the client brought his ten-year-old daughter, Belinda, to the recording session and suddenly Belinda became an expert on phrasing. You never know when talent will surface.

THAT NIGHT JACK and I walk to Lincoln Center. It's my favorite place in New York. On a night when the fountain is on and the Metropolitan Opera House and Avery Fisher Hall and the New York State Theater and the Vivian Beaumont are all lit up, it's the most magnificent place in the world. We get a couple of sandwiches and some beer and sit out by the sculpture pond. The night is warm and the music from Damrosch Park wafts through the air and we eat and drink and listen to the sounds of the summer night.

"Heaven, I'm in heaven," the right side of my brain sings. We walk back uptown and get ice cream cones on the way, a double chocolate chip for me and pistachio for Jack.

"Do you play pool, Mags?" Jack asks as we pass the Broadway Pool and Billiards Hall on Seventy-eighth Street.

"A little. I mean I can chalk up." I laugh and Jack laughs.

"What do you say we play a few games?"

"It's kind of late," I say, although reluctantly.

"It's only ten thirty. Come on. I'll show you a thing or two. Pool is fun."

"Really? It's been years since I've even been in a pool hall."

"Come on."

"All right. But I'm going to need a few beers to loosen up."

"Absolutely," Jack says and takes my arm and hustles me through the door. And hustle, my friends, is the name of the game.

Jack gets us a table and a couple of Heinekens. Then he explains to me how to choose the right size pool stick.

"Oh, I see," I say, measuring the stick. "It should just come to here."

"Right. Now. Easy does it." Jack takes the frame and corrals the balls.

"I'll break," he says. "And you watch to get a feel for it."

"Sure, I'm all eyes." I take a long swig of my beer.

Jack aces the first three shots, then scratches on the fourth. My turn. I take my stick and chalk it up.

"Slow and steady," Jack instructs me. "Here, put your fingers lightly on the table. I suggest you go for the four ball into the corner pocket."

"Thanks," I say. "But I thought maybe I would bank the six ball off the back bumper and send it down the lane into the side pocket. Like this."

I lean over and line up my shot. The six ball kisses the back bumper, marches down the lane, and slips into the pocket like I said it would.

"Four ball in the side." I love this game. I love the geometry of it, the triangles and rectangles. The pretty patterns the balls make.

"You're hustling me," Jack says with a grin.

"You betcha," I say. "I am hustling your ass. Three ball in the corner." The ball glides across the green felt as smooth as Kristi Yamaguchi on ice. It's a three-dimensional algebra problem worked out in bright spheres—an equation in pressure points.

"The last ball off the rail and in the left pocket," I say, and with that I clear the table.

"You're good."

"I know. I need another beer. Loser buys."

"Coming up, Miss Minnesota Fats." Jack kisses me full on the mouth. "Love you." Then he grabs my ass and I grab his.

"Love you too, big guy. And I love whipping your ass."

"This game ain't over yet, Sweet Pea, not by a long shot."

Jack gets us another round of beers and I rack the balls. We play till they close the joint. We're drunk and in love and the night feels like a big warm hug.

When we get to my place, we make love. We really make love. We slowly explore the particular ins and outs of each other's body and then fit them together in a harmony of motion—not the blazing heat of a one-night stand, but the slow burn of desire to make someone, someone you really like, feel really good. And later I sleep in a cool sea of contentment with Jack, the guy from Queens who still lives at home and sells cars for a living, nestled snugly into the crook of my life. I feel happy. Is it possible to be happy? As I close my eyes I think I see Goodie all decked out in a real fairy godmother dress. Not some Barbie thing but chiffon and sequins and a trail of fairy dust from his magic wand. And then just as I sit up he's gone, but there on the nightstand are a few sprinkles of glitter. Did I leave them there? Did they fall off of some costume jewelry, or was Goodie here for a moment spreading magic? I lie back down and circle Jack with my arm and listen to him breathe. Yes, I think, happy is possible.

6

The next morning the alarm goes off at seven a.m. I have to go to Trenton to do *Pinocchio*. Dee-Honey is going to be at the pickup spot at eight thirty. Jack rolls over and puts his arms around me.

"Mornin', Sweet Pea," he says.

"Mornin' to you," I say back and burrow in close to him. We lie like that for a while, breathing in tandem. Then I feel Jack's "manness" get manly. I sing softly into his ear as he makes sweet love to little old me. He is like fine wine. He is a precious substance.

"Oh my God," I say, glancing at the clock. "We've got to fast-forward. It's five to eight." I rush to the bathroom. "I'm going to be late and Dee-Honey has about had it with me; I can't keep her waiting again." I turn on the shower and step in. I start to soap up and Jack slips in behind me.

"I'm doing the Blue Fairy in *Pinocchio*," I tell him squeezing some shampoo on my hair.

"*Pinocchio* the one with the cat in the boot?" he asks.

"Didn't you ever see a Disney film?" I ask. "Pinocchio is the wooden boy whose nose grows when he lies."

"And what does the Blue Fairy do?" Jack asks running his hands down my back and massaging the small section above my pelvis, which indeed feels tight and I wonder how he knows that.

"After Pinocchio learns his lesson, the Blue Fairy turns him into a real boy," I say.

"Hmmm . . . must be fun for Pinocchio. I thought this was a kid's show."

"She hits him on the head with a wand. It's not like a *Here's to you, Mrs. Robinson* moment."

"Your chakra feels tense here," he comments as he deepens and intensifies his touch.

"Really? I didn't even know I had a chakra there."

"Well you do, and it's hard as a rock," he says, kneading it gently with his thumbs.

"I've got to get going." I turn and wrap my arms around Jack's neck. "Thanks."

"Just tell me one thing," he says.

"What?"

"Where the hell did you learn to play pool like that?"

"My brother taught me when I was ten," I say, stepping out of the shower and grabbing a towel. "He was stuck with me one summer because our mom was away. He was eighteen. Every evening we went to the local pool hall and got hot dogs for dinner and played pool. I liked the symmetry and I loved being with my big brother."

"Sounds like a nice guy."

"It's funny, we barely even speak now, but that summer we were pool hall buddies, hangout friends, and by

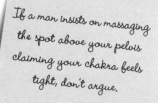

NOTE TO SELF . . .

If a man insists on massaging the spot above your pelvis claiming your chakra feels tight, don't argue.

the end of it, I could whip his butt and he loved it. He thought I was a natural, and I thought he was the best big brother in the world. We hustled everybody in town."

Jack leans down and kisses me sweetly and then hugs me close. "So Pinocchio has a happy ending?"

"Yeah, I guess."

"Well, he gets to be a real boy and maybe one day he finds a real girl," Jack whispers in my ear. "That's a very happy ending."

"Is it?" I say. "What if it doesn't work out? What if they don't live happily ever after?"

"Slow down," Jack says, "you'll get your chakra tight again."

"I just don't think happy endings are what they're cracked up to be," I say, "like we're always looking for a happy ending?"

"And always finding them," Jack says.

"What do you mean?" I ask, brushing my teeth.

"Well, we had a nice evening together and that was a happy ending to the day, and you'll make Pinocchio a real boy and the kiddies will clap and that's a happy ending, and I'll sell a couple of cars today and that's a happy ending."

"Hmmm," I slush some water around in my mouth and spit.

"And now you're teeth are dazzling white and you look beautiful and I'm going to kiss you," Jack says, leaning toward me. "And that's a happy ending."

"Oh, I see, it's the little things."

"Yeah, little things like this," Jack says kissing me gently and then pulling me close. The phone rings in the other room and the machine picks up. It's Dee-Honey.

"Mags, we're on the corner, honey," she announces. "Maybe you're on your way out the door."

"Gotta go," I say to Jack, "got to go make magic."

Jack grabs me and kisses me goodbye. "Happy ending," he says with a wink as I dash out the door.

BUT WHAT *IS* a happy ending, I wonder as I rush out of the apartment. Is it an ending in which everything turns out fine? When the lasagna doesn't burn and the potatoes are done on time? Or do the stakes have to be higher for a really happy ending? Is it the safe end to a difficult journey fraught with life-threatening events that one survives against all odds? Does a happy ending have to be a miracle, or can it be just a pretty sunset at the end of the day and a simple kiss goodnight?

A car horn honks and Dee is waving from the van as she pulls up to the curb. Randall Kent rolls down the window.

"We had to circle the block. Where have you been?" he says getting out and letting me crawl in between him and Dee.

"Sorry," I say, "I had a terrible time finding my keys. You know how you leave then someplace and the next minute they are nowhere to be found. I should keep them around my neck." I don't know why I lie all the time. I don't know why I can't say I had an overnight guest and we had a beautiful morning of lovemaking and I happen to be a little late. Actually, I do know why: lying is easier.

"Put the keys in a special place," Eddie yells from the back. "I always put mine in a dish next to the refrigerator and they are always there. I also have an extra set sewn into the lining of my knapsack, and then my super has a set and my neighbor on the third floor. So if I lose them, I can always get into my apartment."

"I wasn't trying to get in, Eddie, I was trying to get out," I say over my shoulder.

"Aren't we all dear?" Eddie says with a flourish and takes a long drink from his thermos. And off we go to the land of make-believe.

"REALITY IS INDISPUTABLE," Jack says, squeezing a wedge of lime into his Corona Extra. We're having dinner at a village bistro on West Tenth Street with my friends Annie and Ray.

"Whose reality?" I ask, taking a bite of a deep-fried mozzarella stick.

"Careful," Ray cautions. "Those things are hot."

My mouth screams in pain. I take a long pull off my Rolling Rock and try to act nonchalant. But the indisputable reality at the moment is that my tongue is singed.

"Are you okay, Mags?" Annie asks.

"Fine," I answer and toast her with my beer. "You know me. Tough as nails." I reach for another stick of mozzarella to prove my point. Jack stops my hand midair.

"Here let me." He takes the stick and blows on it and then hands it over. I feel like a three-year-old. "There, Sweet Pea, now try it."

Ray and Annie both look up at the same moment and I know what they are thinking: *Did he actually call her Sweet Pea?*

One side of my brain goes, "Ugh" to Jack and "Don't patronize me" and "Stop calling me Sweet Pea." The other side says, "Please stay with me and blow on my food forever."

"Reality is relative," Annie says, getting back to the discussion at hand. Oh boy, I think, here we go, treading down the slippery path of metaphysics—not my strongest subject.

"Relative to what?" Jack asks.

"Circumstances," Ray says nibbling carefully on a mozzarella stick. "A blind man's reality is considerably different than a sighted man's."

"Why?" Jack goes on. "You're living in the same physical world — subject to the same laws of nature."

"Yes, but I, as a sighted man, don't need a white walking stick or a Seeing Eye dog to negotiate the topography," Ray explains. "My reality is that I can drive a car. A blind man's reality is that he needs someone to drive it for him."

"But the reality is the car must be driven. How it's done is irrelevant," my young hero asserts.

"The how is utmost," Ray pontificates with glee. "The where and the when are facts; and, yes, indisputable. But the how and the why are fraught with variables and therefore subject to dispute."

"And what's the other thing of the five things, you know, in journalism?" I ask, trying to hold on to my place in the discourse.

"Yes," says Ray.

"Yes, what?" I ask.

"Yes, what is the other thing. How, when, where, why, and what, and all of it in the first paragraph," Ray explains ever so slowly to me, the three-year-old with the badly burned tongue.

The meal arrives. Chicken wings, well-done fries, and another Rolling Rock. I'm starving, but have go to slow because of the tongue situation.

Ray and Annie have been together for years. They never married, but by now qualify as a common-law couple. They are both smart and work for public radio and have an exotic bird named Ulysses who bit me the first time we met. Annie said it was because Ulysses thought I was patronizing him when I asked if he wanted a cracker.

Annie and I met doing summer stock twenty-some years ago. I

was the girl in the bib overalls painting sets and setting the props and hitting the high notes and Annie was the dark-haired ingénue who sang off-key but could dance like crazy.

"Well, age is indisputable," Jack says. "You can't argue that." I almost bite my already damaged tongue. The last thing I want to discuss is the indisputable properties of age with someone under forty. I signal the waiter.

"I'll have another R-r-rolling R-r-rock," I say with a slight stammer. My tongue is rebelling against the lousy treatment I've been giving it. I can't say that I blame it.

Ray, the intrepid, charges into the age issue. "I have to disagree. Age is indeed relative."

Christ. Where is my beer? I toy with my fork and contemplate thrusting it into Ray's larynx.

"There is physical age, emotional age, perceived age," he continues with the kind of reckless certitude that comes with an Ivy League education. "One is only as old as one feels is a cliché, yes, but it is absolutely true. You cannot measure age with a number."

I've noticed this argument becomes more and more emphatic the older and older the arguer gets. It's a syndrome known as denial. Ray, in this case, will be fifty-one on his next birthday, so he is adamant in his stance as he glares across the table at my twenty-eight-year-old-stud-muffin boyfriend, who is smiling indulgently at him.

"All right, Ray, I'll let you have this point because I don't want to risk your blood pressure going any higher," Jack says good-naturedly. Annie laughs and pats Ray's hand.

"The middle-age crisis is a terrible thing. We better get going. I have to be up early tomorrow." Annie motions to the waiter for the check. I take it from him when he offers it.

"My treat," I say. "I just booked a national commercial, so please let me be the *indisputable* hostess of this soiree. Besides, I played the Blue Fairy in *Pinocchio* today, so I can make all your dreams come true if you're nice to me and don't argue."

THAT NIGHT I WAKE up with a start. I look at the numbers on the clock — 2:30 a.m. The light from the building next door is bleeding through my blinds so I get up and start to close them tighter, but instead I look out into the back courtyard. Most of the windows are dark and the people inside sound asleep, as they should be. There is a light in the third-floor window of the building across from me, the shade is drawn and I can see a shadow moving back and forth across the room — another insomniac passing a sleepless night. I watch as the shadow moves through the apartment. I'm not really an insomniac. I usually sleep well, but now and then I have my bouts of wide-awake nights. When I do, I typically rummage through the kitchen looking for some carbohydrates; a bagel with a slab of butter or a bowl of cereal usually puts me out. But tonight I stand at the window, comforted by the fact that someone else is awake and pacing the hours until morning.

Jack dropped me off after dinner, saying he needed to get back to Queens for an early morning appointment. I did not entreat him to stay. The conversation with Ray and Annie was unsettling. What are the properties of age? What does it mean to be involved with someone younger? Does it mean I'm immature? Does it mean I'm afraid of commitment, or am I just looking for my very own "real boy"? After all, I am the perpetual ingénue. I can be anything as long as I have the right wig and makeup. And where is this relationship going and does it need to go anywhere? Can't it just be?

This train of thought is making me sleepier than a bagel and butter. Bixby is stretched across my pillow. I pick him up gently and put him on the foot of the bed. I turn on the radio. It's late-night talk on WABC. The caller is discussing an encounter he had with a flying saucer on a highway in northern Oregon. Bixby settles into the bend of my knees and the next thing I know it's eight a.m. and my phone is ringing.

The machine clicks on and I hear Jack's voice. "Hey, Sweet Pea, wake up. I miss you. Sorry I took off last night. You and I have to talk. This is getting a little crazy."

I throw the covers off and stumble toward the phone, but I'm too late. He has already hung up. And what can I say to that: "You and I have to talk"? Those are never good news words. In my experience, those words are rarely followed by words I want to hear.

And what does he mean "Sorry I took off last night" like we had a fight? We didn't have a fight, did we? He said he had an early appointment and wanted to be home in Queens when he woke up so he could get dressed and get on the road. Or was that a cover for the fight he was having in his own head about us—about where we are going and why? They were like the thoughts I had standing at the window in the middle of the night. Had Jack been standing at his window in Queens? I begin to ruminate until I look at the clock. It is later than I thought. I need to get a shower and get to my rehearsal session with Thomas. There is no time to ruminate now so I will have to ruminate later. *Ruminate* being another word I don't fully understand, I make a mental note to look it up the next time I'm near a dictionary.

7

So let's take a look at your charts and see what we have," Thomas says, reaching for the brown folder. "I usually like to do my own arrangements when I'm working with a client, but I'm open to anything."

"Great," I say, taking another sip of my coffee and trying to stop myself from screaming. I sometimes have an impulse to scream at the most inappropriate moments, and right now is one of those moments. I don't want to be here. I don't want to be starting with someone new and I don't want to be called a client.

"Interesting," Thomas says as he starts noodling through Goodie's arrangement of "My Funny Valentine." "How's the tempo? Is that about right for you? I like this song to bounce more. Like this." He plays it almost double time, like a happy sort of ditty.

"That seems too perky," I say.

"Well it is a happy song." Thomas continues to pluck it out.

"Yeah, I guess so. Except she's pleading with him to stay, which leads me to believe there is a question as to if he will stay and therefore I think she might not be as perky as she seems."

"So literal," says Thomas with a slight smirk. "Why don't you try it? Just sing through it and see how it feels."

He plays the first few bars in a saucy, upbeat tempo. I come in at the bridge racing a bit to catch up. The words feel strange in my mouth. I haven't sung this song in years. It's Rodgers and Hart, I think, but I'm not sure. I'm standing left of the piano, feeling uncomfortable. I don't know what to do with my hands. I feel self-conscious. The words keep coming out of my mouth and I don't seem to have anything to do with it. Thomas is nodding. We are almost at the end of the song. I'm singing and I'm watching myself sing, and then just like that I'm crying and watching myself cry. Thomas stops playing.

"Are you all right?" he asks.

I shake my head left to right and then shrug.

"I'll get you a glass of water. Do you need a tissue?"

I shake my head up and down this time. Snot is running in rivulets down the back of my throat. This is not pretty and certainly not professional.

"Here, take a sip." Thomas hands me the glass of water and a box of tissues. He watches as I take a drink. He takes the glass, sets it on the little table next to the piano.

"I don't know what's wrong," I say, shaking from the inside out. "I haven't sung these songs in a while—not since . . . Goodie . . ."

The word *died* remains unspoken. I can't get it out and I don't have to. Thomas puts his arms around me and starts to sway me from side to side.

"It's going to be all right, Maggie. You'll get used to singing with someone else. I didn't mean to push you. I think the arrangements are great."

"Can I use your bathroom for a moment?" I ask.

"Sure, absolutely," Thomas says, "it's down the hall on the left."

I go in the bathroom and gently shut the door. I sit down on the toilet, turn on the sink faucet full blast, and start to cry in long, loud sobs. My nose begins to run. I grab a handful of toilet paper and continue to cry loudly.

"Oh for goodness' sakes," Goodie says, pulling at my hair. "Look at me." I raise my eyes a smidgen. I don't want to be interrupted. I want to wail. I want to wallow. I want to cry for the rest of my life. "Give it up, girlfriend," Goodie says, tugging hard on my bangs.

"Ow, that hurts," I say between sobs. I swat at Goodie and he smacks me with his wand, right on my nose.

"Goodie, what do you think you are doing?"

"I'm trying to get your attention."

"Well, you've got it now so stop hitting me," I shout. I hear a knock on the bathroom door.

"Everything all right in there?" Thomas asks.

"Oh, yeah," I say, "I'm . . . getting . . . warmed up. I'll be right out." Goodie is sitting on the edge of the sink wearing a brand-new dress. A sunburst yellow affair, fringed with some sort of feathers — parakeet possibly?

"I'll say you're getting warmed up," he says. "You've got to get over this. You can't keep crying and moaning over me being gone. And it's fine for you to do your show for the kids and this and that, but you're a singer, Maggie, and you need to be in a club with a baby grand piano and spotlight with a pink amber gel singing your little ole heart out. I mean it's flattering, all this crying over me, but it's enough, time to grow up — you can't be an ingénue forever — take off the gingham and put on some sequins."

"Are you saying I'm getting old? Is that what you were sent back to do? Humiliate me so I become an old woman? So I just give it up?" I say.

"Surrender Dorothy, that's all I'm saying, Mags. You've been playing little girls for so long you've forgotten you're a full-blooded woman with a sultry voice and plenty of pain to sing about—sing the blues, sing swing, sing rock and roll. I don't want to see you turn into Bette Davis in *What Ever Happened*—"

"Shush! You don't need to rub my face in it, Mr. Smartie-Barbie-Pants. Don't think I haven't sat in front of the makeup mirror and had the same thought. Why just last week—"

"All right," Goodie says, cutting me off. "Now stop talking and get out there and sing from your soul, from deep down in the dark corner of your heart. Make me cry, Maggie, make me feel it." Goodie flies right in my face and chucks me under the chin with his tiny forefinger. "What do you say, Maggie Magnolia?"

"I'll try," I say in a teeny tiny voice, "but nobody plays piano like you."

"But I'm not here anymore, Mags, not really," Goodie say in his own teeny tiny voice. His little forehead is against mine, "So I want you to sing like the diva you are and stop doubting yourself. Make me proud of you."

"Why can't you come back, Goodie?" I say. "Why can't you drink a gallon of Miracle-Gro and come back to me like before?"

"It doesn't work that way, lovey, I wish it did," Goodie says with a sigh. "You think I don't miss it?"

"Do you?"

"God, yes, I miss my life," Goodie says, and a tiny crystal tear-drop rolls down his cheek. "I miss it all, but now I'm somewhere over the rainbow, like the song says, and believe me, it's a whole new thing, so I keep going, I keep on strutting right down the yellow brick road."

"And nobody could strut like you, Miss Goodie-Two-Shoes," I say, nuzzling Goodie's little neck, "nobody, nowhere . . ."

"No how!" Goodie squeals and then stands tall on the lip of the sink with hands on hips. "Now let's go out there and sing." I turn off the faucet and we leave the bathroom. Goodie perches himself on the piano for a while and taps his plastic-stiletto-encased foot and smiles at me and encourages me, and then at some point I realize he is gone and I'm still singing—singing in my grown-up deep-down voice with a vibrato that purrs real pretty when I let it.

For the rest of the session Thomas and I work through the songs, and I let him offer suggestions. A few times I have to stop and dab my eyes and nose, but all in all I sing as best I can. "It'll be easier next time," Thomas says at the end of the hour.

"Thank you," is all I can manage as I gather my things and leave. When I get on the street I feel as if I'm going to collapse into an emotional pile of mush right there on the corner of Twenty-second and Eighth Avenue.

I punch in the number of Charles's gallery on my cell phone. Tosh, his assistant, picks up.

"Is Charles available?" I ask. "It's Maggie."

"Maggie—hold on," Tosh says. "I'll see. I think he's finishing up with a client."

Ethel Merman bursts into song when Tosh puts me in the hold loop. Charles always has show tunes piped into his phone system. My mind wanders to the message from Jack. It sounds like the beginning of the end. You know the old where-is-this-going-I-like-you-a-lot-but-maybe-we-can-just-be-friends discussion. I wonder if Jack and I will end up very good friends. I have a feeling not, as we don't live in the same generational neighborhood, much less zip code. Tears start to well up again.

"Mags," Charles says, breaking in on Ethel Merman singing "No Business like Show Business." "What can I do for you?"

"I was wondering if you were free for lunch."

"Are you in the neighborhood?"

"No, I'm in Chelsea, on Twenty-second Street, but thought I would come down. I haven't seen the gallery in ages."

"I'd love to see you, darling, but I do have plans for a late lunch with a new client."

"Everybody's a fucking client."

"Why so much anger so early in the day, Mags?" Charles asks in an even tone.

"I just had my first session with a new accompanist." My voice breaks just slightly. I don't mention Goodie. I don't want Charles to know that I'm angry and crazy.

"I see. Come on down, my lunch isn't until three. Let's have a glass of wine. I think you need a port in the storm."

"Thanks, Charles. That's exactly what I need."

I walk over to Seventh Avenue and take the number 1 train downtown. It's very crowded. I stand and hold on to the metal bar above my head. The man sitting in front of me is smacking his chewing gum and reading the *New York Post*. The woman next to him is rolling her eyes and cursing under her breath. A trio of black men sing, "This little light of mine, I'm going to let it shine," in three-part harmony and pass a hat as they move through the car. The train arrives at the Franklin stop and I get off. Charles's gallery is on Walker Street. I stop at a deli and buy a 3 Musketeers candy bar. I eat as I walk and am once again struck by how perfect the consistency of the 3 Musketeers center filling is. I love it. I dig in my bag and find a cigarette; sugar and nicotine, nicotine and sugar—what more can I say? I arrive at the gallery in a pleasant haze. Charles hands me that promised glass of Chardonnay and I accept. I take two sips and settle back on his couch as the combination of substances kicks in.

"So what's the new piano player like?" Charles asks as he pours himself some wine.

"He's great. Everything is great." I inhale the rest of my wine and reach for the bottle. "I'm a funny valentine, let me tell you. I'm a funny little valentine." I pour another glass. "Things couldn't be more terrific. Have I told you about my guy? The twenty-eight-year-old?"

"Well you've hinted, but do tell all." Charles is a big sucker for a good romance.

"He calls me Sweet Pea and he gives me massages."

"The massages sound great, Sweet Pea is questionable."

"And he lives at home with his dad."

Charles chokes slightly.

"And he smells like fresh mowed grass."

"Does he live on a golf course?"

"Queens."

"Hmmm," says Charles as he refills my glass.

"Sometimes I stare at the back of his neck because I love the way his hair grows in a comma at the nape and the way the muscles of his neck look like two strong ropes suspending a colossus."

"A colossus. How big is this young man?"

"Plenty big."

"I see," says Charles with a grin.

"And when he leans down to kiss me his eyes are always wide

open so he doesn't miss a thing, and it makes me not want to miss a thing."

"Oh my, Mags, you're, as they say, 'head over heels.' What's happened to that tough outer shell you always wear so fetchingly?"

"Are you making fun of me?"

"No, not at all. It's great to be in love, to be infatuated. Enjoy it. Just don't expect it to last forever."

"Like you have to tell me that." In my head I count to ten, take a deep breath, and light a cigarette. "I know all about things not lasting forever," I say, exhaling smoke out of my nostrils like I saw Joan Crawford do in a 1940s film.

"And then yesterday while we were waiting on the corner for the light to change," I continue, "he started talking to a little girl in a stroller. She was about a year old and she cooed and laughed at Jack, and he cooed and laughed back, and I had this outrageous thought. I thought, I want to have this man's child."

"What's so outrageous about that?"

"First of all I've only known him a few days, barely a week."

"Love happens fast," Charles says, holding his wineglass up in a salute to the heart.

"And second of all, that's not my thing, the mother thing, that's not who I am. I'm a nonmaternal type woman. I wasn't born with the *mommy* gene, at least I don't think so, and if I was it is very recessive. I've never wanted to have a child. I didn't even play with dolls when I was a kid."

"Not even Betsy Wetsy?"

"No, I played dress-up and then I played detective, and sometimes my friend Ann and I played bomb shelter because she had lots of miniature canned goods and paper products."

"Oh, that sounds fun."

"We put Barbie and Ken in a cardboard box alone with the canned goods and waited for the all clear siren." I wonder to myself if that is why Goodie decided to haunt me in Barbie attire. He knows it strikes a chord.

"Well, maybe it wasn't the all clear siren you were waiting for," Charles is saying as I tune back in, "maybe it was your biological clock and now it has sounded and it's time for *Barbie and Ken* to stop waiting and get to work."

"Funny. That's funny. You forget I'm on the flip side of forty."

"Everyone has babies in their forties now. Besides, you're barely on the other side."

"Well, I'm not everyone, and I'm not having a baby."

"Oh go on. It will be fun. It will be a hoot. I'll give you a baby shower."

"This is easy for you to say. I'm not sure I have any viable eggs anymore. They could all be rotten by now. Dried up."

"I think you'd be surprised. I bet a couple of survivors are in there just waiting for a chance to meet the right Mr. Sperm."

"What's happened to *your* tough outer shell, for goodness sake? You sound like a besotted grandmother."

"Here's to babies," Charles says, raising his wineglass. "Here's to sweet round cuddly babies."

"To babies," I say reluctantly and click Charles's glass.

Charles's client shows up for lunch and I head back uptown. I'm more than a little tipsy and can't wait to lie down and take a nap. On the subway stairs a woman is struggling with a baby stroller. I offer to help and she gratefully nods. I grab the bottom half of the stroller and start down the stairs. The boy sitting smugly in the seat kicks his work boots and hits me square in the forehead and giggles with baby glee. The mother apologizes. I shake my head and smile sweetly as in *don't worry about it.* At the bottom of the stairs I put my end of the stroller down and rush off to catch the train, my head throbbing from the impact of baby's boot.

I sit on the train. My head is not only throbbing but pounding as well. I wasn't completely truthful with Charles about the baby issue. I had considered having a baby before—years ago. I was actually pregnant for five months and seventeen days. And I was married. I often forget that detail of my personal biography. The marriage. It was brief, ill advised perhaps, but ultimately fairly painless. Fairly, except for the miscarriage. A late miscarriage. Something went wrong and the baby had to be aborted. It was a girl. She died in vitro and fortunately the doctor was able to do the procedure immediately. Sometimes when it happens, the *nonviable fetus,* as it is referred to, has to stay put for a time and then labor is induced and the baby is delivered, a nightmare I was lucky enough not to have to endure.

I was twenty-six. Hugh, my husband, was twenty-seven. He was a graphic designer. He had a sheepdog named Ernie and lived in a duplex apartment on the Lower East Side. We met in Tompkins Square Park on a Saturday afternoon. I was reading Kurt Vonnegut's *Breakfast of Champions* and smoking a joint.

"That's a great book," Hugh said as he sat down next to me on the bench. "I've read it four times."

"Wow," I said and offered him a toke of my joint and thus began our relationship. We were inseparable for six months, I moved my things into his duplex apartment, then I got pregnant and we went to city hall one Thursday afternoon and got married. I never even told my family. I figured I would surprise them the following Christmas. Most of my friends didn't know because Hugh and I spent all of our time one on one. We picked out names for the baby; Hugh worked on freelance assignments; I stopped getting high and made beaded bracelets that I sold on commission out of a shop on Eighth Street.

Then at five months, just after I started to show, I experienced some pains and went to the doctor and three days later was in Roosevelt Hospital having the *procedure.* Hugh was devastated. I was numb. The doctor told us it was a girl. We named her Abigail and then had her little nonviable body cremated. Hugh, a lapsed Catholic, still believed, if not in God, at least, in the power of ceremony. I put some of the ashes in a locket. Hugh had an urn made for some and the rest we took to St. Luke's on Hudson Street and scattered on the rose garden next to the parish house. I still visit the garden at least once a year when the roses are in bloom. At the time I didn't know why we decided to put ashes there, Hugh's love of ceremony perhaps, something guided us, maybe Abigail herself, but for whatever reason, I'm grateful we did. The train stops at Eighty-sixth Street. I'm so lost in thought I almost miss my stop, but I manage to get out just as the doors are closing. I make my way out of the station and into the daylight again.

Hugh got a job offer in Chicago a month after the *event* as we came to call it. He decided to take it. I stayed in New York and got cast in a tour of *Godspell,* and three months later I filed for a divorce. It was a mutual decision. A month after that I ended up in the psych ward of a hospital in Des Moines, Iowa. That came about because one night during the tour I started screaming and couldn't stop, so the company manager took me to the emergency room of the local hospital and from there I was admitted to the psych ward and spent a month putting together jigsaw puzzles and talking to a shrink once a day. Hugh flew out from Chicago and got me out and took me back to New York and life went on. I have never told Charles about any of this. I think he would be shocked to learn how fragile that tough outer shell he says I wear so fetchingly actually is.

8

*D*o you want mushrooms?" Jack asks, standing in the middle of my living room, buck naked, with his cell phone pressed to his ear.

"Sure, and extra cheese." I am sitting on the toilet with the door open a few inches so we can talk. "And get some beer."

Jack came over about eight o'clock. The minute he walked in the door he took off his shirt, I took off my blouse, he took off his jeans, and I took off my pants. It was like strip poker without the cards. We made love on the couch and on the chair and on my grandmother's maple Ethan Allen coffee table.

"And ask them to put in lots of napkins. I'm all out." I wash my face and apply lotion and then quickly powder and put on some blush and a little lipstick. I have a feeling the *conversation* is coming and I want to look pretty. Hell, I want to look drop-dead gorgeous. I squint into the mirror and realize that pretty will have to do. I slip into my Victoria's Secret red silk bathrobe (on sale for $24.95) and fluff my hair.

"Mags," Jack says, looking up from the paper as I enter the

room and head for the kitchen. "Let's go downtown and hear some music later."

"Great," I say, reaching into the kitchen cupboard and pulling out a bottle of scotch.

"Want some scotch?" I ask.

"Scotch?"

"Yeah, you want a shot of scotch?"

"Yeah, sure."

I pour two glasses.

"Straight up or on the rocks?"

"Straight up, baby," Jack says with a laugh.

"What's so funny?"

"Nothing. There is nothing funny about a shot of scotch."

I hand him his glass and sit down in the chair across from him.

"Cheers." I drain the glass. Jack does the same.

"Another round?" I ask.

"It's your call, Sweet Pea."

I go into the kitchen and get the bottle and pour us two more shots and set the bottle on grandma's coffee table.

"Here's looking at you, kid," I say.

"And you too, kid," Jack says.

And we look at each other like gunfighters in a face-off. We finish the drinks. Jack picks up the bottle and pours again.

"Mud in your eye," he says.

"Mud in yours," I say. We finish at the same moment and slam the glasses on the table.

"We are getting drunk," Jack declares with a slur. I pour another round and look him hard in the eye.

"What did you want to talk about, Jack?"

"What do you mean?"

"Your message this morning. You said and I quote, 'You and I have to talk.'"

"Ahh, yes," he says and, of course, just then the buzzer rings.

"It's the pizza man," Jack says getting up too quickly. He takes a moment to steady his balance and then crosses to the door.

"You got any money, Sweet Pea? I don't think I'm going to have enough."

"I have a little money. Just a tiny bit. Four dollars and thirty-seven cents."

"So precise," Jack says, opening the door. The delivery guy is holding the pizza and a brown bag with a six-pack of beer. Jack hands him a couple of twenties that he got out of the jeans he quickly stepped into on his way to the door. He gets the change and closes the door with a flourish.

"Pizza, at your service," he announces placing the box on the coffee table.

"I thought you said you didn't think you had enough money? I would say forty dollars is plenty of money."

"Well the forty dollars has to do me for a while. I have to pay for the parking garage and the tolls every time I come here. I know I look like a million bucks but looks are deceiving. I thought maybe you could contribute to the cause," Jack says as he opens a Rolling Rock.

"So is that what you wanted to talk about? You want to talk about money and how I don't contribute to *the cause*?"

"No, it wasn't about money."

"Because I would like to point out that I have some overhead myself. I do pay the rent on this love nest, after all."

"All right."

"I'm not living at home with my parents."

"Parent."

"Parent. What's the difference really?"

"Look, this is getting off base. You have no idea what I want to say. You can't even listen long enough to hear," Jack says.

"Go on then, I'm listening. I'm all ears," I say putting my hands behind my ears and pushing them forward like the three-year-old child I've become.

"I don't have to defend my life to you."

"Am I asking you to? I'm just making observations," I say punctuating my statement with a swig of scotch.

"Look, Mags, I think I'm going to take off."

"Boy, it doesn't take much to get rid of you, does it?"

"Don't do that. This is your call, not mine. I thought we were having some pizza and maybe hear some music and maybe have an adult discussion. It's called a date. Not a showdown."

"This is just a stopover for you, isn't it? A drive-by fuck on the way to the rest of your life. Go on. I wouldn't want to keep you," I say taking another mouthful of scotch. I feel my toes getting numb. "I wouldn't want to keep you from the rest of your life in Queens, which I would like to point out I have never been invited to visit. Do I embarrass you? Is that it, Jack?"

"What are you talking about? Do you even know what you're talking about? We've only known each other a week. When did we have time to go to Queens?"

"I'm talking about us. About you and me and how miserable I feel right now because there really is no you and me, is there?"

Jack starts untangling the clothes on the floor, finds his shirt and puts it on. He pulls on his socks.

"You're drunk," he says. "And this is out of hand."

"And who are you to judge what's in and out of hand?" I say, not knowing what the hell I'm trying to say, but trying nonetheless.

"I think you're right. I think I should leave and let you cool off and then maybe we can talk. Now where are my shoes?"

"I don't know? Are you leaving? Is that it?"

"Didn't you tell me to?"

"Well if you want to leave, you are certainly free to leave. Go right ahead."

"I am going right ahead the minute I find my shoes," Jack says.

I get up and start looking. I pull the cushions off the couch.

"I'm sure they're here somewhere. Aha," I exclaim, seeing them under the bookcase next to the bathroom. Jack turns and looks. I throw them, one at a time, directly at his head.

"There are your fucking shoes," I say. I don't hit him—the half bottle of scotch I have ingested impedes my aim—but my intention is dead on.

Jack doesn't say a word. He gathers up the shoes, checks his pockets to make sure he has everything he came in with, and exits through the front door.

I sit down on the couch and try to figure out what just happened. How did it get so crazy so fast? Bixby, my cat boy, jumps on the couch next to me and kneads my leg with his paws.

"What have I done, Bix? What the hell have I done?" Bixby settles against me and starts to purr. Goodie lands in the middle of the coffee table and shakes his wand.

"Why do you have to be so dramatic all the time? Life is a lot simpler than you make it," he scolds.

"Simple? Life isn't simple."

"Sure it is," Goodie says, picking some lint off his feathered skirt. "All you have to do is keep both shoes on and be home before midnight."

"Don't make jokes," I say

"All right, let's not joke. Let's be dead serious," Goodie says. "I am seriously worried about you, Maggie. I'm worried that you're all tied up in a tight ball of yourself, and you're so afraid that life is going to pass you by and you're not going to get what you want and maybe you don't even know what you want and all you can think about is what you don't have and not what you do have and you can't stop for a second and really see what's right in front of you."

"Are you done?" I ask.

"I'm only telling you what I see, and telling you what I learned. You and I were a lot alike, Mags. I didn't see my life most of the time, and then it was gone. I know this is one big cliché, but sweetie, wake up and smell the roses. I only say this because I love you."

"You're living in a fairy tale."

"No, you are, stop living in some bad movie version of what you think the drama of your life should be. It doesn't have to be a tragedy."

"I think I want to be alone right now."

"Oh, that's smart," Goodie says. "Wallow."

"That's enough, Goodie," I say. "Get the hell out of here and leave me the fuck alone."

"All right. I know an exit line when I hear it. But be careful, Maggie Mae," Goodie says with a wave of his wand. "I'm warning you." And with that Goodie is gone.

"What's that supposed to mean? Is that a threat?" I yell over the trail of fairy dust.

Somewhere in my scotch-soaked brain I remember I'm supposed to be taking care of Mr. Ed for the next couple of days. There was a message on my machine from Sandy. Shit. The thought of getting up and even putting my shoes on seems too much for me. What does it matter if Ed takes a walk or not? An uninvited picture of dog dung smeared into the delicate pile of Sandy and Dick's eight-thousand-dollar imported oriental rug gets me on my feet and looking for my Dr. Scholl's.

Mr. Ed is frantic when I open the door to the apartment. He rushes by me and is down the stairs without a word. I look around for the leash. I have to keep one eye shut and one hand on the countertop to steady myself. I am a wreck. I squint at the clock on the wall. It's 10:17 and I'm drunk as a skunk. I hear three sharp barks from next door. Mr. Ed is furious. I grab the leash and stumble down the stairs. I open the front door of the building and Mr. Ed is gone in a flash.

"Eeeedieee," I yell. "Wait for me." Terriers have terrible tempers, and Mr. Ed is fit to be tied, indeed. I am also fit to be tied—as in tied to a chair and beaten with a stick. How did I let this happen? How did I get to be forty-one years old, single, drunk, running after an angry Westie in a pair of ill-fitting Dr. Scholl's at 10:17 on a Saturday night on the Upper West Side of Manhattan?

There is no time to ponder—Mr. Ed is halfway across Columbus Avenue and heading for the park. Terriers not only have tempers, they are also spiteful. I clickity-clack after him in my wooden-soled shoes. The light changes and as I'm about to dart across the avenue, a wall of cars motor toward me forcing me back on the curb. Mr. Ed is half a block ahead of me moving at the speed of light.

"EEEEEEEDD!!!" I scream as loud as I can. The light changes

and I careen across the intersection. My head is spinning and I feel nauseous. I would like nothing better than to sit down and put my head between my knees and hyperventilate for a few minutes. Where is Goodie when I need him? He could fly ahead and knock Mr. Ed out with his magic wand, but no, Goodie has renounced me because I'm living in the movie version of my life. Well if this truly was the movie version of my life, even a bad movie version, I would be richer, younger, and thinner, and I sure as hell wouldn't be chasing a dog. I'd have my servants do that.

I get to the entrance of the park at Eighty-sixth Street. Ed is nowhere in sight. It is well past sunset and streetlamps illuminate the park. I weave along the soccer field, past some benches where two elderly gentlemen sit smoking cigars.

I head toward the Great Lawn. I pat my pockets and find a crushed pack of cigarettes. I get one out but discover I have no matches. Shoot. There is nothing worse than having the drug but not the means of administering it. I consider circling back and asking the cigar-smoking gents for a light but the thought of circling makes me woozy. I put the cigarette between my lips and am momentarily comforted by the warm rush of anticipation. I get to the Great Lawn and start around the perimeter.

"EEED!" I yell into the tranquil evening. I spot an older woman sitting on a bench having a cigarette with her toy poodle perched in her lap. The two of them sport matching pink hair ribbons.

"Excuse me. Do you have a light?" I ask.

She reaches into her bag and produces a half-empty book of matches and hands it to me.

"Here," she says. "Keep them."

"Thank you." Smokers are always happy to accommodate other smokers—we are a band of outcasts linked by our common need.

"Oh," I add as I turn to leave. "Did you see a little Westie, off the leash? Out on his own?"

"I did see him. He stopped and barked at my Azalea and almost scared her to death."

"Sorry, he has a thing about poodles. Which direction was he headed?"

"Over towards the castle," she answers as she snuggles up to Azalea. "Yes, he was a brute, wasn't he? Just a brute," she baby talks to the trembling poodle.

Belvedere Castle sits on a promontory rock above the Delacorte Theater and is quite a hike from where I stand, especially considering I'm drunk, tired, and wearing inappropriate footwear. The way I feel it might as well be Mt. Everest. I know Mr. Ed is doing this on purpose.

I start toward the castle with Ed's leash draped around my neck. At least I have my cigarettes to keep me company. I go past the theater and around the side and up the path that leads to the back of the castle. As I get to the top I hear a familiar bark to my left and turn down an adjacent path.

"Ed," I call out. The streetlamps are not as plentiful in this part of the park. I head in the direction of the bark and find myself in the middle of the Ramble. My drunkenness has mellowed into a mild headache and a very dry mouth. I would give anything for a glass of water. I hear voices to my left, and see a man and woman walking hand in hand. That's sweet. A moonlit walk with the one you love.

I amble along, not knowing where I am. I'm Gretel minus Hansel, lost in the forest. I turn down another path and move further into the darkness. A couple of streetlights are out and it's suddenly pitch black. I suspect Ed is hiding from me, playing his own doggie version of hide-and-seek. I call out again but my mouth is so dry I can hardly muster his name.

Then I hear footsteps behind me and as I turn I'm pushed to the ground. Someone is on top of me breathing into my ear. The breath is foul and acrid.

"Don't move," a harsh voice says.

I'm too stunned to do anything. My arm is twisted behind my back. I can feel my heart beating against the ground; it feels like it's going to explode. I try to scream, but I have no air because the knee in my back is pressing my lungs flat in my chest. I fear I'm going to pass out, that this is my last moment, my last chance. My drunken mind clears. I try to roll over; my fingernails dig into the ground for leverage. The body on top of me is heavy, too heavy for me to throw off.

"Don't fucking move, you bitch!" the voice hisses. I lie still. Oddly, I flash on an article I read once about people in life-threatening situations and how they don't implore God for help as is widely thought, but rather their mother. That's usually the response. They cry for their mother.

And indeed, "Mother!" is what comes out when I muster enough air. "Help me, Mother." I pray the couple I saw earlier is still in the vicinity. I kick my legs to make noise and try to scream, but my mouth is too dry and fear has gripped my throat, the only thing I manage is another barely audible "Mother." I'm sure the couple is too far away by now to hear. A hand grabs my neck, fingers clamp into my windpipe.

"Shut up!" commands the voice. I try to bite the hand but get only a mouthful of glove. I feel the leash being pulled tight around my neck like a noose. I try to get my free hand out from under my body. My pants are ripped down from the back. I know what is about to happen and I can't stop it. The hand tightens the leash. I can't breathe. I try desperately to relax. I know struggling will make it worse. Panic is the enemy in these situations. At least that's what I have read, but when in the situation it is hard to do anything else. I will myself to relax, and as I do my attacker seems to do the same and air finds its way down my windpipe.

"That's right, just lie still. Try to enjoy it," says the voice and the hand that has ripped my pants down now moves between my legs. Oh my God. It's going to happen and I can't do a thing.

At that moment loud staccato barks cut through the air coming right in my direction, then snarls and yipes.

"Shit!" the voice grunts. The barks are emphatic and then a low growl and then the hand is pulled from my throat, releasing the noose and my attacker curses in pain. I turn my head to see Mr. Ed biting down hard on the hand that is attached to the body that is holding me hostage. The body picks Mr. Ed up and lobs him into the air.

I roll to my right and get up on my knees in time to see Ed recover his footing and take off after my assailant. I'm too shaken to stand. Mr. Ed's barks are like high-pitched warning signals, mixed with snarls and yelps, and then abruptly they stop. No sound. I taste blood in my mouth. My lip is bleeding and my left wrist is throbbing in pain. I listen for Ed. Nothing. Then I hear footsteps again, this time from the path to my right. My heart almost stops. I frog walk into the underbrush just as a large golden retriever comes bounding toward me.

"Abby!" the owner calls. "Come here, girl."

I make out a young man coming up the path. Abby, the

retriever, circles back to him. I'm sure this isn't the same person who attacked me. At least, I'm almost sure, and I'm very sure I need help.

"Hello?" I call out, struggling to my feet and pulling my torn pants up as best I can. "Excuse me. Can I walk out of the park with you? I was attacked and I've lost my dog." I move into what light there is.

"My God!" he says. "What happened?"

I start to shake all over. My teeth chatter. My wrist is still throbbing and my lower back feels like someone hit it with a two-by-four.

"I was attacked and Mr. Ed saved me. He chased the guy off. I heard him barking and then he stopped and I don't know what happened." Tears are coming out of my eyes, but I'm not conscious of crying. I'm just leaking. The body is 80 percent water and I feel so liquid with fear that very soon I might be reduced to the 20 percent of matter left after all the water leaks out.

"When did this happen?" the young man asks. He is tall, Afro-American, and wearing a Mets cap.

"Five minutes ago, maybe."

"Look, my name is Spider, and you're going to be all right."

"Your name is Spider?" I ask, thankful to note I haven't lost my sense of humor. I mean, really, is anyone actually named Spider?

"What direction did they go in?"

"That way. The barking was coming from there." I point up toward the castle.

"Well, let's go see if we can find your dog."

"What about the guy that attacked me? What if he's waiting there?"

"He won't be," Spider says with assurance. "He'll be long gone."

I follow Spider up the path. I reach out and take hold of his shirttail as we make our way up to the castle. Abby is sniffing and running and sniffing and running. She senses a hunt, and sure enough in a few minutes she starts barking. Spider and I follow and find Mr. Ed lying on his side, laboring to breathe.

"Oh, no, Mr. Ed." I squat down next to him. "Oh my God, Ed." I put my head next to his. "You'll be okay, you'll be fine."

Mr. Ed opens his eyes and looks at me and tries to get up.

"Don't move, Eddie. Stay still," I say.

Spider squats next to me and puts his hands on Ed's chest. Ed winces in pain, and that is a good sign. At least I hope it is.

"Hey, little guy," Spider says. "I'm going to pick you up, is that okay?" Ed's eyes are fixed on me.

"It's okay, Ed. Spider's not going to hurt you. He's going to take you home."

Abby is dancing around us, proud of herself for retrieving what needed to be retrieved. Spider cradles Ed in his arms and carefully gets to his feet. As we make our way out of the park, I hold onto Ed's front paw and tell him everything is going to be fine.

I cringe to think what happened to my little friend. I imagine he was kicked very hard in the chest, and I wonder if, in that moment of fear, Mr. Ed, like me, cried out for his mother.

When we get to the entrance at Central Park West where the traffic is whizzing by, and doormen are standing in front of the luxury buildings that border the park, I begin to breathe again. I realize I haven't taken a full breath since the whole thing started.

"What were you doing in the park at this hour?" Spider asks waiting for the light to change.

"I was looking for Mr. Ed. He got off the leash and took off and I wasn't thinking about the time. You know how it is."

"I have to say it was pretty crazy to be back there in the Ramble by yourself."

"You were there by yourself," I point out in my defense.

"I think that's a little different and don't pretend it isn't. I'm a six-foot-two, 230-pound, twenty-three-year-old male with a black belt in karate."

"Yeah, but you're a Mets fan," I say, trying to divert attention from the obvious.

"Don't do that. Don't pretend you don't know what I'm talking about. I don't want to find you next week after it's too late. Do you hear me?" Spider stops and looks hard at me. Even Mr. Ed turns his head and casts a scolding eye.

"Yes, I hear you."

"All right?"

"All right," I say in agreement. The agreement being I am an idiot.

"So where are we headed?" Spider asks, hoisting Ed higher in his arms.

"Halfway down the block," I say, pointing in the direction of my building. I see someone standing out front smoking a cigarette. It's Jack.

9

"Mags?" Jack is coming toward us. "What's up? Where were you?"

"In the park with Mr. Ed," I say trying to keep my voice steady. "We ran into some problems and Spider here helped us out."

Jack and Spider nod at each other. If Spider's hand were free, they'd probably shake, but Spider is still cradling Mr. Ed.

"Here." I reach out. "I'll take him now."

"Maybe you'd better let your friend," Spider says handing Ed off to Jack. "And I think you should call the police and report this. Okay? I better get going." Abby is doing a little let's-get-a-move-on dog dance.

"Thanks, Spider. I don't know what else to say. I just . . ." I put my arms around his neck. "Thanks."

"No problem. Take care, now." Spider nods at Jack again and then heads down the block toward Amsterdam Avenue.

"Maggie, what is going on?" Jack asks.

"I got attacked in the park and Mr. Ed saved me and in the process got the shit kicked out of him."

"Jesus."

"Yeah. Jesus."

We take Mr. Ed to his apartment. I look down the list of emergency numbers next to Sandy's phone. There is a number for the Westside Animal Hospital. I dial and talk to someone who tells me the location of the twenty-four-hour clinic that will see Mr. Ed. I jot down the address.

"I have to go to the bathroom before we go," I tell Jack. "And change my pants."

"Did you get . . . I mean did he?" Jack asks, struck with the possibility. "Oh, Maggie." He puts his arms around me.

"No, but it was close," I say, fighting with myself to stay calm. "Can you go ahead with Mr. Ed? I'll meet you there. I'll take a cab."

"No," Jack says. "I'm not leaving you alone. Go change. Ed is okay for the moment."

I get to my apartment and turn on the shower. I pull off my clothes and step in. My hands are still bleeding, but the wounds are superficial, and my wrist is throbbing, but I can still move it, so I'm pretty sure it's just sprained. I grab a bar of soap and scrub and scrub down there where he—I don't want to finish the thought. I squeeze my eyes shut, trying to erase the image of his hand between my legs. I wish I could stay in the shower and let the water cleanse me of the whole experience, but Mr. Ed is waiting. I dry off quickly and dress and go back to Sandy's.

"Let's go," I say.

"You all right?" Jack is sitting on the couch. Ed is wrapped in a blanket lying next to him.

"Yes. Fine and dandy." Did I say that? Amazing what stress will make us do.

Jack bundles Ed in his arms and off we go. The clinic is on

Tenth Avenue at Fifty-third Street. The veterinarian on duty is a young Asian man with DR. CHANG printed on a name tag. He takes Mr. Ed into an examining room. I'm not sure if I should follow. I think it might be best if Ed has a chance to speak with the doctor one on one.

"You should report this," Jack says. "You need to talk to the cops."

"I didn't even see the guy. He was behind me the whole time and it was dark. I don't know what I could tell them."

"It's an incident. They should at least know it happened. There might be a pattern. The next girl won't be so lucky."

"Girl?"

"Woman. I don't think this is a time to get into semantics, Maggie, and besides maybe it will be a girl and then how will you feel?"

"How is it that I'm suddenly the guilty party? Jesus, Jack, give me a break."

"Do what you like. Don't report it. Don't say a word. Don't tell the cops a madman is roaming Central Park attacking *women.* Go home and have another shot of scotch and stare at the wall and maybe it will all disappear."

"Go, Jack. I don't want to sit here and listen to you lecture me on my life."

"Mags, I'm just trying to help. You can't act like nothing happened."

I get up and walk across the waiting room and look at the bulletin board that is peppered with pictures of abandoned dogs and cats looking for homes. There is a snapshot of a little black and white dog with spiky ears and a pink tongue dangling out of his mouth. He looks happy. I guess he hadn't been told yet he was about to be abandoned. I had a feeling I was about to suffer the same fate and it wouldn't be the first time. I could feel Jack behind me. I could feel him making up his mind to leave, to walk out and abandon me. I wouldn't blame him. Besides, I had told him to leave, so I don't know if you can really call that abandonment. I've never been good at relationships. I don't like it when people get too close. I start to feel smothered. I stop making eye contact. I stop talking and I try to stop feeling and that is what I am doing now.

Jack comes up behind me and puts his arm around my shoulders. I feel my body stiffen. I can't stop it. Jack kisses me on the crown of my head.

"Do you have money for a cab to get home?"

I nod. I can't respond verbally because there is a big lump in my throat that won't let the word *yes* get out, or more importantly, *don't go.*

"So long and take care of yourself, Mags." He leaves. I don't turn around. I continue to look at the pictures on the board. One calico cat is hunkered down in a corner with her face to the wall. I suspect she, unlike the black and white dog, has been informed of her fate. I wipe my eyes, bite my lip, and sit down to wait for Mr. Ed. The lump in my throat drops to the pit of my stomach and the words I wanted to say before finally slip out. "Don't go, Jack," I whisper. "Please, don't go."

WE GET HOME about three a.m. Mr. Ed is bruised and hurting, but nothing is broken, and Dr. Chang assured me that Ed would be fine in a few days. He handed me some pain medication to give him and suggested that I go see my own doctor the next day.

I go to my apartment to check on Bixby and then go back to spend the night with Mr. Ed in Sandy's place. I don't want to leave the little guy alone.

THE NEXT MORNING around ten the phone rings and wakes us both up. Mr. Ed is sleeping against my right leg. I answer with a groggy, "Hello."

"Sandy? Is that you?" a man's voice on the other end asks.

"No, it's her neighbor. Sandy's out of town and I'm feeding the dog."

"Oh, well, I'll call back. When will she be home?"

"Tuesday afternoon," I answer, momentarily wondering who in the world this is.

"Thanks, I'll call back then," he says and hangs up.

I turn over and stare at the ceiling. Mr. Ed stirs and nuzzles my hand.

"How are you feeling, little fellow?"

He scrunches up along my side and puts his face next to mine and we lay there for quite a while

"Thanks, Ed," I say. "Thanks for saving my life."

Ed licks the side of my face and I hug him close.

"So CAN YOU give us any description at all?" Officer Kelly asks. I'm sitting at his desk in the One-hundredth Precinct. Ed is curled up at my feet. On our morning walk I decide to go by the precinct and then I decide to go in and then I decide to report the incident as long as I'm there. Sometimes I have to trick myself into doing the right thing.

"I didn't see him. All I can tell you is it was about eleven last night; it was a man; and it happened in the Ramble near the

castle. And he was wearing leather gloves. I know because I bit
down on his hand."

"Do you think you broke the skin?"

"No, I'm sure I didn't. I barely got a hold of the glove. That's
when Mr. Ed found me and started barking and grabbed the guy's
leg or hand or something and he took off with Ed at his heels.
Maybe Ed broke the skin somewhere."

"You're lucky."

"I know."

"Well, fill this out. We didn't have any other reports last night.
Thanks for coming in." Officer Kelly hands me a clipboard with
an incident report on it. I fill in my name and address and number
and leave it with the desk clerk. On my way out I notice a bulletin board with pictures of missing children and the FBI's most
wanted list. I guess being abandoned isn't the worst thing.

When I get back to my apartment there is a message from
Dee-Honey. "Just checking in with you, honey, to remind you
about the *Snow White* tomorrow. Early call." Boy, she must think
I never write anything down anymore. For goodness sake, she
really is Mother Goose checking on all her goslings, or is it geese-
lets? There is also a message from Texas Joe.

"Maggie, how are you? Give a call. I, uh, I have something to
tell you. I . . . well . . . give me a call."

He's getting married. I know it. That's what he wants to tell
me. He's going to marry the dentist. Damn, I think, damn, damn,
damn. I take Mr. Ed back to his apartment so he won't have to
see me get all weepy and ugly, which I have a feeling I'm going
to do.

I wait an hour before I call Joe back. I drink two beers and listen to Sam Cooke sing "You Send Me" about a half-dozen times.

Once, after we had spent a couple of weeks together, Joe called me from Texas and sang that song into my answering machine. I saved the message and played it when I was feeling blue and then my phone broke and the message was lost, so I bought a cassette of Sam Cooke's *Greatest Hits*.

"Hey, Joe, what's up?" I ask as nonchalantly as I can when he answers.

"Well, I just wanted you to know . . ." he falters.

I decide to help the poor guy out.

"You wanted me to know that you're getting married. Am I right?"

"Boy, you know me."

"Like the back of my hand." I say. "So, wow, is it the dentist?"

"Yeah."

"I thought that was over."

"It was, but then we decided that we really should give it a shot."

"Sure, why not? So when is the happy day?"

"Well, actually . . ." Joe sounds sheepish. "Today."

"What? And you waited until now to tell me. Why didn't you tell me the last time you called? I mean . . ." I can't finish.

"I'm sorry. I'm real sorry. Every time I started to tell you I chickened out. It hasn't been easy."

"I know," I say, and then we are both quiet. I can hear Joe breathing and I know he can hear me, and for a few moments we just breathe together.

"Look, I'm happy for you," I say finally. "I really am. Best wishes, I guess."

"Thanks. I love you," Joe says.

"I love you too."

"So you're okay?" Joe asks.

"I'm fine," I say and then my voice breaks.

"What's wrong?" Joe asks.

"Nothing, it's just that . . ."

"Tell me, I got time, tell me."

"It's your wedding day. And I'm happy for you."

"Thanks. I'll call you soon."

"Sure. We'll talk. Bye, Joe." And we hang up. The clock over the kitchen sink ticks off the minutes. Bixby catnaps on the sofa. I sit and stare at the wall, remembering every sweet thing I can about my Texas Joe. He slept on his left side and snored only when he had a cold, was a good lover, made an excellent peach pie, and could sing harmony to all the Beatles' early tunes. But the sweetest thing I would always remember about Joe was the night Goodie died. The whole family was there: Charles, Goodie's and Joe's parents, all the siblings, two nephews, and myself. Goodie had requested not to be put on life support. He had been in a coma for twenty-four hours and his breathing began to fail. Joe walked into the living room where we were keeping vigil and announced that it was time. He went over to his mother, took her hand, and led her into the room. Goodie's breath was labored. Joe's mother got very agitated and started to cry.

"Please, we have to do something, give him oxygen, I can't just let him go," she sobbed. She had been so strong, but momentarily her strength deserted her. Joe gently took her by the shoulders.

"Goodie needs you to help him, Mom. Remember how you used to read from the Bible when you put us to sleep. Do you think you could read to Goodie now?"

"He always liked the Twenty-third Psalm," she said. "It was his favorite." Charles handed her the Bible from the bookshelf next to the bed.

"The Lord is my shepherd; I shall not want," she began from memory, her voice now steady with purpose. The rest of us gathered around the bed and gently placed our hands on Goodie's frail and struggling body. Charles sat against the headboard with Goodie's head in his lap, and Joe stood behind his mother, his hands still on her shoulders, giving her the courage to bear the unbearable grief.

"Yea, though I walk through the valley of the shadow of death, I will fear no evil: for thou art with me." Her voice intoned as Goodwin Albert DePugh, her precious firstborn son, surrendered his final breath.

Then, later, Joe was the one who called the coroner and the ambulance service. He was the one who reached out and gently closed Goodie's half-opened eyes and held Charles and comforted his father. He was the one who was there for us all. "But you're not here for me now, Joe," I say out loud. "You're not here for me now and I need you, I need somebody. How come you get someone and I don't?" But I know the answer to that question. I push away from people when I should try to pull closer. It's a reflex. Like not knowing your left from your right and always turning the wrong way.

"Goodie? Are you here somewhere?" I ask between sobs. "Did you hear? Joe is getting married. Isn't that dandy? You said we were made for each other. You said we were perfect for each other. Why can't you wave your magic wand now? Why, Goodie, why?"

I stumble into the kitchen and get a beer. I swig it down.

"Here's to you, Joe," I say. "Here's to you and little wifey." Snot drains down my throat along with the beer. I open another and chug it. I get down on my knees and bury my head in my arms. I want to disappear. I want to not feel *anything*.

"Goodie, dammit, where are you?"

There is no answer.

"Miss Goodie-Two-Shoes, I need you."

But there is nothing. Just the damn clock over the sink tick-tick-ticking off the minutes. I close my eyes. The room spins and I'm out.

I wake up at three a.m. in the middle of the kitchen floor. My back is in spasm and my mouth is so dry I can't swallow. I stand up but my left leg is so profoundly asleep there is no feeling in it and I fall against the counter. Shit! I get to the bathroom and splash water on my face. I use the toilet and limp to my bed. By a miracle I remember I have a show in the morning, so I manage to set the alarm before I pass out.

10

*D*ee-Honey, as usual, is driving. She is weaving in and out of traffic, making a beeline for the Fairfield Junior Civic Center where we are scheduled for a *Snow White* performance. My stomach flip-flops as the van zooms along on the Major Deegan Expressway. We stop at a Dunkin' Donuts a few blocks away. I order a large coffee and two Bavarian crème donuts. I wish I had a beer to settle my stomach and a shot of scotch to ease the pain, but a megasugar hit will have to do.

Helen Sanders is standing next to me, shaking her head. "You kill me, the way you eat."

"Well, Helen, I'm lucky. I don't have to squeeze into that wood nymph costume the way you do."

"Coffee and a low-fat blueberry muffin," Helen barks at the counter girl. "And be sure to put skim milk in the coffee."

"You are so disciplined, Helen, I don't know how you do it," I say, biting into my Bavarian crème. The sugar plops to my stomach and immediately jumps onto the express lane spreading happy glucose molecules as it goes.

"I hate you, Mags."

"I know, Helen."

We get back in the car and head to the civic center. My left hip hurts like crazy from where I fell against the kitchen counter, and my spine feels like a pretzel from sleeping on the kitchen floor last night.

Right before the show starts I bum a cigarette from Frank. I lean out the fire exit and take a few puffs. It's so hard to smoke anywhere now it's almost not worth it, but *almost* is the operable word because I'm still not humiliated enough actually to kick the habit, especially now when all my underpinnings seem to be coming unpinned.

I hear Frank call, "Places, please," and I stamp out the cigarette and head to the stage left wing, ready for my entrance. Helen has the first scene as Snow White's dying mother. She's very moving and does a lovely job with the ballad. She declares the baby's name to be Snow White because her skin is as white as snow and her hair as black as ebony. (However, today Snow White is a blonde, as I forgot the black gel I usually put in my hair to darken it.) Then Helen dies as the huntsman reaches for baby Snow White.

In the next scene I skip onstage and sing my little Snow White happy song. Then Dee-Honey sweeps onstage as the evil stepmother, or as Frank calls her (never to her face of course), "Herself, the Ancient Evil." We do our scene and then I scrub the stage while Ron, the handsome play prince, arrives. My hip starts to throb as I scuttle around the stage on hands and knees. And then my stomach does a few more flip-flops.

"Is that Snow White?" I hear a girl whisper in the front row. I glare out at her.

Don't you dare, I think, don't you dare say a word. The girl looks at me and I look at her and then smile my adorable ingénue smile and she smiles back. She can't resist. I'm a star, dammit, and nobody, not even a spoiled rotten six-year-old, can resist star power. I finish the scene and exit stage left. I head for the dressing room for another cigarette while the Ancient Evil and the huntsman plan my demise. Helen is in the dressing room struggling out of her wood nymph costume.

"Maggie, could you help me? I think the zipper is stuck." With a good bit of tugging and yanking and grunting I get Helen unzipped and out of the leotard. She collapses into a chair.

"I hate doing this show. It's not worth the trouble. Dee-Honey has got to do something about this costume."

"Helen, you're lovely as the dearly departed mother and be thankful you don't have to wear the Dorothy pinafore."

"Why, Mags, you're adorable in pinafores," she says with a hint of snideness. It's her way.

"Well at least this Snow White costume fits the whole way around," I say.

"Yes, this one is much more flattering, the gingham makes you look . . ."

"All right, Helen, that's enough."

"Too angelic, I was going to say."

"Uh, thanks, Helen." I smile. "Your voice was to die for in the ballad today."

"Really? I thought I was flat today. In the bridge."

"Flat? You were dead on and your vibrato has never been sweeter."

"Thanks, I do think I bring a kind of . . ." she trails off, waiting for me to supply the appropriate term of flattery.

"Delicacy?" I venture.

"Yes, delicacy. It's tricky. You don't want to be too melodramatic, but for goodness sake the woman is dying."

"No, Helen, really, you do it just right. If you milked it anymore, it would be criminal."

"What?" She turns as I am out the door and rushing down the hallway to the fire exit to get a few hits of nicotine. I need it. I've had a hard week and now I can't stop thinking about Joe. About my Texas Joe. Damn him, damn him, damn him. Not that I thought it would work out for us. I knew we weren't going to end up together as Mr. and Mrs. on El Ranchero Drive in Houston, Texas. But it never occurred to me that Joe would end up with anyone else either. I figured maybe after all was said and done we'd retire together to Sarasota, Florida, and take up golf.

"Mags, you're on," I hear hissed behind me. Frank's head is poked out the stage door.

"Shit," I push through the door and run onstage for my scene with the huntsman.

"What a beautiful forest," I say, and then I hear that little girl.

"She's smoking, Mommy." And then I hear lots of muttering from the peanut gallery. Randall (as the huntsman) does exaggerated eye acting and I realize I am still holding a lit cigarette in my hand.

"Look at this, Mr. Huntsman," I say, raising the cigarette for anyone who hasn't yet noticed it. "Someone has been smoking in the forest, and we all know that is not good, is it?"

"No, Snow White," Randall indulges me, "it's not good."

"Nobody should ever smoke these evil cigarettes," I say. Frank is standing in the wings shaking his head. I continue: "I better take this over to the stream and drop it in so it won't cause any harm." I turn to exit and hear Randall.

"Oh, fair maiden, be sure to drop the dampened butt into a trash receptacle because thou must never litter either."

"Yes, kind sir," I say from the wings where Frank is ready with a half-drunk cup of coffee. I plunge the cigarette in and go back onstage.

"And now as I was saying, what a beautiful forest." And we continue the scene without further incident.

"What the hell were you doing out there?" Randall snaps at me when we're offstage.

"You can never have too many public service announcements about smoking," I say with a wink.

"Maggie, wake up! You were smoking onstage as Snow White in front of five hundred children."

"I was setting an example," I yell after him. "It wasn't *my* cigarette. I found it in the forest."

Frank walks by me still shaking his head.

"What?" I say.

"That was definitely a first," Frank says. "I give you credit for that. No one else has ever smoked as Snow White."

"She wasn't smoking," I say at the top of my lungs. "She found it in the forest! The big bad wolf was smoking it."

"Mags, there is not a big bad wolf in *Snow White*," Frank says.

"Well there should be!" I say and stomp off to the dressing room.

I GET HOME LATE that afternoon and go straight to the kitchen and pour myself a tall scotch. So big deal Snow White is a smoker. Wait until they find out what else she does. I'll save that for my next performance. The whole cast serenaded me back with a three-part arrangement of "Who's Afraid of the Big Bad

Wolf?" I check my message machine and find it empty. No one has called, not a soul, and especially not Jack. And why should he? We are hardly even friends. I mean, it's not like I even know him well enough to miss him. Besides, he probably heard via the grapevine that Snow White is a smoker and a slut. Who cares? It's just bad timing what with Texas Joe announcing his marriage. It would be nice to have a warm body nearby to absorb the shock. I go next door and knock on Sandy's door. Maybe a neighborly chat will do the trick. "Hi, how are you?"

"Come on in." Sandy opens the door.

"I wanted to see how Mr. Ed is doing."

"He's mending. He's asleep in the bedroom."

"The vet said he would sleep a lot."

"Well, then he's doing exactly what the doctor ordered. How are you doing?" She gestures to a chair. "Sit down. Can I make you a cup of coffee? I was about to have one."

"You go ahead." I indicate my glass of scotch. "I brought my own libation." Sandy makes herself a cup of coffee and we sit and talk. She tells me all about her garden up at their country house in Ulster County. All about the tomatoes and the herbs and the hibiscus and her prizewinning rhubarb. Sandy and I aren't really friends, but we are good neighbors. She gets my mail and feeds my cat when I'm gone, and I do the same for her. And now the other little thing is that her dog saved my life. Maybe someday Bixby will do as much for her. I can't imagine the circumstances in which that would occur, but I'm sure if called into service Bixby will do his damnedest to deliver Sandy from harm.

When I get back to my apartment the message light is blinking on my answering machine and my heart almost stops. "It's him, it's him, it must be him," the Vikki Carr classic plays over and over in my mind. I don't listen to the message right away. I wait, get a beer out of the refrigerator, circle the phone a few times, then I hit the button.

"Maggie, I wonder if we could reschedule our session tomorrow? Could we do it from eleven to one instead of noon to two? Let me know. Oh, it's Thomas. Call me."

It's my accompanist, not Prince Charming. "But it's not him and then I die, again I die," Vikki sings in my head. I look up Thomas's number on my Rolodex. I dial and his machine picks up.

"Hi, it's Maggie. Tomorrow at eleven will be fine." I pour myself another scotch.

I can't believe I have a club date coming up. I haven't even contacted anyone. I haven't sent out announcements to the throngs of people who have been holding their breath waiting for me to come out of retirement.

I open my cupboard and find a stack of publicity postcards left over from the last time I did a mailing to casting directors. I count out twenty-five and sit down at my desk. I tune in the Yankee game and then write out twenty-five notes with the show information. I go through my Rolodex and get addresses. It's the old-fashioned way—no computer, no Xerox—just pen and ink and hand cramps. I get to the last card and write out Jack Eremus, and then realize I have no idea what his address is in Queens. But I remember the business card he gave me, and sure enough it's stuffed in the D-E-F section of my Rolodex: AJ Auto Sales, 3120 Greenpoint Avenue, Long Island City, NY.

The Yankees are losing five to three to the Tigers in the bottom of the eighth inning when I finish addressing the cards, but Derek Jeter is on first and the top of the order is coming to bat. In baseball you have to hit the ball only 30 percent of the time to be a great hitter. That is a source of comfort to me when I'm playing this other game called life. Then Derek steals second, the second baseman drops the ball, and Derek slides into third, so it ain't over yet.

THE NEXT MORNING I get to the post office bright and early, buy thirty stamps, and mail off the postcards. I hold Jack's aside, considering whether to put a lipstick kiss under my signature. Maybe not, I decide, maybe that's not such a good idea. I do caress his name with my thumb before I put the card through the slot and head over to Central Park West to catch the C train downtown.

I get off on Twenty-third Street and stop at a Starbucks a block from Thomas's studio. I treat myself to a grande skim latte and a chocolate chip scone. If I can't have a boyfriend, at least, I can have sugar. And if I have enough sugar I probably won't have to worry about a boyfriend ever again because I'll be two hundred pounds and living in a trailer park outside of York, Pennsylvania, working in the home decor department at the local Wal-Mart. Not that there is anything wrong with that; in fact, it's a rather pleasant fantasy I indulge in more than I'd like to admit. There is something so addictive and relentless about trying to "make it" in this great big city on the Hudson that on some days a job at Wal-Mart with profit sharing and a double-wide trailer with a patch of green around it feels like a trip to Maui. The session with Thomas goes pretty well.

"Slow down in the verse. I think you're rushing it."

"Really? I think it sounds too sentimental if it's slow."

"Your voice sounds great, really great. Let the audience enjoy it."

"Does it?" I ask. "I'm not fishing for a compliment, honest. It's just been such a long time since I've really sung that I was afraid maybe I'd lost it."

"No." Thomas smiles. "You certainly haven't lost it. You've got it in spades. Now let's go back to the verse."

He starts to play and I sing it again, slowly, savoring every note. It feels so good to be singing again. It feels like my soul is wearing chiffon and dancing in the moonlight. I have two auditions in the afternoon. One is for an on-camera spot for Fleet Bank. I am the mother of two with a mortgage and station wagon and worry lines on my brow. I can do that and I do. The second is a radio voice-over for Toyota at five p.m. I finally get in to see the casting director about five forty-five. It's June Enders. She's pretty nice, but she's never been a big fan of mine. I smile more than necessary and ask about her husband.

"He walked out five months ago."

"Sorry," I say wiping the now unnecessary smile off my stupid mug. I consider mentioning my own recent heartbreak, actually a doubleheader what with Joe getting married and Jack walking out, but it's never good to upstage someone's pain. We all like to feel special when we suffer.

"We celebrated our twentieth anniversary and the next week he left."

"I'm so sorry. I remember when you got married. You were assistant casting director at B and D. Can't believe that was twenty years ago, June. We were kids."

"Yeah, I know. Thanks, Maggie."

"Well, you look great," I say and then realize I might be pushing it, but June smiles and I exit as quickly as I can.

I can't believe I've known June for twenty years. I feel as old as dirt as I make my way down Seventh Avenue. I catch the number 1 train uptown at Twenty-third Street. It's almost seven, not rush hour, but the train is still crammed with people. It seems like the subways are always crowded now. When I first moved to New York it was different. The subways were dirtier and there was more graffiti, but they weren't as crowded. I loved getting on a subway car that was almost empty and hurtling through the underground tunnels of New York. Back then people smoked if the cars weren't full. That seems very romantic to me now—to be on a subway smoking a cigarette and to be young. And that's the real romance of it—not being on a subway car smoking, but being young.

Sitting across from me is a bland-looking man in his late forties with dirty blond hair. He's wearing a beige nylon jacket with coffee stains down the front. He's staring at me staring at him. He looks vaguely familiar, like maybe we dated way back when, or met at a party and smoked a joint together and discussed Nietzsche for a few hours. All I remember about Nietzsche is that he said God was dead, but he didn't really mean God was dead or something like that, but now Nietzsche is dead and if he was wrong I bet Nietzsche had some explaining to do when he got to the pearly gates: "I am really, really sorry God, but I really, really thought you were dead." A large black woman with dyed orange dreadlocks moves between Mr. Beige and me, straining to read the poster about the Harlem Museum above his head. She gets off at Fifty-ninth Street. Mr. Beige is starting to drool.

Someone a few seats down curses at a Macy's shopping bag. The train stops in the tunnel between Seventy-ninth and Eighty-sixth Street. A garbled voice comes on the PA system saying something about a delay.

A man perched on a small pushcart comes rolling down the aisle. His body is severed at the waist. I give him a quarter and he

rolls on. He is amazingly adept at ma-
neuvering through the car. And there
it is — evolution and adaptation — the
human condition. We loose some
gills, get some lungs, loose the tail,
get better balance, start to walk, lose
legs, get wheels. Get old, get wrinkles,
and get cosmetic surgery.

NOTE TO SELF . . .

*Find out
if Botox can be
self-administered.*

The train starts to move again.
Mr. Beige puts his fingers in his ears and barks like a Chihuahua,
which illustrates evolution can work both ways.

We finally arrive at Eighty-sixth Street. I get off. I hate riding
the local; it gives me too much time to think. I stop at Lou's Deli
for a beer. I walk over to Riverside Park and sit on a bench facing the New Jersey skyline. People are out walking their dogs. A
golden retriever comes over and sits on my foot. I pat his head and
he licks my hand, then his owner whistles and he trots off without
a backward glance. Dogs are so fickle.

I sit and watch the sunset behind the New Jersey skyline. The
world looks flat from here and only as big as I can see, like a giant
finite piece of real estate. As I watch the sun set, I imagine it being
lowered down on a system of pulleys by a beefy stagehand with
a cigarette poking out of his mouth. Then the nighttime canvas
is prepared. The stage manager cues "Night!" and the canvas is
unfurled across the sky like it has been every night for millions
of years.

There is no message from my young friend Jack on my phone
machine when I get home. There is one from Brian O'Connor.
We worked together in summer stock ten years ago. We did *Boeing
Boeing,* a play about an airline pilot who dates lots of stewardesses,

and on one fateful weekend he and the stewardesses all end up in the same apartment with about seven different doors. It's a traditional farce. I played the Swedish "stew" who kept getting shoved into the bathroom while wearing a pair of men's pajamas, just the top — no bottoms.

"Mags, *It's a Mad Mad Mad Mad World* is playing at the Thalia tonight at 7:45. Do you want to join me? It'll be fun," he says. God, I could sure use some fun.

An hour later I'm sitting with Brian in the Thalia Theatre on Ninety-third Street. We're sharing a large popcorn. And we have smuggled in some beers. The movie starts.

"This is great, isn't it? They just don't make movies like this anymore," Brian whispers as the opening credits scroll across the screen.

"Yeah," I agree, and settle down in my seat. The minute Jimmy Durante kicks the bucket down the hill and Ethel Merman climbs into the back of her son-in-law's convertible I start crying uncontrollably and continue for the rest of the movie.

"It's one of the best comedies of all time, and you were crying through the entire movie. That's a symptom of something," Brian says as we leave the theater.

"Do you think?" I say and hook my arm through his. Brian is a good friend. He's the universal brother. He knows when to listen, and he knows when to put an arm around your shoulder and say, "Get over yourself." He grew up in a large Irish Catholic family in Long Island.

We buy a couple more beers and a bag of Fritos and walk over to the war monument on Riverside Drive.

"Something is wrong with you," Brian says, twisting the top

off his beer bottle. "Slapstick comedy is funny. Your censors are off. You need help."

"It struck me as so sad," I say. "All those people looking so desperately for the hidden treasure." We sit and drink our beer and munch our chips. The city night hums with traffic and snippets of passing conversations. Dogs bark, horns honk.

"I'm worried about you, Mags. That movie is funny, even Peter Falk is funny in it," Brian says, finishing off the last of his beer. "Are you in therapy?"

"Not right now, I'm taking a break. My last therapist kept dozing off during my sessions and then she moved to Michigan."

"Well, you need to talk to someone. Call mine. His name is George. He's great. Tell him you cried through *It's a Mad Mad Mad Mad World*—he'll probably see you immediately. This is an emergency. Geez, Mags, it's so funny and you cried and sniffled through the whole damn thing. I gotta run," he says, checking his watch. "I'm meeting some friends downtown. Want to come along?"

"No, I think I'll pass. Thanks, Brian." I give him a hug.

"Call George—I'll get you his phone number—and for Christ's sake, get a grip." I walk him to the subway stop on Eighty-sixth Street, we hug again and then Brian disappears down the stairwell.

I should call George. Brian is insightful about these things and, besides, there is a great deal of mental illness in his family so he knows the symptoms. I stop at the Dublin House and sit at the bar. I order a scotch on the rocks. The Dublin has a big old jukebox with the same tunes it's had since 1979. I put in a quarter and select the Eagles' "Tequila Sunrise."

I sit back down at the bar.

"Another shot?" the bartender asks.

"Sure, hit me again," I say.

"Put that on my tab." A man at the end of the bar picks up his drink and approaches.

"Will you let me buy you a drink?" he asks.

"Sure, why not?"

"You look familiar. I've been sitting down there wondering where I know you from and then I realized you're—"

"Nurse Mom—"

"Yes, on the cough syrup commercials." He smiles. "Wow, that's right."

"I don't think they're still running, are they? I mean they didn't renew the cycle. Have you seen it recently?" I ask. My interest is piqued because sometimes commercials go off the network, but a smaller market picks it up, and it can be running somewhere and you don't know it and nobody tells and you aren't getting paid.

"Well, maybe not for a while. But you are definitely Nurse Mom."

"I am indeed."

"You must have made a fortune."

"No, not really. I did all right for while, paid off my credit cards, but now I'm back to the same old grind, picking up nickels and dimes off the sidewalk. The commercial business is a harsh mistress."

He laughs at this. I think he's trying to ingratiate himself. Maybe he's hoping for some sample cough syrup.

"I'm Sam," he says, flashing a smile.

"Mags."

"Want to dance?"

"Right here in the bar?" My left eyebrow arches up to my hair-line.

"Sure." Sam puts his arm around my waist and helps me off the barstool. I need help because in a short time I have ingested several beers and four scotches on a relatively empty stomach.

I put my head on his shoulder as he maneuvers me slowly through the box step. Sam is wearing English Leather. It's about the only aftershave I recognize, that and Old Spice, which my older brother always wore until his second wife introduced him to Ralph Lauren Eau de Toilette for men. Sam's shoulder is com-fortable. I close my eyes but open them quickly, as I'm drunk enough that my head spins when they're shut. Shit, I haven't had any scotch since the park incident. I haven't wanted to chance it. Just beer. But now here I am again—in the arms of a strange man with my head spinning. Don't think about it. Don't think about it. Don't think about it. My tired and true mantra kicks in.

"Are you all right?" Sam asks.

"Fine, but I think I better get going."

"Come on. Have one for the road. Then I'll see you home."

"No, I just live a few blocks from here."

"Then you have to have a nightcap before you go."

The smell of English Leather mixed with all the scotch sloshing around in my belly seduces me into the haze of bygone days when I was on the homecoming court in high school and dating Denny Spangler and all was right with the world.

"All right, one more for the road." I drop my head back onto Sam's shoulder and momentarily drift off as we sway to the music.

I come to abruptly when Sam shakes me.

"Mags?"

"What?"

"I think you passed out for a minute or two."

"Possibly," I say in my thick, throaty, late-night voice. "I got to go."

"I'll walk you," Sam offers.

"No, I'm fine." I grab my bag and head as directly to the door as I can. "See you," I say.

"Right," says Sam.

"And thanks for the drink, buckaroo," I toss over my shoulder as I make my exit. God, I'm good at exits.

11

When I wake up the next morning, my head is pounding and I feel like I have cat hair growing on my tongue. I try to focus. I'm pretty sure it's Friday, and I think it's still June, and I'm in my own bed. All right. That's good for starters. I switch on the radio next to my bed. I dial to 1010 WINS. Their slogan is, "You give us twenty-two minutes and we'll give you the world." Seems so easy. Right now it's Lisa, with traffic and weather on the 10s. The midtown tunnel is jammed, the FDR Drive is slow, and the George Washington Bridge is backed up due to a two-car collision on the lower level, but the skies are blue and the temperature is seventy-eight with only 20 percent humidity. And it's 10:50 a.m.

I get up and head for the bathroom. My left knee throbs. It is scraped and bruised. I look in the mirror. My eyes are red and puffy and my wrist hurts. There are more scrapes on the palms of my hands. I must have fallen. I light a cigarette and put on water for coffee. I sit and smoke, looking out the window. My apartment is in the back of the building so I look out on a little courtyard.

Old Mrs. Vianey, who lives in 3E, is sitting on a bench reading
the paper.

I remember being at the Dublin House and then I left, I
guess. I don't remember getting home. The kettle whistles. I
pour the water through the drip coffee cone. My mind locks
for a minute. It's not the first time I have stood and tried to
reconstruct what happened the night before. Usually it comes
back to me. I'm sure it will. I must have fallen on my way home,
no big deal. I put my coffee on the edge of the sink and turn on
the shower. I get in. I keep the cigarette in my hand and hold it
outside the shower curtain. I cock my head back and let the hot
water hit my face full blast. I take a couple of deep breaths, then
poke my head out of the shower curtain and take a drag on the
cigarette. I repeat this a few times, and then drop the cigarette
butt in the sink. I get the coffee and place it on the soap dish in
the shower stall. I turn around and the shower caresses my back,
I cradle the coffee cup in my hands, sipping slowly, then I place
it back in the soap dish and drop down to my knees and let the
water pour over me.

I wonder how "old Mrs. Vianey" got to be old. How did she
make it through? She must have been young once and then not—I
don't know if I'm going to survive this middle passage. Maybe I
should ask her. Maybe I should sit in the courtyard with her and
let her tell me how to negotiate this part of my life, because right
now I don't have a clue. And Brian's right—I have lost my sense
of humor. Nothing is funny. I feel scared and alone most of the
time, and strangely comfortable in the discomfort. Will I ever
learn to be myself and feel safe? No funny hats, no gingham pinafores or pigtail wigs, no script? Is it too late to learn? I close my
eyes and press the palms of my hands together. "Help me," I pray

into that void between regret and resolve as the hot water washes over my body. "Please help me."

I eventually get up off my knees, wash my hair and shave my legs. Starting today I'm going to take better care of myself. I'll take my vitamins and I'll eat broccoli and I'll vacuum my apartment and I'll clean Bixby's litter box and I'll go over all my songs for my club date and I'll pay my bills and . . . I won't drink. Not even a beer.

Life is good, I remind myself as I dry off. I make another cup of coffee and pull Bixby up on my lap and hug him to my chest.

"You're a good kitty. You're my good kitty." Bixby curls up in my arms and purrs. The phone rings. It's Dee-Honey.

"Hi, honey." Her standard greeting leaps from the phone. "I'm going to change the pickup time to three o'clock instead of two. Gloria has an audition, and you know I always try to accommodate that. It just means we'll get there a little later."

"Pickup time?" I ask.

"Maggie, we're going to up to the Cape to do *Cinderella*. You're playing Tilliebelle. I'm sure I gave you the dates."

"Oh yeah, sure. I'm just waking up. Don't listen to me." I find my bag and look through it for my day planner. My God, I'm living in some kind of perpetual purgatory, I think as I rifle through my things.

"So we're set. It's three instead of two," Dee says.

"I'll see you then," I say. "The usual corner?"

"Yes, Ninety-sixth Street on the northwest corner. Are you all right, dear?"

"It was a late night and I overslept this morning. Some caffeine and a winning lottery ticket and I'll be fine."

"You and me both. See you at three." Dee-Honey indulges me

with a quick laugh and then rings off. Sure enough I see that Friday and Saturday are blocked off in my day planner with *Cinderella* written across them in bold letters.

Also in my bag I find an orange, two apples, and a pineapple. What the hell? I must have gotten them on my way home last night. But did I pay for them? I check for my wallet. It's there with a few nickels and dimes and a couple of singles and my emergency twenty stuffed under my driver's license. It wouldn't be the first time that I've helped myself to fruit from the outdoor bins of the numerous Korean delis along the street. But I had never brought home a pineapple. That's like big game. That's like fishing for trout all your life and then one day harpooning a whale.

Oh well, I peel the orange and slice up some apple. Then I feed Bixby and get out my overnight bag. It's almost one o'clock.

By pickup time I'm bright eyed and bushy tailed. When I get to Ninety-sixth Street, Dee-Honey is already there. The back of the van is crammed with suitcases, and the cast is milling around on the sidewalk with coffees and sodas. Dee and Helen Sanders are discussing sinus remedies.

At this moment Gloria arrives at a trot.

"Sorry, I'm late. Thanks for waiting."

"How'd it go?" Helen Sanders asks, nibbling on some carrot sticks.

"Gosh, I think they really liked me, but who knows."

"Well you've hit the nail on the head there," Helen says. "Who the hell knows?"

Dee-Honey honks the horn and we take our positions in the van. Randall holds the front door for Pauline.

"Your carriage awaits, Madame," he says as Pauline scoots in next to Dee and Randall assumes his place next to Pauline.

"I'm riding shotgun, kids, so fear no evil," he says as we take off toward the Westside Highway.

I'm sitting between Helen and Gloria in the backseat. Glo plays Cinderella because she insisted that she get to play at least one ingénue in the Little Britches repertoire even though she is five foot nine and has to sing all of Cindy's songs an octave lower than written. Dee-Honey agreed to her request and sewed a ruffle on the bottom of Cinderella's ball gown. Ron, Mr. Prince Charming, is wedged in with the suitcases in the far back. He falls asleep almost immediately. Helen gets out a crossword puzzle and Gloria puts on her earphones and cues up her iPod. I stare straight ahead. It's a six-hour drive to the Cape. If I had a gun, I'd shoot myself.

We stop for gas near Providence, Rhode Island. Everyone gets out for a bathroom break and some food. Gloria pulls me aside.

"I've got to talk to you. My agent thinks I should move to LA. He says I could really do well out there. They have an office there. What do you think?"

"Glo, I don't know. Would you like to live in LA? Do you have friends out there?"

"Not really. It's just that my agent thinks I'm more of an LA type than a New York type."

"Well, think about it. You don't have to decide right now, do you?"

"The lease is coming up on my apartment so . . ."

"Then do it. Give it a shot. You're young. You're tall. You've got an agent who's helping you. You go, girl."

Gloria hugs me. "Thanks. I knew you'd know what I should do."

People always think you give good advice when you give them

the advice they want to hear, and besides it's easy to be decisive when you're dealing with other people's lives.

I go the ladies' room and then get a fish sandwich, a small fries, and a Diet Coke at McDonald's. I also buy a 3 Musketeers bar and a bag of peanut M&M's.

I switch places with Pauline. Randall takes over the driving and Dee-Honey rides shotgun.

We get to the Cape about nine o'clock. We check into the motel and then all head out to Spanky's Fish Net for lobster dinner. Randall orders a pitcher of beer. He hands me a glass. I consider declining it for a moment, but, instead, I toast my fellow actors and drain the glass. It's only beer. It's only one beer, for heaven's sakes. Besides, it's not the beer that gets me in trouble, it's the scotch.

The next morning we assemble in the parking lot. It's eight a.m. Dee-Honey comes rushing out.

"Oh my goodness. Frank just called. There has been a mix-up and the sponsors think we are doing *Rumpelstiltskin*. I'm sure I gave them the right schedule. *Rumpel* is next week. Oh, dear, Frank said the woman in charge kept asking him where the spinning wheel was."

We all look at each other and for one moment try to calculate if we could actually do *Rumpel* with this cast. I know Randall has played the king and I've played the princess, of course. Ron has done the prince, and it doesn't really matter because if you've done one prince you've done them all. But no one has played Rumpelstiltskin. I guess Gloria could pull it off if she had to — although she'd have to walk on her knees. But then there is a matter of the costumes and, of course, that damn spinning wheel.

"Well, they'll just have wait until next week for Mr. Stiltskin. Besides *Cinderella* is so much more fun. Don't you think?" Dee says getting into the car. "But maybe we could do a little preview for them at the end of the show. Randall, you could sing the king's patter song and, Maggie, you could recite a section from the tower scene," she suggests.

"Dee, the kids are eight years old. They're not going to care all that much," Randall says.

"Oh, all right, honey. I guess it will work out," Dee says. I catch Randall's eye, mouth a big thank-you, and off we go.

Frank is standing by the stage door finishing a cigarette. "Can you believe it?" he says. "If one more person asks about that damn spinning wheel I'm going to shove Cinderella's glass slipper up somebody's —"

"Hi, honey," Dee chirps.

"Ass," Frank mumbles under his breath and takes a drag on his cigarette.

The Cape Playhouse is reputed to be the oldest summer theater in America. It was built in the 1920s when Broadway actors fled the hot city for the cooler New England summers. The walls in the backstage area and dressing rooms are full of production pictures featuring Henry Fonda, Bette Davis, Tallulah Bankhead, and many more.

I stick my head in one of the dressing rooms. Gloria is wiping off the mirror.

"Anyone claim this other seat, yet?"

"It's all yours," Glo says. "I don't know what is on this mirror. It looks like someone blew their nose on it."

"Ugh," I say unpacking my makeup kit. "I'm going to run downstairs and see if the coffee is ready. Do you want a cup?"

"Please, black with two sugars."

The staff at the Cape Playhouse always provides a fresh pot of coffee and an assortment of sticky buns and donuts in the green-room. Eddie Houser, who plays Ashes the cat, is sitting at the table eating a powdered donut. He drove up with Frank in the truck.

"Hey, Eddie, how are you? How was your trip up?"

"Well, Frank drives like a maniac, but aside from that it was fine."

"But I thought you liked that. Living dangerously."

"Oh, I do, Mags, indeed I do." Eddie bites into another donut as Pauline enters in full costume.

"Eddie, dear, do you have any false eyelashes I can borrow? I must have left mine in Yonkers last week. I don't know what to do. I've looked all through my things and they're just gone, gone, gone," she says. "Oh, are these pecan rolls? They look delicious."

Pauline takes one and wraps it in a napkin. "Yummy, yum. I'll save this for later."

"I double lash for Ashes, Pauline, I really can't spare them for you. Just use a lot of mascara. Besides, the fairy godmother is not a beauty queen."

Pauline purses her lips and takes a deep breath. "I'm not intending to be a beauty queen, but I do think it's important that the children see my eyes when I'm working my wonderful magic for our dear Cinderella, but if you think it's more important that Ashes, the cat, has his lashes, that is fine, but mind you—and I'm sure you don't know this or care—cats don't have eyelashes, so that's how silly you look, and I've wanted to tell you that for years but I didn't want to hurt your feelings, but the truth is, dear, you look perfectly ridiculous in that costume—and you always have."

"Pauline, for goodness sakes," I say, trying to ease the situation. "Maybe Gloria has an extra pair."

"No, I'll go on without them. Maybe Eddie's right, no need to pretend I'm pretty. There is nothing wrong with the children seeing a homely fairy godmother."

"Pauline, you look beautiful with or without your lashes, doesn't she, Eddie?"

Pauline doesn't wait for a reply. She sweeps out of the greenroom in a huff.

"Eddie, how could you?"

"Really, Mags, how couldn't I? She'll get over it." Eddie refills his coffee cup and heads upstairs to the dressing rooms.

Frank sticks his head in the greenroom. "Half hour to show time."

Geez, I haven't even started my makeup. Fortunately I'm not on until the third scene. Gloria is already backstage doing her vocal warm-ups. She really does take this so seriously.

I throw on my costume and start to paint my face. I put on a light pancake base and then draw on arched eyebrows. I make rosebud lips and place a beauty mark on my chin. I pull on my wig cap and then the bright red wig that screams "comedy." I make it to the stage as the show is starting. I find my hoopskirt positioned on the floor next to Frank's booth. I step into it and tie it around my waist while holding the skirt of my costume under my arms. I can't believe hoopskirts were actually once worn in everyday life. But back then they weren't riding subways or elevators. Dee-Honey is at my side. She is playing the ugly stepmother.

"Remember, honey, you help Frank with the throne right after Ashes enters with the pumpkin."

"Yes, Dee, I remember."

The great thing about a theater company like this is you get to do everything. Nobody's a star. I just wish Helen would remember and, speak of the devil, here she comes. She plays Gladiola, the other ugly stepsister, and no one can flounce a hoopskirt like Helen. The last time we did *Cinderella* she almost knocked me into the orchestra pit when she exited the ballroom scene.

Randall Kent rushes up to Dee with his arms extended. "I can't get these damn cuffs buttoned."

"All right, honey, relax."

"I told you the last time I did this show that this costume needed major repairs. The pants are practically falling apart."

"I'll look at it between shows. There dear—all buttoned." Dee finishes with the cuffs as the second scene starts. He rushes on-stage.

"Do I have lipstick on my teeth, Dee?" Helen asks in a back-stage whisper. She peels her lips back in a chimpanzee grin.

"No, none at all, dear, you look lovely," Dee-Honey whispers back as we line up for our entrance.

In the final scene, Randall, the prince's manservant, tries the glass slipper on the ugly stepsisters in a desperate attempt to find the mysterious woman who left it behind. Oh, you know the story. Gladiola goes first. After much jamming and cramming she gives up and then it is my turn as Tilliebelle. Of course this takes some mighty fine acting from me because Gloria's foot is much larger than mine because she is much taller but there is no rationale in the land of make-believe. So I push and grunt and Randall turns his back to me and straddles my leg and tries to get the shoe on my foot. I put my other foot on his buttocks for leverage and, of course I fall on top of him, which gets a big laugh from the audi-ence. Then I grab the shoe and attempt to try it on myself and at this point Randall is supposed to wrestle the shoe away from me, but at that moment one of the kids in the audience has an accident (euphemism for vomits) and there is scurrying around and a run up the aisle by the kid and the kid-wrangler. Randall loses his place for a moment and forgets to get the shoe back. So when Cinderella sits down to try on the shoe there is no glass slipper to try on. I have it hidden in my pocket. The children know I have it and I know I have it, but no on else does. The show comes to a standstill. I look at Randall who is blustering about. I can't believe he doesn't know where the damn glass slipper is. I have to admit I'm enjoying this immensely. He blusters a while and I wink at the audience and finally they can't contain themselves and give me away.

"She has it! She has it!" they scream pointing at me.

"Give me that shoe," Randall booms in his best baritone. And the audience squeals with delight and bursts into applause.

I hand the shoe over and we maneuver our way to the end of the show. I think the bit is very funny and suggest we keep it in. Randall is not amused.

"Dammit, Mags, the show is long enough as it is," he says the minute we get offstage.

"Yeah, but it was funny. The audience loved it and you should have seen your face."

"Funny for you, my dear," Randall snaps.

"Yes, Mags, it wasn't humorous for the rest of us," Helen says, stepping out of her hoop. "Not at all. Some people get piggy when they get in the spotlight, don't they?"

"Piggy, indeed," Eddie agrees and snorts a few times for effect.

"I thought it was hysterical," Pauline says. "I loved it. You were very in character. Feel it, I say, let the moment take you."

"Well thank you, Pauline, I appreciate that. And fuck the rest of you if you can't take a joke," I say heading for the dressing room.

"Temper, temper, Mags. It's not pretty," Randall calls out after me.

There is an hour between shows. I get out of my costume. Gloria comes into the dressing room with a big grin on her face.

"I just checked my service. I got a callback. I got a callback for a big national TV commercial!"

"That's great," I say, pulling off my wig. "Good for you."

And since Gloria is in such a good mood, I ask if I can borrow her cell phone to check my messages since I have misplaced my own phone again. I'm sure it's here somewhere, but why waste time looking when I can use Gloria's minutes instead.

"Sure, no problem, I'm going to be rich."

Little does she know how short-lived that feeling can be, but I'm not going to tell her. I dial my number and then punch in the code.

"Hey, Maggie, just wondered how you are doing? Call me," Jack's voice says. My heart almost stops. It's him. He called.

I decide Gloria is going to be rich enough to afford me another call so I quickly dial Jack's number and take a deep breath to steady my voice.

"Jack Eremus, here."

"Hi, it's me, Mags."

"Hey, where are you?"

"I'm on Cape Cod doing *Cinderella*. I have another show in about forty-five minutes, then we're driving back."

"Oh, I called you last night and when I didn't hear from you . . ."

"Well, I just got the message."

"Look, I've got a meeting with my boss in a few minutes. Can I call you later?"

"You don't have to," slips out before I can stop myself.

"I want to," Jack says.

"I want you to," I say, abandoning my comfortable state of abandonment. "I miss you."

"Look, why don't I just come by tonight."

"All right. I'll be back around seven."

"Great. I'll see you then, Sweet Pea."

We say goodbye. I sit and let the sound of Jack's voice saying "I'll see you then, Sweet Pea" pass through my brain and travel straight down to the center of my heart. I return Gloria's phone and go to the greenroom in search of sugar. I pour some coffee and take a glazed donut and stroll out behind the theater. The scene shop is about fifty yards away and the sound of buzz saws and staple guns emanates from its doors. The crew is building the set for the next production. Loretta Swit of *M*A*S*H* fame is going to be starring in *Driving Miss Daisy*. I sit down at one of the picnic tables on the side lawn.

My first experience in summer stock was as an apprentice, which meant I sewed costumes, painted sets, built props, sold tickets, pulled the curtain, ran the spotlight, and anything else that had to be done. And then in the last show of the season, *South Pacific,* I got to play the lead, Nellie Forbush. The actress they hired fractured her ankle the second day of rehearsal and I had to jump in. It was the perfect end to the perfect summer. And I did it all for nothing but room and board because I loved the theater. I loved it unconditionally. And it was the summer I met Randall Kent.

As that thought pops in my head, Randall pops around the side of the building with a McDonald's bag.

"I was just thinking about you, Randall. About the summer we met. Remember?"

"How could I forget? I was playing Tevye." Randall sings the first few bars of "If I Were a Rich Man." "That was some season. I also played Don Quixote in *La Mancha*. Now there's a role. I'd love to do that again. I love the score. Remember the girl that played Aldonza? She had webbed feet. Did you know that? Oddest thing. They were completely webbed." Randall sits down across from me.

"I didn't know that, but I do remember that her mother made all of her underwear. She had never bought a pair of underpants in her life. I mean who makes underwear?"

"Funny what you remember about people."

"Yeah, it is. I remember you were wonderful as Tevye."

"You're a dear," Randall says. "Look, I'm sorry, Mags, about the shoe thing. I didn't mean to be an asshole, but you really threw me for a loop. If there is no glass slipper there's no damn show."

"You have to admit it was funny. I mean the kids loved it."

"All right. It was funny," Randall says opening his McDonald's bag.

"I'll forgive you being an asshole if I can bum a cigarette."

"Hmmm. I don't know that I can go that far." Randall smiles, then hands me his pack of Marlboros. "Take two, they're lethal."

"Thanks." I light the cigarette as Randall bites into his hamburger.

"I don't know which will kill me first, smoking or eating fast food," he says chewing a mouthful of poison.

"Half hour," Frank calls to us from the back door of the theater. "And don't forget the throne this time, Mags. Helen almost fell on her butt when she went to sit down and it wasn't there."

"Oh, is that what happened?" I ask, innocent as a baby. "Sorry, Frank, I'll remember." Randall catches my eye and winks at me.

"You're wicked, darling." He snorts with glee. "You're wicked as hell."

12

That night Jack and I walk over to Broadway and get Chinese food. We drink tea and eat shrimp with broccoli and rice. The fortune cookies arrive at the end of the meal. Mine says, *Friends surround you.* And Jack's says, *Be open to opportunity.* I smile when he reads it.

"That's a good one," I say. "Be prepared, isn't that what the Boy Scouts say?"

"I don't know, I was never a Boy Scout. I just know that when opportunity knocks be ready to open the door. Don't get caught with your pants down."

"What?"

"That's what my grandmother always said," Jack says. "She had a real fear that something great would happen and she'd miss it because she was in the bathroom."

"You're kidding."

"No, I'm serious. She was a little crazy. She always kept the bathroom door ajar so she could hear what was happening."

"I do that, come to think of it."

"I've noticed," Jack says with a smile. Gosh, he has good teeth. How does someone get such good teeth?

We walk back to my apartment. Jack comes in and we sit on the couch. Bixby jumps in my lap.

"So," I say. "What's next?"

"I don't know," says Jack. "I wanted to see you to make sure you were all right."

"So this is just a courtesy call."

"No. Well . . ."

"Thanks. I'm fine and now you're free to go."

"Look, you're the one—"

"I know. You don't have to say another word. I'm the one that asked you to leave before and I'm asking you to leave again. So go . . . and thanks. Thanks for checking up on me." I wish I could cut my tongue out.

"All right . . ." he gets up. The back of his neck is moving out of my reach and I love that neck.

"Wait," I say. Jack stops and turns. I get up and put my arms around him.

"Please wait," I say.

He bends his head to mine and I place my face next to his. "I love you," I whisper into his ear.

He picks me up in his arms and carries me to the bed. He lays me down and then lies on top of me. Very gently. His body feels weightless on me, like a warm goose down comforter. He folds me in his arms and kisses me. It's like oxygen, vital to my existence, like something I've always needed and have finally found.

"I love you, Maggie. I think about you all the time," Jack whispers in my ear.

"I think about you too. I love you, Jack, I really love you," I say it so quietly that only the consonants are audible. I feel tears on my cheeks and I'm not sure if they're mine or Jack's. I love you, I love you, I love you, our bodies say in perfect harmony.

Sometime during the night, I wake with a start. Jack is beside me. I have dreamed my old recurring nightmare. I open my front door and in front of me is an impossible journey, a swinging footbridge over a large chasm, then a steep, forbidding path up a glacier of ice, but this time, as I step on the bridge, a man appears. It's Jack, but it's not Jack. It's a middle-aged, more rugged Jack. He stands at the edge of the chasm and reaches out his hand to me, and that's what wakes me.

I get out of bed and go to the kitchen for a drink of water. As I pass my little fireplace I hear something lightly fall down the chimney. I squat and see a small pile of soot as more sifts from above. That's odd. I haven't used the fireplace for months. I wait a moment and all is still. I stand up and go back to bed.

I curl myself up next to Jack. He turns slightly and kisses me and then drops back into sleep. Bixby nestles against my back. I am surrounded by friends, like the fortune cookie said, and I'm in love with a wonderful guy, like Rodgers and Hammerstein said.

THE NEXT EVENING I'm sitting across from George, the therapist that Brian recommended. He's agreed to work me in when he has time. I'm leaning forward with my elbows resting on my knees; the cup of coffee in my hand is lukewarm. It's a hazelnut blend with whole milk in it, not skim. I hate skim milk in my coffee. It looks weak—ambiguous.

"Lately," I confide in a hushed tone. "Lately I've been feeling invisible."

"Invisible how?" he asks.

"You know, when I'm walking down the street and people bump into me and they look surprised, like they hadn't seen I was there. I think, my God, I am invisible. And I wonder if they see me even after they bump into me, or do they just pretend to see me because it's too disconcerting to bump into something that isn't there. So they act as if I'm there but I'm not. I mean, I am there, but they don't know I am. Like for instance, I think this is your dinner break and you don't know I'm here."

George wipes his mouth and clears his throat. "You know we worked out a lower rate if you came at this hour. But if it bothers you, I'll—" He starts to push his sandwich aside.

"No, no don't stop eating," I interrupt, not wanting to get into discussion again about being lucky to get the odd hour here and there. Apparently George is a busy man. "What is that? Ham and cheese?" George pulls the sandwich apart and offers me half.

"No, thanks. I don't eat red meat and ham is red meat, isn't it? I'm never sure. For a long time I thought red meat was meat from animals that bleed and the blood made it red. But, of course, chickens bleed and that's what? White meat actually. I wonder, do fish bleed?"

I find a perverse pleasure in discussing animal blood while George eats his dinner. I notice a vague look of discomfort as he considers his next bite.

"I know they're amphibians or reptiles or something, and of course they bleed, but is it red? The blood? Because blood is really blue until it's exposed to oxygen, so then fish blood would still be blue 'cause they're in the water and there is no oxygen or rather . . . yes . . . there is oxygen, it's H_2O, so it's hydrogen with some oxygen. God, isn't it amazing how ninth-grade biology comes rushing back into your brain."

I take the last gulp of my lukewarm coffee. George folds the rest of his sandwich into the wax paper and pushes it aside.

"But you know what I'm really concerned about?"

"What?" George asks.

"I'm really concerned about the fact that I'm paying you seventy dollars an hour to discuss the color of meat," I say smiling. George doesn't appear to be amused.

"What's really going on?" he asks, very businesslike. Geez, I think, can't we have a little friendly banter? I don't feel like getting into it right now.

George is midsixties with a trim figure and a handsome face. Brian told me that before he was a therapist, he was a photographer's model and lived mostly in Paris. His apartment is a floor-through in a renovated brownstone on West Tenth Street. He conducts his sessions in a cozy living room with overstuffed chairs, ottomans, and an abundance of silk flowers.

He is looking at me with his head tilted, waiting, ready for me to spill the beans. Goodie is now sitting primly on the mantel of the fireplace, also waiting. Well here goes, I think. If you want beans, I got beans.

"What isn't going on?" I say with a self-conscious giggle. "I'm in a relationship with a guy who is much younger, and I don't think there is much chance that it's going anywhere, but I'm absolutely crazy about him. The fellow I was seeing before, who lives in Texas, called me recently to tell me he had married his dentist girlfriend. He's been sort of an insurance policy for me. I knew that no matter what, I could always move

NOTE TO SELF . . .

Just because your therapist eats lunch during your session doesn't mean he isn't listening.

to Texas and marry Joe, and now that's gone, I mean, because he married someone else. He loved me. And I loved him." I take a breath. Shit, I can feel it. I'm going to start crying. But I can't seem to stop this litany.

"And I was attacked in Central Park and Mr. Ed got hurt and it was all my fault because I was drunk and shouldn't have been there in the first place and my career is going nowhere and I have a club date coming up and I have to sing for grown-ups and I'm not sure I can because my accompanist died and I don't know if I can work with someone else and I'm over forty and I haven't done anything exceptional in my life and I want to disappear and maybe that's why I feel invisible all the time. Oh, and I've been hallucinating." I take a breath. "Do you have any water?" I ask. "My throat feels really dry."

"Of course." George gets up and heads toward the kitchen. Goodie flies off the mantel and perches on my knee.

"Good, Mags," he says. "And don't forget to mention the baby."

"What baby?"

"The one you dream about." He places a tiny kiss on my cheek and then disappears in a cloud of fairy dust.

George returns with a large glass of water.

"Thank you," I say and take a long drink. "Ah, there is nothing better than a tall drink of cool water. There is a song by that title or something like that from a musical based on *A Streetcar Named Desire*. Do you know it? It's beautiful."

"Let's try to stay right here in the room," George says picking up a little notebook.

"Are you writing down what I say?"

"Not every word, I take notes. Jot down the details. It helps me help you."

"Oh."

"Now, you were saying . . ."

I take another drink of water. I look at George and then I notice the Georgia O'Keeffe print on the wall behind his head. It's one of her cloud series. Beautiful. Tranquil.

"I love that print," I say. "I'm a big fan of hers. I went to see the retrospective of her work at the Metropolitan a few years ago. It was amazing. You could see her whole life in her work, in her exquisite colors and compositions and brushstrokes."

"Yes," George agrees. "Why don't you let me see your story, Maggie? What do your brushstrokes look like?"

Corny, I think to myself, but before I can stop it my mouth opens and I hear myself saying, "When I was in tenth grade, there was this guy, his name was Danny Panther. He was an artist. In fact his nickname was Picasso. He was a senior. And in the yearbook under his picture it said, "To create is to breathe, this I believe." When I read that, it hit me like a bolt of lightning, and I knew that I felt that way too, but had no idea what I wanted to create, and every time I remember that phrase it makes me cry."

And I start to cry sitting in the overstuffed armchair in George's living room. George hands me a box of tissues. I don't shed a few ladylike tears; I cry loudly and messily for the remainder of my fifty-minute appointment.

"Well, I think this is a good beginning," George says at the end of the session. I gather my things and take the wad of tissues out with me as I don't see a wastebasket and don't want to ask.

"We'll continue this next time," he says, showing me out the door.

Great, just what I want to spend my money on, a sob session with a strange man once a week. I need a drink. I need a scotch on the rocks and make that a double. I call my friend Patty from a pay phone to see if she can join me because, of course, I don't have my cell phone with me. Christ, no wonder I don't have a career—at least that's what my agent would say.

Patty lives on Charlton Street a few blocks away. Her machine picks up. "Patty?" I say into the receiver. "Are you screening?" No answer. Damn. I check the coin return on the pay phone like I always do and then head for the nearest bar.

Rose's Turn on the corner of Grove and Seventh Avenue is a piano bar with a cabaret space upstairs. It used to be the Duplex but the Duplex moved across the street and down the block fifteen years ago. Rose's Turn refers to the big eleven o'clock number at the end of the musical *Gypsy* that Mama Rose sings.

The bar is pretty empty. It's early for the drinking, show tune crowd. I order a scotch. The clientele at Rose's Turn is primarily gay men, so it's a good bet I won't end up in some compromising position later tonight with too much to drink in my belly and too little to wear on my patooty. I glimpse myself in the mirror behind the bar. A character in Sondheim's *Follies* sings a song called "I'm Still Here." She's an old showgirl who's seen it all and survived it all and gets to sing about it. Wouldn't that be a great way to go? What if everyone got one last number at the funeral? Everybody got an eleven o'clock showstopper song, and then keeled over into the coffin as the lid snapped shut—so long, end of show. I'd want a great costume too. Sequins and feathers and a pair of killer Joan Crawford fuck-me pumps.

"Can I get you another drink?" the bartender asks.

"Sure, thanks," I say. "When does the piano player come in?"

"Not until nine o'clock."

"Do you mind if I noodle a little?"

"Sure . . ." he says with a slight hesitation. Piano bars can be frightening places because the talent isn't selected; it's random and sometimes very random. Anybody can get up and sing their heart out, anybody who's ever wanted to sing the whole score to *Music Man* or the aria in the third act of *La Boheme,* or the love duet (both parts) from *Phantom of the Opera,* any tone-deaf son of a bitch with enough nerve can get up and sing. It's a piano bar and that's what it's about, making dreams come true for the drunk and less than gifted.

I put my scotch next to me on the piano bench; I'm an okay piano player and, baby, I got rhythm.

"Oh, excellent!" Goodie exclaims perching himself on the C above middle C. "Thought I might find you here. Let's sing that arrangement of 'Red Robin' we used to do."

"I'm not sure I know it. I wish you could play it," I say.

"Sorry, but I need a much smaller piano," Goodie says. "Go on, you can do it."

I pound out some chords. Goodie repositions himself on the top of the piano.

"Now make it swing," he says.

"Oh when the red, red robin comes bob-bob-bobbin' along, along," we sing together, Goodie in an interesting tenor and me in my throaty semi-soprano. We swing into the second verse. By this time the bartender and one old guy dressed completely in black studded leather are singing harmony with us.

And without taking a break I go right into my Cole Porter medley, which always makes Goodie cry. The bartender buys me a drink. The old guy in leather asks, "Do you know 'Fifty-Percent' from *Ballroom?*"

"You betcha." And we sing and sing and sing until the real

piano player shows up for the evening shift. I thank the bartender and he invites me to come back anytime.

"I'm doing a show at Don't Tell Mama soon."

"Good luck." He waves as he pours another vodka for the old man in leather.

Goodie rides on my shoulder as I walk to the subway.

"That was fun," he coos. "Like old times. I love being down here in the Village. The Upper West Side is a little buttoned up for my taste."

At that moment a large black man wearing an orange boa and platform shoes comes walking toward us. On the corner a fellow in lederhosen and kneesocks is playing a banjo, and as we get to the subway entrance a young woman with short spiked orange hair and fishnet stockings talking on a cell phone rollerblades through the intersection.

"See what I mean, these are my people," Goodie says. "I've got to go. I'm meeting with a few friends on Cornelia Street. You know that bakery with the most delicious coconut cream pie?"

"Your friends?" I ask. "Little friends or big friends? More fairies? I never thought there were more of you."

"Mags, my love, the afterlife is complex and way too hard to explain until you've been there. Lots of levels, off-ramps, holding pens."

"Sounds like a board game," I say.

"Kind of," Goodie says, "but then that's the way my mind works. You might find it completely different. It's perception, perception, perception—like life, darling."

Goodie gives me a peck on the cheek, then spreads his gossamer wings and flies south.

I stop at the Village Smoke Shop and buy a pack of cigarettes for what seems like a hundred dollars. I have got to quit smoking. Again. I have quit before. Hasn't everyone?

Mark Twain said, "Quitting smoking is easy, I've done it a thousand times." And so have I. I decide to walk for a while. It's a beautiful summer evening, and Seventh Avenue, as Goodie has pointed out, is an entertaining stretch of road.

I stopped smoking for a year while Goodie was sick. I didn't want to smoke around him, but then at a wedding reception in Connecticut I picked up the beast again and haven't been able to kick it since. I made the mistake of going to the wedding alone. That's how it started. I knew the bride from an ad agency I had done some commercials for, and I thought it would be politic for me to show up, but couldn't convince anyone to go with me. Texas Joe was back in Houston, so I was on my own. It was a few months after Goodie died.

The wedding guests were all rich and privileged, all except me, of course. The groom was a graduate of Yale and the bride of Smith College. So the conversation was clever and witty and very Ivy League. I stared straight ahead most of the time and tried not to make eye contact with anyone. I didn't want to be sucked into some conversation I couldn't keep up with.

Then a handsome Yale guy whom I had been introduced to earlier asked me to dance. I shook my head explaining I had twisted my ankle when I tripped on a baby stroller on my way into the tent and was going to sit it out. That wasn't the truth. Truth was I was wearing a pair of black-and-white checked pants that made me look like a table for four in contrast to all the fitted designer dresses and slacks.

Then I noticed an abandoned pack of Marlboros lying on the table where I was sitting. I reached for it. I fingered the oblong package. I ran my hand over the cellophane. I guiltily sniffed the three last cigarettes nestled cozily in the corner. They smelled delicious, like a forest glen after a rainfall, like roses in full bloom at the height of the summer, like honeysuckle along a country road, like freshly mowed grass.

The three-piece band started to play "Smoke Gets in Your Eyes." That did it. I pulled one of the cigarettes out. I rolled it around in my fingers for a while. I put it in my mouth. Dormant desire came to life. My lips curled longingly around the filter. Ah, sweet Jesus, it was like running into an old lover on the street in the middle of a late afternoon summer rain shower and ducking into a bar for a glass of sherry and some sweet memories. Like standing on the beach at the end of the day with the sun setting and the warm ocean breeze brushing against your face. It was like heaven.

I looked around for some matches, a lighter, or some dry kindling. A bespectacled overweight accountant type bumped into my chair.

"Got a light, big guy?" I asked.

"I sure do," he said as he fumbled in the pocket of his seersucker suit and pulled out his Bic. He flicked the igniter wheel, a flame jumped up and kissed the end of my cigarette, and the Hallelujah Chorus started playing in my brain. I inhaled deeply, pulling the hot smoke into my lungs where it filled every nook and every cranny. I coughed once, then twice, then relaxed and took another drag. And just like that, I transformed myself back into a pack-a-day, devil-may-care, what's-your-problem, get-out-of-my-way-or-I'll-knock-you-down, hard-ass-cigarette-smoking broad. The bespectacled accountant watched in wonderment. I imagine it must have been like witnessing Dr. Jekyll turn into Mr. Hyde.

"Let's dance, big guy," I said.

"I was getting a drink for my wife. I have to get back. She's expecting her white wine spritzer," he gasped as I shoved him into the electric slide line dance.

"Oh, sorry," I shouted over the music. I waved him off as I slid once and clapped and rocked back and forth and slid, slid, slid.

"Hey watch that damn cigarette," a guy in a khaki suit admonished.

"Yeah, and watch your mouth, buddy boy," I snapped. I got out of the electric slide line and headed back across the dance floor in search of that abandoned pack of cigarettes. Smoking felt like a vacation. The months since Goodie's death had been difficult. I cried all the time. I had watched him wage a long, excruciating battle against his disease, but could do so little to ease his pain. No one could. In the end he was shrunk to the bare minimum of flesh and bone. Frail as an eighty-year-old man, his skin became translucent, but his eyes were still hot with hope. Hope for a cure, for a reprieve, for a day free of pain, for a new melody to play on his beautiful baby grand piano sitting silent in the tiny living room of his apartment.

I found a pack of matches on the table and lit another cigarette. I took a long drag and was reminded how cigarettes neutralize emotion and put everything into park and let you idle for a while.

The band started to play a pretty decent arrangement of "Light My Fire." The Yale grad sauntered over to my table.

"How's the ankle?" he asked.

"Much better, thanks." I smiled. "How about that dance?"

He put down his drink and slipped his arms around my waist

and sang, "Come on, baby, light my fire," slightly off key into my left ear.

The Yale grad and I danced the last dance with our heads pressed together, two lonely ships at the end of a long and tedious day of nuptial bliss. He held me tight, but all I could think about was another cigarette and another and another to numb the pain. I have been smoking ever since.

I'm on Twenty-eighth Street by the time I shake my head clear. I have been walking for fifteen minutes lost in memory. I need another drink. The scotch from Rose's Turn is long gone. McManus's Bar is on the corner. "A scotch on the rocks," I shout to the bartender over the U-2 tune blaring on the jukebox. And before I know it I'm sitting on someone's knee in the corner of the back booth as the night folds me in its arms and I am gone.

13

wake with a start. Someone is licking my hand. I'm lying on my back, my hand is dangling over the side of the bed or sofa or whatever I'm lying on, and a large wet tongue is exploring my right hand. I open my eyes for a second. My head is pounding and the light makes it worse, so I close my eyes quickly.

"Come here, girl." I hear a voice call and the tongue stops and goes off to find the voice. I hear clicking noises on the floor. I open one eye. The ceiling is mirrored. Oh my God. I close my eye again. I take a deep breath. Where the hell am I?

I remember being in the Village, at Rose's Turn, and then walking uptown and then? Oh, right. I went into the bar on the corner of Twenty-eighth Street. McManus's. I ordered a scotch. And then I was with someone I didn't know. I think he said he was a lawyer, but I'm not sure.

I open my eye again. I avoid the ceiling and look in the direction of the voice. There is a partially opened door. A bathrobe is hanging on the back of it. And then the tongue, which is attached to a large golden retriever, comes bounding back into the room.

"Abby, come here," the voice commands. And Abby turns around instantly.

I slowly sit up. Light is pouring in through the window. Hasn't anyone heard of blinds for Christ's sake? I squint and manage to stand up. My head is pounding like the clichéd bass drum. I'm dressed except for my shoes.

NOTE TO SELF . . .

When you wake up in a strange bed with mirrors on the ceiling, find your sunglasses — quick!

I take steps toward the open door. I have to find a bathroom.

I venture through the door, and there sitting in a big wicker chair is a young black man. He is drinking what I assume is coffee out of a large mug and has a newspaper open on his lap.

"We meet again," he says.

I take a moment to let my eyes focus. "Spider?" I say.

"That's right."

"Ah, of course, Abby. And you. How did I get here?"

"I'm the night manager at McManus's. You were passed out in the back booth when I was closing. I got you up, poured you into a cab, and brought you home with me."

I don't know what to say. This feels very awkward. I blush and drop my eyes. Funny how quickly embarrassment turns into shame, and then how quickly a clever girl like me can turn it right back.

"Geez, this is crazy. You are my . . ." Eyes back up, I smile with all my might.

"Guardian angel?" Spider finishes the sentence.

"Yeah, is there a bathroom?" I ask. "Because I really have to . . ."

"Through there to the left," Spider says, pointing to the hallway in front of me.

"Thanks. I won't be a minute."

"Take your time," he says, glancing down at the newspaper. "Coffee's on the stove. I hope you like it strong."

The bathroom is painted avocado green. Ugh. I sit on the toilet and put my head in my hands. Ugh. Ugh. Ugh. I notice a framed comic book cover on the wall across from me. It's Spiderman. Well that makes sense.

I stand at the sink and splash cold water on my face. I find a tube of toothpaste and squeeze some on my index finger and brush my teeth, prisoner-of-war style. I wish I had a Water Pik. That would feel great. I look through the medicine cabinet for some much-needed aspirin. Thank God. I find a small bottle of Bayer. I take three.

"I'll have a cup of that strong coffee, if you don't mind," I say as perkily as I dare on reentering the living room.

"Be my guest. The cups are in the cupboard over the sink."

"Thanks." I pour the coffee and then join Spider. I sit on the sofa. Abby plops down next to me. "This is a great dog," I say patting her head. "Aren't you, aren't you a good doggie?"

Spider puts his newspaper aside, and I can feel it coming. We're going to have a discussion, and I have a suspicion it's going to be about me.

"Do you know where you are, right now?" Spider asks.

"I'm in your apartment, which is really lovely, and thank you so much for your hospitality. It's funny how we keep bumping into each other."

"No, it's not funny, Maggie, it's dangerous. For you."

"Why, what happened? Did something . . ."

"No, something didn't, but something could have, and you wouldn't have known. You were in a blackout—could have ended up dead from a gunshot or a knife wound or you could end up with HIV from unprotected sex or pregnant or any number of things. Are you with me? Are you listening to me?"

"Are you a high school guidance counselor or something?" I ask.

"Maggie," he snaps.

"I'm listening," I say.

"You have a problem. You get drunk and you do stupid things."

"I get drunk sometimes and once in a while I do something stupid," I counter.

"And what are you going to do about it?"

"I'm going to go home," I say, getting up. "I guess my things are in the other room."

"I guess," Spider says. "But before you take off I have something to say and I'll just say it once. I'm a recovering alcoholic. I know the game, and I'm telling you if you play it much longer you're going to lose. It's time for you to get help. AA. Alcoholics Anonymous. It's cheap and there are meetings around the clock or you can check yourself into a rehab or you can go to a monastery, shave your head, and take a vow of abstinence, but do something, Maggie. I'm not always going to be there."

"What are you doing working in a bar if you're a recovering alcoholic, Mr. Smart Guy?" I ask in an accusatory tone. "Isn't that against the rules?" I can't help being a smartass sometimes, especially when people are telling me what to do when I haven't asked for their opinion.

"Well, the money's good and it gives me a chance to help poor wretched souls like yourself," Spider says with a smile. "Remember the show *Cheers*? The character Ted Dansen played? He was a recovering alcoholic, so you can think of me as the black Sam Malone."

"Right. Yeah. I never liked that show after Shelly what's-her-name left. It wasn't the same. Anyway, that's funny, you being the black Sam Malone," I say, hoping to end the discussion.

"Do you believe in miracles, Maggie?" Spider continues, much to my chagrin.

"No, not really," I say in a pleasant what-me-worry tone, "although, lately I'm more inclined to believe in unexplained events."

"Well, you should, because in one week a total stranger has saved your life, not once but twice. A total stranger who is a nice guy and who is offering you some good advice so maybe you can end up living the rest of your life and not pissing it down the drain. If I were you I'd get down on my knees and thank God and say, 'I do believe in miracles and I'm not going to waste these.' All right. That's it. End of discussion."

I get my things together. I pet Abby behind the ears, and then extend my hand to Spider. "Thank you."

"Don't thank me, Maggie, thank the big guy upstairs," he says, shaking my hand. Then he opens the door and I leave.

I get out on the street. "Big guy upstairs." Please. I don't believe in that personal God concept. The universe is just math. A big bang, lots of molecules, some aberrant forms of intelligence, and plenty of algebra. Nobody is looking out for anybody. Well, maybe sometimes drag queens who die of AIDS; maybe they are looking out for someone. What did Goodie say about up there?

"I said it's computerized," Goodie says, flying close to my ear.

"Where have you been?" I say. "Why didn't you help me out last night? I ended up having to be rescued again by this guy who claims I have a problem."

"Really, well, even fairy god-queens can't override free choice— even if the choice is downright stupid."

"Goodie, do you believe in God?" I ask. "I mean now that you've been up there?"

"I don't know, Mags, it's different once you've crossed over. It's a much bigger picture, and you know what they say about LA?"

"What? That there is no there there?"

"Well, it's kind of like that—there is no there up there."

"Weren't you angry about dying? I mean, did you mention that to someone?"

"That's where the bigger picture comes in. It didn't seem relevant anymore."

"Well, I don't believe, and if Spider thinks I'm going to go to AA, he's crazy. I had a friend who did AA and ended up selling her condo and moving to Montana. Besides, I'm not an alcoholic. I'm a drinker, yes, and once in a while I get drunk. Big deal. So what? And I'm still angry you're dead even if you aren't. And if somebody is up there pulling the strings, they've got an evil streak."

"You need a bigger God, Mags," Goodie says and flutters off.

"It's all luck anyway," I shout after him. It's where you happen to end up on line. If you're near the beginning, there's a chance there'll be some hot food left, and if you're near the end, well too bad for you.

As it turns out I'm just a few blocks from my apartment, so there is some luck—it's lucky that Spider and I happen to live a few blocks from each other and lucky he was in the park that night and lucky he works at McManus's Bar and lucky I'm a nice person and not bad to look at so it wasn't so hard for him to be gallant and rescue me and make himself feel good. Hell, he should thank me. People like Spider need people like me. It's obvious he likes being a hero as evidenced by his nickname and the framed comic book cover in the bathroom. So it works out all around, and I don't think it has anything to do with the big guy upstairs—or Sam Malone. And so far Goodie the fairy god-queen hasn't made much of a difference except to make me feel more crazy than usual—so there you have it. It's math and a few random mutated cells.

A car horn honks loudly as I step off the curb. I jump back. Yikes. I definitely need another cup of coffee. Yeah, I need more coffee and a shower and I should go to the gym. And I won't drink today. I don't have to. I'll show him. I'm not an alcoholic. I don't need to drink every single day like alcoholics do.

I stop at the Amsterdam Deli for a cup of joe. I also get a bagel with cream cheese because I'm starving. My stomach is begging for fuel. I tear open the plastic tab on the to-go cup and snap it back. I sip the coffee as I walk. The sun is shining. It's a beautiful day, dammit, and everything is great. I turn the corner onto my block.

"Maggie," I hear yelled. I see Jack coming toward me at a run walk. "Where the hell have you been?"

"What are you doing here?" I ask, stopping in the middle of the sidewalk.

"I was calling you all last night. At home and on your cell. You didn't answer."

"Damn, batteries are dead again, I'm the worst cell phone person," I say.

"I was worried. I drove into the city. You weren't home. I waited for you."

Damn, I forgot that Jack still has a set of my keys.

"I stayed at my friend Patty's place down in the Village. We went out and it was late and I stayed down there. I do it a lot.

Have you met Patty? She's great. Want a sip of my coffee? Have you eaten? We can split this bagel."

I say all of this as nonchalantly and quickly as possible in an attempt to defuse the situation. I'm not an actor for nothing.

"I'm sorry, Jack, I wasn't thinking," I continue as I take Jack's arm and steer him toward my apartment. "We didn't have plans to get together, so I didn't let you know. I'm so used to being on my own. Here, have a sip of coffee. It's very good. Hazelnut. I got it at that place on Amsterdam."

The ease with which I lie amazes me, and when I get on a good roll, I go on and on.

"Patty has such a wonderful apartment. You'll have to see it someday. She has a little backyard. We had coffee out there this morning and it's so lovely. Jessye Norman, the opera singer, used to live right behind Patty." At some point in this fiction of an explanation I have taken on an English accent. "Their gardens butted up against each other and Patty used to hear Jessye singing right outside her — "

"Maggie, stop talking, will you? I don't care what Jessye Norman was singing. I haven't slept. I was very worried about you. And I don't believe a word you're saying."

"You don't believe me?" I stop and look hard at Jack. "And who are you not to believe me? Huh? Who are you? I have a life. I had a life before I met you, and if I want to stay at my friend Patty's, I don't have to get a release form from you. Does your daddy know where you are every moment of the day? Do you check in with Daddy? And where is your mommy? Huh? Is that what this is all about? You miss your mommy?"

The slap comes hard across my face and it stings like crazy. My eyes tear up.

"Stop it!" Jack yells as he delivers the blow. "Stop it, Maggie."

The doorman standing in front of the building on the corner comes walking quickly toward us.

"What's going on? What's wrong with you, mister?" he says. "Leave her alone or I'm calling the cops."

"Thanks," I say. "It's all right. We're just having a fight, you know."

"I know he hit you and that's not right," the doorman says.

"Thank you. I appreciate your concern. I really do. But I think we're all right now." He goes back to his post. Funny thing, I don't even know the doorman's name. All these years we've just nodded in passing. But here he is, ready to defend me. Maybe he wouldn't be so quick to help if he knew the truth.

Jack has turned and is walking toward my apartment. I catch up with him.

"I'm sorry, Mags," he says, his voice still trembling with anger. "I'm sorry I hit you. I don't do that. I just don't know what is going on, and I don't know why you are lying to me. I live with my dad because it's financially good for both of us and, when my mother walked out on him a few years ago, he was suicidal. I was afraid for him so I moved back home. And I don't know where my mommy is. She went to Las Vegas with a man, a man who played the saxophone. Now there's a bad made-for-TV movie for you, but I don't think seeing you has anything to do with that. I like being with you, but that seems to irritate you, so now I'm going to get my things and I won't be back. You've got problems and so do I. Who doesn't?"

We are in front of my building. Jack unlocks the door then hands me the keys. We get up to my apartment and I unlock that door. Jack goes in and gets his backpack.

"So long, Bixby," he says, reaching down and giving the cat-boy a chuck under his chin. "So long, Sweet Pea," he says under his breath, and then he gallops down the stairs before I have a chance to make the situation any worse. Well, there's a blessing.

Bixby stands at the front door looking up at me. He knows. I can feel it. Like I can feel the sting of Jack's slap. Cats are intuitive and he knows exactly what a shit I am. I'm a liar. I'm a cheat. I'm a fake. And the closer someone gets the louder I squeal. I don't even know why anymore. I go in the kitchen and get a beer out of the fridge. I pop the top and drink it down in one big gulp. Then I get another one and pop the top and drink it down in one big gulp, and then I get a third beer and pop the top and sit down on the couch and drink it down in one big, long, lonely swig.

The phone rings. I don't answer. The message plays and then the beep and then Dee-Honey is talking very fast.

"Where are you, Mags, honey? We're all waiting for you at Ninety-sixth Street? I'm sure I gave you the call. *Robin Hood.* You left me a message saying you'd be here."

Did I call her and not remember? Shit, shit, shit. I take a deep breath and I pick up the phone.

"Dee, I'm on the way. I'm sorry. There was a leak in my bathroom this morning and I had to wait for the plumber. He's just finishing. I couldn't leave because water was pouring into the apartment downstairs. Look, can you meet me at Eighty-sixth and Broadway? What? Sorry, Dee." I actually cover the phone with my hand for a minute and pretend to talk to the plumber. I am a shit for sure.

"He says he'll be another two minutes. So I'll see you in a sec, okay?" I hang up the phone. Where is that bagel? I need to put something in my stomach. The brown paper bag is lying next to

the sink in the kitchen. I open it, unwrap the wax paper, and bite
into the bagel. I hope the dense dough will soak up the three beers
sloshing around in my belly. And then for a second I have a brain
freeze, I can't remember what I'm doing. Then, yes, right—I have
to meet Dee-Honey. Fuck. Maid Marian. Why do I have to keep
playing these parts? Let's see, Marian falls in love with Robin
Hood and Mary Elizabeth Mastrantonio (or Olivia de Havilland
in the classic) played her in the movie. What else do you need to
know? I hate my life.

I grab my shoulder bag and shove the rest of the bagel and an
overripe banana in the side pocket. I can't find my keys. I can't
find them anywhere. I look everywhere. I start to hyperventilate.
The phone rings again.

"What?" I bark into the receiver.

"Mags, honey, we're on the corner. Are you on the way?"

"I'm almost out the door. The plumber is finally leaving."

Fuck. Where are my fucking keys? Then I see the spare set Jack
gave me back, on the table by the door. Big tears splash down
my face. Shit! I pick them up, shove them in my pocket, where
much to my surprise I find my own set of keys. All right. Calm
down, put the spare keys in the drawer, and get the hell out of the
apartment. Randall Kent is standing outside the car smoking a
cigarette when I arrive.

"Mags, darling, nice of you to join us."

"Can it, Randall, I'm having a difficult day."

"Aren't we all, dear," he says, climbing into the car.

"Sorry, everybody. It was a mess. The whole ceiling was pouring water."

"I thought it was leaking to the apartment below," Dee-Honey
says, catching my eye in the rearview mirror.

"It was both places—my ceiling and theirs. The pipes burst—all of them. It was a fucking flood. Who's playing Robin Hood?"

"Wally Greig, you know him. He was out in LA for a while and now he's back. He's riding up in the truck with Frank. Didn't you do *Pied Piper* with him a few years ago?" Pauline Letts asks. She is sitting on my left, straightening out her needlepoint.

"Oh, yeah, sure. Isn't he kind of chunky for Robin Hood?"

"Fat, is that what you're trying to say?" Randall asks. "Yes, he's a plump Prince of Thieves, but Ron is out with the *Rumpelstiltskin* cast. Isn't that right, Dee?"

"Yes, honey, we are short on handsome princes right now. He'll be fine. Wally is a wonderful actor."

"Yeah, but he's fat," I contend. "He should be playing Friar Tuck, not Robin Hood."

"Think how thin you'll look playing opposite him. Maid Marian will look absolutely anorexic." Randall laughs. My head feels like it's going to explode.

I reach in my bag and get out the bagel. I finish it in four or five bites and then eat the banana. I feel better, but not much. I don't know how I'm going to get through the day.

"Where's the show?" I ask.

"Albany."

"Albany?" I moan. "That's three hours away."

"Plenty of time for a line rehearsal," Dee says cheerily. "Does anyone have a script?"

As usual there is not even one script to be had among the whole cast. Dee-Honey's company believes in the oral tradition of theater. You learn the lines by saying them over and over onstage in front of five hundred screaming children. Once when I was going on for the first time in *Little Red Riding Hood,* I asked Dee for a script. She had to call five people before she could rustle one up, and it wasn't a Xeroxed copy. It was mimeographed. The way they made copies back in the Dark Ages. It was like reading something printed on the Gutenberg press.

Three hours and 150 miles later we arrive in Albany. We've been through the play three times, with Dee-Honey filling in as Robin Hood.

Frank and the crew from the theater are putting up the set. Wally Greig is sitting in the front row of the theater eating a bag of potato chips and a turkey club on rye. He's as fat as I remember. He's going to look like Robin Hood, the Macy's Thanksgiving Day balloon.

"Hey, Wally." I wave. "Looks like we're the lovebirds today."

"Hiya, Mags," he says through a mouthful of sandwich.

"Do you want to go over anything?" I ask. "We have that duet. We should definitely go over that as soon as Frank gets the sound set up."

"Sure. Want some chips?" Wally offers me the bag.

I shake my head no, and just like that my stomach starts to turn. I have got to find a bathroom.

"Frank, bathroom?" I yell across the footlights.

"Stage left, down the hall."

I walk, then break into a full-out sprint. I get there just in time. I heave it all—the beers, the bagel, the banana, the two cups of coffee. I heave and heave.

Then I hear a voice from the other stall.

"Is that you, Mags? Are you all right?"

It's Pauline. Shit.

"Fine," I say. "It's food poisoning. I had some seafood last night

and I guess it was spoiled. I don't know. It was expensive. Geez."
I'm lying, lying, lying.

"I have some Tums in my bag if you need them."

"Thanks, Pauline. I think I'll be all right now that it's out of
my system. Seafood. I should never even order it, but I do love it
and my boyfriend was paying, so, you know." Lie, lie, lie. If fairy
tales came true, my nose would be four feet long.

THE SHOW GOES pretty well. At least until we get to the
archery contest between Robin Hood and Sir Guy of Gisborne,
the bad guy henchman of the scheming Sheriff of Nottingham.
Randall Kent plays Sir Guy with a swagger and bite that would
put Basil Rathbone to shame, and Wally's Robin Hood isn't so
bad—he's just fat.

But, alas, in the archery contest it is revealed that Wally isn't
only fat, he is also blind. As Robin Hood, the hero of our tale, he
has to shoot the arrow offstage into a blanket that is draped over
a ladder.

You don't actually have to hit anything, just get it in the right
direction and, of course, get it offstage. Wally's first arrow lands
below the curtain line and slides off the apron of the stage onto
the floor. A child in the front row throws it back.

As Maid Marian in the disguise of a young lad of court, I catch
it, thank the girl, whom I pretend is one of the townspeople, and
ceremoniously hand the arrow back to Robin Hood, who puts it
in the bow, shoots it offstage, but misses the blanket and hits the
back wall. The arrow bounces off the wall with such force that it
lands back onstage at Robin Hood's feet. The whole cast is shaking now with repressed laughter, Randall has turned his back to

the audience so he can bite on his hand to try to stanch his guffaws. One boy in the audience shouts something obscene and he
is quickly escorted from the auditorium.

I, as the young lad aka Maid Marian, am keeping score of the
match. Sir Guy of Gisborne is way ahead so I have to cheat the re-
sults in order for Robin Hood to win. It's terrible to have to do this
in front of children. The kids in the audience start booing Robin
Hood. On his third attempt Robin shoots the arrow straight up
in the air; it comes down and hits Pauline, who is playing the
Sheriff's daughter, right in her wimple hat. Pauline dives for the
floor and the kids roar with laughter.

It's a train wreck. Dee-Honey is standing in the wings shaking
her head and pulling at her hair. I run offstage and bring back
the target, which is preset with an arrow, stuck in the bull's-eye.
I declare Robin Hood the winner, explaining that the last arrow
went up, came down, hit the Sheriff's daughter, ricocheted off
the wimple hat, turned left, and hit the bull's-eye. A little like
the magic bullet theory in the JFK assassination. The audience
grumbles, a few girls applaud, and the show goes on.

After Robin Hood and I sing our final duet and the curtain
comes down, Wally Greig gives me a hug and says, "Great show."

"Not only is he fat," I say in an aside to Randall. "He's also
stupid."

Pauline and I retire to the dressing room. She hands me the
roll of Tums.

"Maybe you should take a couple. It's a long trip back."

"Thanks."

By the time we hit the road it's almost five o'clock. We stop
at a Taco Bell on the strip outside of town. I order two chicken

tortillas and a large Coke. We all sit at a big table and chow down. Wally is a sport about the archery contest.

"Next time, wear your glasses, for Christ's sake," Randall says. "Don't you have contacts?"

"Contacts don't help, neither do glasses. I have cataracts. I'm supposed to get surgery the end of this month," Wally explains between bites of his supersized, extra cheese taco.

That shuts us up. My God, the poor man *is* going blind.

Then Pauline chimes in. "Well, you sounded wonderful in the songs, Wally. Your voice is as beautiful as ever."

We all nod in agreement and quickly finish our meals. I take two more Tums. Then our not-so-merry band of men and women climb into the station wagon for the long trip home. Three hours, I think to myself, in three hours I'll be able to crawl into bed and forget the whole damn day.

14

I'm up at the crack of dawn. I look at the clock. It's 6:20 a.m. I get up and put water on for coffee. Then I sit in the chair by the back window. The courtyard is brimming with summer flowers. I don't know if someone plants them every year, or maybe they're perennials. The sun is coming up. I do my morning sits and stares. Bixby leaps into my lap, all twenty pounds of him.

"You're my big cat-boy, aren't you, Bix?" I snuggle my face next to his. "I love you . . . and I love Jack." Bixby puts his paw on my shoulder and purrs.

"Where is he, Bixby? Where's my handsome prince?" I say and then recite in oval tone:

> *O fortune, fortune! all men call thee fickle:*
> *If thou art fickle, what dost thou with him*
> *That is renowned for faith? Be fickle, fortune;*
> *For then, I hope, thou wilt not keep him long,*
> *But send him back.*

It's *Romeo and Juliet,* act three scene five. I pride myself on still remembering all the lines, and Shakespeare, like Hallmark, has a stanza for every occasion.

When I was seventeen and played Juliet, I was sure that love should be hard won, and that the most romantic thing in the world was strife. I don't believe that anymore. Or do I? If I hadn't told Jack to leave, he would be here right now.

My whistling teapot whistles. I put a filter in the coffee cone, add two scoops of grounds, and carefully pour the hot water through the top. Then I put a scoop of cat food in Bixby's dish. This is not a happy ending. In fact it's a lousy ending.

"A walk in the park is what I need to clear my head," I say to Bix while looking through the cupboards for the insulated coffee mug my sister-in-law gave me last Christmas.

"I'll go over to Riverside Park and walk down to the boat basin. Maybe even get a paper on the way and sit by the river," I tell Bix, who is now fully concentrating on his breakfast and not listening to a word I'm saying.

I haven't been back to Central Park since I was attacked; it's too soon. But I need to see some open space, and the boat basin is lovely early in the morning. And it's safe.

As I come out my door, Sandy and Mr. Ed are coming out theirs.

"Good morning, you're up early," Sandy says. Mr. Ed just nods.

"Yeah, I couldn't sleep. Thought I'd go over to Riverside Park for a walk. Are you two going for a run?"

"Rollerblading actually," Sandy says, indicating the bootlike shoes she is carrying in her hand.

"Oh, of course, you're going to have to hustle to keep up, Ed." I lean down and ruffle his fur. Ed stares at me. I look up at Sandy.

"I think Mr. Ed is still upset with me. He's been very hot and cold. Has he said anything?"

Sandy smiles at me. "You know Mr. Ed. He's very private in affairs of the heart."

"Oh, Mr. Ed," I say into his ear. "I'm so sorry about what happened. You're my hero."

Ed turns his head to me.

"What do you say, Ed? Are you going to forgive old Mags?"

He cocks his funny head to one side, considering the proposition.

"Come on, boy, forgiveness is good for the soul." This is the kind of chicken soup philosophy that Ed is a sucker for, and sure enough he leans in and gives me a sloppy dog kiss right on the mouth.

"Oh, Ed." I pick him up in my arms. "I love you, little guy."

I look over at Sandy and she is crying.

"That is so sweet," she says between sobs. "That is just so sweet. The two of you."

It's not even seven o'clock and we are having a love fest right in the hallway. This is too saccharine for my blood.

Goodie lands on my shoulder. "Go with it, Mags, there is nothing wrong with a little love in the morning. Besides, the dog saved your life for goodness sakes."

I shrug him off my shoulder and put Ed down. Sandy hugs me tight. Thank goodness I have a no-drip top on my coffee mug.

"What would have happened if Ed hadn't been there? You are so lucky."

"I know, Sandy."

We start down the stairs. When we get out front, Sandy sits down on the stoop and puts on her Rollerblades.

"Beautiful day," she says.

"Absolutely," I agree. Sandy and Ed go east toward Central Park and I head west.

"Oh, by the way," Sandy says, turning back for a moment. "Dick and I are going away—spur of the moment. Four days in the Caribbean. Do you think you could take care of Ed? I know it's short notice but since, you know . . ." She trails off, not saying the obvious.

The obvious being "since he saved your life"—as in, since he saved my life I am now an indentured servant to his owners. I feel manipulated, but who am I to squawk? He did come through for me in a big way.

"Of course, no problem," I say. I look down at Ed. "My pleasure."

And Ed takes this moment, as if on cue, to run over and lick my knees.

"Sweet," I say.

I get a paper at the corner deli on my way to the park. Goodie is buzzing along beside me.

"Well that's done, now we have to concentrate on Jack," he twitters.

"Goodie, I don't think Jack is going to be back," I say, sorry the unintentional rhyme makes the statement sound comical, because there is nothing comical about it. I know Jack is gone for good this time. Why would he come back to a lying sourpuss like me?

"I think he deserves an apology, and then you never know. Sugar attracts more flies than . . ."

"Don't finish that phrase, please, I'm all chicken-souped out this morning. I don't want to hear one more aphorism."

"Well, then fine, I'll be on my way. I won't worry about you anymore. A fairy godmother knows where he isn't wanted, even if he is needed, but you'll see, oh yes, dear, you'll see," Goodie says as he flies off into the morning.

"Is this a curse? Are you putting a curse on me?" I yell after him. Fairy godmothers (aka god-queens in Goodie's case) can turn on a dime. One minute they're all in pink chiffon, waving magic wands, and the next they're wearing deep purple and riding brooms.

"Maggie, is that you?" a voice behind says.

I turn too quickly. I'm still very jumpy.

"It's me, Bob, I didn't mean to scare you. I thought it was you. I've been following you since you turned into the park. You walk fast. Are you power-walking? It's the best exercise isn't it? You remember Piper, don't you?"

Piper is, of course, the teacup poodle yapping at my feet. He's so tiny and yet so noisy.

"Of course I do." I kneel and pet his head. "How are those kidney stones, little fellow, all cleared up? They don't seem to have affected your enthusiasm."

Piper is dancing up and down and up and down, yapping a blue streak.

"Oh, he's fine and dandy," Bob says. Fine and dandy. There's that silly phrase that came to me in my time of need and gave me comfort. I told Jack I would be fine and dandy. And I am, aren't I? I'm fine and dandy, just like Piper.

"Mind if I walk with you a while, Bob? We haven't had a chance to catch up. What's going on with you, my friend?"

Bob coos in appreciation of the attention. I suspect a lot of people dismiss Bob quickly, anxious to get away from his perpetual good cheer and, like me, seek their daily comfort in more cynical places. But today I am in need of cheer and Bob is what the doctor ordered, in a small dose, of course, and to be taken only until the symptoms subside.

"Well, I got a job as company manager for a tour of *42nd Street.* It's going to Japan. I'm so excited. The cast is first-rate. And I love the Japanese culture. And I'm very into sushi. What are you doing? Anything coming up?"

"I have a club date at Don't Tell Mama."

"Oh my goodness. I just saw Mary Ballou at Rainbow and Stars. You know I was the assistant stage manager when she did *Sunset Boulevard* on Broadway. What a magnificent voice!"

Bob chirps on about Mary Ballou and the tour and a new low-carb diet he's on. We get to Seventy-second Street and he and Piper have to take off.

"I have rehearsal at nine o'clock. It was great to see you, Maggie. You're the best. You have me on your mailing list, don't you? I'll be there, if I can. I'd love to hear you again. It's been a while. And you look great, never better. Life is good, isn't it? What a glorious day! Enjoy."

And off he goes. Thank God, because, truthfully, a girl can take only so much good cheer, no matter what the doctor says.

I sit on a bench by the river and open the paper. I glance through the national news, read page six, and then turn to the sports page. The Yankees are in second place in the American League. Boston is in first, but that won't last. I look out over the river and take a deep breath. Life is good, I concede, like Bob says, and on any given day those of us still standing are lucky as hell even if it doesn't feel like it.

WHEN I GET BACK to my apartment I go the kitchen and open the cupboard over the sink where I know a bottle of red wine is standing at the ready. Ready for me. It's good for you — four out of five doctors say so. I pour a glass. I'll sip it. To take the edge off. I sit by my window and sip it for an hour. The bottle is empty and the edge has melted and gone runny and sentimental.

I pick up the phone and dial Texas Joe's number. A woman's voice answers. His new wife. "Hello," she says with a warm southern twang. She sounds nice. I wonder why she is home and not in her office filling someone's cavity or executing a painful root canal.

"Grandma? Is that you, dear?" I ask innocently.

"Oh, I'm sorry you must have the wrong number," she seems to hesitate but says it very nicely.

"Really? I'm calling long distance. Damn is this . . ." I recite the number and reverse the last two digits. Honest mistake.

"No this is . . ." and she gives me her number.

"Thank you so much. I'm sorry to inconvenience you."

"No problem," she says almost like asking a question and hangs up before I have a chance to continue my charade. Well, that's kind of rude. Yes, she was helpful, but isn't it rude to hang up before formal goodbyes have been exchanged? That's so like Joe to get himself a woman with minimal manners, not like me, the absolute definition of politeness.

I look through my Rolodex and find Joe's cell phone number. The phone rings and she answers again. She answers Joe's personal phone. Has she done away with him? Killed him for his money? Why the fuck is she answering his phone?

"Mr. DePugh?" I ask in my best-disguised phone voice.

"I'm sorry, Mr. DePugh isn't available at the moment. May I take a message?"

"No thank you. I'll try him later," I say in an officious tone and hang up. There, I showed her, I guess.

Three minutes later my phone rings. It's Joe.

"What do you want?" he asks, irritation dripping off the words. How dare he? How dare he be irritated at me! He's the one who went off and got hitched and left me alone.

"What do you mean?" I ask right back with as much irritation.

"You called the house and then you called my cell and you pretended to be someone else. We have caller ID for crap's sake, Maggie. Look, I don't want to be angry, but you can't do this. My wife doesn't care if you call me. She knows all about you. Just leave your name and I'll call you back. Don't complicate it or make it dramatic. I don't have any secrets from Ruth. It's okay if you call me."

"Really? Did you tell her about the time we made love in the hot tub at Disney World? Remember? I was wearing my Minnie Mouse ears and nothing else. And you said you would never love anyone the way you loved me? Did you tell her that?"

"Maggie, we're leaving for the airport. We're going to Hawaii for ten days. I can't talk right now."

"Fuck you, Joe."

"Are you drunk? Is that what's going on? Are you drunk and feeling down? I understand, but there is nothing I can do for you, kid."

"Don't you fucking call me kid. Don't you ever do that again. And don't you ever call me again."

"You called me." Joe's voice is louder.

"Well I won't ever again," I shout back. "Oh and I've been seeing Goodie. You do remember your brother Goodie, don't you?"

"What do you mean, you've been seeing him?"

"Well, he's smaller now, about eight inches high. He tells me he's living in the Barbie department at Toys R Us. He's got the cutest outfits."

"Maggie, you're worrying me. Goodie is dead. A long time now."

"I know he is d-e-a-d. But he's come back. He's my fairy god-queen or whatever. He was assigned to my case. He's helping me."

"Helping you do what?"

"Get by . . . in this little old life of mine. I'm going to sing again. I've got a club date. Goodie's helping me. Remember when we used to sing. We sang all the Beatles."

"Maggie, you are drunk, aren't you?"

"No," I lie. "I'm just . . . just lonely."

There is a long pause. I hear Joe take a couple of deep breaths. I feel my face tighten up into an angry fist. Then very quietly Joe says, "I've got to go. I'm sorry, Maggie, and I'm sure Goodie would help you if he could. He loved you. And I love you but things changed. I am sorry I can't be there for you right now, but it was inevitable."

"Oh really? Well so is this." And I slam down the phone. Done. Over. Shit.

I stagger into my bedroom and open the top dresser drawer. Under the jewelry tray are stashed four oversized Valentines from Joe, along with an empty matchbook. It's from Flamingo Vic's Tex*Mex*Tropical Restaurant, Deep Ellum, Texas. Joe left it at my apartment after our first night together. He flew back to Houston the next day and I didn't see him for another week. He left the matchbook beside the bed. It was like a talisman until I saw him again. So here it is, stashed in the dresser with the Valentines and a pair of rhinestone earrings Joe gave me for Christmas the first year we were together.

I sit and finger the matchbook. I open and close it and hold it against my face. I breathe deeply and take the empty matchbook into the kitchen and place it in the sink along with the four over-sized Valentines, then I deactivate the smoke alarm in my apartment, which goes off at the least provocation. Ceremoniously I light a match to the whole mess and stand and watch it burn. The Valentines curl up, the matchbook turns black. I run water over it and stuff the charred remains into a plastic bag and put them in the trash can. I keep the rhinestone earrings. A girl has to have something to show for the pain. Chapter closed.

Two hours later I wake with a start. It's five in the afternoon and I have one of those dull wine headaches. God, this day started out much better than it ended up. It seems like a month ago that I saw Bob Strong and heard his message of cheer. Life is good. Ugh. My stomach is growling like a Bengal tiger. I pick up the phone and dial information. I wish there was an eight hundred number like 1-800-BRING FOOD. Nothing specific, whatever is in the oven that night. I'm not a picky eater, but I am impatient. I get the number for the Chinese place up the street. I've gotten the number a hundred times but I always forget to write it down. I punch it in and order. Instant gratification. A half hour later I'm eating House of Noodles sesame chicken. It's so good I can't help but moan. Wait until I tell Goodie what a son of a bitch his brother is. And, of course, Joe wouldn't believe Goodie was back. He has no, none, nada imagination. He's a civil fucking engineer. Well, I'll show him. I'm going to clean up my act. I'm going to be a big star and then Joe will be sorry he left me. Sorry he stayed in humdrum old Houston. I'll show that son of a bitch. I stuff the last of the chicken in my mouth and then slink off to bed.

15

The next morning I get up and get rid of all the liquor in my apartment, including my last three bottles of Rolling Rock. I take my pack of cigarettes and crush them up and flush them down the toilet. If I'm going to burn some bridges I might as well burn them all. Fresh start. I put on my power-walking togs and head to Central Park. It's nine in the morning and the sun is shining. I fear no evil. I set a good pace. I swing my arms and keep my head high. Life is good, life is good, life is good. This is where I came in yesterday morning, before the red wine sucked my brain out. I have a terrible headache but I concentrate on not thinking about it and just breathing. I run/walk by Bethesda Fountain and stop in front of the *Angel of the Waters* and say a silent prayer.

"Please purify me like you purify the waters. Let me be washed clean so I can start fresh." The Angel's face is radiant in the morning sun and for a moment it seems she inclines it slightly in my direction. I bow my head and take a deep, long breath and then run/walk home. I'm meeting Dee-Honey and the cast at noon. We're going up to Stamford to do *Pinocchio,* in which I once again play the Blue Fairy who turns our diminutive hero into a "real boy." Never an easy task considering the little fellow is played by Eddie who is sixty-five years old, or rather sixty-five years young as the saying now goes—but young or old Eddie's still sixty-five. I pop three aspirin and drink a big glass of water.

The children's theater is fast becoming full-time employment, which is just as well. Summer is always slow in the commercial voice-over business. I haven't heard a word from my agent lately. I also haven't heard from Jack. Even my fairy god-queen has deserted me.

"Goodie," I say out loud in case he's lurking about and listening. "Look, I'm sorry. I have been having a hard time, as you know, but I'm cleaning up my act and I would love to see your little face."

No answer, no flutter of wings, no sprinkle of fairy dust. Oh well, guess I'm on my own. At noon the station wagon is waiting on the corner of Ninety-sixth Street. "Don't anybody give me a cigarette today, even if I beg," I announce to my fellow actors as I climb into the backseat of the station wagon. "I've quit smoking as of early this morning so don't give me one no matter what. Okay?"

"Well, we've heard that before," Randall says with a snort.

"I mean it this time. This is it," I counter.

"Great. No cigarettes from me. My pleasure. And don't bitch when I refuse you. So everybody in? All arms and legs? We're not missing anyone?" Randall asks as he pulls into traffic and heads for the Westside Highway. Dee-Honey is with *Pied Piper* today so Randall is acting as camp counselor for this group. "How about a line run-through? I haven't played Gepetto in a year."

"Can't we wait until after we're on the road a while? I'll need a second cup of coffee before I can focus," Eddie says from the far backseat, brandishing his Superman thermos. When you're a sixty-five-year-old Pinocchio, you need all the help you can get. Eddie's been playing the wooden puppet for thirty years. He has his own set of rubber noses, which he had designed by a Broadway prop master back when dinosaurs roamed the earth. He had them made in three different lengths, signifying the first lie, then the second lie, and then the third lie that lands him right in the belly of the whale. The noses travel in a custom-designed wooden box with red velvet lining. Once, after a show, in a moment of anger, Randall, who's been playing Gepetto for at least twenty years, threatened to throw the noses, case and all, out of the car if Eddie didn't stop referring to Randall's Gepetto as "my old man." They didn't speak for three years. Eddie and Randall, I mean. Not the noses—they never speak.

Forty-five minutes into the trip we stop at a Dunkin' Donuts for breakfast. I get three chocolate donuts and a large coffee.

"Careful, Mags," Helen says. "I gained twenty-five pounds when I quit smoking."

"I know," I say.

"Well, I've managed to lose most of it, but it hasn't been easy," Helen says, nibbling on a toasted bran muffin. "It's not easy at all, that's why I have to be so careful."

Helen doubles as Jiminy Cricket and Tommy the Tuna in the show. She's adorable as the Tuna, but her Cricket looks like a freak of nature. The audience often gasps when she enters. She thinks they're surprised, but I think they're scared.

"How did the *Agnes of God* audition go?" I ask.

"Great, really great. I'm still waiting to hear," Helen says. "You know how slow they can be getting back to you."

"Sure," I say, finishing the first of my chocolate donuts. We do a line run-through when we get back on the road. We arrive at the civic center in plenty of time. Frank is in the parking lot, lounging in a beach chair, catching rays. The civic center provided him with three union stagehands, and the set for the show was up and ready to go in about twenty minutes. The center also provided a buffet in the wings backstage. Coffee, more donuts, bagels and cream cheese, and fresh squeezed orange juice. I get a coffee, two donuts, and a sesame bagel and head for the dressing room. Helen's right, I'm going to gain fifty pounds by the end of the week if I don't watch it.

The show goes pretty well. Eddie has trouble getting his nose off in the blackout before the last scene, so as the Blue Fairy I have to come on, tap his head with my magic wand, declare him a "real boy," and rip his nose off all in one graceful swoop. The spirit gum that the nose is attached with pulls off skin as well and Eddie lets out a yelp. Puberty is painful even for a wooden puppet.

I fall asleep on the trip back to the city. We get there about four o'clock. So I've had no cigarettes and no alcohol for about twelve hours.

"Good luck with the no smoking," Randall says when he drops me off on the corner of Eighty-sixth Street. "Think of all the money you're saving."

"Thanks," I say and lean back in the car. "Sorry about the nose, Eddie. I didn't mean to pull so hard."

"It wasn't your fault. I used too much spirit gum on the last one. I'm sure it will heal in no time," Eddie says, touching the Band-Aid on his nose. "Be brand-new in a day or two."

I get home and check the clock. I have a therapy appointment at six. That will be good. I can't smoke there, and then it will be just a few hours before I can call it a day and climb into bed.

GEORGE IS ENCOURAGING about the smoking. He tells me he gained only ten pounds when he quit. I don't mention that I'm also giving up alcohol. I don't think it's any of his business, and besides, I don't want to label it a problem in case I decide to go back to it when I get things under control.

"And I haven't heard from Jack. I guess we're finished and I think it's just as well," I tell George.

"Why is that just as well?"

"Because it wasn't going to last. He was too young, or rather I was too old. He should be going with someone more appropriate, someone he could start a family with."

"You could still have a family. You're not over the hill."

"No, I can't. It's not my thing. You know."

"Why?"

I shrug my shoulders. This subject keeps coming up. It's the biological clock syndrome. It seems the last of my viable eggs are kicking up a fuss and sending messages to my brain and to everyone else's too.

"Well, that's it for this session," George says, getting up and heading for the door. "Think about the family thing. You're not out of the running. And good luck with the smoking. Lemons help. Cut them into quarters and suck on them."

On my way out of the building I remind myself that not all women are destined to have children. Look at Katharine Hepburn, Georgia O'Keeffe, Virginia Woolfe, for goodness sake—brilliant and talented women, and not a bundle of joy among them.

But I know there is something going on for me. The other day I was in Macy's looking for housewares and found myself in the baby department pricing cribs. It's last call at my fertility factory. The foreman does one last sweep of the eggs and then locks it down, system over and out—estrogen drops, skin shrinks, closing whistle sounds, and the old factory grinds to a halt.

Standing in the checkout line at Gristede's recently, I read an article in *Ladies' Home Journal* written by a woman who claimed in spite of winning a Pulitzer Prize for literature, earning two advanced degrees, nursing the sick in Calcutta with Mother Theresa in the late '80s, and single-handedly navigating the English Channel in a one-person wind skiff, that it wasn't until giving birth to her son, Malcolm, at the age of forty-eight, that she felt she had done anything worthwhile with her life. I usually avoid those kinds of stories, but lately I'm drawn to them, like fingernails to a scab. I walked out of the store without my groceries and headed straight for the intersection planning to impale myself on the hood ornament of a speeding BMW. Fortunately I ran into Marge Meghin on the corner and she told me what a great job I did on the last voice-over I booked with her. Sometimes flattery can save your life.

I stop at Dunkin' Donuts and order a tea with lemon. I put the lemon in my mouth and suck like crazy.

I call Patty from a pay phone on Christopher Street.

"Hello?"

"Patty, how are you? How's the cold?"

"Better, thanks."

"I'm in the Village and I wondered if you might be free for a bite to eat. We could have that gab."

"Hmm that's an idea. I've been cooped up for three days. I'd love some of that homemade soup from Caffè Sha Sha on Hudson Street. Meet me there?"

"Sounds good."

Caffè Sha Sha is a wonderful little restaurant that has an outdoor garden in the back. I get there first and settle into a table next to the fountain, which is an adorable little boy carved out of stone, taking a leak into a fishpond. The owners have an interesting sense of humor. I order another tea with extra lemons.

"How are you?" Patty says, arriving in a flurry. "I'm not going to hug you. I'm still full of germs. No fever, just a runny nose and a bit of a hacking cough. But it's great to be out. So what's going on? I love your hair. Is that a new color? Why are you down here? Did you have an audition or something?"

"Not exactly," I answer. "I'm seeing a therapist."

"Really? Who?"

"George . . ."

"George McMann?"

"Yes. How'd you know?"

"Just a guess. He's good. Jim saw him a few years ago for a while."

"Your husband Jim?"

"Of course."

"That is so amazing. I mean there must be thousands of therapists in Manhattan and I end up with the same one as Jim. It feels incestuous," I say.

"Not unless you and Jim are having an affair. Which I don't think is happening," Patty says with a smile.

Patty and Jim have been married for almost twenty years and have a teenage daughter and are one of those couples who seem like they were made for each other. Of course, you never know what goes on behind closed doors, and I have to say I'm curious why Jim was in therapy, but I think by any standard they are the real thing when it comes to two people in love and in it for the long haul.

The waiter stops at the table. Patty orders a bowl of the home-made chicken soup and I get a grilled tomato and cheese.

"Oh, and could I get some bread right away to nibble on? I'm starving," she asks.

The waiter nods and heads to the kitchen.

"Jim was having trouble with his work. He was completely blocked and Tom Hansen . . . do you know him?"

"I don't think so."

"Anyway, he suggested George. Turns out it all had to do with Jim's mother and her suicide when Jim was a teenager, and within a couple of months he was back on track. That's exactly the time he got the commission to design the new shopping mall in Akron, Ohio. Remember?"

"Yes." Patty is a talker, that's for sure. It's nice to let someone else fill the space. All I have to do is suck the lemons and listen.

"Anyway, I know you were curious about Jim. I didn't want you speculating something deep and dark. Really it was the midlife thing. He was despondent. And, of course, it was the mother thing too. She was forty-nine when she offed herself. Sorry, but there is no better way to say it. Devastating for the whole family and between you and me I'm sure that was her intention. She was absolutely stunning and apparently couldn't face everything go-ing south. Our Sarah looks a lot like her. So why are you seeing George? Midlife thing?" she asks, back to the subject at hand.

"You might say I'm having a bit of a midlife thing."

"Well, it happens. I'm going through that short-term memory

loss they talk about. I can't remember what I did ten minutes ago, but I can still recite all of *Beowulf* in Old English."

"I'd love to hear that sometime."

"Sure, the very next time we're in front of a fireplace on a long winter's night and all the power lines are down. So what's the story with you and therapy? Is this your first time?"

"No, but it's been a while since my last fling with it. It's just stuff, you know. For instance, career, as in I'm still playing Dorothy and Snow White. Still the ingénues, but I'm getting heckled and the last time I played Miss White, I went onstage with a cigarette in my hand!"

"That's brilliant," Patty says.

"Well no one else thought it was."

"Those kids need some reality. Did you know teen girls have one of the highest percentages of smokers? It's shocking."

"These were six and seven years old."

"It's still brilliant."

"And relationships," I say, "or rather relationship." Then I hesitate.

"And?" Patty coaxes.

"And babies keep coming up."

"For you? Babies for you?" Patty asks, incredulous.

"Well, I do have the equipment. It might be a little rusty, but . . ."

"I don't mean you can't, I just never thought you wanted to," she says.

"I think it's the biological clock thing. It's starting to sound the alarm."

"Well, haven't you heard?" she says. "The biological clock is of no consequence now with all the new scientific options. There is no alarm, no more ominous ticktock."

The waiter plops a basket of bread on the table.

"Thank goodness. I'm so hungry," Patty says. "I haven't eaten a decent meal in days. This cold knocked me out." She grabs a piece of bread, lathers it with butter, and takes a big bite. "Hmm. That's better. There is nothing like a big wedge of carbohydrates to make me feel better. Warm bread and butter. It's like mother's milk. Speaking of which, did you read that article in the magazine section a few weeks back? About a sixty-year-old woman giving birth to a newborn. I say *newborn* because it is so hard to imagine. I find it easier to imagine a sixty-year-old woman giving birth to a twenty-five-year-old somehow."

"No, I didn't see that," I say, sucking a lemon wedge. I am dying for a cigarette. "How did she manage that?" I try to stay focused on the conversation.

"Artificial insemination—really artificial. They got an egg from some farm in Jersey and a sperm off the Internet and combined them into a kind of Baby Gap designer ovum and planted it in that antiquated womb and presto—pregnant at sixty! Amazing. Can you imagine? I guess the good news is eventually kids won't have to worry about housing for their aging parent because a lot of them will be in their teens and still living at home when their mothers are eighty."

Our meal arrives and we chow down. Our conversation moves from babies to recent movies to the price of produce.

"Broccoli is almost two dollars a head at the Union Square Farmers Market. And forget the cauliflower. I might as well be buying truffles."

"Isn't it because of a drought or something? Isn't that what drives the prices up?"

"Greed is what drives prices up," Patty says between slurps of soup.

"Well, everybody has to make a living. We're not all trust fund kids." The minute I say it, I realize it's the sour chord that could end this friendly meal. Patty's grandfather made a fortune in ball bearings. I'm not sure what they're used for, but apparently they're essential to something.

"I'm not going there, Mags, because I'm too happy to be out of my sickbed to let anything offend me. But, yes, I have money and, no, I didn't work for it in the traditional sense, but that doesn't mean the price of broccoli can't get my dander up. Okay?"

Patty and I have known each other for fifteen years. We met in a pottery class at the School of Visual Arts. I was there preparing for a role at the suggestion of Pauline Letts.

I had been cast as Hedda in *Hedda Gabler,* and I was so nervous because the part is huge and a classic and I was going to be doing it at a prestigious regional theater in Minnesota. Pauline and I were doing a *Peter Pan* together about a month before I was to leave town for the start of rehearsals and when I told her how nervous I was she told me to take a pottery class and forget about the acting and concentrate on the clay. I did and it helped and that's when I met Patty. She was six months pregnant and using the clay to prepare for her role as mother.

"I'm sorry. I'm a mess lately and, of course, you can complain about the price of broccoli. I can't believe how expensive toothpaste is; it's over three dollars a tube. I've gone back to using plain old Arm and Hammer baking soda."

"I'm sorry too. You know it's my Achilles' heel," Patty says. "And since I'm going to pay for our meal because I'm so filthy rich . . ."

"You don't have to, please," I protest. "I won't let you, absolutely not."

"I insist," Patty says. "And for dessert I'm ordering us a round of napoleons and cappuccinos."

We sit and gab for another hour. The napoleons are fantastic. We order seconds. I have been living on sugar for days. I might as well accept the fact that I'm going to weigh two hundred pounds by Thursday. Patty walks me to the subway.

"That was fun," she says.

I give her a big hug. Screw the germs. Friends like Patty are worth the risk.

"A baby might be the right thing for you," she says. "But remember, it's a long-term contract. Did you know Sarah is going to be fifteen next month?"

"That's amazing. I always think she's eight."

"Well she's not. And we're all coming to your show," Patty says as she waves and heads down Seventh Avenue.

I get the train uptown. The local stops at Times Square and the conductor announces it is going out of service.

Damn. Everyone grumbles and then exits to wait for the next train.

On the now-crowded platform a fellow is playing guitar and singing "Sittin' on the Dock of the Bay." A large black woman is sitting on the bench with two huge Kmart bags at her feet. She starts scatting along with the guy on guitar. She has a drop-dead voice. For a moment I think it actually might be Aretha Franklin. A guy in a tie-dyed T-shirt starts whistling. A young black kid improvises the percussion section on top of a metal trash can. I catch Aretha's eye, she nods and invites me along for the ride. We sing an improvised counterpoint through the chorus. The guy on guitar sings the last verse in a deep rumble of a voice and Aretha and I and the whistler back him up in a tight three-part harmony, and then the whole place starts to jive for the final chorus. The whistler takes eight bars followed by the trash-can percussionist, who whacks out a sixteen-bar riff that sets the whole platform rocking. It's Times Square, New York City—smack dab in the heart of the universe. Then the train pulls into the station, the tune ends, and we subway rockers disperse. Just the guitar player remains, sittin' on his dock of the bay.

When I get home, I get a call from Charles. "I have an open-ing this Sunday night. Come and see it. I think you'll love the work. It's a wonderful artist. She makes beaded tapestries. They're amazing."

"Sounds lovely. What time?" I ask.

"Starts at eight but it doesn't get interesting until around ten. I'll see you then."

Charles has lavish openings with lots of booze so I'll have to be careful. I check the clock. It's half past ten. Pretty soon I'll have a whole day without a cigarette or a drink. I feel like Bernadette, the patron saint of Lourdes.

I go to bed at midnight but I can't fall asleep. I think through the conversation I had with Patty about artificial insemination and the woman who had a baby at sixty. Pretty soon self-fertilization will be common practice. All you will need is a kit like over-the-counter early pregnancy tests. It will be an over-the-counter Get Yourself Pregnant Kit. It will be about the same size as a Lady Clairol hair coloring kit, but rather than the smiling model on the cover, there will be the smiling sperm donor and a list of his vital statistics.

Of course, they'll be available in a range of prices; the top end being Ivy League graduates, movie stars, professional athletes, then white-collar workers, blue-collar workers, and, bargain basement, you guessed it, politicians and prison parolees.

Directions read: Take sperm and egg (check the refrigerator next to the frozen peas—remember you harvested these after seeing a special with Diane Sawyer). Place ingredients in plastic petri dish, like the ones from ninth-grade biology. Whoever thought those lab classes would actually be of use? "Warm to room temperature over Bunsen burner or, if a Bunsen burner is unavailable, substitute fondue warmer," I say aloud to Bixby, who is kneading my right thigh with his paws. "Now carefully coax the sperm to swim toward the egg with the sterilized end of a straight pin; put on a little music. If the sperm seems reluctant, add an eyedropper of scotch or bourbon. Once the sperm has made contact and done its job, you'll know because the little sucker will turn on its side and fall asleep." Bixby frowns at me and I scratch his ears.

"Take the customized turkey baster," I continue, "and insert the mixture into the vagina with a gentle squeeze. And remember, the directions caution, this is a delicate procedure, so take your time, Bixby. Because what's the hurry? You have all the time in the world, which is exactly the point."

Bixby nestles himself next to me and falls asleep (typical male response). I wonder if it will ever be possible to crossbreed species. Now there is a new frontier waiting for intrepid explorers. All right. That's it. Stop thinking.

I turn on the radio. The Yankees are playing San Diego in California so the game is only in the third inning. I fall asleep listening to the Bronx Bombers whip the San Diego Padres. I wake up and look at the clock. It's three a.m. Art Bell is talking to a caller from outer space or so the caller claims. I get up and go to the bathroom. Then I shuffle along to the kitchen and get a lemon out of the refrigerator and suck it dry. It's over twenty-four hours since I've had any nicotine, and my brain is crying out for a fix. I wish I had a big wooden mallet that I could hit myself over the head with so I could pass out for a week and skip all this withdrawal. I go back to sleep until the phone awakens me at seven a.m. It's Sandy.

"We're just leaving for the airport," she says. "I wanted to remind you. We'll be back on Sunday. There's plenty of dog food and you know about the antiseizure medication. Break up one pill in his food every day."

"Right. That's great. Have a wonderful trip. I'll see you when you get back," I say with as much perkiness as I can muster on four hours of sleep. Mr. Ed has been on the medication ever since he was hurt saving my life. His brain was swollen and the medication is preventative. I don't know how long he has to take it, but I do know I paid for it and his clinic bill as well. It was the least I could do. That and dog-sit whenever and wherever necessary for the rest of his life.

I lie in bed and stare at the ceiling for about an hour. I'm afraid to make a cup of coffee because nothing is a stronger trigger for a cigarette than a cup of coffee. But without coffee I may never be able to function again. Maybe I should go out to the coffee shop on Columbus Avenue and get coffee and sit there and drink it because you can't smoke in the coffee shop. It would be like a demilitarized zone. That way I wouldn't have to chew my right hand off to keep it from picking up a cigarette.

I manage to get up and get out and walk up to Columbus Avenue without turning around and running to the deli on Amsterdam that has supplied me with nicotine ever since I moved into the neighborhood. When I get to the coffee shop, I order a double espresso and sit at the counter that looks out on the street.

"Guess who?" a voice says as two hands are clamped over my eyes.

"I don't know, Harrison Ford?" I say.

"No. Come on. You can get it," the mystery voice says.

"Javan?" I say, prying the hands off and turning around. "It's you. How are you? Long time no see."

Javan Jones is an actor and a stand-up comic. We met in a production of *Carousel* in Boothbay, Maine, one summer and later shot a few commercials together. We had a lucrative Chef Boy-Ar-Dee that ran for years. And then I lost track of him for a while. He stopped doing commercials because his "type" went out of fashion. The industry works like that. One minute you're hot, hot, hot, and the next you can't even book a spot for a local carpet cleaner. I also heard via the grapevine that he ended up in drug rehab for a couple of months. He got straightened out and the last time I ran into him he was back doing stand-up.

"I'm hanging in. How are you?" he asks, giving me a kiss on the cheek and a big hug. Javan is nice to hug and I linger for a second.

"How's Deb doing?" I ask, reluctantly stepping away.

"Oh, you haven't heard? We split up. About a year ago."

"I'm sorry," I say as sincerely as I can. I was never a big fan of Deb's. "Gosh, is it possible I haven't seen you in a year?"

"It's very possible. I've been on the road doing comedy clubs, working nonstop. I was opening for George Carlin for a while."

"Wow. That's great."

"Yeah, the money's decent, but the road gets pretty gruesome. I'm back in town for a month. I'm booked at the Comic Strip for the next week."

"I'll have to come see you."

"What are you up to? I see your commercial for Special K all the time. You must be rolling in dough, baby."

"Not really. I'm doing okay. But the summer is dead. I've been doing children's theater."

"That's fun. Hey, I've got to run," Javan says, looking at his watch. "I have an audition in a half hour downtown. Come over to the Comic Strip. I'm doing the nine p.m. show every night starting Wednesday. Check it out. I'll buy you a drink. We'll catch up."

"Sure." We hug goodbye and off he goes. Javan and I had a fling the summer we did *Carousel*. I played Julie Jordan and he played Billy Bigelow and our characters fell in love and so did we, briefly. It's not unusual to fall for a costar; I've done it dozens of times. It's also not unusual to unfall the minute the show is over. It's summer stock romance and it happens a lot, especially when you're young; you learn to get over it. It was awkward for a while when we got back to New York because we were constantly running into each other at auditions.

Actually Javan was seeing someone before he went to Maine, and started seeing her again when he got back. The "her" was Deb, and that explains why I was never a fan. But eventually Javan and I booked the Chef Boy-Ar-Dee spot and made a lot of money and that bonded us in a positive way, so I forgot about the affair and Maine and Deb. Except now I remember because Javan looks great; and feels great; he has what is known in the pumping iron business as a good pair of pipes, and, let's face it, I'm lonely. I'm lonely without Jack and I'm lonely without my cigarettes. And I'm craving another diversion. Someone else might say I'm horny, but not me because I was raised Presbyterian, so I'll just say I'm craving a diversion.

I gaze out the window of the coffee shop. People are hustling up and down Columbus Avenue. Mothers with strollers, kids in shorts, men in summer suits, guys in work clothes, women in sling back heels, girls in midriff shirts, dogs on leashes, boys on tricycles, little girls with play strollers and dolls. Humanity, that divine comedy. My dad loved watching people. It was a pastime we often indulged in together. Saturday afternoons we would go downtown to Thompson's Bookstore and browse for a while, then get a coffee to go at Grounds & Beans on Hanover Street and sit on one of the benches in front of the First Presbyterian Church and watch the parade pass by.

My dad said people were like plants. You could tell by looking at someone if they were raised in the light or if they had been deprived and kept in the shadows. And how some people seemed to flourish and others had to struggle even if they had the exact same soil and nutrients. And there were always those poor plants that never seemed to take hold even if conditions were optimal, and then those hearty souls that grew and blossomed even if they landed in a pile of rocks. And while he mused and speculated and philosophized, he smoked and so did I. We smoked together and talked together and that's why I'm thinking about him now, be-cause I'm lonely and I want to smoke and I miss my dad. I don't miss him all the time, I'm used to him being gone, but every so often I smell a certain blend of pipe tobacco or get a whiff of Old Spice aftershave or I sit and watch people and I remember him. Vividly. And the other thing I remember is that he died of lung cancer when he was fifty-seven. So, maybe I can make it one more day without a cigarette—one more day for Dad.

When I get home, I rummage through the kitchen drawer to

find Sandy's apartment keys, and then I go next door to visit Mr. Ed. He is napping on the couch.

"How about a walk, little guy? It's a nice day out. What do you say we go to the park?"

Ed's tail starts to wag like a metronome set to a fast three-four meter beat. I grab his leash and off we go. Ed beats me down the stairs by two flights, and when we get outside he runs to the corner with me hanging on for the ride. We get to the park and Ed starts his happy dog-sniffing dance. I let him off his leash when we get to the dog run next to the Great Lawn. About fifteen other dogs frolic in the fenced area. I sit on a bench and watch Mr. Ed socialize with his canine friends. A man sits down next to me and lights a cigarette.

"Is that your Westie?" he asks.

"Not exactly. He belongs to my neighbor."

"You mean Sandy? I thought he looked familiar. How is Sandy? I haven't seen her in a while. Everything okay?"

"Yeah, sure. She and Dick are out of town for a few days. So I'm on dog duty."

"Oh, I see," he says puffing thoughtfully on his cigarette. It's all I can do not to reach over and wrestle it out of his hand and take a good long drag. "She didn't mention she was going out of town. We often have our morning coffee together right here on this bench. She didn't mention a trip."

"Well, maybe it slipped her mind."

"She's a good woman."

"Yes," I agree. I am getting the feeling a little more is going on between Sandy and Mr. Dogwalk than just walking dogs. Of course, it could be one-sided and Sandy is oblivious to the attention, or maybe she is having a wild and passionate affair. Either way it's none of my business. What is my business is the cigarette thing. I have to get going or I'm going to knock this guy out and steal the pack of Marlboros he has stashed in his pocket.

"Well, I've got to head out. Nice talking to you. Come on, Ed, let's go," I call to my four-footed friend. Ed comes running over and Mr. Dogwalk reaches down and ruffles his ears and pats his head.

"Good boy," he says. It's obvious he and Ed are friends.

"Tell Sandy I said hello when you see her. And tell her I'm still here every morning at the usual time, in case she's interested."

"Yeah. I sure will." This guy has it bad. I think the affair ended and Sandy decided to get back with Dick and that's what the sudden vacation in the Caribbean is about. But I'm sure Mr. Dogwalk hasn't completely given up. Gosh, there is a soap opera sitting on every park bench in this big old city of dreams.

Ed and I stroll around the ball fields and then I head toward Belvedere Castle. And before I know it we are going to the scene of the crime. My feet seem to be leading me there, and it's as if I have no choice but to follow. Mr. Ed starts sniffing furiously as we get close to the knoll where I was attacked.

"It's okay, Ed," I say. "I think it might be good if we go together and take a look at it. I think it might be therapeutic. What do you think, little guy?"

Ed stops and cocks his head up toward me. I squat down beside him and pet his head. "Are you nervous about being here with me?"

"Arf, arf, arf," Ed replies.

"I see. You are apprehensive. Well, so am I, but they say it's good to face your fears. I don't always agree with that, but I know you are still upset with me and I was hoping this might open a door for us to have a dialogue about our experience." I look around for a second, momentarily self-conscious about speaking so frankly with a dog. It might seem strange to someone watching us. But then again, maybe not. I don't know anyone who doesn't talk to his or her dog, especially if the dogs talk back.

"Arf," Ed says moving in the direction of the knoll.

"I'll take that as a yes." We find the spot together. Mr. Ed circles around a bit and then starts to bark as if to say, "This is it, this is where I saved your life." The spot is isolated even in the full light of day. What a fool I was to come here in the dark and jeopardize my safety and Mr. Ed's. What a fool. It's a miracle we both survived. I get down close to the ground and watch him exorcise the ghost of bad things past. He barks and yaps and then comes over and licks my face and pushes his body against mine. I hold him in my arms and rock him back and forth.

"You are a good boy. You are my hero," I say. Ed perks up his ears and licks my face some more.

"Arf, arf, arf, arf, arf," he says and nestles in my arms.

"I love you too," I say. "You're the best dog in the whole world."

16

The next few days are a blur. I sleep a lot and spend time with Mr. Ed. We walk all over Central Park and Riverside Park. I don't smoke and I don't drink and I don't breathe as much as I should. I find myself holding my breath, waiting for something to happen. For one thing I'm waiting for Jack to call, but I decide it's better that he doesn't, although it hurts like hell, because the truth is, I'm in no condition to be with another person. I can barely stand myself—why should anyone else be able to? Then I realize what I'm really waiting for is a cigarette. I think if I don't smoke I'm going to smother to death. I call my friend Brian who quit smoking a few years ago.

"I'm breathing too much oxygen. It's making me light-headed. I'm not used to it. It's giving me a headache," I say.

"You need to breathe more," Brian tells me. "People light a cigarette when what they really want is a deep breath. Just open up your lungs and take a good, long, slow breath, and then drink a glass of water. You'll feel better. Have you tried meditating?"

Brian is very into eastern practices. He studied Hinduism, and then Buddhism, traveled to Tibet, has a poster of Richard Gere and the Dalai Lama in his living room. He buys his incense at a little shop in SoHo. In the late eighties he spent a year at an ashram up in the Catskills and was briefly married to a Pakistani woman who was a professional belly dancer.

"No, I'm not meditating, are you crazy? I can barely sit still long enough to go to the bathroom. I have to keep moving because if I stop for a moment I'm afraid I'll open the oven door, turn on the gas, and stick my head in."

"Don't do that. Promise me you'll call me before you do that," he says. "I've got to go. But keep in touch, and remember, you can do this."

Right, of course I can. I can do this. There is a knock at my front door. It's Sandy. She looks relaxed and pleasantly sunburned.

"It was magnificent, the whole trip, too short but very sweet. Have you ever been to the Caribbean? It's so beautiful and so romantic."

"That's great," I say.

"Here, we brought you something." She hands me a package.

"You didn't have to get me anything."

"Well, I saw it and thought it was perfect for you."

I open the box and see a lovely silver bracelet with pink coral inlay.

"Oh, Sandy, you shouldn't have. It's beautiful."

"Well, I wanted to get you something special because of, well, you know . . ." Her voice trails off and then she adds, "Dick picked it out."

I don't know what to do. I'm speechless. I give Sandy a hug.

"Thank you."

"Dick and I had a great time. We really needed to get away." Sandy says this with a big smile. "And it's always nice to go someplace new."

"I'm glad it was a good vacation. Oh, by the way, I ran into a friend of yours at the dog run. He said to tell you hello. Tall guy. Do you know who I mean?"

"Ah, yeah, sure," Sandy says and drops her eyes. She doesn't move, and then I notice a tear trickle down her cheek.

"Oh, Sandy," I say. "I'm sorry. I shouldn't have said anything."

"No, it's all right," she says, dabbing at her eyes.

"Come in and sit down for a minute," I say, gesturing to the couch. "Do you want to talk? I know how those things can be."

"It was just something that got out of hand." She perches on the arm of the sofa. "But it's behind me now."

"Good. Because I think you and Dick are a wonderful couple."

"We are," Sandy says. "Oh, God. I don't know what to do, Maggie. Todd, that's his name, is so intense, and he makes me feel so alive."

"I see."

"We were talking one day, and before I knew it we were under the trees next to the dog run, having sex."

"In the morning? Oh my gosh — right in the park? Did anyone see you?"

"The undergrowth is very dense."

"Where was Mr. Ed?" I ask.

"The dogs were in the dog run. I know it's crazy."

"Did it just happen that once?"

"Oh, no. It's been months."

"For months? In the undergrowth?" I ask, trying not to sound appalled.

"At first, then we started going to Todd's apartment. His wife is gone during the day and he works at home."

"He's married too?"

"Yes. It's so complicated."

"Do you love him?"

"I don't know. I told him it had to end. That's when I started rollerblading. I couldn't go to the dog run anymore. And I thought the vacation would put a spark back in my marriage. Dick doesn't know, but I think he suspects."

"Did it?"

"Did it what?"

"Put the spark back?"

"It was great. Dick was so relaxed, and we were together the whole time. You know our schedules are so opposite. We really are like two ships in the night. It was great to have real time together. Even at the country house we're so busy doing chores that . . . oh God." Sandy lets out a cry and slides off the arm onto the sofa and collapses among the cushions.

"Can I get you some water or something?"

"I don't know how I feel. I miss Todd, I ache for him, but I love Dick. Does that make sense?" she says between sobs.

"Make sense? That's the plot of just about every romantic comedy ever written."

"I better get back," Sandy says, righting herself on the couch and dabbing at her eyes. "Dick's waiting for me. We're going to that new Vietnamese restaurant on Eighty-fourth Street. Have you eaten there?"

"No, I haven't, but it must be good because there is always a line out front."

"Thanks for listening," Sandy says sotto voce, as if Dick might be standing outside with his ear pressed against the door.

"Sure," I say in a whisper, in case he actually is. "And, Sandy, if you need me to deliver any sort of message, I'd be happy to," I offer.

"Thanks. I'll think about it," Sandy says.

"Well, you look great," I say, back to full voice as I open the door. "I think the Caribbean agrees with you."

And when I open the door, Dick is indeed in the hall, leaning against the wall skimming through the current issue of the *New Yorker*.

"Hey, Maggie," he says.

"Dick," I say as I nod in greeting. "Sounds like you had a great time. And thank you so much for the beautiful bracelet."

"Well, we wanted to bring you back a little bit of paradise," he says, leaning over and giving me a peck on the cheek.

"I appreciate it." And with that the happy yet not-so-happy couple exits down the stairs and out the front door for a lovely meal at the new trendy restaurant down the street. And I go back to not smoking and not drinking, and not thinking about not smoking and not drinking, while quietly obsessing about how I'm not smoking and not drinking, and most definitely going completely insane.

THAT NIGHT THE OPENING at Charles's gallery is packed. I get there about nine thirty and have trouble making my way through the crowd. I look for Charles but can't spot him. The usual folks are crammed in next to a new group, the artist's friends and fans of the tapestries. They are exquisite. The beads refract the light so the pieces shimmer with motion. The artist is a petite woman with cornflower blue eyes and wispy blonde hair. She is talking with a group about the process of beading. Tedious, I think as I examine one of the pieces. It is completely hand sewn. "Ten thousand beads," I overhear her say as I pass by. Ten thousand beads hand-sewn in one piece. I look around the room and count about twenty tapestries and then do a quick calculation. Two hundred thousand beads sewn one by one onto the fabric. Wow, that's impressive. Or is it just compulsive? What is art anyway? One person's cockeyed view of the world, expressed over and over in slightly different variations, then framed and lit and sold for a price, a really good one if you're lucky and get the right agent.

"Mags!" I hear shouted from across the room. It's Charles. I wave at him above the heads. Waiters are weaving in and out of the crowd with glasses of wine and trays of hors d'oeuvres.

"Do you have any club soda?" I ask one as he offers me a glass of wine.

"You'll have to go to the bar in back. I think there's some Pellegrino," the waiter says.

"I know you. We did a couple of shows together at Maryland Stage a few years ago?" I say.

"Oh, my God, of course, you look so different. Is it your hair?"

"Could be. It's longer and blonder, maybe. I think that's the summer I was a redhead."

"Yeah, you were. But I like this look."

"Really? I've been thinking about going all the way to pure platinum, but I'm getting old for that," I say popping a clam puff in my mouth.

"And aside from your hair, how are you?" the waiter/actor whose name I can't remember asks.

"Great. Okay. You know. I see you're making a buck."

"Oh, yeah. Hanging in. And you?"

"I'm doing some theater. And I've got a club date at Don't Tell Mama."

"Did you hear about Marty? He played opposite you in *Promises, Promises*. Remember?"

"Of course I remember; he stepped on every laugh line I had. I haven't seen him since Maryland."

"He went out to LA. He's got his own series. On ABC. It starts this fall."

"What? That's amazing," I say, my eyes wide in genuine amazement.

"I know," he says with nod. "I've got to circulate these clam puffs. We'll talk later. You look great."

"Thanks, you look great too."

Marty has his own series? Shit. How does a guy like Marty Lancer get his own series? Not only did the guy have the worst timing in the world, he was also tone deaf and couldn't act his way out of paper bag. God I want a cigarette. Why is it so hard to be happy for other people? Why? Why? Why? Shit, he's set for life if the show goes into syndication.

"Good for him," I say out loud through clenched teeth. "Good for him."

"What?" The fellow standing next to me asks, turning toward me.

"Good stuff, good beads," I say. "What do you think?"

"I think it's very seventeenth century. You know tapestries were almost always made by nuns, long hours of sewing in the isolation of a convent. Makes you wonder about the artist doesn't it? What is she isolating from?"

"Does she have to be isolating? She is in dialogue with her art, isn't she?"

"That's interesting."

"To create is to be in communication with the world. What did Emily Dickinson say? 'This is my letter to the world that never wrote to me.' I'm sure there are many interpretations of that line, but I think it means the artist is communicating," I say, happy to note I still have a brain. "They are leaving a mark regardless or even in spite of the response. So how can one be isolating when one is saying through art, 'Look at me, here I am, and this is what I have to say'?"

"Oh, God, I want to make love to you right here."

"What? Are you crazy?" I say.

"I want to put my hands all over you and lick your essence. I want to soak up the poetry of your skin. You're so beautiful. I need to feel you. I need to be inside you."

"Excuse me. But I think you must have me confused with someone else."

"I live right around corner. Please."

"Sorry." I quickly move away and look for Charles. I catch sight of him and head in that direction.

"Please," I hear the insane man say behind me. "I'm wild for you and I don't even know your name."

"And doesn't that tell you something," I say over my shoulder as I make my way toward Charles.

"Maggie, what do you think?" Charles asks. "I love these things and I know they are going to sell."

"I've got to go."

"You just got here. We haven't had a chance to talk."

"We'll have lunch soon. Besides, you

NOTE TO SELF . . .

Time to leave the art exhibit when a stranger tells you he wants to "soak up the poetry of your skin."

have to do your thing. I've got an early call in the morning. I'm off to West Virginia for three days with *Snow White*."

"You have got to get back into grown-up theater," Charles says, kissing me on the cheek. "Thanks for coming down. Oh, I noticed you talking to Chad. What do you think of him?"

"Chad?" I ask. "You mean the guy in the paisley shirt?"

"Yes. I'm in love. He's the best thing that has happened to me in years. I've known him for a while, but the other night we suddenly clicked."

"What about the guy from Spain?"

"Too Spanish and too much au naturel body odor—if you know what I mean," he says with a grimace.

"Charles," I say, "Chad, propositioned me. He said he wanted to lick my essence."

And at that moment Chad joins us.

"I really had you going didn't I?" he says, laughing. "You should have seen her face, Charles, she was appalled. I'll show it to you."

"What do you mean? You'll show it to him?"

"Chad is a video artist," Charles says. "He captures people's reactions to inappropriate sexual advances in public situations. It's fascinating stuff. Some of it is hysterical and also very touching. Heartbreaking. You wouldn't believe how people respond."

"And you'd be surprised how many times people say yes," Chad adds. "It all speaks to the innate loneliness of the human race and how desperate people are to make contact. It's sort of a blue candid camera—and get the double meaning of blue, huh? Blue like sad and blue like soft porn but not real porn."

"Who are you?" I say. "You're an idiot."

"You were ready to say yes weren't you? I could feel it," Chad goes on, oblivious to my comment. "You're really a very attractive woman."

"This is unbelievable. How dare you talk to me like that? Charles, will you say something?"

"Maggie, don't get so high and mighty. It's art. You understand that."

"Charles, I would appreciate it if you see that my footage gets destroyed," I say with haughty indignation, and the more I talk the more indignant I get. "Do you know I was attacked recently in Central Park and almost got raped? I wonder if that was some video artist looking for reactions from the lonely public. Someone making art. Fuck you, Chad. And fuck you, Charles." By now I'm shaking all over and my voice is loud and shrill and people are staring.

"Maggie, calm down," Charles says, holding me by the shoulders.

"Take your hands off of me," I say and spit out each word into Charles's face. Then I turn and walk out, arm in arm with my righteous indignation. People stand aside and let me pass, and all the while I'm sure the whole tirade is being recorded on Chad's hidden camera. For "art." I get outside and continue walking. I walk twenty blocks without breaking stride. If I don't walk, I'll smoke. I dig in my purse looking for my cell phone but can't find it, but I do find change so I head for a pay phone on the next corner and pray that it's working. By some kindness of the local Verizon god it is. I dial Jack's number. It rings. My stomach turns over.

"Jack here," he says.

I don't say anything. My throat constricts.

"Hello? Hello?" Jack says. I hear music in the background. "Who is this?" he asks and then hangs up.

I wait. The pay phone rings. I know it is Jack. He dialed the number that showed up on his cell phone. Sometimes public phones block the caller's number. Not this one because I know it's Jack. Maybe he thinks it is one of his buddies and they had a bad connection. Or maybe he knows it's me. I let it ring. I don't dare answer; I can't let him know how desperate I am.

I signal the next cab and head home. It's almost five full days without cigarettes or alcohol. I don't think I can make it much longer. I wish I could lock myself in a room for a few weeks. I guess I actually could, because I think that's exactly how rehab works. Well, I'm not doing that; besides I have to go to West Virginia tomorrow and put on pretty-girl makeup and wrestle with the evil stepmother.

When I get to my building, Jack is sitting on the front stoop. I pay the cabbie and get out of the taxi. My knees feel weak. Jack walks over and puts his big, warm arms around me. I bury my poor aching head in his chest. We stand like that for quite a while.

"I'm sorry," I say finally.

"Love means never having to say you're sorry," Jack says. "Didn't you see the movie?"

"You mean *Love Story*?" I say. "Of course I saw it. I'm surprised you did."

"My first girlfriend made me watch it," he says.

"I haven't had a cigarette for years."

"Really?" Jack says. "Years?"

"Well," I say, "it feels like years."

"Is that why you called me?" he asks.

I don't answer. The words are stuck in my stupid, nicotine-deprived throat.

"You did call me, didn't you?"

"I called you because . . ."

"Because?"

"Because I love you," I manage to say, and then look Jack right in the eyes and he looks me in the eyes and suddenly we both grin. Grin like two silly kids. I wish Chad were here with his fucking video camera, because *this* is art. This is something worth seeing. Then we wrap ourselves around each other and take a deep breath.

We finally make our way up to my apartment and continue holding on to each other long after we are inside.

We make love slowly, passionately, and then lie on the bed with the window open and let the cool summer breeze play against our skin. Eventually we start to fall asleep.

"Goodnight," I whisper to Jack.

"Goodnight," he whispers back to me, "and goodnight moon, goodnight socks."

"Goodnight bunnies, goodnight light," I say. Jack hugs me close and we drift off to dreamland.

I wake up around five to go to the bathroom. As I step out of the bedroom something rushes past my face. I take a quick breath. Then something bangs the windowpane and flutters across the room.

"Goodie?" I whisper loudly. "Is that you?" No response. I let out a little scream. Jack is quickly by my side.

"Something is in the room," I say.

"Turn on the light," he says. I reach over and switch on the table lamp. We stand squinting into the room. I see dark marks on the ceiling.

"Up there," Jack says, pointing to the bookcase. I look up and there perched on the top shelf is a bird covered in soot and shaking, shaking almost as much as I'm shaking.

"You scared me," I say to the bird.

"Not as much as you scared him," Jack says, moving closer to the bookcase. The bird flutters across the room, hits the ceiling, and comes to rest on top of the coatrack.

"Poor thing," Jack says. "How'd he get in here?"

"Down the chimney," I say piecing something together in my mind. "The soot, remember, I told you I had noticed soot in the fireplace. Last week maybe. It must have been this bird. He's been stuck in the chimney."

"Well, we've got to get him back outside."

"Open the window the whole way. See if he'll fly out."

Jack wrestles to get the window up and I get a piece of newspaper to try to wrangle the bird toward the opening, but birdie is confused. He flies back to the bookshelf.

"Come on, little fellow. We're trying to help you. Just fly out the window and you'll be okay," I say. The bird looks at Jack and Jack looks at me.

"I think we're going to have to take him outside," Jack says. "Maybe we can catch him in a towel."

It's still pitch black out. I look at the clock. It's now 5:15. Dee-Honey is picking me up at eleven to go up to West Virginia. I'm sure I won't be getting back to sleep.

"I'm going to put on water for coffee," I say. Jack goes in search of a towel and I fill the kettle with water. Birdie doesn't move.

"Let's take him out to the courtyard," I say, getting out the coffee and filters.

"Why do you think it's a boy bird? I mean how can you tell?" Jack says, going toward the bathroom.

"Oh, I know it's a boy. A girl bird would have stopped on the third floor and asked for directions. But the boy bird just kept on going, too proud to ask for help."

"Or, you could say our intrepid boy bird sensed an adventure and kept exploring. You know if Christopher Columbus had stopped and asked for directions, we'd all be living on a small island in the West Indies."

"Well, we are living on a small island," I say, "and it's very early in the morning, and boy-birdie just pooped on my carpet." I grab a paper towel to clean it up. The kettle whistles.

"Can you imagine being stuck in the chimney. Poor fellow probably didn't know which way was up or which way was down after a while," Jack says, towel in hand.

"Not that one, that's a bath towel. Get one of the big beach towels," I say. "There's an orange one on the bottom shelf." Then I finish making the coffee.

"This one?" Jack asks, holding up the bright orange towel with blue shellfish.

"Yes, now see if you can catch the bird," I say. Jack springs into action, all the while sweet-talking the bird about the open air and endless blue sky and far-off horizons. Amazingly he is able to wrap boy-birdie loosely in the towel, and boy-birdie seems to know he has found his savior because he doesn't resist as Jack cuddles him in his hands. I get the coffee and we head out of the apartment, down the stairs, and out the back door that opens onto the court-yard. The sun is peeking up over the rooftops. Jack squats on the ground and opens the towel. The bird looks around, then flaps his wings and tries to fly. He gets airborne for a moment and then crashes down.

"Maybe he's hurt," I say, "broken wing or something."

"No," Jack says watching him, "he's too heavy with all the soot. Watch, he'll figure it out." And sure enough the bird makes his way to a puddle left from yesterday's rain shower and begins to take a bath. He ducks down into the water and then shakes himself off and ducks again and again and again. Then he tries his wings once more and this time he flies up and lights on the fire escape of the synagogue, sits for a moment, and then soars up and over the building, headed for the blue skies and far horizon that Jack promised him.

"Go, little fellow," Jack cheers as boy-birdie disappears into the morning.

Jack and I sit and drink our coffee and stare off in the direction that birdie flew. I think we are both half expecting him to fly back for one last look, or to sail over and dip his wings at us like pilots do in the movies as a kind of salute to the people waiting below. We sit in silence for quite a while.

"I guess he's going to be all right," I finally say.

"Oh, yeah," Jack says, clearing his throat, "he'll be fine." Then my handsome young man reaches up with his strong left hand and wipes away a tear.

"Are you crying?" I ask.

"Yeah, I guess I am. It's pretty powerful to watch something reclaim its freedom. To be back where it's meant to be."

"Yeah," I say, "must have been scary in that chimney, not knowing which way to go."

"Well, he's not scared anymore," Jack says.

"No, I guess not," I say.

"Lucky bird," Jack says and smiles up at the morning sky.
Jack and I sit and watch the sun come up, and then I offer to make breakfast.

"I have some English muffins," I say, surveying the contents of my fridge when we get back upstairs, "and some leftover Chinese. And some cottage cheese. Oops, no, this is way over the expiration date."

"An English muffin," Jack says. "Mind if I jump in the shower? I got to get on the road."

"Sure." I put a muffin in the toaster and look for some butter. I find margarine and grape jam. I go to my window to see if our bird has circled back into the courtyard.

"I smell something burning," I hear Jack say. I rush to the kitchen and sure enough the toaster is smoking. Jack pulls the plug and waves the smoke away with his towel.

"Damn," I say. "This is my life in the kitchen." Jack upends the toaster and the two blackened muffin halves plop out into the sink.

"There," he says. "Breakfast is served." Then he kisses me on the forehead. "I've got to run; I'll pick up something on my way." Jack goes to the bedroom and starts slinging on his clothes. I'm still standing in the kitchen looking at the dead muffin when Jack comes up behind me and kisses me on the top of my head.

"Sorry," I say.

"It's okay," Jack says. "You win some, you lose some."

"But I bet you win most things," I say.

"Hell no," he says, pulling on his socks, "my life is a mess."

"What do you mean?"

"I'm just a guy who is trying to get by."

"Oh," I say, and bite hard on my lip so I don't say something I'll regret.

"I'm no prize. That's what I'm saying."

"Well neither am I."

"Good, we're even." Jack steps into his shoes by the door. "I got to go."

"Wait," I say, "don't leave now."

"I have an appointment," Jack starts for the door.

"Stop," I say, "stop, please."

"I'm sorry. I'll call you."

"I want to say that you're a prize to me."

"You wouldn't say that if you really knew me."

"What?" I say. "What does that mean?"

Jack looks at me for a moment. Takes a step, then reconsiders.

"Sorry, forget it," he says and ducks out the door. I follow him and yell from the landing as he gallops down the stairs.

"That's a lousy thing to say. I *do* know you."

"All right," he yells back, "have it your way, Sweet Pea. Love ya." And he exits quickly out the front door of the building.

"Love ya too," I yell back. Mrs. Vianey pokes her head out of her door two flights down.

"What's going on?" she asks. I lean over the railing and she looks up at me. What's going on? I think. I wish I knew.

"Sorry, Mrs. Vianey," I say. "I was . . . just rehearsing a scene and it got a little loud." Which I realize is absurd.

"Shakespeare?" she asks hopefully. "I love Shakespeare."

"Well, this was more like Sam Shepard."

"Oh," she says, looking up at me. "I saw Laurette Taylor in *Glass Menagerie*. Did I ever tell you that?"

"Yes, you have," I say. "Many times, actually."

"Oh," she says.

"But I always love hearing about it," I say.

"She was wonderful," Mrs. Vianey says. "I was a young girl, but I remember it like it was yesterday."

"I'm sorry to have disturbed you," I say, moving toward my door. I reach out and steady myself against the frame. My knees feel weak and my stomach is growling and I'm having that flickering sensation in my peripheral vision again. I make my way to the kitchen and open the refrigerator and look for a beer, something to ease the angst in my head, and then panic hits me. I threw it out. I threw the beer out, along with the rest of the booze. Shit! I close my eyes and count to ten . . . and then remember my special secret. I open the cupboard over the sink, shove a chair next to the counter, and climb up. I reach into the big pot that I would make spaghetti in if I ever made spaghetti. Eureka. There it is, my emergency bottle of scotch. What a smart girl I am. "Be prepared," I whisper. My old girl scout leader would be proud. I climb off the chair. I hug the bottle for a moment and take a deep breath. Just for now I'll drink this. Then I'll quit again. I promise I will. What's the big deal anyway? I unscrew the top and take a deep swallow and slide down the wall and sit on the floor and let the scotch work its magic. No thoughts — open, drink, slide. The scotch rolls down my throat and hits my belly, and immediately I feel a wave of nausea. I run to the bathroom, lean over the toilet, and throw up. I close my eyes, the room spins, I squat holding my head between my hands. Bixby meows. I open my eyes. He is looking at me, his cat face so close to mine that he looks huge, like something out of a Japanese sci-fi movie — *The Cat That Ate New York*. I gasp and lie back. My head hits something hard. It takes a moment to realize it's the tub. I struggle to my feet and start searching for a cigarette thinking that will steady me, and then I remember I quit that too. Shit. And, I didn't hide any anywhere. I call Brian.

"I really want to smoke. I am not smoking but I really want to. I just wanted to tell you."

"What time is it?" Brian groans.

I squint at the clock. "It's six fifteen," I say.

"In the morning?" Brian snaps.

"I think," I say. "And I haven't had a cigarette. I have a headache but no cigarettes." I don't tell him about the scotch.

"Hot milk," Brian whispers into the phone. " I know it sounds corny, but it really works, and if you have a nice slice of toast with it, dip it. It's like eating baby food. Call in the morning . . . the real morning. Like around ten." Then he hangs up.

I drink some hot milk—adding a medicinal splash of scotch. The milk eases that scotch into my stomach and this time it stays down. I eat a piece of toast and then I decide I should lie down and get some sleep before I have to meet Dee-Honey. I set my alarm. And it seems to go off before I even close my eyes. I stumble to the shower, turn it full blast. I don't know why I feel so upset; after all, Jack did say he loved me. Maybe that's what upsets me. He said it like he was saying goodbye.

IN MY RUSH to get packed and meet Dee-Honey, I scratch my right eye with the earpiece of my sunglasses. It hurts like hell. My eye waters and stings and my head is pounding. This is punishment for my bad behavior. And I have to go to West Virginia and pretend to be an ingénue. I should call the funny farm right now and make a reservation

"Bye, Bixby," I say as I close the door. "Sandy will be in to feed you and visit and perhaps have a tryst with her lover, but don't judge, Bixby. Remember, you can't judge a man until you have walked in his moccasins, or her Dansko clogs, in Sandy's case." I can't get the idea of Sandy and Mr. Dogwalk out of my mind, especially the image of them having sex under the trees next to the dog run bright and early in the morning. I wonder if that's against the law? Don't you need a permit from the parks commission to fornicate in the undergrowth?

By the time I get to Ninety-sixth Street to meet the cast, my eye is throbbing and my head is pounding louder and louder by the minute. Also, I'm having trouble seeing and the sunlight is giving me a terrible headache on top of the pounding.

"Good morning, fair damsel," Ron says as I approach.

"Funny," I manage to say, but talking makes it worse.

"Hey, I just had a great audition for Alabama Shakespeare. *Henry V.* That would be awesome," Ron says, helping me get my bags into the van.

"Ahh," I say, "*Henry V.* I know it well," and despite my throbbing eye and pounding head I quote a few lines. It's an affliction common to actors, the irresistible urge to spout lines from past performances

"Wow. That's impressive," Ron says when I finish.

"I played the chorus at San Diego Rep about ten years ago. I hope you get the part." Now my head feels like a raccoon is chewing on my frontal lobe and I'm seeing in triplicate, which is alarming because this is exactly how my friend Dan's brain tumor started.

"Are you okay?" Ron puts his hand on my shoulder. "You look a little off."

"To tell you the truth, I hurt my eye this morning. I was in a hurry and when I put my sunglasses on — "

"Let me see," Ron interrupts me. "Take off your glasses." I pull off the glasses and the sunlight about knocks me out. I can't even open my eyes.

"Wow," Ron says. "We need to take you to the emergency room."

"Look I think I—"

"Dee, Maggie scratched her eyeball and she needs to go to a hospital."

"I think you're overreacting," I say.

"It's your eye. You don't want to mess around," Ron says. Dee-Honey comes over and takes a look. Then Randall Kent inspects the damage.

"Oh, God," he exclaims. Pretty soon the whole cast of *Snow White* is examining my bloodshot, weepy eye.

Helen Sanders offers to call her eye doctor and see if I can get a drive-by appointment. The receptionist says if I can be there in fifteen minutes, the doctor can see me right away.

"You scratched the cornea. That is very painful. Are you nauseous?" Dr. Trostle says after he examines my eye.

"No. It just hurts like hell."

He cleanses it and gives me a painkiller and then bandages my eye.

"You're not going to have any depth perception, so you have to be careful. Take the pills and put the drops in twice a day. I'll give you a prescription. And keep the eye bandaged."

"Am I going to be able to see? I mean is it damaged permanently?"

"No, it's a deep abrasion but it should heal fine," Dr. Trostle says, writing out the prescriptions. "Drops twice a day, and be sure to keep it bandaged."

We stop at a Duane Reade and get the prescriptions filled. We are an hour behind schedule, but Dee-Honey has a heavy foot so that's no problem. We'll make it. Besides, the first show isn't until tomorrow morning. As we settle into the drive all I can think is three days with my fellow thespians, a scratched cornea, and nicotine withdrawal. Thank God for the painkillers! I have to be careful no one steals them. I close my eyes, the good one and the injured one, and try to sleep.

We get to the Days Inn outside of Wheeling, West Virginia, about eight p.m. We check into the motel, then we assemble and head for the IHOP we spotted on the way in. Helen orders a short stack with a side salad. Her reasoning: roughage flushes out the carbohydrates, thus canceling the meal. Interesting. You just have to get a look at Helen from the back end to know that this theory is only true in, well, theory. I order a short stack of blueberry pancakes and a side of whipped cream because my eye needs the comfort of sweet, fluffy food. It's called the sweet and fluffy diet.

"So what do we tell the kiddies?" Randall asks.

"About what?" Helen says, shoving a big spoonful of pancakes in her mouth.

"About how the lovely young Snow White lost her eye," he says looking at me.

"I haven't lost my eye," I say. "I hurt my eye. In a domestic accident."

"So mundane, run of the mill," Randall says frowning. "I think it should be a curse, a curse from the wicked stepmother because of your beauty. The one flaw. And yet even with only one eye you see clearly. Good lesson for the kids."

"Maybe you should tell them you lost it to cancer because Snow White used to smoke and she got cancer of the eye," Ron offers in reference to my last outing in the part.

"I told you, Snow White found the cigarette in the forest," I say getting irritated by the whole discussion.

"Maybe we could say it was eaten out by a rat," Helen offers. The image of a rat eating my eye causes my throat to constrict and the pancake that was starting it's way down gets stuck in my windpipe and I realize I can't breathe.

"I like it," Randall says leaning back in his chair. "A rat that was cursed by the evil stepmother. Or maybe it *is* the evil step-mother."

I look wide-eyed around the table. I put my hands to my throat. I can't even cough. I have no air. It's eerily the same feeling as with the man in the park. No air. I pound the table and then throw my arms in the air.

"My God, she's choking," Helen says. I wag my head up and down.

"Who knows the Heimlich?" Randall booms in a panicked voice. Everybody freezes for a second. Eddie Houser yells for the waiter. Helen gets behind me and places her arms around my waist.

"Higher up," Ron says putting his hands over hers and together they strike sharply below my rib cage. Pancake debris flies out of my nose and mouth. I take a deep breath and shiver out a long exhale. I put my head down on the table and take a few quick breaths.

"You're okay," Helen says, patting me gently on the back. "You're going to be fine."

Ron slumps back in his seat. Gloria, who has been huddled in the corner of the booth, talking to her boyfriend on her cell phone, never misses a beat on her phone. She is giving her boy-friend a play-by-play of the near catastrophe.

"Then Ron and Helen administered the Heimlich and saved Maggie's life," she says.

Oh, God. It dawns on me what happened. I was choking to death.

"How do you feel?" Ron asks.

I nod.

"Wow," Helen announces with gusto. "That was great. That's the most exciting thing that has happened to me in years. I saved someone's life. Maggie, I swear I saw your life pass in front of my eyes. Weird, huh? And I knew we were about to lose you, but thank Jesus I had the strength to save you."

"And Ron, you and Ron," I say getting my voice back.

"Of course, Maggie," Helen says. "We both saved you." She reaches over and puts her hand on mine and gives it a squeeze. "And it's always going to be something special between us."

I momentarily wish they had let me choke.

"So did you really think you were going to die?" Gloria asks between phone calls.

"Yeah, I guess, but it wouldn't be the first time. Seems be to happening a lot lately," I say. "Does anyone have a cigarette?"

"Now, Maggie, remember, you quit," Randall says. "We didn't save you to have you poison yourself with nicotine. We're your protectors now." I look around the table and everyone is nodding at me in a patronizing, disgusting way.

"Does anyone have a cigarette?" I say at the top of my lungs to the whole room. "Huh? Does anyone have a fucking cancer stick I can smoke?"

All the activity in the restaurant skids to a stop like in those old E. F. Hutton commercials. Fifty people sit with forkfuls of pancakes suspended in midair. Then a big guy in a flannel shirt with the sleeves cut out reaches in his breast pocket and pulls out a pack of Camels.

"Here, little lady, have one of mine."

I walk over, take the pack, and shake out a cigarette.

"Thank you, sir. I appreciate it." And then I turn and make my grand exit out of the restaurant. Prince "Ron" Charming is right on my heels.

"Don't smoke that, Maggie," Ron says. "Come on, hand it over."

"If you come near me, I'll bite you," I say, holding my hand up. "Don't you dare try to stop me!"

"All right I won't get any closer, but let's at least talk this through," he says. "Look, you had a traumatic experience, and of course you are on edge and want a cigarette, and it's hard I know. I remember when my mother quit."

"Fuck you. I don't want to hear about your mother."

"Well, it's just that she's about your age."

"That does it. I'm not listening to another thing you have to say." I turn and stomp off in the direction of the motel.

"You're not going to walk, are you? It's more than two miles."

"You bet I am," I yell over my shoulder. "These boots were made for walking, kid. Ask your mom about that."

"You're wearing sandals," he yells back. "And you're blind as a bat with only one eye."

I turn around and stomp my foot and say with a snarl, "I'm not listening to you or anyone."

"All right. Have it your way," Ron says and starts back into the restaurant. "Oh, FYI, Mom said the first week is the worst." And he is gone.

Now I have to walk back to the motel. I've made my stand. Damn. Take a deep breath I tell myself. "Drink some hot milk and have a piece of toast," I hear Brian's voice say. I'll give him a call when and if I get back to the motel without being kidnapped and sold into a white slavery.

I think about Jack and the bird stuck in the chimney. And Mrs. Vianey, old and alone, and up every morning at five a.m. And the whole lousy world that seems so damn . . . lousy.

I start to cry big wet tears out of my one unbandaged eye. I walk against the traffic, crying and cursing. Headlights hit my one eye. I squint and keep walking and keep crying and keep cursing. Then I hear a car horn. It's my merry band of fellow actors. They pull over on the opposite side of the road

"Maggggiiee," I hear Randall shout out the window. "Come on, get in. This is silly."

"I am walking!" I yell back. "Just leave me alone!"

They sit for a minute, deciding; then Randall honks twice and off they go. Obviously the group consensus is to let the hellcat rot and that's fine with me.

"And you're welcome," Helen says out the back window.

"For what?" I say.

"For saving your life, dear, and I'm not going to let you forget it," she yells as the car speeds off.

Oh my God, if I had any sense I'd lie down in the middle of the road and pray for a six-wheeler to flatten me like an IHOP pancake. Ha, ha. My little joke makes me laugh, which hurts my head and makes my eye throb.

I sing the score to *Sweeney Todd, the Demon Barber of Fleet Street* as I trudge along the highway. I make it back to the motel in one piece. About halfway there I throw my pilfered cigarette on the ground and stomp it to bits.

When I arrive at the room we are sharing, Helen is sitting on her bed, tweezing her one big eyebrow into two small ladylike ones. I don't say a word.

"So, the prodigal ingénue returns," she says, not looking up.

I go in the bathroom and sit on the toilet for fifteen minutes.
I wash my face, then open the door, and see Helen doing sit-ups,
military style,

I grab my wallet and head out of the room to the motel bar I
noticed off the wood-paneled lobby. I perch myself on one of the
barstools. *The Late Show with David Letterman* is playing on the
TV over the bar. The guy at the desk, who is also the bartender,
takes my order.

"Scotch on the rocks, please." He pours me a double.

"Thanks," I say and stare at the TV. Dave is interviewing some
gushing starlet with long blonde hair extensions. I go over to the
cigarette machine, fish out a handful of coins from my pocket,
and buy a pack of Marlboros. I sit and smoke and drink two more
scotches. The desk guy/bartender joins me for a drink.

"What happened to your eye?" he asks.

"A rat ate it," I say.

THE FIRST SHOW is at nine the next morning. There are
two shows here, and then we will drive for a few hours and do an
evening performance in Buckhandle. We arrive at the theater by
eight. My head and eye are throbbing in syncopation. The sponsors have provided coffee and two big boxes of breakfast pastries.
Everyone is being very nice to me this morning. Helen offers to
carry my coffee because of my depth perception handicap. There is
one large dressing room, boys on the left and girls on the right sort
of thing. I find a spot and start to unload my makeup kit. Helen
places my coffee in front of me along with a big sticky bun.

"Thanks," I say with as much warmth as I can muster, which
believe me wouldn't melt a pat of butter.

I squint into the mirror. Which is worse, I wonder, looking like

Baby Jane or like an escapee from a zombie movie? What the hell am I going to do about the big white bandage on my eye? Maybe I could put some pancake makeup on it and then draw an eye. That'll be pretty.

I'm still staring in the mirror when Randall sits down next to me and opens his kit. He roots around for a while.

"Aha, I knew I had one of these," he says, pulling out a black eye patch. "Here, Mags, try this on. It should do the trick. And I think I have some glitter here somewhere. That with a little spirit gum will do the trick." He hands me the patch. "I think we'll have to take the bandage off and put some cotton over your eye. Who has some cotton?"

"I have cotton balls," Eddie pipes up.

"Look, I can do this myself," I say.

"Shut up, missy," Randall says. "Now I'm going to apply a little base before we do the patch." Randall gently covers my face with a layer of makeup. Then he applies the rest of my makeup, including blush and lipstick. And manages to attach plenty of glitter to the patch with spirit gum. I look rather splendid.

"Fifteen minutes, please," Frank yells into the dressing room.

"Thanks, Randall," I say.

"My pleasure, sunshine."

"Goodness," Helen says. "I haven't even started my hair."

I make my way to the backstage area where Dee-Honey is setting the props.

"How are you, honey?" she asks. "Oh, I like the eye-patch. I had an uncle who lost an eye in the war."

"How did that happen?" I ask.

"Bayonet. It just missed his brain. One of the Nazi hordes. Came out right in front of his ear." She rummages through the trunk of props. "He used to take his glass eye out and roll it be-tween his fingers and then pop it back in the socket."

Why did I ask? I wonder. The thought of it makes my eye pulse with pain.

I GET MY CELL PHONE and walk out of the building so I can get reception. I call Jack's number.

It rings about five times, then the message plays. "It's Jack. Leave a message and I'll call you back."

"Jack, it's Maggie. I just want to say I'm sorry. I'm sorry about everything. Oh, I don't know what I'm saying. Just wanted to say hello. I'm in West Virginia to do some shows, but I'll be back in New York some time tomorrow. Maybe we could talk. And . . . and . . . I love you, Jack."

I flip my phone closed as Randall Kent comes around the corner.

"Frank just called five minutes," Randall says. Then he stops and gets a look at me. "For goodness sake, what's wrong?" he asks.

"I'm having . . . a difficult day."

"I'll say," Randall puts his arm around me and walks me back into the building. "Is some of this difficulty in the affairs of the heart?"

"You could say that, definitely the heart."

"Well, you'll survive, my dear. And you'll live to love another day."

"Places, please," Frank yells from stage right. I shake out my hands and stretch my lips. The theater is packed with kids waiting for me and my eye patch. If I can't hold onto prince charming in real life, I can at least snag one onstage.

• • •

WE GET BACK to New York late the next afternoon. Dee drops me on my corner. When I get home I have a message on my machine from Javan inviting me to the Comic Strip that night to watch his set. There is still no word from Jack. It's been over twenty-four hours since I called him, so I think it's a wrap. He is not going to be calling back and I don't blame him. I think the bird did it. Seeing birdie fly free made Jack want to be free. Free of me. Bixby curls up next to me and makes biscuits on my thigh. I scratch behind his ears the way he likes and we rock back and forth. "I love you, you love me, we're a happy family," I sing through my tears.

I GET TO THE Comic Strip that night about a half hour before Javan's set. He is sitting at the bar drinking a beer.

"Hey, how you doing?" I say, coming up behind him.

"Mags, you made it?" Javan says, getting up and giving me a hug. "I'm trying to get in the zone. I love the eye patch, especially the glitter. It's very sexy."

"Thanks, it's all the rage in West Virginia," I say. "Look, I'll leave you alone to prepare. We'll talk after."

"No, no. It's fine. Sometimes I zone out too much and the set is a real sleeper. I'm always trying to find the absolute best combination of beer, concentration, memorization, visualization, prayer, and sugar. I have to have a candy bar right before I go on. Snickers. And then I say three Hail Marys and—this is very important—I always pick up the microphone with my left hand. That's a must. Oh, and I have to wear red socks."

"It's amazing you remember all of that *and* your material," I say.

"Comedy is tough. Believe me."

I sit down on the barstool next to Javan. The bartender comes over and asks what he can get me.

"I'm just visiting. Here for the show."

"It's on me," Javan says. "Have a drink."

"I'll wait for the show. Don't I have to order something in the club?"

"It's all the same whether you order it out here or in there," the bartender explains.

"Well then, I'll have a . . ." I hesitate. I can't remember how long it's been. I know I started my count over in West Virginia, but since I've lost track maybe it won't matter. Still I should try, even though a drink and a cigarette seem very attractive right now. "Anytime today," the bartender says.

"Club soda . . . with a splash of cranberry juice and a twist," I say.

"One Shirley Temple coming up," the bartender says.

"Right. Great. That sounds good." I feel like such a nerd.

Javan looks at his watch. "I better get backstage. We'll talk after my set. Sit up front so I can see you. And be sure to laugh."

"Of course I will." And then Javan leans over and kisses me on the lips which throws me completely off. In fact, I almost slide off the barstool. The bartender delivers my Shirley Temple. Javan heads backstage and I try to regain my balance. God, I wish I had a cigarette.

At ten of nine I go into the club with my Shirley Temple and sit at one of the front tables. The room is two-thirds full, mostly with thirty-somethings in suits, all of them drinking too much beer. There are some older folks dressed primarily in synthetic blends, tourists from the polyester belt. A group of Asian couples occupies the table to my left. They are having a lively conversation in what I think is Japanese. One of them appears to be quite a comedian in his own right, and every time he says something the whole table squeals with delight. Javan definitely has his work cut out for him.

The MC comes on and delivers a couple of lukewarm jokes and then introduces Javan. "Just back from a nationwide tour, shared a bill in Las Vegas with George Carlin, here's the funniest man I ever met from Marysville, Minnesota—Mr. Javan Jones."

There is a splatter of applause. Javan appears onstage, removes the microphone from the stand with his left hand, swallows the last bite of his Snickers bar and begins.

"So I was in Pennsylvania a few weeks ago and driving behind this Amish buggy." Javan goes through his Amish material and his Laundromat material and his divorce material. The audience responds here and there and I laugh like a madwoman. The Shirley Temple is starting to kick in; I signal the waitress and order another round.

"And do you have any peanuts or beer pretzels," I whisper to her when she delivers my drink. Javan glares at me. I guess I was louder than I thought. Then the Asian couples get out their money and begin to tally up their check. Javan is losing us and he knows it, so he pulls out the blue material. He tells a joke about two waitresses with big breasts and a bald short order cook. The Asians laugh. I smile and the folks from the polyester belt signal the waitress for their check. Javan finishes up and exits quickly. The MC comes back and introduces the next act, a woman who appeared on two episodes of *Friends* and opened for Joan Rivers in Atlantic City last month. I meet Javan back at the bar. He is guzzling a beer.

"So what did you think?" he asks.

"Great. You were great," I say.

"It was a tough crowd. That Amish stuff usually kills and the divorce bit is new, of course. I need to work on that. Well thanks for coming. It was great to have you out there."

"My pleasure."

"Are you hungry?" Javan asks. "I'm starving. Do you want to get a bite?"

"Sure. Why not?"

We go to a restaurant on East Sixty-fifth Street. Javan orders another beer and I get a coffee.

"I have to check my messages," Javan says, getting out his cell phone. "Sorry."

"I'll forgive you if you let me check my machine."

"You mean you don't have a cell phone? How can you live?" he asks, looking at me like I have two heads.

"I do have a cell phone. Sometimes I forget to put it in my bag. Like now," I say.

Then he holds up a finger while he listens to his voice mail. He hands me the phone and I dial my number.

"You never like being too available," Javan says. "That's why you forget your phone. It's Freudian."

"Oh, please," I say, holding up a finger to shush him.

"You have two new messages," my machine announces. I punch in the code and hold my breath. I just know one is from Jack. The first one is from Patty; the second one is Dee-Honey. No Jack.

"What's wrong?" Javan asks. "You look crushed."

"It's nothing. Nothing at all."

I order french fries and Javan gets a hamburger and we eat and talk, and when we leave Javan invites me back to his place. "For old times' sake," he says.

"I don't think so," I say. What I thought was horniness a few days ago has morphed into low-level irritability.

"Come on, we're grown-ups. It would be great."

"I'm sure it would. I'm just not in the mood for love, know what I mean?"

"All right, I hear you." Javan hails me a cab and hands me a ten-dollar bill. "My treat, kiddo. And thanks for coming to the show."

"Thank you." I don't comment on the "kiddo," although it rankles, but then what doesn't in my present condition?

When I get home there are no new messages on my machine. I light a candle and sit with the phone in my lap and will it to ring. It's almost midnight. I dial Brian's number. He answers on the first ring.

"Hello?"

"Bri? It's Maggie."

"Hey, how was West Virginia?"

"Awful, then not so bad, then awful again. Look, I don't think I can do this, this no smoking thing. I had a few in West Virginia."

"A few?" Brian says.

"All right, a pack. I almost choked to death at an IHOP. I had to smoke. I was very stressed, but I haven't had any since then and now I'm feeling suicidal. I'm so unhappy and I'm not sleeping and I'm drinking too much coffee and I can't stand myself."

"Great. You're in withdrawal. Ride it out—the whole way. Stop cheating."

"I'm telling you I can't do it. I just wanted to call you before I go to the corner to get a pack of Marlboros and a six-pack of Miller Lite."

"Don't, don't do that. Look, I'm going up to the mountains

tomorrow for a retreat. It's a monastery. I've never been, but a friend said it's awesome. Come with me. It's what you need. You need to change your perspective."

"And how!" I say, not really listening. "I need to do a lot of things, but mainly I need a beer and a cigarette."

"Come on, Mags," Brian says. "You can do this. Remember, I was the one that drove you to Pennsylvania for your dad's funeral. You remember that, don't you? And the way he looked by the end. Come to the mountain with me; it'll help."

"I'll think about it."

"Fair enough. Now make some hot milk and some toast and then off to beddie-bye, okay?"

"Okay," I say. "Okay, dammit, I'll eat some toast." I hang up the phone, pour a glass of milk, put it in the microwave, and pop a slice of bread in the toaster. Baby food, ugh.

I don't like remembering my dad in the last six months of his life. He was frail, bloated, and full of regret. That was the hardest part, his regrets. He was sorry he hadn't taken better care of himself, sorry about my mother, sorry he wouldn't see my brother's kids grow up or me get married, sorry he hadn't expanded his business and made more money. Sorry, sorry, sorry. Would I feel that way? I already have plenty of regrets. Another ten years, I could be drowning in them.

I cut up the toast and drop it into the warm milk and add sugar. It's warm, sweet comfort food, and after eating it, I go to bed. I get through the night without a cigarette. Brian's right. I can do this.

At eight the next morning I call Brian and tell him I think the trip to the mountain would be a good idea.

"What do I bring?"

"You don't really need anything other than clothes and a tooth-brush. And be sure the clothes are comfortable. You're going to be meditating, doing some yoga, and then doing a work assignment. It will be really good for you."

"My mother used to go on retreats and she was always calmer and saner afterward," I say.

"Well, there you go," Brian says.

"Until she went to one and decided to stay. It was a Catholic retreat, a convent actually," I say, remembering my father's face as he informed my brother and me that mother was going to be staying with the Sisters of Bethany for a while.

"Your mother is a nun?" Brian asks.

Jesus, I'm leaking information like a sieve. I try not to talk about this family footnote unless someone is holding a gun at my head. No wonder I smoked; it kept my mouth busy.

"Can you believe it?" I say with a laugh. "My mother, the nun, which is exactly the reason I've never done *The Sound of Music* even though I'm perfect for the part."

"But you weren't raised Catholic, were you?" he asks.

"No, Mother converted. The Presbyterians didn't suffer enough for her. Besides, she wasn't actually a nun, she just lived in a con-vent for a while. She was sorting things out. My brother called it a religious lobotomy. And then she came back home — refreshed as she said — and then after my father died she moved to Florida. We exchange Christmas cards and she calls me on my birthday."

"I'll pick you up at noon tomorrow. This is going to be good for you."

I don't have another show with Dee-Honey until next week, Sandy can feed Bixby, and Jack isn't interested in where I am, so there is no reason not to go. I've never meditated before, but I'm pretty sure you're not allowed to smoke during it, so that's more time without the devil's weed. I just have to remember to keep my mouth shut. Brian can be so nosy, and the mother stuff is such old news—no wonder my last therapist fell asleep during my sessions. I pop two pieces of bread in the toaster and put on the kettle for coffee.

17

At noon the next day I'm packed and ready to go. I take my toothbrush, eyedrops, clothes, and Kathleen Norris's book *The Cloister Walk,* about her experiences at a Benedictine monastery. It's a book my mother sent me a few years ago. One of her attempts to convert me, but what the hell, I figure I can use it as a guidebook; every journey needs a map so you have at least some chance of finding your way back home.

Brian rings the buzzer; I grab my suitcase, give Bixby a goodbye smooch, and head for the hills, literally.

Two hours later we make a stop at Brian's country house. It's a cabin in the Catskills that he and his brother bought years ago so they would have a place to go trout fishing.

"I have to do some chores at Two Dogs. I have a new tenant coming in next week. I'll make you a cup of coffee and you can relax."

The cabin is called Two Dogs because Brian and his brother both had Labradors when they bought it, and the dogs ran the place. Since then the dogs have died and Brian's brother got married and moved to Ontario, but the name remains. Brian kept the cabin and rents it out a few months of the year.

I lie in the hammock in the sun and wait for Brian to finish his work. The sun is hot and the summer afternoon feels like a warm blanket. I have no makeup on, in preparation for my spiritual journey. I'm still wearing the eye patch, which I'm beginning to like. It makes me look exotic. We are going to a Buddhist monastery. Brian tells me the motto is "Life is suffering." Boy and how. I hope the Buddha will smile on me.

After Brian finishes his chores we head for the monastery, traveling higher into the mountains along the Beaverkill River. Finally we turn onto a long dirt road that is guarded by a large stone statue sitting at the entrance.

"Say hello to Buddha," Brian says as we drive by.

"Hello, Buddha," I call out the window.

We pass a lovely lake. "That's Sangha Meadow," Brian tells me, pointing to the left. "The burial grounds."

"That's a bit ominous."

"The alpha and the omega," Brian comments. "The circle of life."

Why can't I just smoke and listen to Joni Mitchell for the rest of my life? That's all I really want to do. That and eat homemade brownies.

"There it is," Brain says.

"Gosh," I say, seeing the monastery in the distance. It's beautiful, sitting serenely on a hill above the lake. It is built in the traditional Japanese design, with simple, clean lines. The grounds around it are impeccably groomed. "Well," I say, taking it in.

"Indeed," says Brian. "By the way, did I tell you this is a silent retreat? I don't think I mentioned that. Once we get inside the monastery, no talking, understand?"

"Are you kidding? I can't go days without talking. It's scary being in my head by myself."

"You only talk to the roshi, your Zen teacher, when you meet privately with him."

"I could strangle you right here at Buddha's front door," I say. And I mean it.

"Come on," Brian says with a laugh. "Have faith. This is just the thing for you. Have I ever steered you wrong?"

This is going to be a nightmare. I can feel it. We park the car at the bottom of the hill, get our things, and hike up to the main entrance. A young man in robes, with a shaved head and a cheery smile, greets us at the door. We deposit our shoes in the shoe room and are taken to our assigned quarters. Mine is on the first floor—very small with a cot, one light, an incense holder, a tiny closet, and a bathroom down the hall. It is, indeed, monastic.

"Well," I say. And this is my last "well," as the cheery young man in robes reminds me that silence is now the rule. I nod, unpack my comfortable clothes, and wonder—silently—what the hell I'm doing here.

We have dinner in the dining hall. There are about twenty-five participants. Another cheery monk explains the schedule and work assignments. It seems the monks are allowed to speak when instructing us, but we can't respond. We must only do. After dinner we go to the meditation hall for zazen, which I'm told is the term for the sitting meditation practice we will be doing for the next three days.

When I get back to my cell—oops, I mean room—I lie down

on my cot and stare at the ceiling. I concoct a plan to sneak into Brian's room and steal the car keys for my getaway, but then abandon it. I'm sure he has hidden them. He knows me. I decide to keep a diary. In case I don't make it out alive and end up in Sangha Meadow at least there will be a record.

My Silent (I have really lost my mind)
Retreat Journal

Day One: I realize I didn't bring a notebook so I am writing on the back pages of my day planner. I will write small. This morning we got up at four thirty a.m. Awakened by someone running up and down the corridors ringing a bell. I thought it was a dream. It is now eight fifteen a.m. We have already meditated and chanted and eaten breakfast (some sort of porridge with cabbage and hot sauce and seaweed sprinkles). Now we have a half-hour break. I am dying for a cigarette and a nap. I'm sitting by a beautiful, peaceful lake. It is incredibly quiet, which makes me want to scream. My body is in pain from sitting cross-legged on the round meditation cushions. The fellow sitting on the cushion next to me looks and smells like he hasn't washed in weeks. And he breathes through his mouth.

My sublime peace was just interrupted by a monk diving into the lake. A large splash and then his bald head resurfaces. His breathing is labored. I gather my thoughts and my sandals and start back to the zendo for another three hours of meditation. I hope lunch is better than breakfast.

Day Two: I am still here, although last night if someone had offered me a ride back to the city I would gladly have gone. Another day of this and I'll be catatonic. I met with the Zen master last night for a one-on-one talk. I said I wanted peace of mind. He told me to think about nothing and count my breaths (at first I thought he said breasts). Count my breaths and breathe out through my tailbone. I wish I had a shot of scotch. That would help me relax more when I meditate. I think about cigarettes and I think about Jack.

During the next two hours of meditation I feel very peaceful and very close to Buddha, except my neck is stiff and my shoulders are going in and out of spasm, my eye throbs intermittently and my right leg has gone to sleep. The man sitting opposite me in the meditation hall has only one leg. He walks with crutches when he's not sitting. I wonder how he lost his leg — maybe a car accident or combat, or maybe he was here at a retreat and his leg went to sleep and the circulation stopped but he couldn't move or speak so gangrene set in and the leg was amputated. The price of enlightenment can be high. I concentrate on nothing and breathe in and out. I feel like I am in the Buddha's belly.

The food is organic and mostly brown. I miss the morning coffee and get herbal tea instead. You have only one chance when the server goes by, and I was confused which server had tea and which had coffee. It was six a.m. I'll probably have a caffeine headache in about an hour.

I'm at the lake. It's still placid. I breathe in and then I breathe out through my tailbone. The trees are blowing in the wind. The leaves look like tiny ballet dancers moving in slow motion; in fact, the whole world looks to be moving in slow motion. It is v-e-r-y b-e-a-u-t-i-f-u-l. I am a tree.

Day Two and a Half: I don't want to ever talk to anyone again. I'm glad this is a silent retreat. Brian is becoming unbearable. I hate him. He is refusing to talk. I can't stand it. He just sits quietly during quiet time and reads *The Three Pillars of Zen.* My Kathleen Norris book about her three-year retreat at a Benedictine monastery is redundant. I can't bear reading it. I wish I had Sue Grafton's new murder mystery instead.

I am beginning to get some clarity here in all this silence, clarity about other people, and it is not pleasant. People are irritating. I've always thought that and now Buddha has confirmed it. I just killed a big water bug in the women's restroom. The blood is dark orange, not red but a rich burnt sienna. This will probably set me back a few years on my journey to Nirvana. God, I wish I could shave my legs, but showers must be short, silent, and every other day. I want to burst into a medley of Broadway tunes.

It's our afternoon rest period. I sit on a big rock. Two monks are swimming in the lake. I sit with my face to the sun and listen to the buzz of Buddha's lesser creatures, and the heavy breathing of the swimming monks magnified in the quiet of the day. I wish I had some Anne Sexton to read. I am desperate for some loud, unbridled neurosis. The rest period draws to a close, and I must return to my sitting cushion and breathe through my asshole. I think about Jack for the whole meditation period and have a silent sitting orgasm which is very pleasant. I wonder if the man sitting next to me with the dirty hair finds me attractive.

Day Three: I'm worried about the graham cracker supply. I brought a box with me as I anticipated the food situation, and Brian keeps eating them. He sneaks into my room and steals them. One thing I know about my true nature is I don't like sharing—especially food, and especially when it is in short supply. I'm going to have to hide the crackers.

I go for a walk during my forty-five minute break. It has been raining and a thick layer of mist and fog gracefully drapes the lake. The beaver dam is fecund with baby beavers. It looks to me like the mother beaver is smoking a cigarette. I must be hallucinating. A large bumblebee stings me on the head. I can't remember if I'm allergic or not. I take my pulse. What if my heart stops right here? I breathe in and out and feel like I'm going to faint. I am overdosing on enlightenment.

Day Three and a Half:

The sitting meditation is very painful. I think I'm developing arthritis in my left hip. Tonight during quiet time Brian pointed out a passage from his Zen book that says women can achieve enlightenment sooner than men because they have fewer ideas in their heads. I had to bite my tongue and suck the blood to keep from committing a mortal sin.

Day Three and Three-quarters: It is the last evening of the retreat, and my body is so racked with pain that I can't feel the profound hunger in my belly. I would kill for a chocolate éclair. The person I'm most jealous of is the man with one leg sitting opposite me. He has only half the pain—no wonder he is so serene. He sits like a rock. I focus on his stillness to calm my mind. The fellow next to me never has washed his hair. But it doesn't bother me anymore. I am beyond caring. I hope this is the closest I ever get to being a prisoner of war. I know now that by day three I would tell them anything and everything. Brian found the graham crackers last night and finished them. I am going to kill him as soon as we are alone.

In my last meeting with the roshi he talked about breathing again. I told him I was too depressed to breathe. I told him I was depressed because I was in love with this guy, but I had been mean to him and now there wasn't much chance of things working out. I also told him that I wanted a cigarette and some scotch and that I didn't think I could go on living. I said I wanted to put my head in the oven and turn on the gas. He smiled and said, "Be here and breathe." He's kind of like a respiratory therapist. I've never really thought about breathing before. I didn't realize it was so important, but I guess it is. Maybe I don't need to smoke; maybe I need to breathe more.

Final Entry:

In the final meditation period I am very still and breathe in and out through my tailbone. And in a mental flash the phrase that was under Danny Panther's picture in the high school yearbook pops into my head: "To create is to breathe, this I believe." Maybe this is what it means, why the Zen master keeps talking about breathing. I breathe and create life, create my life, moment by moment. I am a creation, the creation of my life. My life is a canvas. My life is a poem. I think Henry David Thoreau said that, after years of living alone on Walden Pond. Stop it, I tell myself. Stop thinking. Concentrate on nothing. I look at the one-legged man across from me. He is Buddha. God, I want a cigarette. No, I want a breath. I breathe in and out and in and out. I hope there is a message from Jack when I get back home. I would like to lie down and breathe next to him again and think about nothing.

WE HAVE A FINAL meditation very early Monday morning and then we have cleanup chores assigned. I have to clean the slate stairs and polish the railing. The once quiet monastery is now bustling with activity. Then the bell rings and we all gather for our final meal. It is an informal breakfast and everybody is talking. It's like an explosion after so much silence. I sit next to Brian.

One of the monks offers a toast to our Zen master, who is sitting at the front table. He bows his head in gratitude. Then different participants get up and talk about how the retreat affected them. The fellow with the dirty hair gets up and bows to the room.

"This has been a beautiful time," he says in a thick Polish accent. "I am renewed and I offer this in gratitude." He pulls out a violin and starts to play the most beautiful music I have ever heard. Maybe it's because it's the first music I have heard in days, or maybe the air is so much thinner in the mountains that every note seems to shimmer, or maybe it's because my dirty-haired friend is a god. Zeus with a Stradivarius. I close my eyes and float to heaven.

I don't see the man with one leg at the buffet. I wanted to tell him how much he helped me. I'm not sure I would recognize him in his street clothes. Everyone looks so different in a verbal, animated state.

On the drive back to Two Dog Farm, Brian and I compare notes about the retreat. We stop at a diner and order a huge meal. Brian gets a cheeseburger with onion rings and a chocolate shake.

I order a grilled Swiss cheese with a side of fries and a root beer float.

"It was awesome," Brian says between bites of his burger. "I was dead by the second day. I thought I would never make it, but then something happened. I gave in to the pain like it was my friend, like the pain was teaching me. Wasn't it amazing?"

"It *was* amazing. Although I thought I was going to kill you a couple of times," I say.

"Really?" he says. "I didn't sense any hostility from you, and usually I'm very sensitive to that sort of thing."

"I liked the chanting. And the man with one leg. If he hadn't been sitting opposite me I don't think I would have made it." I stuff a handful of fries in my mouth.

"A guy with one leg? I didn't even notice him. You know I spent a month at an ashram in India and it was great, but nothing like this. So intense. The sitting. The zazen. It's like a Berlitz course in spirituality. I mean, Mags, don't you feel incredibly evolved?"

"My legs feel sore and my neck is out of whack and, yeah, I guess I do feel more evolved than usual. I think the incense made me high."

"And you haven't smoked, have you?"

"No, I haven't. It's a week today."

"Wow, it was great. And the guy with the violin. Wasn't that fucking amazing?"

"It was. It really was amazing."

We spend the night at Two Dog Farm. We both are dead tired and go to bed about nine o'clock and sleep until noon the next day. We have a huge breakfast at Sally's Pantry Kitchen. French toast and eggs.

We get back to New York in the late afternoon. Brian drops me off in front of my building.

"Thanks," I say, getting my bag out of the trunk. "It was good to get away—way away."

"You're doing great, Mags. Call me if you need me." And off he drives. And here I stand on the curb in front of my building. It feels strange to be in the city after days in the silence and peace of the mountains. I get up to my apartment and unlock the door.

"Maggie," a voice calls out. It's Sandy and she is sitting on my couch. Mr. Ed dances around at my feet. "I didn't want to startle you. Ed and I have been waiting for you to get back. I thought you said you'd be back this afternoon."

"How long have you been here?" I ask.

"An hour maybe. Look, all hell broke loose. I'm going downtown to stay at a friend's place. She is out on tour with a show and she said I can stay at her duplex, but I can't bring Ed. So I was wondering if—"

"Hang on a sec." I cut her off midsentence. "What hell broke loose, and why are you going there?"

"Dick told me to get out. I saw Todd again," she says. "It was going to be the last time, but when I got home Dick was waiting for me. He had packed a couple of suitcases for me and told me to leave. That he was disgusted." Sandy sobs and buries her head in her hands. "So I've stayed here the last two nights, and then I heard from Kelly that I could stay there, but the building doesn't allow dogs and Dick said he won't take care of Ed because he's really my dog and besides he was a witness to my indiscretion. In fact, Dick said Ed was an accessory. Can you believe that? I don't know why I didn't leave him years ago. He's an idiot. Do you know we only have sex once a month? For years. Once a month? Is that normal?"

"Wow. I'm sorry. Of course I can look after Ed." I reach down and pet Ed and then look for Bixby. I find him lying in the bathtub, his favorite hideout. Sandy is getting her things together when I go back to the living room, carrying the Bixer. "Are you all right? Do you want to talk? Have a cup of coffee?"

"I need to get going. Thanks, Maggie. I'm sorry," she says.

"Are you going to see Todd again?" I ask.

"I don't know. It seems so complicated now. It takes all the joy out of everything. Why bother? What's so great about love and sex, anyway? I've been married to Dick for twenty years. Twenty years. We've worked and saved. We've eaten thousands of meals together and filed joint tax returns, then one day this somebody comes along and wants me. Really, really wants me, and makes me feel beautiful and sexy, and he wants me more than once a month. And I give in for a while, but then I let it go, and that's when Dick, Mr. I-love-you-but-only-on-the-third-Saturday-of-the-month, tells me to get the hell out of his life."

"He's probably hurt."

"I'm hurt too. I'm going to go. I'll call you, and here, take this." Sandy hands me a wad of bills. "Here's money for dog food."

"You don't have to."

"It's Dick's money. Take it." Sandy leans down and gives Ed a hug. "You be good for Mags." Then she picks up her bags and leaves.

"Well, Ed," I say, "welcome to your new home."

I unpack my bag and put some water on for coffee. I'm dying for some caffeine. The light on my answering machine is blinking, which means I have messages. I walk over and look at the display window. The number seven flashes on and off. I wait until I make my coffee before I listen to them. I'm sure one of them is from Jack. I feel it. I press the play button. The first one is from Charles, saying he's sorry about the whole video art thing and that Chad is in fact a great guy. "We want to take you out for a really expensive meal. What do you say? Please, you know I can't live without you. Call me." Charles knows I'm a sucker for pleading. And expensive meals.

The next two are from Dee-Honey giving me the call times for the *Pied Piper* show this weekend and then calling back to give me the revised time. "Call me to confirm," she says.

The fourth call is a hang-up. I hate that. Maybe it's Jack. The next is my friend Patty, followed by a message from my agent: "Call me as soon as you get in. I've got an audition for you on Monday."

The next message is a voice I don't recognize. "You don't know me. My name is Bob. I'm a friend of Jack Eremus. Call me when you get this. It's important."

My heart almost stops. I quickly copy down the number he left. Why in the world would a friend of Jack's call me? I sit down and take deep breaths. I feel anxious. Free floating. Like I could pass out.

Bixby climbs in my lap and I scratch his head. "I'm sure it's nothing, Bix. Maybe it's a surprise birthday party. I can't remember when Jack said his birthday is or if he ever did."

"It's in December," I hear a tinkling voice say. Goodie is standing on the arm of the sofa. "December seventeenth."

"Well, where have you been? And how do you know Jack's birthday?"

"He told you the first night you met."

"Oh, right. I don't remember much about that first night."

"I do," Goodie says rolling his eyes. "I saw the whole thing."

"You were there?"

"Don't you get it yet? I'm everywhere." He puts a little hand on my shoulder. "I think you better make that call."

"Do you know what it's about?" I ask him.

"Just call, Maggie," Goodie says flying onto my knee. "I'll be right here."

I dial the number. It rings six times, and then the same voice that was on my message machine answers.

"Hi," I say. "This is Maggie. You left a message for me. About Jack."

"Yeah, this is his friend Bob. We went to high school together. I got your number off his cell phone. I'm sorry to tell you . . ."

"Oh, God," I gasp.

"Jack died two days ago. He had an aneurysm. It was very quick. I thought you would want to know."

I feel like I'm going to faint.

"Do you want to take some time and call me back? I'm sorry, I know this is a shock. Everyone is in shock."

"Yes. I'll do that. Where was he?"

"He was driving and luckily he was able to steer the car off the road before he hit anyone. The doctors said the pain would be paralyzing, but Jack managed to get off the highway before he went unconscious. Someone stopped and called for help but by the time they got there he was . . ." Bob's voice trails off. I can tell he is crying.

"Thank you for calling me, Bob." My voice breaks. "Oh, God. I'm so sorry."

"Me too." Bob sobs and we hang up.

"I'm sorry, Maggie," Goodie says.

"How could you let this happen?"

"I didn't let it happen. I have no control over these things."

"What about all your magic?"

"I don't have that kind of magic, Maggie, nobody does."

"You're my fairy god-queen. You're supposed to take care of me."

"I can't take care of you Maggie, I can only love you. That's all anyone can do for anyone else."

"I've got to get out of here," I say, getting up and stepping into my sandals. I grab my wallet and keys. "And don't you come with me, Goodie. I want to be alone." Mr. Ed whines and follows me to the door.

"Sorry, Ed. I'm not taking you with me," I say. He sits back on his haunches and looks so miserable I relent.

"Okay," I say, getting his leash. "But no talking; I don't feel like any chitchat. Understand?" Mr. Ed nods.

I get out on the street, I can barely walk, my legs feel heavy and my chest is tight. It's early evening. The air is warm and the sky is turning a pretty sunset pink. Slowly Ed and I walk over to Riverside Park. I have to stop every half block or so and take big gulps of air. Ed sits quietly at my feet until I can move again. When we get to the river, we sit and watch the sun go down. Jack told me once that as a kid he thought God pulled a big circus tent over the earth at night to make it dark, and that the stars were little in the tent where the sun peeked through. I sit completely still in meditation like at the monastery. People pass me by, people on rollerblades, on bicycles, pushing baby strollers — people living their lives.

NOTE TO SELF . . .

Don't expect your fairy godmother to have all the answers.

Ed curls up next to me on the bench. The sun slips behind the buildings across the river. The sky turns from pink to mauve. The streetlights come on and reflect off the river as the warm summer evening rests an arm around my shoulders. I wonder if I'm in shock. The tears have stopped but I can't move. I can only sit and stare. Maybe if I don't move, nothing else bad will ever happen. Maybe if I don't move, Jack's soul will return to earth and reclaim its place, and the corpse that is now cooling at some funeral home in Queens will start to breathe again and the heart will pump and Jack will rise up from the dead. A miracle, a medical anomaly, a mistake by the coroner—it happens. People have been buried alive. Doctors make mistakes and so does God, if indeed God is the one who determines fate, the one who gives and takes life. God made a mistake with Jack, dammit, and if I sit still enough and pray hard enough and believe deeply enough God will perform a miracle and Jack will take a breath and live. I sit perfectly still and stare straight ahead. Ed sits next to me. We say our separate prayers. Finally Mr. Ed stirs and licks my face. It's dark and the lights in the buildings across the river have started to come on.

"Okay, Ed," I say. "Let's go." Ed jumps off the bench and we leave the park. I decide not to go home. I walk down Broadway to the Dublin House. I could use a drink. It's been almost a week since I've had a one. I won't smoke. I just need a shot of scotch. I can't give up everything. Ed and I sit at the end of the bar and I order. Scotch straight up. The bartender delivers my drink. I take a sip. It burns going down, which is the way I like it. I like to know that something is happening. Then it hits my empty stomach and goes to work. I take a deep breath and feel the neurons leaping back and forth between the synapses in my brain, and everything slows down and I relax. I don't need all that information—all those feelings. I take another sip and I can feel my shoulders drop an inch or two. Mr. Ed looks at me from his position on the floor. I reach down, pick him up, and put him in the barstool next to me. The Dublin is slow this time of night.

"Bowl of water for my friend," I say to the bartender. And then I smile my million-dollar smile. In the half light of the bar I can still pass for a pretty young thing, especially with some scotch in my belly. I drain the glass. "And another round for me," I call out. He brings the drink and a bowl for Ed.

"My name is Artie," he says. "And we're really not supposed to serve anyone with more than two legs, but I'll make an exception because the boss isn't here and your friend looks thirsty. I had a Westie when I was a kid. They're cool."

When Artie was a kid wasn't long ago. He looks like he's about eighteen, but I'm sure to be serving liquor he has to be older.

"Thanks. Mr. Ed appreciates it, don't you Ed?" And sure enough Ed barks in agreement. God, he's a smart dog. I should try to find him an agent—as long as he's going to be living with me for a while he should earn his keep.

I finish my drink and Artie buys me another round. "On the house," he says, putting the glass down in front of me. "You're the woman on the cereal commercials, aren't you?"

"Special K? Yeah that's me," I say.

"Wow, I'm an actor too."

"Great." I say. Someone from the other end of the bar orders another brew and Artie hops to it. The scotch has definitely done its job. The room seems fuzzy and I feel hot. Mr. Ed has dozed off on his barstool. One drink and he's out.

One night Jack and I came into the Dublin for a drink. We played the vintage pinball machine in the back and walked home

to my place holding hands — one evening in a whole series of
evenings. We made love and fell asleep and woke up and took a
shower and made love again. We made love a lot. It was electric.
Exciting. Jack made me feel like nothing had passed me by, that
everything was in the future; that forty-one was just a number,
an illusion, that you really could be as young as you felt, and that
the feeling would last forever. Where was Jack going? What was
he thinking in the last moment before he was struck with pain?
Was he happy? Was he wondering what's next? What was the next
thing going to be? Did he get my message? Wow. I'd forgotten
that. I had left him a message on his voice mail when I was in
West Virginia, saying I was sorry. Did he get it? I hope he did.

"Hey, Artie," I say too loudly. "Got a cigarette?"

"Sure, Special K, but you got to smoke it outside." He bounds
back with a cigarette and a light.

"I know," I say as he lights me up. "Come on, Ed." I pay Artie
and leave a five-dollar tip. Mr. Ed and I head up Broadway. I'm
drunker than I thought, and now the cigarette is making me more
light-headed. Why am I doing this? Why? I get to my corner and
Mr. Ed turns, but I pull him in the other direction.

"We're not going home, Ed," I say. I walk a few more blocks
and find the building I want. It's almost midnight. I perch on the
front steps of the brownstone and Ed curls up next to me. A few
people pass. I bum another cigarette. Then I see a familiar figure
coming down the block with a dog in tow.

"Hey, remember me?" I say with a slight slur.

"Sure," Spider says. "My damsel in distress."

"Jack died. Remember Jack? You met him that night. Something happened in his brain. It was sudden."

"And you've been drinking," Spider says, sitting down next to me. Abby and Mr. Ed sniff at each other.

"I didn't mean to, but I went to a bar because I didn't know where else to go and, dammit, it's not fair. Everybody keeps dying, why is that?" I start to cry, and then I cry and cry and cry. "Do you know that his mother abandoned him, ran off with a saxophone player. Mothers!" I say. "They get away with murder and yet . . ."

"Yet, what?" Spider asks, rubbing my back.

"In a crisis, that's who you want. When I was attacked in the park that's who I cried out for."

"Is that a bad thing?"

"Only if there is no mother around to help. Then you're on you own, like Jack was in the end."

"We're all alone in the end," Spider says.

"Yeah, and yet we're all still waiting for Godot."

"Who?"

"Godot. It's the name of a play by an Irish existentialist," I say. "It's a comedy."

"I see," Spider says in a soothing voice.

I cry some more and then he walks me home. He helps me find my key and gets me into my apartment.

"I'm going to write my phone number here. Get some sleep and call me in the morning. You're going to be all right. I'm sorry about Jack, and you're right, life isn't fair, but that doesn't mean you get to quit and go home. It ain't that easy."

Spider leaves and I sit and stare at the wall, and I want to do as Spider said and get some sleep, but I can't. Not yet. I put my sandals back on and head for the door. Mr. Ed is right at my heels.

"I'm just going down to the deli for a few things," I say. "You stay here and keep Bixby company." And I am out the door. I am definitely feeling the effects of the scotch, but it's not enough. I weave my way down to Amsterdam Avenue and go to Vinnie's Deli, which is a happening place at one a.m., with the lottery machine running at full tilt. The New York jackpot is over ten million, so everybody thinks they're a winner. A couple of guys from the hood are leaning on a car in front of the store talking about shit. It's hard to figure out exactly what shit, but from the pitch of their voices and the animation of their conversation it is some pretty important shit. I get a six-pack of Miller Lite and a pack of Marlboros. Vinnie behind the counter smiles and I smile back.

"How's it going?" he asks.

"It's going," I say.

I've been coming into this place for the past ten years for cigarettes and beer, and the past two weeks are the longest time Vinnie and I have been apart. His brother runs the place during the day and Vinnie is the night guy. "Have you been out of town?" he asks.

"Upstate for a while," I say, taking my change from the twenty-dollar bill I handed him.

"Have a good one," Vin says.

"Yeah, you too." I leave with my contraband. At least it feels like contraband. I don't wait to get home to open the cigarettes and light up. I fumble around in the bag for the matches and light one as I walk, then I sit out on the front stoop and crack open a beer. I'm drunk but not too drunk. I'm high enough to feel like I'm in an alternate universe, but not so high I'm stupid. And for now I like being in a different universe, the one where things don't happen—nothing happens and nothing goes wrong and life is one endless evening with the person you want to be with and the food you want to eat and the music you want to listen to and the place you want to be and you stay there forever.

I hear laughter down the block. A couple is coming in my direction. They are wrapped around each other and giggling and stumbling toward me. As they get closer I realize it is Dick and a young woman with strawberry blonde hair. She is probably early twenties, and seems to be wild about Dick—no pun intended. I wish I could disappear. Dick looks up and sees me and freezes.

"Hey, Bucko," I say. "How's it hanging?" Oops. Now that's not nice.

"Maggie," Dick says, poison darting off the word. He searches in his pocket for his keys. Miss Strawberry Blonde gets very quiet and prim. The whole picture is getting clearer. Apparently the fact that Dick was having sex with Sandy only once a month doesn't mean he was having sex only once a month. I suddenly have reason to think he is actually quite active in that department. They make their way past me and get the key in the door and escape from my knowing gaze. The things one learns on a summer's eve.

I take the rest of my six-pack and go up to my apartment. Mr. Ed and Bixby are asleep on the couch. I open another beer and sit by the window and smoke another cigarette. I fold myself into the chair and place the ashtray on the overstuffed arm. I take a long pull on the beer and lean back and smoke and smoke and smoke. The nicotine and beer and scotch have successfully conspired to ease my mind and numb my feelings, but they haven't made me truly drunk. At least not so drunk that I can just pass out. So I sit and watch the lights flicker off in the apartments around the courtyard as one by one my neighbors brush their teeth and pat the cat and kiss the kids and fold down the sheets and go to bed. Day is done.

When I was in high school I competed in poetry reading competitions. The poetry readers and the debaters traveled to events at other high schools. And if you were good enough you competed in the districts and the states. I made it to states my junior year. I won second prize and lost my virginity in a Ramada Inn to the captain of the debating team. I always find that expression interesting. Lost my virginity. Like something happened, I didn't see it happen, couldn't remember what happened, but one minute I had my virginity and next minute it was gone, and now as I reflect maybe *lost* is the perfect word. Because often it does happen like that, and before you know it you're searching around on the floor, under the bed, in the medicine cabinet for something you thought you had a minute ago but now it's gone. And once you've lost it there is no getting it back.

I can still recite the poem I read or rather "interpreted" when I won second prize. It begins,

> *The day is done, and the darkness*
> *Falls from the wings of Night,*
> *As a feather is wafted downward*
> *From an eagle in his flight.*
>
> *I see the lights of the village*
> *Gleam through the rain and the mist,*
> *And a feeling of sadness comes o'er me*
> *That my soul cannot resist.*
>
> *A feeling of sadness and longing,*
> *That is not akin to pain,*

And resembles sorrows only
As the mist resembles the rain.

It's Longfellow's poem, "Day Is Done." I recite it slowly in hushed tones. Bixby climbs in my lap and Mr. Ed snores on the couch.

Come, read to me some poem,
Some simple and heartfelt lay,
That shall soothe this restless feeling,
And banish the thoughts of day.

I don't even have a picture of Jack. Not one snapshot. I'm not a picture taker. My sister-in-law carries a camera with her at all times and constantly records moments. She has hundreds of photo albums filled with snapshots of her kids eating at McDonald's, swimming in the ocean, standing at the bus stop, sleeping in a chair in front of the TV. I would give anything to have one picture of Jack. His face recorded forever. I have an umbrella he left by my front door and a pair of tube socks. And I found my virginity. Yes, and it's not the beer talking. I felt like a virgin again when I made love to Jack, I guess because he made me feel young, he made me feel the world was new and fresh, not burdened with loss.

I open another beer and light a cigarette. All the lights in the buildings are out. I, alone, sit with a flickering candle watching, waiting.

"Jack," I say in the darkness. "I'm so sorry." The candle sputters out. Bixby shifts gently in my lap then settles back to sleep. Day is done.

18

*A*pollo and his chariot screech through my bedroom window right at the break of day. I put a hand over my injured eye, which is still very sensitive to light, and turn on my side to find myself nose to nose with Mr. Ed. Bixby is on the other side, still traveling in dreamland. I have become a single woman with pets. Oh, God.

I get up to go to the bathroom. My head is full of mothballs and my mouth tastes like old shoe leather. Before I make it halfway across the room I remember what I wanted to forget. I remember Jack is dead. I sink down to my knees as the weight of grief settles on my shoulders. I know this feeling. It's like a shackle on the heart. Breathe, I tell myself. The phone rings. I let the machine pick up and hear the voice of Jack's friend say, "Maggie, it's Bob. I wanted to let you know."

"I'm here," I say grabbing the phone.

"How are you doing?" he asks.

"Okay. And you?"

"All right, I guess," he says.

"Tell me more about what happened. Do you mind?"

"Sure. It helps to talk about it. Makes it more real. Like I said, he had sort of a seizure from the pain, it just came over him. But he was able to get off the road. Thank God. Sheryl didn't know what was happening."

"Sheryl?" I ask.

"Oh, right. Didn't I mention that before? He was with a friend. She wasn't hurt. Just shook up, in shock. She and Jack have known each other since high school."

"Were they a couple?"

"Off and on," Bob says.

"I see. And were they on?" I ask.

"Yeah, I think they were back on," he says. "Look, I'm sorry. I know that you and Jack were . . . well, he told me about you . . ."

"Really?" I say.

"He was confused. Jack was a great guy, and he certainly wouldn't have wanted you to be hurt. He got your last message."

"How do you know? He never called me."

"He had saved it, so I know it meant a lot to him."

"I see. And, yet, he was back with Sheryl."

"For the moment. What's it matter now anyway?"

"You're right. What's it matter?"

"I called to tell you about the service today. If you want to come," Bob says. "It's at Green Lawns Funeral Home. At four p.m. The address is 188-11 Hillside Avenue."

"Thanks. I'll see," I say.

"I shouldn't have said anything. I didn't mean to mention Sheryl, but it's just that—she and Jack—I've known them both for so long, since junior high."

"It's okay, Bob. Jack was a great guy, and I only knew him . . . what? A month, maybe. I'm sorry for you and I'm sorry for Sheryl."

"Thanks. Maybe I'll see you later."

"Maybe."

We hang up. My scratched cornea is throbbing. I put in eye-drops. I've stopped wearing the eye patch. It itches like crazy and I got tired of people calling me Old One Eye and the like.

I'm oddly unaffected by the revelation of Sheryl. Every guy has a Sheryl, the high school sweetheart, the girl next door, first love, first sex, and first heartbreak. It all makes sense now. I was the stopover between sweetheart and wife. The older woman with no strings attached. A cliché. Joke's on me. However, it's hard to act the victim when the other player is lying in a coffin, stiff as spray starch, at the Green Lawns Funeral Home in Queens. Joke's on Jack.

I get dressed and head to the park with Mr. Ed. I stop at the Columbus Café for a coffee to go. It's a beautiful day. The sky is crystal blue; it's seventy-five degrees with very little humidity. Perfect, a perfect summer day. Ed and I walk over to Bethesda Fountain. The Angel glistens in the sunlight and the fountain water sparkles as it cascades under her feet. I dip my hands in the water and splash it on my face.

"Forgive me, dear Angel of the Waters. And carry Jack's soul swiftly to the bright shining light of forever." I dip my hand again and sprinkle some water on Mr. Ed. "And bless my four-legged friend with happy days and long life."

Ed barks and bites at the air. I take him to the dog run on the other side of the park. When we get in the enclosed area I take off Ed's leash and set the little guy free. He runs in a circle and then does a double hop and chases a poodle back and forth the length of the run. I sit down on a bench, close my eyes, and tilt my face to the sun and try to think about nothing.

"Nice day," a voice says, and I feel someone sit down on the bench next to me. I nod in agreement and keep my eyes shut, hoping whoever it is will get the message that I want to be left alone.

"Not too much humidity," the voice continues. Apparently the message has not been received. I open one eye and peek at the intruder. Oh God, it's Todd, Sandy's paramour. I'm trapped.

"Hi," I say.

"Hi yourself," Todd says. Well, it certainly wasn't his witty banter that got Sandy all hot and bothered.

"I'm just getting a little R and R," I say hoping he'll take the hint and leave.

"How's Sandy? I haven't seen her," he asks, plunging into the meat of the matter.

"Look, I don't really know. She's moved downtown for a while."

"Without the dog? She left her dog behind?" Todd asks.

"Well, the building, you know, rules, couldn't take him," I say, desperate to get back to thinking about nothing.

"I think that is irresponsible," Todd says. "You don't really know anybody, do you? I mean, you think you do, but then the seams start to fray and the insides start to show and the picture isn't so pretty, is it?" Todd reaches into a pocket and pulls out a silver flask. He unscrews the top and takes a nip and then offers it to me.

"Chivas Regal," he says. "I only drink top shelf because otherwise it's just booze, know what I mean?"

"It's a little early, don't you think?"

"Early? What difference does it make? I haven't slept in two weeks."

"God," I say. "You must be exhausted."

"I'm never exhausted," he says, still offering the flask. "I have too much energy to be exhausted. I could launch a rocket to the moon with my energy."

I take the flask and suck down some scotch. It is definitely top shelf. "That's nice," I say, handing it back to him.

"Finish it," he says. "There's more where that came from."

"Well," I say. "Here's to love." Shit I don't know what made me say that.

"Yeah, love," Todd says. "It will kill you, but what a way to go." Then he puts his head back and laughs the dirtiest laugh I've ever heard. This man oozes sex. I wonder if maybe he's in the porn industry. Boy, I can see how Sandy didn't have a chance; she probably got down on her knees and begged. Oh, my God. What am I thinking? I shake my head a couple of times. The scotch has really hit me. Maybe it's laced with something, what's that new designer drug? It starts with an *O*.

"So what's your story?" Todd asks.

Boy, what a lame line, I think to myself. This guy is a sleaze machine. "Well, you know . . ." I say.

"Are you in love at the moment?" he asks, looking directly at me with his ice blue eyes surrounded by long black lashes. He looks like a youngish Paul Newman, like Paul Newman in *Cool Hand Luke*. I love that movie.

"No, not really. The guy I was seeing . . . died," I say.

"Really?" Todd says. "I'm so sorry. Was it sudden?"

"Very," I say, looking right into the ice blue eyes.

"So sad. You must be heartbroken."

"I am. Except I found out he was seeing his old girlfriend again."

"Oh, that's too bad."

"Yeah. I guess I really don't know how to feel about it." The heat from Todd's body is palpable. "But now it seems so incidental, considering."

"Feelings are never incidental," he says, looking me up and down. "Why don't we take a walk?" He takes my arm and gently pulls me off the bench. "The dogs are fine in here. I want to show you something."

"Okay," I mumble. I'm sure that scotch had some of that O drug; otherwise he would never be able to get me to go with him because I know exactly what he is doing. He wants to get me in that underbrush. Well, let's see how far he gets. I hate men who are so smug they think they can get whatever they want. We leave the dog run and, sure enough, he starts walking toward some trees that are surrounded by thick shrubs.

"There is this wonderful little copse over here and underneath it is the most magical spot in the whole park."

Copse, I think who the hell uses a word like *copse*?

"It's like something out of *Alice in Wonderland*," he says, pulling apart some branches. "Right in here."

Sure, big guy, let's see who gets what in the magical copse. I bend down and duck walk into the brush and sure enough there is a little open space. The sun filters through the leaves and shadows dance on the ground. There are even a few wildflowers, delicate pink blooms. I think they're called coralbells. And then I feel a hand on my backside as I crawl toward the center. The hand moves down my leg. He's got to be crazy if he thinks I'm as easy as Sandy. Then both of his hands are on my upturned butt, petting and caressing. His breathing is getting heavy.

"You have an amazing ass," he says. I sway to his touch in spite of myself. His hands move to my underside and cup my breasts. Then he fondles them slowly. I moan. He finds my nipples and pinches them gently. A chill runs down my spine. Todd pulls me up toward him. Our bodies move in rhythm, his underside against my backside. He kisses the back of my neck while he explores my body, running his hands across my breasts, lingering, then moving south. He inches his way down to my soft spot, my happy house, my mound of pleasure. And when he reaches it he begins his work. I'm putty in his hands. I turn my head to the side and find his mouth. The heat from his lips is like fire. I'm lost in it. He rips my shirt open down the front. I turn and am on my back facing him. He is a god. He pulls his shirt over his head to reveal a torso that is ripped and rippled. He pulls down my jeans. I open his belt. He groans with pleasure. I unzip his fly. His cock springs out fully erect. It's magnificent. Todd is about to guide his bigness into my love canal when a loud voice interjects itself into the scene.

"What the hell is going on in there?" it says. "NYPD. Come out of there at once."

Oh, my God. My mind clears. Todd rolls off me and scrambles to get his pants on. My clothes are strewn over the ground. I reach for my shirt and start to put it on.

Goodie buzzes onto a low hanging branch. "Really Maggie," he says, shaking his head and tsking. "This is not pretty, not pretty at all. Get your clothes on and get out of here."

"Save the lecture, Goodie," I hiss at him. I struggle to get in my pants. Todd has already gone out to face the music. I manage to get dressed and then crawl out of the "magic place." Amazingly, I hear laughter and look up to see Todd and the policeman buddying up. Todd offers the cop a cigarette and the cop lights up. I get to my feet and have the instinct to start running. But I don't, mainly because I can find only one of my sandals.

"Look, I don't want to cause you any grief," the cop says and winks at Todd, "but we can't let this go on in broad daylight. Get it? Broad?"

"Yeah, broad . . . daylight," Todd says. "That is funny." And the two of them collapse again in guffaws. I have the awful sensation of being the butt (and more literally than I'd like) of a fraternity house prank.

"So what's the story, guys?" I say with as much chutzpah as I can muster. Todd turns to me as if I'm just a grace note in the duet that he and the officer of the law are now performing.

"What's that?" he says. I notice for the first time that his hair is dyed, yes, dyed. Well tinted at least—maybe Grecian Formula or Just-for-Shoes? And he is wearing, oh my God, pancake makeup and a thick gold chain around his neck. Why didn't I notice that before? That must have been why he looked momentarily like a god to me. The sun reflecting off the cheap gold chain and then refracting off the Grecian formula "summer blond" dye on his thinning hair. I wish I could disappear. I can't believe that not three minutes ago this bozo (is he actually wearing madras clam diggers?) had me in the hot throes of unbridled ecstasy.

"Sex is just biology," Goodie whispers in my ear. "It makes you stupid—that along with the scotch on an empty stomach. Now find your other glass slipper and let's get out of here." And for once I couldn't agree more.

"Well, then, fellas, I'm going to get going." I see my sandal

NOTE TO SELF . . .

*No more drinking
before noon and never
at the dog run.*

sticking out of the magical copse. "I have some appointments this afternoon." I reach down, retrieve my sandal, and put it on my foot. And then put that foot in front of my other foot and keep walking. I get to the dog run where I find Mr. Ed panting mad.

"How dare you go off and leave me with this mangy pack of dogs!" he barks at me as I fasten his leash onto his collar.

"Sorry, little guy, just momentary insanity, God help me!" Then Ed and I hightail it out of the park with Goodie buzzing along beside us. We get to Central Park West and I stop to catch my breath. What the hell was that about? How did I end up half naked in broad daylight with Todd, the sex maniac, working his mojo on me? Thank goodness for NYPD's coitus interruptus or rather cop-us interruptus. What is a grown woman with two brain cells to rub together doing having sex in the park with a strange man wearing pancake makeup? I feel like I just dodged a bullet—again. I need something to eat. My head is pounding, and my eye is starting to throb.

"You need some protein," Goodie says. "Meat and potatoes. A good old-fashioned meal."

"I don't remember when I ate last."

"Get a good meal. You'll feel better. I've got to scoot. I'm due at a christening across town."

"Goodie, you knew about Jack, didn't you?"

"What do you mean?"

"When I got the message to call his friend, you already knew Jack was dead, didn't you?"

"I had a feeling."

"What kind of feeling?"

"A sense of change in the air. A flicker of light that flashes then disappears. A slight disturbance in the atmosphere. It's happening all the time, Maggie, you know that, and sometimes it happens close to home. Get something to eat, and not just pretzels. I'll check with you later." And off he goes.

A slight disturbance in the atmosphere? Not so slight when you're standing nearby. I wonder how Jack's dad is doing. He must be devastated. And his mother, I wonder if she will fly back from Las Vegas for the service. Jack mentioned her only once when he told me she ran off with a saxophone player and that his dad was suicidal. Geez, it's always the mother.

When I get back to the apartment I call information in Queens and ask for a listing for Eremus.

"E-r-e-m-u-s," I spell for the operator.

"I have a Donald Eremus or a John on Forty-third Road."

"John, I think."

She gives me the number.

"Can you give me that address?"

"142-53 Forty-third Road."

"Thanks," I say jotting it down on the back of a take-out menu from the House of Noodles. Luckily there aren't hundreds of Eremuses listed in Queens. I'm sure the name was John. It's got to be. And it makes me feel better, like having his address will somehow keep him safe. I strip off my clothes and jump in the shower. I let the hot water wash away the feel of Todd's hands on my body. Grief is a powerful aphrodisiac and can drive a person to some very unexpected places. Geez, what was I thinking? But I tell myself I'm not going to feel guilty about this Todd thing.

I'm not, I'm not, I'm not. Poor Sandy. Poor me. Poor all of us, out there looking for love in all the wrong places. I don't think Jack was a wrong place, just a wrong time. Chemistry is a funny thing. The elements don't have to be compatible in order to create heat—after all, it takes a lot of friction to make fire.

I scrub myself with a loofah sponge and lavender soap. Should I go to the funeral? What would be the point? I can mourn for Jack in my own way; besides, I was just a detour in his journey, a coffee break along the short road he traveled. A big sob wells up in my throat, I heave a heavy sigh, and the tears start to pour out.

It's almost one o'clock when I get out of the shower. I open my refrigerator and look for something to fill my belly. There is a half-eaten container of Cozy's rice pudding. I get a spoon and settle down on the couch. I eat one tiny bite at a time and let the pudding warm in my mouth before I swallow it down. It's comforting and sweet and milky. A few years ago I became a rice pudding connoisseur. Wherever I went I ordered it, and graded the restaurant by the quality of its pudding. After a few years of investigation I discovered that the best rice pudding in the continental United States is served five blocks from my apartment at the New Wave Diner on Broadway. It's very smooth. They serve it warm and top it with Reddi-wip. It's as close to heaven as you can get for $2.95.

I tried to turn Jack on to rice pudding, but he was a Häagen-Dazs man and had no desire to switch. Another heavy sigh escapes my lungs, followed by more tears, more grief, and more tiny bites of pudding. I finish what's left in the container. I have three hours before the funeral. I don't know what to do. I find my pack of Marlboros from last night and light one. I get a beer out of the refrigerator. Then I remember I was supposed to call Spider.

I find where he jotted down his number. I dial. The phone rings three times.

"Hello," he answers.

"Spider? It's Maggie."

"How're you doing?"

"Not great. You told me to call. I didn't want you to worry."

"Thanks. What's going on? Did you get some sleep?"

"A little," I say. "I've already been through a day and a half and it's only one o'clock."

"I see," Spider says.

"Jack's funeral is today at four. I can't decide whether to go or not. I'm not very familiar with Queens. I wouldn't even know how to get there."

"The subway goes to Queens. Or take a cab."

"I didn't think of that."

"Look, I've got to run. I'm working an early shift. Maggie, try not to drink. That will only make everything worse."

"I'm gonna try."

"Good. It won't bring Jack back and it won't make you feel better."

"I had some rice pudding. That sort of helped." I don't tell Spider about the earlier part of my day. Or the beer I just took out of my refrigerator.

"Good," Spider says. "Lay off the scotch and stick to rice pudding. That's an excellent plan. Call me tomorrow."

"Sure, okay." We hang up. There's something comforting about Spider wanting me to call him tomorrow. I bet he figures that if I say I'll call him, I won't get drunk and kill myself, and, who knows, maybe he's right. And maybe tomorrow I won't get drunk, but today all bets are already off so I finish the beer.

"I'll think about it tomorrow," I say aloud in my best Scarlett O'Hara imitation. "Because tomorrow is another day."

The phone rings and I pick it up. It's Patty.

"Where have you been?" she blurts out. "I've been worried about you. I had a dream that you were in a boat and it started to sink. Isn't that crazy? Anyway, I wanted to make sure you weren't treading water somewhere, waiting for me to rescue you." Then she laughs. And I laugh too. And then I cry. Big loud sobs right into the phone.

"Maggie, what's wrong?" she asks.

"You know that young guy I was seeing?" I say.

"Yeah, sure."

"He's dead."

"What?" Patty asks incredulously.

"Dead," I say. "Died of an aneurysm three days ago. I was at a monastery in the mountains, and when I got back there was a message from a friend of his asking me to call him, and when I did, he told me Jack was dead. The funeral is today at four in Queens. I don't know whether or not to go. Oh, my God, Patty, I don't know what to do."

"I'm on my way," she says without a moment's hesitation. "I'll be there in half an hour and we'll figure it out. Go in the bathroom and rinse your face with warm water and then sit on the couch and wait for me. Don't think about anything until I get there. All right?"

"All right," I say in a very small, very fragile voice. "Thanks, Patty."

But she is already off the phone and out the door. Help is on the way. I go to the bathroom, like Patty told me, and wash my face with warm water, get another beer out of the fridge, and then I sit on the couch and wait. I think about nothing. I take one breath after another, between sips of beer, like I learned at the retreat. Less than half an hour later my buzzer rings. I get up and talk into the intercom.

"It's Patty," she says back. I buzz her in the building and then open my front door. Mr. Ed runs out into the hall and looks through the stair railing with his tail wagging. I hear Patty making her way up the four flights of stairs.

"Mags, honey," she calls.

"I'm here," I say looking over the railing. And there she is, my dear friend Patty. She is carrying some pink tulips wrapped in paper.

"I'm so sorry, my friend," she says, handing me the flowers. A new round of tears pops out of my eyes.

Patty puts her arms around me and rocks me gently. "I knew you were in need of help in some way. I just knew it," she says. "I was so worried."

We go into the apartment. I hunt under the sink for something to put the flowers in. "Let me do that," Patty says. I sit down on the couch and let her fuss with the flowers. "I'm going to put some water on for tea." Then she comes over and sits next to me.

"Tell me about it," Patty says, taking my hand. "Tell me everything."

And the words come pouring out. I tell her how Jack came into my life and how he changed it and how wonderful he was and how unfair I was to him and how I sent him away and how he came back and how I sent him away again because I was so afraid of how good it felt and couldn't let myself trust it and how I left him a message when I was in West Virginia asking for his forgiveness and telling him I loved him and then the call from

Bob about Jack being dead and then finding out Jack was seeing his old girlfriend again and that's who he was with when he died and how I've been drinking and smoking again after I tried to quit and how I ended up in the underbrush with Todd in the park having sex and how disgusting that was and that the funeral is at four o'clock and I have no idea how to get to Queens or even if I should go because I don't know anyone and I don't want to see the girlfriend but I do wonder how Jack's dad is doing because Jack told me he was suicidal when his wife left so I can imagine what he is feeling now and I'm curious if Jack's mother will show up for the funeral with her saxophone-playing boyfriend from Las Vegas. It all comes pouring out, nonstop, in one breath.

Then the teakettle whistles and Patty gets up to pour the water. "Let's let it steep," she says, sitting back down. "And let's figure out how we're going to get to Queens."

"You'll go with me?" I ask, dabbing my eyes.

"Are you kidding? I wouldn't miss this for the world. It's sounds better than the last season of *Dynasty*. I'm going to call my cousin. She lives in Queens and will be able to tell us exactly how to get to the funeral home. You go change into something appropriate, and I'll get the directions."

I go in the bedroom and look through my closet. I have only one black dress without sequins, and even that seems dressy for a four o'clock funeral, so I put on a pair of black slacks, a pair of strap sandals, and beige silk jacket. Simple yet sophisticated. My eyes are blotchy and my skin looks like I'm about to break out in chicken pox, and the scotch and beer are forming thunderclouds in my head. I need aspirin.

"I have to put on some makeup," I say to Patty on my way to the bathroom.

"Well, hurry. Angie says to take the number 7 train to Woodside Avenue and get a taxi from there. It's not too far, but it's too far to walk. It's almost three. We need to hustle."

I do a quick makeover, but it doesn't help. I'll keep my sunglasses on, which I have to do anyway because of my scratched cornea. I'm sure I won't be the only person there with puffy eyes. I pop three aspirin, put a pack of breath mints in my pocket, and figure I'm good to go.

Patty and I take the train to Times Square and then transfer to the number 7. We make it to the Woodside stop by five to four. We hail a cab and get to Green Lawns Funeral Home ten minutes later. The service is starting as we walk in. Folding chairs and flower arrangements line the walls, and in the front of the room is the casket and it's open. It never crossed my mind that the coffin would be open. I can see Jack's head resting on a pillow, his hands folded on his midsection. I'm about thirty feet away, which is more than close enough. I freeze. Patty grabs my hand and leads me to the back row where there are two empty chairs.

The officiating minister is offering a prayer for Jack and for Jack's family and friends. Then there is sound from the back of the room like someone dropping a bag of coins. Everyone turns around to see a tall woman with jet-black hair, on her knees, trying to gather the nickels and dimes and lipsticks and keys and put them back in her handbag. A fellow wearing a sharkskin suit and cowboy boots is helping her. They are both deeply tanned. The minister pauses in the middle of the prayer to wait for the woman and her helper.

"I think that's the mother and her boyfriend from Las Vegas," I whisper to Patty.

"Oh, I'm sure of it," she whispers back.

Mama Rose finally manages to get everything back in her bag, and she and the lounge lizard make their way to the second row of seats. Someone moves over and motions for them to sit down. Mama keeps her head down, not once looking at the coffin; the boyfriend puts his arm around her shoulders and whispers in her ear. Then I notice the man in the front row aisle seat. I can just see his profile. He never once turns around to see the woman who entered in a commotion. His eyes remain fixed on the young man in the coffin. It's Jack's father—the same profile, same broad shoulders, same curly brown hair but with flecks of gray. When he senses that Mama is settled, he nods to the minister to continue.

"God giveth and God taketh away," the man of the cloth says. "His purpose is a mystery and his means sometimes painful, but his power and his glory are unquestionable."

I always find it hard to listen to this type of rhetoric, but I keep my eyes down and my tongue silent.

"In every season there is a time and in every death there is a birth," he goes on in solemn oval tones. "Let us be reborn here today in the presence of God Almighty, our heavenly Father, who keeps us all in his loving arms and who taught us to pray by saying . . ." Then the minister leads us all in the Lord's Prayer. I fumble along as best I can. It's not a prayer I say easily. Patty's head is down and her eyes are closed as she recites the words. I keep my eyes on Jack's father. His head is bowed, but his lips are still. The broad shoulders slump and his fingers fidget with impatience. This is a man holding on—barely holding on. The prayer ends and the minister moves to the side. A tall young man about Jack's age approaches the front of the room. He is holding a few pages of typewritten text. His hands are shaking as he places them on the podium.

"My name is Bob McNabb," he begins. Of course, I think,

Jack's friend. "Jack Eremus and I met when we were in sixth grade and have been best friends ever since. He was the best man at my wedding six months ago." Bob's voice breaks. A woman in the front row sobs loudly. I'm sure it is Bob's wife. A slight blonde woman sits next to her. I have a feeling it's Sheryl. The two of them sit close together, shoulders touching. Jack's mother reaches forward and puts a hand on Sheryl's shoulder. Sheryl turns and looks at her. Jack's mother cups Sheryl's face in her hand. These relationships are deep and go back a long way. Jack's father doesn't move. He is by himself on the other side of the aisle. No one reaches out to him.

Bob recovers his voice and continues the eulogy. When he finishes, he walks over to the coffin, crosses himself, and kneels briefly. Then he rises, touches Jack's hands for a moment, and returns to his seat. His wife kisses him and puts her arm around his shoulders. Bob shudders. A stocky woman with dyed platinum hair gets up and sings "Amazing Grace" in a lovely alto voice. At the end of the song she introduces herself as Jack's Aunt Gladys. She thanks us all for coming and invites us to her home to share memories of Jack and partake of refreshments. The actual interment will take place tomorrow morning at eleven at the Calvary Cemetery. The minister offers a final benediction. Piped-in music plays, and people get up to mingle for a few minutes, offer kind words, and then take their leave. Jack's father stands and shakes hands and accepts condolences.

Mama Rose rises from her seat and tentatively approaches the casket. Her boyfriend steadies her with his arm tightly wrapped around her waist. She falls to her knees on the prayer rail next to the coffin and shakes with emotion. She reaches out and strokes Jack's face. Tears roll down my face.

"Maggie, are you all right?" Patty asks. I nod and smile at her. We are still seated in the back row.

"It's just so sad," I say.

"I know," she says, and pats my hand. "Look, I have to find a ladies' room. Do you want to come with me?"

"No, I'll wait here," I say. Patty leaves through a side door in search of the restrooms. Jack's mother is still kneeling by the coffin, obviously struggling to maintain a grip but losing the battle. Her shoulders shake convulsively. The boyfriend strokes her hair and looks completely useless. Then suddenly Jack's father is standing beside her. He extends his hand and she takes it. He gently helps her to her feet. The boyfriend has the good sense to step aside and disappear into the crowd. The father kisses Mama Rose on the cheek and they embrace for a long moment. The shaking stops and she seems to find her spine. Then the father gently releases her and turns to leave. He walks down the aisle. I see his full face now. He looks familiar and not just because he resembles Jack. Then I notice the limp. His knee appears to be stiff; he walks as if he is wearing an artificial leg. Oh my God! I take a quick breath and my heart skips the next beat. Jack's father is the one-legged man who sat across from me at the monastery, the man who sat with such serenity and stillness. As he passes me, I bow my head in acknowledgment and heartfelt sympathy. He doesn't see me. His eyes are fixed on some distant spot. He is willing himself to get from one moment to the next, one step at a time, and obviously trying to think about nothing.

"Excuse me," someone says. I look to my left. It's Bob. "Are you Maggie, by any chance?" he asks.

"Yes, I am," I answer. "What a lovely eulogy. I can tell you loved Jack very much."

"I did," Bob says. "He was my best friend." I stand up and we hug.

"Thank you for letting me know," I say after a moment. "It helps to be here."

"Are you going to Gladys's house?" he asks.

"I don't think so. I feel awkward. You understand, don't you?"

"Yes," Bob says. "Jack was very conflicted about . . ." He doesn't finish.

"About the women in his life," I offer.

"I think he didn't know how to deal with his feelings. When his mother left, he never got over it. It made it hard for him."

"I'm glad she came today," I say, looking across the room to where she is standing. Aunt Gladys is now offering her comfort, and it occurs to me Gladys is her sister.

"Well," Bob says. "Better late than never."

Then Patty is at my side, back from the ladies' room. I introduce her to Bob and she offers her sympathy and Bob excuses himself to rejoin his wife. I notice Sheryl is now standing with Gladys and Jack's mother. The lounge lizard boyfriend is nowhere to be seen. Most likely he's out front, smoking a cigarette. Not a bad idea, I think. I look to the front of the room. For the moment no one is near the coffin. This is my chance.

"I'll only be a minute," I say to Patty.

"Take your time," she says.

I walk up the side aisle and approach the coffin slowly. Jack is wearing a pin-striped suit, a pale blue shirt, and gray tie. I never saw him wear a suit. I wonder if this is even his. Of course it is, but he looks so out of place in it. But not as out of place in the suit as he looks out of place in the coffin. Life out of order. I kneel down on the prayer rail and bow my head. The tattoo that I saw on Jack's shoulder the first night we were together turned out to be the Citipati, as he told me. Tibetan. Two dancing skeletons, the Lords of the Cemetery. Did he know? Did Jack sense he was in jeopardy? Is that why he tattooed the macabre duo on his shoulder? The thought gives me a chill.

"Happy trails, my friend," I say as I reach out and place my hand on Jack's. I can't believe I'm quoting Roy Rogers, but it was the first thing that came to mind, and it's better than thinking about the eeriness of the skeletons. I stay like that with Jack for a few more moments and then leave. I don't look left or right as I move to the back of the room in search of Patty. I don't want to catch anyone's eye. I don't want to speak to anyone. I just want to get out of this funeral home as anonymously as I arrived.

When we get outside, Patty says she's hungry as hell and needs fuel. I need something too, but it's not food. I'd prefer something stiff and on the rocks. An older gentleman smoking a cigar directs us to Eats & Drinks a few blocks away. And just then the blonde, fragile-looking girl, who I'm positive is Sheryl, comes out of the funeral home with Bob's wife. When they see Patty and me they stop and whisper to each other. Then Sheryl comes toward me.

"You're Maggie, aren't you?" she asks.

"Yes, and I guess you're Sheryl," I say.

She nods and we stand like that in a kind of stalemate for a minute, not wanting to acknowledge each other and yet feeling some need to connect. Finally Patty extends her hand to Sheryl and tells her how sorry she is. Sheryl takes Patty's hand, but she keeps looking at me and I keep looking at her.

"You were with Jack when he died, weren't you?" I say.

"Yes," she says, tears forming in her eyes. A part of me wants to lunge at her and shake her and ask her why the hell she didn't save him? Why the hell she didn't give him CPR or mouth to mouth, but I don't. Because I can see in her eyes that she has been asking herself those same questions ever since it happened, and by the strain on her face I know she hasn't found any answers and probably never will.

"I'm sorry for your loss," I say, and she nods again, then turns and rejoins Bob's wife by the front of the church.

"Come on, let's get something to eat," Patty says, taking my arm and we walk in the direction of Eats & Drinks.

We walk in silence. I can't talk. I can barely breathe.

We get to the diner and take a back booth.

"I'll have a BLT on toast," Patty tells the waitress. "Coffee and an order of fries. Well done. I don't like them underdone. If they're underdone, I'll send them back." The waitress is standing on one foot then the other as she writes Patty's order on her pad, then she turns to me.

"Just coffee," I say.

"You've got to eat something," Patty says. "Get a piece of pie or a turnover."

"No, coffee's fine," I say. "And a scotch on the rocks."

"For goodness sakes, Maggie. Bring her a slice of a pie," Patty says, looking at the waitress. "What kind do you have?"

"Cherry, apple, and uh, banana cream," the waitress says with a roll of her eyes.

"Banana cream would be perfect," Patty says.

The waitress manages a half smile and walks away. Her feet are killing her. I know because her shoes look brand-new, and by now blisters have formed on one or two of her toes and on the backs of her heels.

"Well, the funeral was certainly interesting," Patty says, arranging the salt and pepper shakers next to the ketchup and restacking the sugar and Sweet 'n Low. "And the poor mother. She looks so damaged. How long since she has actually been in the picture?"

"I don't know. Jack moved back with his dad when she left, or 'ran off,' as he put it. He said his dad was suicidal."

The waitress delivers my drink and I take a swig and hope it hits the spot. The spot being right in the middle of my aching heart.

"Really? That sounds difficult for Jack," Patty says.

"I'm sure it was," I say.

"The human condition. It's not always pretty."

"I think she left six or seven years ago, at least that's what his friend Bob said. I didn't ask Jack about it. Truth is, Patty, I didn't really know him that well. Amazing, isn't it?" I say. I feel a catch in my throat. I take a deep breath. I don't want to start crying. "I only knew him a few weeks. And now it seems surreal. Like it was a movie I saw." Patty reaches over and pats my hand.

What is it with women and hand patting? Like that makes everything better. We sit quietly for a few minutes, hands patted, and say nothing. The sounds of the diner percolate in the background.

"The mother is glamorous in a kind of rough-cut way," Patty says. "She looks like she's been in the desert sun too long with no moisturizer—and that boyfriend—straight out of central casting."

"Apparently he is an awesome sax player. He plays in the house band at one of the big casinos in Vegas."

"Well he looks like a reptile in a cheap suit," Patty says, and then the food arrives. Our waitress, Irene of the sore feet, drops it (literally) on the table. Several fries bounce off Patty's plate and roll toward the edge of the table. They look brown and crispy and very well done. Irene scoops them up and puts them in her apron pocket.

"I'll be back with the coffee," she hisses under her breath.

"She must have quite a stash in that pocket by the end of her shift," Patty says.

My banana cream pie is six inches high. The top layer looks like it's made of Styrofoam. Irene returns with two cups of coffee, which she places too firmly on the table; a few drops splash out of the cups onto the saucer.

"Enjoy your meal," she says with a frown. I finish my drink and order another.

"Aren't you even going to try the pie?" Patty asks, taking a big bite of her BLT. I poke at it for a minute, wondering where the bananas are hiding.

"The strange thing is, Patty," I say, "I've seen Jack's father before."

"Really? Where?" she asks, her mouth full of bacon, lettuce, and tomato.

"At the retreat I went to last week. He was sitting across from me the whole time."

"Wow," she says.

"It's eerie. It was a silent retreat so we never spoke, but I noticed him in particular because he has only one leg."

"Oh my God," Patty says between bites.

"Today he was wearing a prosthesis, but at the retreat he used crutches. And the last day he wasn't there. He must have gotten a call from the hospital or the cops, because that was the day Jack died."

"That *is* really strange," Patty says.

"I'm sure this is horrible for him."

"The worst," Patty says. "The worst kind of loss."

And just like that I'm crying again, big sloppy tears coming out of my eyes and falling onto my Styrofoam pie. Patty reaches over and pats my hand again.

"I'm going to the ladies' room," I tell her and slide out of the booth. I look around for the restrooms. I see Irene behind the counter, scowling at a customer.

"Ladies' room?" I ask. She points to a hallway. I follow her direction. A sign points down a steep set of stairs. I make my way down and find the door with "Dames" on it. Once inside I start to sob uncontrollably. I sit on the toilet and let it happen. I weep and cry and sob and sputter and moan. I don't know how long I stay in there, but when I get back to the table Patty is having a refill of coffee and finishing off a piece of cherry pie à la mode.

"Irene said the cherry pie was homemade and she was right. It's delicious." Patty says. "Here have a bite. Get ice cream with it. It's heaven." I take a big bite of the pie.

"Feel better?" Patty asks.

"Yeah. Shall we head back to the big city?" I say finishing off my second scotch. But the scotch hasn't done its job. The spot in the middle of my heart is still aching, my head is still pounding, and I feel stone cold sober.

"You betcha, I'm right behind you. Just let me pay the check. My treat," Patty says, getting her things together and heading for the cash register.

"I'll leave the tip," I say. I look around and spot Irene standing at another booth, shifting her weight from one foot to the other. I pull out a ten-dollar bill and put it under the saltshaker. Irene's going to need a little extra for Band-Aids by the time this shift is over. Patty and I catch the number 7 back to Manhattan.

"Thanks for coming with me," I tell Patty when we part company at Forty-second Street. "I wouldn't have made it without you."

"Anytime," Patty says. She gives me a quick hug and then catches a downtown train. I get an uptown train and head home. I notice the clock in the station. It's seven thirty but it feels like midnight. When I get home I get my last beer out of the fridge and decide that this is it. I'll drink this and then I'll call Spider and tell him that I'm quitting this time for sure, because it doesn't seem to be working anymore. I wish it did, I really wish it did, because I could use some help right now. I could use a ticket to paradise. Then somewhere between the beer and my call to Spider I remember my cell phone. I haven't seen it since my trip to West Virginia. I used it to call Jack and then I went up to the monastery and didn't take it there. I look through my bag and then the backpack I took to West Virginia and realize I'm drunker than I think because I have trouble with the zippers. I concentrate and finally get the front one open and sure enough there is my cell phone and as per usual the battery is dead. I get out the charger and plug it in. Then I sit and drink the beer. I'm exhausted and drift off to sleep. Sometime during the night I wake up. I go to the bathroom and then go to the fridge for another beer but there are none left. Damn. Then I notice the cell phone. I unplug the charger and open the phone. The voice mail message flashes. I press 1 and send and put the phone to my ear. It's from Jack. He did call me back. He called my cell because he had the number on his phone. "Hey, Maggie Mae, got your message. Don't be sorry. Life is just a river of dreams. Like your friend Billy Joel says. So take it easy. I'll talk to you soon." I play the message again. I can't believe it. It's Jack's voice. I take a breath and try to take another and then another. He called me on the day I got back from West Virginia and my trusty little cell phone was jammed in the bottom of the pocket of my backpack and I went to the monastery never once thinking to check it and then Jack died that Sunday. I lie down on my bed and hold the phone close to my ear and play the message again and again, so it's like Jack is lying close to me, whispering it in my ear, over and over. I eventually fall asleep, but not until the battery on the phone has gone dead again.

19

*S*unday morning I meet Dee-Honey and the rest of the gang at our usual spot. We're headed up to Connecticut to do *Pied Piper,* the show du jour. I'm not in a great mood. I've spent the last few days sleeping and eating, listening to Billy Joel, and watching Alfred Hitchcock movies. And not drinking. Or smoking. And talking to Spider every few hours. I even went to a few of those meetings he keeps mentioning. But so far I prefer staying in my apartment and watching movies.

Today nobody in the Little Britches tribe is in a particularly good mood. At least not until we have coffee and some carbs and get on the road and realize we have no choice, so why not enjoy it? That's the way it usually works. It's like the Stockholm syndrome—happy prisoners. Then we arrive at the theater and the smell of the greasepaint quickens the pulse, and our actors' blood begins to churn because, after all, there is an audience waiting and a wig to be brushed and eyelashes to glue on and a show to be done.

We don't always get it up, but mostly we do because we're actors and we act.

"All aboard," Dee-Honey chirps in her happy morning voice.

I slide in next to Sam Stoner in the backseat. Sam plays the Piper and a damn fine Piper he is. He has a wonderful tenor voice and he looks great in tights and when he's not on the road with a national tour, he works for Dee. I'd say Sam is close to sixty, but I can't be sure and I don't dare ask. Never ask an actor his or her age, especially her, because you could get hurt . . . badly.

We get to the theater. I don't smell the greasepaint and my pulse doesn't quicken, so it's going to be one of those times when I'm going to have to slug my way through it. "Can we go over the duet?" Sam asks, startling me out of my joyless reverie.

"Sure," I say.

"Good. I'll find Arnold," Sam says. Arnold is the composer and accompanist. For some shows the music is on tape and for others we have the luxury of a live piano player. Arnold has written the score for most of the shows in Dee's repertoire. He's a curmudgeon with a genius for melody. He lives by himself in a cramped one-bedroom apartment in Hell's Kitchen; his baby grand piano swallows up the whole living room in one bite. At Christmas time he has a holiday party. We all gather around the piano (there is no place else to gather), holding song sheets with the dirty lyrics Arnold has devised for the traditional carols. It's amazing what the Herald Angels sing.

Sam comes back with Arnold in tow. The piano is in the orchestra pit in front of the stage. Arnold runs his fingers up and down the keys with a few arpeggios to warm up. Sam and I stand center stage and do a couple of la-la-las to wake up the old voice box. Then we begin our duet, which is entitled "Rats, Rats, Rats." It's a lovely song, although you wouldn't know it by the title. It's has a nice two-part chorus that Sam and I do with the rest of the cast singing "rats, rats, rats" in counterpoint.

"Go back to the bridge," Arnold says as we finish. "You were off the tempo. Don't slow down so much."

"I need more coffee," I say.

"I need more money," Sam says. Then we sing through the bridge again and Arnold finishes with a flourish.

"I love it," he says. "You're great."

"No, you're great," I say.

"I know," Arnold says. "I'm always great. Now where are the donuts?"

"Your voice sounds wonderful, Mags," Sam says.

"Thanks, I really haven't been singing much."

"Well, you should be. You don't want to lose it. It's important for a singer to sing."

"A lot's been going on. And everybody's dying lately," I say without thinking. It slips out.

"I know," Sam says sadly. "Everybody's always dying." Then I remember Sam's lover died about four years ago. Shit. How could I forget?

"I'm sorry, Sam," I say.

"People die, so it's important to live while you can."

"Is it? Even if you can't feel anything?"

"Don't worry about feeling; live and sing, Maggie, sing. Dig deep. Wake up. Praise the Lord and pass the potatoes," Sam says throwing his arms around me. "Shall we dance?" he asks and then we waltz across the stage like Anna and the King of Siam.

"Half hour," Frank calls from the wings.

"Let's do a show," Sam says, hugging me tight. "Live, Maggie. It's the best revenge."

"If you insist," I say, hugging him back. "I'll try."

"And sing," he says as we head to the dressing room. "Sing your heart out."

The show goes pretty well except the parade of rats gets bogged down when they make their exit across the stage. Fifteen brown felt rats on roller skates are pulled from stage left to stage right as the Piper lures them out of Hamlin town. Today the second to the lead rat falls over and the rest follow so rather than rolled across they are dragged the whole width of the stage. Poor creatures. No choice but to follow.

I play Fastidia, the mayor's wife, and have to stand center stage and watch the whole scene unfold. The last two rats slide off the apron of the stage so Frank has to jerk hard until they bounce back up and shimmy-shake their way offstage. I can't look at Randall Kent, who is playing the mayor, because if I do I'll start to laugh and I won't be able to stop and then the children in the audience will never know what becomes of the poor citizens of Hamlin town because all the actors will be laughing uncontrollably and unable to deliver the rest of the lines. Finally the last of the rats are pulled offstage and we maneuver our way to the end of the play.

When I get back to New York I have a message from Sidney at Don't Tell Mama. I dial the number.

"Maggie, thanks for calling back. Could you help me out this Friday night? I have the eight p.m. slot open, and I know we'll have hotel people and some regulars. It should be a full house, so we'll both make some money. Tina Rush came down with bronchitis. Could you do it for me? It will be like a dress rehearsal for your show on the twenty-fifth and twenty-sixth. I'll throw in an extra fifty bucks."

"I don't know. I'm not sure I'll be ready."

"Get back on the horse, Maggie. It's time."

"All right, I guess, but I'll have to check with my accompanist."

"Great. This is great. Our Friday customers are steady and I'd hate not to have a show. And you know, doll, you're the best."

I love it when Sidney calls me "doll." It makes me feel like I'm headlining at the Copacabana show with Tony Bennett.

"Can I get some rehearsal time?" I ask, getting back to business.

"Sure. How about one to four Thursday afternoon?"

"I'll check with Thomas and get back to you."

I look through the papers on my desk for Thomas's phone number. I know I jotted it down somewhere or else it's in my appointment book. I really have to remember to put numbers in my Rolodex instead of leaving them on scraps of paper. I look through another stack. I don't find Thomas's phone number, but I do see an address written on a take-out menu from House of Noodles. It's Jack's address, and his father's. Then I find Thomas's number and leave a message. This is good. It will be like a dress rehearsal and sooner than I thought. Like jumping into the ocean in March rather than July. I take Ed for a quick walk down the block and back. Then I feed Ed and Bixby and make a grilled cheese sandwich for myself and sit at the window and eat.

I fiddle with the scrap of paper that has Jack's address on it. An odd thought pops in my head. I wonder what Jack's dad is doing right this very minute. Is he all right? I picture him sitting across from me at the monastery. It's so odd to think that was Jack's father, the man with one leg. Small world? Flat-out minute. I look at the clock. It's past six. I grab my bag.

"I'll be back soon," I say to Ed as I close the door.

I take the number 1 train to Forty-second Street and switch to the number 7. It's the same way Patty and I went to the funeral home. I study the map on the train and find the nearest stop to the address on the slip of paper I'm holding in my hand, 142-53 Forty-third Road. When I get off I ask a young man in a suit if he knows what direction Forty-third Road is. He points north.

"It's about three blocks and then make a right, I think."

"Thanks." I walk north and then turn and start looking at numbers. The fellow who directed me was right and I find myself on Jack's street in no time. The houses are nice, with well-kept lawns. I pass 138, then 140, and then 142-53, the address on the scrap of paper I'm clutching in my hand. The house has a garage and a small front porch and window boxes on the second story.

It's almost seven o'clock and still light. The summer evening is warm but not hot. It's that kind of intoxicating night air when the sun is about to set and the sky is a calliope of color. I stand still and study the house. It's newly painted, but the lawn could use some attention. Rows of impatiens are planted around the house like a daisy chain necklace. The front porch is devoid of furniture and the blinds are drawn on the downstairs windows.

It doesn't appear anyone is home. Where is John? I wonder. Is he in the kitchen eating a frozen dinner, or is he out with some well-meaning friends, or is he sitting serenely in meditation with his mind bent toward Nirvana? I wish I could see him, talk to him. Ask him how he lost his leg. Ask him how he is coping with Jack's death. Ask him if he is all right or if he is suicidal like when his wife left him and Jack moved back home to help dispel his pain. I let out a gasp at the thought. Oh God, I think, is he hanging from a rafter in the attic? Has he already played his cards and cashed in his chips?

A car turns into the driveway and stops. I don't move. John gets out on the driver's side and slams the door shut. I watch from my place behind a tree across the street. He opens the trunk of the car and lifts out a bag of what I imagine are groceries. He is not more than thirty feet from me. He goes to the front door of the house. He puts a key in the lock and opens it and disappears inside. I still don't move. He comes back outside, hesitates, and then looks in my direction. He sees me. At least I think he does. His head moves to the side like he's wondering who I am and why I'm watching him, yet maybe he doesn't see me at all and merely cocks his head to the side as a reflex, a response to a slight pain in his neck, a cramped muscle, a movement that has nothing to do with me. I don't move a muscle. He opens his mailbox and gets out letters, a magazine, and then disappears back into the house. I take a breath.

I feel foolish, standing across the street, spying. What am I watching for? An SOS flashed on the venetian blinds? A distress flag waved from the roof? John is alive and well and buying groceries and getting the mail. I can stop worrying. He's fine.

"He's fine, Jack," I whisper into the evening air. "Well, maybe not fine, but coping."

I turn and head back to the subway. I study the sidewalks and houses and lawn ornaments and then I paint a picture of it in my mind and put Jack in the center as a young boy, riding his bike, skateboarding down the sidewalk, playing kickball in the street with his friends on lazy summer days or cold winter mornings, every day of every year of his life. I pass an empty lot where some boys are playing a pickup game of baseball. The evening is fast becoming night, and the sky in the west is bruised a deep purple.

Miniature golf flashes in my mind. Jack told me he and his best friend built a miniature golf course in his backyard the summer before junior high. I bet that best friend was Bob. I stop dead in the street. I want to see the backyard. I want to see if the miniature golf course is still there, if there is something that Jack built still standing in this world. It's imperative.

I turn around and head back to the house. A light shines through the blinds in a room on the second floor. Maybe John is sitting on the side of his bed, tying a noose and contemplating the end. Stop it, I tell my self, stop thinking like that. I tiptoe quietly up the driveway and make my way to the backyard. I could get shot for trespassing with no questions asked.

I hear a television or radio as I pass by one of the windows. I crouch low and flatten myself against the wall and peek around the corner like a cat burglar. The coast appears clear. I take a few more steps and gently open the gate leading into the yard.

There are four lawn chairs and a barbecue grill, a picnic table, flower beds with pink petunias, and a bicycle leaning against a toolshed. Jack's I'm sure. I sneak in further—the gate creaks as it closes behind me, and then falls silent. I need to, have to see the golf course. But when I look, there is no sign of it. I crouch low to the ground and steal around the yard like a piglet nosing for truffles. Still no golf course, no jerry-rigged putting green built by innocent, adolescent hands. It was probably dismantled years ago and deposited at the local dump. I take a deep breath and sink down on the ground. A few stars are twinkling overheard now and the crickets are cricketing in the bushes. I hear a door open in the next house over. A woman's voice calls out, "Here, Ginger, come on, come on, girl." A dog barks in response and trots home. The door closes.

I decide to leave but I'm disappointed I didn't find that piece of Jack I was looking for. Then, as I start toward the gate, I see it—a little wooden windmill in the middle of the petunias. The paint is peeling and one of the propellers is missing, but it's still there, still standing, one last remnant of Jack's miniature golf course. I reach out and run my hand slowly over the wood. It's almost two feet high with a red base and white trim. "Thank you," I whisper. "Thank you."

I hear a noise inside the house. Someone is moving about. It's John. Oh God, don't let me get caught. I turn as quickly and quietly as I can and fast walk my way out the gate and down the driveway. Then the front porch light snaps on and I hear a door open.

"Excuse me," I hear from the porch. "Can I help you?"

Shit. I turn slowly. John Eremus is standing on the top step of the porch. He's bigger than I remember. *Formidable* might be a better word, and much to my relief he is not holding a shotgun. Yet due to some perverse reflex on my part I throw my arms up in the air anyway and yell, "Don't shoot."

And due to some perverse reflex on his part, he raises his right hand, cocks his finger, and pretends to fire. "Bang, you're dead," he says. I stumble back in surprise, my foot trips over something solid on the ground, and I land flat on my back. I remain still, praying the earth will swallow me whole. When I open my eyes, John is standing over me. He reaches out a hand to help me up.

"You've got to be careful of those sprinklers," he says. "They'll get you every time."

"Thanks," I murmur as he hoists me to my feet.

"You knew my son," he says. It's a statement, not a question.

"Yes, I did."

NOTE TO SELF . . .

When trespassing in someone's life, watch out for the sprinkler system.

He nods and turns toward the house. "Would you like to come in?" he asks. "I was about to make dinner. Are you hungry?"

"Yeah, a little. I didn't mean to intrude. I was just . . ."

"It's no intrusion," he says, interrupting me. "In fact why don't we fire up the grill and cook some chicken?"

"Sounds good, but I don't want you to go to any trouble."

"I like the trouble. Trouble helps, trouble and keeping busy," he says, leading me to the kitchen. The house has low ceilings and hardwood floors and lots of small Persian rugs. "You were at the funeral weren't you?"

"Yes, but I didn't think you'd noticed me."

"Skin or no skin?" he asks when we get to the kitchen, which is a large room with oak cupboards and white tile counters.

"Pardon?" I ask.

"You like your chicken grilled with the skin or without?"

"Without," I answer. "No skin for me."

"That's smart. Animal fat doesn't do you a bit of good. Do you eat red meat?"

"Absolutely not," I answer, knowing I'm going to get an A on this test.

"Good girl," he says.

I like that. I like being called a girl.

John gets the chicken out of the refrigerator and hands it to me.

"Why don't you take off the skin and wash this and I'll get the charcoal hot." He goes out the back door and I turn on the water in the sink and wrestle with the chicken.

I find a pan to put the meat in and take it out back. John is standing with his back to me. The grill is greased and fired up.

"Shall I put these on yet?" I ask, coming up behind him. He jumps slightly. I caught him off guard.

"Yes," he says. "Please do."

I place the chicken on the grill.

"How well did you know Jack?"

"Not all that well really. We were just . . ." I stop midsentence. I'm at a loss for words. Were we friends or lovers or merely acquaintances? What is the proper term? How do you label a relationship? You don't—that's the thing. At least not until it's over. "I only knew him a few weeks," I say in conclusion.

"I see." John nods.

"I'm so sorry for your loss," I offer.

"Damn." John's eyes fill momentarily, and then he tightens his jaw and narrows his eyes. He's fighting the tears. I remain still and wait. I know the next lines are John's if he can manage them.

"I can't look at anything," he says finally. "Or hear anything or read anything that doesn't remind me of Jack. Like the bicycle over there. A few weeks ago he asked me if I'd help him change the chain on it. It took us a couple of hours. We couldn't find the right wrench, and by the time we did and got the damned thing replaced, we were starving so we ordered pizza and sat out here and ate it. It was the last meal we had together."

The chicken sputters on the grill. John swipes quickly at his eyes and then goes in the house. Men are awkward with tears; they don't seem to know what to do with them. Women are better schooled in tear tending: a quick touch of the finger under the eye to catch them before they fall, a careful dab with a tissue so the mascara doesn't get blotched, a delicate brush with the forefinger, or we go ahead and dissolve into mewling messes.

"There's lettuce in the refrigerator and oil and vinegar on the counter," he says, returning with a spatula. He flips the chicken and I go inside to prepare a salad. The refrigerator door is full of magnets holding snapshots and grocery lists and laundry slips and old receipts. There is a picture of Jack with his dad next to the jib or the jibe (I can never remember which is what) of a sailboat. There on the boat standing side by side they look remarkably alike. Photos seem to pick up a subtle family resemblance that isn't as apparent in life. I run my finger over Jack's face. I don't know how John can stand being in this house. Jack is everywhere; I can almost feel his breath on the back of my neck. A shiver runs down my spine.

"Everything all right?" John says, standing in the doorway.

"Yeah," I say, turning quickly away from the refrigerator. "We just need some plates and silverware." But I've not moved quickly enough, and he notices I've been looking at the photographs. He eyes wander to the refrigerator and then back to me.

"What am I going to do?" John says in a whisper. "What am I going to do without my boy?"

I take two steps toward him. His head falls forward as if it is too heavy for him to bear. I put out my arms and pull him toward me and place his head on my shoulder. I cradle his head in my hand and rock him gently from side to side. John takes a few short breaths and then begins to weep. Tears pour out of his eyes and splash onto the collar of my shirt. No wonder he can't wipe his tears away with a graceful brush of the forefinger, there are too many, too many tears to brush away.

We stand locked together, rocking back and forth for what feels like hours. Then John inhales deeply and we slowly part, disentangling our arms and moving a half step back. John looks at me. His eyes are green or greenish brown. Hazel, I guess. The skin beneath is puffy, but the rest of his face is firm with wrinkles and lines etched in his tanned skin. His hair is grayish and brown, and his gaze is unsettling. I drop my eyes and feel a blush in my cheeks. I hate this. I hate feeling awkward and exposed. I bite the inside of my cheek.

"I need to put some cold water on my face," he says. He walks toward the door that leads to the rest of the house. "I hope that chicken's not burned."

"I'll check," I say.

John stops and turns. "I bought all these rugs after my wife left me. I wanted to cover everything up, the floors, the past, the feelings, the shit." He spits out "shit" like a firecracker, he spits it the whole way across the room. "I can't go through that again. I won't make it this time."

"Then let it out," I say. "Don't cover it up. You don't have to."

"No, I don't," he says quietly. "I thought you were an angel when I saw you in the yard. Sent to help me, to help me find some . . ." His voice trails off.

"Serenity," I offer.

"Yes," he says, his voice breaking. "A little serenity."

He lowers his head for a moment to regain his composure, then looks up with a smile. "You better check on the chicken or it'll be toast."

Then he disappears into the darkness of the hall and I disappear into the backyard. The chicken is definitely toasty, but not ruined. I place it on a platter and put the platter on the picnic table. The back door opens and John comes out with the plates and silver.

"I have some candles in the toolshed. I'll get them if you'll bring out the salad," he says. We get everything assembled and then sit down to eat our meal.

"Wait," John says, jumping up. "We need something to drink.

What can I get you? Ice tea, beer, Coke, which I think I have, or seltzer?"

I hesitate. What I would really like is a pint of Johnny Walker with a beer chaser but I smile sweetly and say, "Seltzer would be fine."

John leaves to get the drinks just as Goodie buzzes up and settles on my shoulder. "Whee, so this is Queens," he says, puffing for air. "What a time I had finding you. You know I hate the boroughs."

"Am I glad to see you," I say. "This is getting intense. It's so strange being here in Jack's house, and his father is really in pain. I feel for him, and I also feel awkward."

"Well this is great, Mags. Very Eugene O'Neill, I have to say."

"What does that mean?" I whisper.

"Trust yourself and for goodness sake stick with the seltzer, Mags. Oh, here he comes. Got to fly. I love you."

"Ah," John says pushing open the screen door. "One seltzer with lime. I hope you don't mind. I put it in without thinking. I always take lime in mine."

"Great," I say. "I love lime."

We talk about baseball during dinner. We talk about Derek Jeter and Joe Torre. We talk about the Red Sox and the pennant race, and I tell him about the time I went to Fenway Park with my dad, a staunch Red Sox fan, and the foul ball I caught. It's the quick, desperate talk people talk when they can't talk about what they really want to talk about. After my father died, my brother and I discussed recipes for split pea soup and the best way to make potato salad, talking as if our lives depended on it. And in a way they did. So John and I talk about batting averages and RBIs and strikes zones and by ten o'clock we've finished eating and we've washed the dishes and we don't mention Jack once.

"You a decaf person?" he asks, getting out a container of coffee from the refrigerator.

"Yes, I'd have a cup if you made it. Where's the . . . ladies' room?" I ask stupidly. I hate using the word *bathroom* in social situations but *ladies' room* sounds so formal when you're in someone's home. But, really, what are the options? I could say *latrine* but that's so military. And this guy's name is John, so that's out.

"Upstairs," he says. "Second door on the right."

"Thanks," I say, as *powder room* pops into my head. Damn, why didn't I say *powder room*? I go through the living room and up the stairs and find the bathroom. It's just a sink and a toilet and is, in fact, a powder room. I guess there is another, larger one somewhere, but since I'm not planning to shower or bathe, this will do. I finish my business and head back to the stairs. The door at the end of the hall catches my attention. It's ajar and the light is on. It's the light I saw from the street. I tiptoe down the hallway toward the door. I push it open a few more inches and look inside. I know immediately this is Jack's room. I knew it when I saw the light from the street. I knew it. I knew John was in Jack's room. I look, and yet don't want to look. I take a deep breath and do a quick survey of the contents. I recognize Jack's Doc Martens on the floor by the closet door. T-shirts are thrown over the desk chair. I recognize a Yankees cap and a faded yellow bandana.

A computer sits on the desk and on the wall behind it is a U2 poster. Car magazines are stacked next to the computer. An empty can of Coke and a half-eaten bag of potato chips are on the nightstand. There is a bulletin board on the closet door with slips of paper—what looks like a work schedule and a Gold's Gym schedule—and in the middle, tacked up with a red thumbtack, is a picture of me. It's the publicity shot I sent out about my gig at Don't

Tell Mama. I wonder if Jack had been planning to come, or had he tacked it up as reminder to stay away from me? I wonder if I had been with him instead of Sheryl when he was stricken if I could have saved him because I am an older woman. I would have known to cradle his head in my lap and call 911 and stroke his brow and hush his fears and ease his pain. I would have kept him alive until the ambulance arrived with the paramedics and the doctors and the surgeons. I would have saved his life. I would have tried.

"Do you take it black?" I hear John ask behind me. I turn. He is standing in the room with two mugs of coffee. "I can go down and get you some milk if you need it."

"No, black is fine," I say, reaching for a mug.

"Good," he says, looking around the room. "I haven't moved a thing. I can't. Not yet. Jack said you were a dynamite pool player."

"Really?"

"Yeah. He said you beat him fair and square."

"Well, he was pretty good himself."

"State champion his junior and senior years in high school," John says with pride. He walks over to the bookcase and picks up a gold trophy and hands it to me.

"Wow," I say. "I think he might have been hustling me while I was hustling him."

"I taught him to play when he was a kid," John says. "There was a poolroom on Continental Avenue, Joey's House of Pool; it's not there anymore. Every Saturday afternoon we would go to Joey's. And sometimes during the week I would pick him up from school and we would go shoot a few games."

I hand the trophy back to John. He studies it for a minute and places it back on the bookcase.

"I was recovering from an injury," he says. His hand subconsciously touches the side of his leg. "So I couldn't play ball with Jack, but I could still play pool. He was good. He was a natural."

The air in the room is so still. Neither of us speaks for several minutes; we just sip our coffee.

"I guess I'd better get going," I say finally.

"I'm glad you came by this evening, Maggie," John says. It's the first time he has said my name. I wasn't sure he knew it.

"I'm glad too." We get up and make our way downstairs. I take my cup to the kitchen and rinse it out in the sink.

"Let me drive you back to the city," John offers.

"No, I'm fine. I don't mind taking the subway."

"Are you sure?"

"Absolutely," I say. "I'll be home in no time."

"Maybe I'll come hear you sing," he says to me at the front door. "I saw the postcard on Jack's bulletin board. That's how I knew who you were; you were the face on the card."

"Sure, please do come," I say, wondering if I should mention the show this Friday.

"Music soothes the . . ." His voice trails off.

"Soul?" I say.

John nods slowly, his eyes fixed in some middle space of seeing and not seeing.

"Thank you for dinner." I reach my hand out and John takes it in his. I can't look at his face as I leave because I know if I do, I will dissolve into tears.

"Goodnight, John," I say quickly. Our eyes meet for a second, and then I turn and walk down the sidewalk and to the end of Forty-third Road and back to the subway station. I stand on the tracks and wait for the number 7 train to take me home to Manhattan.

THE NEXT MORNING I sit across from George, my therapist, a cup of black coffee cradled in my hands. No more milk for
me. I want it straight and strong. George is staring at the floor,
waiting for me to have a revelation. There is none coming. We've
been sitting like this for about twenty minutes.

"Life goes on," I say finally.

"Yes," George agrees. He looks at me, then smiles, and we lapse
back into silence.

"I'm not smoking or drinking," I say a few minutes later.

"That's good, I guess," George says.

"I feel numb. I have no desire for anything. Flat," I say. "I feel
flat."

"That's understandable."

"I went out to Queens last night. To see Jack's house, and his
father was there and he invited me in for dinner."

"Really?" George moves forward in his chair. "And how was
that?"

"It was surreal. I had never been to Jack's house, and there I
am in the house he lived in and in his bedroom and talking to
his father."

"What's his father like?"

"His father is grief-stricken."

"I see."

We sit for another twenty minutes or so. George glances at
his watch and makes a move. I take a deep breath and get up to
leave. When I get on the street I realize I'm shaking, and I feel a
sensation of being unsafe, unsafe in the world, and mortal, very
mortal.

I have to meet with Thomas in a half hour and go over the
songs for Friday night. I stop at a pay phone and dial Charles's

number at the gallery. My cell phone is, of course, nowhere to be found. Tosh answers.

"Is Charles there? It's Maggie."

"Hang on a sec, hon, he's just finishing with a client."

"Maggie, darling. What's up? I've been worried. I called and left a message on your cell. I haven't heard from you. You're not still angry about the video thing. Chad's a sweetheart and so talented. You'll like him when you really get to know him."

"It's been a tough time. The young guy I was seeing, remember?"

"Sure. The one that had you thinking about babies."

"That's right. Well he died. Suddenly."

"Oh my God. Maggie, my love, I'm so sorry. What can I do?" Charles asks. "Are you all right?"

"It was a few days ago. I'm okay. You know."

"Yes," Charles says. "I do know."

"I'm singing Friday at Don't Tell Mama," I say. "Sidney asked me to help him out. He needed a show. He's got the hotel crowd on weekends. Do you think you can be there? It would mean a lot to me."

"Be there? I wouldn't miss it. I'll be in the front row," Charles says. "Oh, I have an appointment. I have to run. Let me know if you need anything. Anything at all."

"Just for you to be there Friday."

"You can count on it. Love you," Charles says.

"I love you too," I say.

I meet with Thomas and we work out a running order for the songs and go over the arrangements and practice a couple of the numbers.

"Nothing fancy," I say. "Let's keep it simple. I hope I can sing for an hour. I feel like it's been years since I've done this."

"You sound fine," Thomas says. "Just don't push. Think of it as a dress rehearsal."

"Goodie always said to sing from the heart and everything else would fall into place."

"He was right," Thomas says. "Do you want me to wear a tux or a jacket?"

"Anything you like except sequins. I'll be wearing the sequins."

"Gotcha. How about a black shirt and jacket?" he asks.

"Sounds good," I say, getting my things together. "I'll see you at the club on Thursday for rehearsal."

The next three days fly by. I vocalize and take Mr. Ed for walks in the park and cuddle with Bixby. I drink lots of black coffee and suck on cinnamon sticks, which someone recommended for cigarette withdrawal. I let the phone machine take any messages. My agent calls with some auditions for the following week. I call her back to confirm and invite her to the show Friday night.

"Thanks, Mags, but I'll be at the beach for the weekend. Maybe next time," she says. I call Patty and tell her about the gig. I also call Bob Strong.

"Wow," he says. "I can't wait. See you then."

I call Spider and leave the information on his machine. "And I haven't had a drink today," I say as if it's a joke, and yet I know it's not a joke. I know it's dead serious. And I've been leaving that message on Spider's machine every day for over a week now. Then I sit and look at the phone for a while. I screw myself into a tight little fist. Thinking, thinking, thinking. Should I call John Eremus? I feel a blush run up my neck. He said he might come to hear me sing; maybe he would like to come Friday. I look around in my desk drawer for the piece of paper I jotted his number down on. I finally find the House of Noodles menu. I have got to organize my life, I think once more as I dial the number. I take a breath and try to relax. After five rings the machine picks up. "Leave a message at the beep," John's voice says.

"It's Maggie. Turns out I'll be singing this Friday night at Don't Tell Mama. It's on Forty-sixth Street at eight o'clock. It's short notice. I'm filling in for someone. Just wanted to let you know," I say and hang up the phone like it's a hot potato. There, I did it.

The rehearsal on Thursday goes pretty well. My voice holds out, and Thomas and I are finding our own music shorthand with each other. I debate with myself over wearing the sequins. Is it too much without Goodie to balance it out? Oh, hell, why not? I have an electric blue dress that looks pretty damn good on me, especially now that I've lost about five pounds. The "grief" diet. It works every time.

The show is at eight p.m. so I get to the club around seven. I get a cup of coffee for Sidney and one for myself at Amy's Bread Shop on the corner. The bar is hopping when I enter. Several well-tanned guys with spiked hair are hanging on the barstools, flirting with Jim, who is behind the bar wearing very shorts pants and a muscle shirt. There are some couples at the tables and a few are leaning on the piano, singing a medley of Elton John hits. I go in the back to Sidney's office. I tap on the door.

"Come in," he says.

"Brought you a coffee," I say.

"You're a doll," Sidney says, getting up from his desk. I hand him the coffee and he toasts me with the cardboard cup. "To a great show."

"Thanks."

"I really appreciate you helping me out on this one," he says. "It's going to be packed."

"Terrific," I say. I can feel the dread rising in my throat—that terrible dread known as stage fright which erases all rational memory and leaves you with only the horrid fear that you will be standing on the stage stark naked with nothing to say.

I make my way to the dressing room and deposit my makeup kit on the counter and hang up the garment bag that contains the pretty sequined dress that will magically transform me into a dynamic, confident performer. I check my watch. I have an hour before the show. I walk outside to get some fresh air and exorcise the dread. I sit on the steps of the stoop next to the club entrance.

I look down the block and see someone walking toward me. I'm looking west into the sunset and the figure is silhouetted in the beams. It's familiar, very familiar, and suddenly out of the sunset steps Goodie, full-sized, wearing his long white raincoat and his yellow high-top Converse sneakers. He leans over and kisses me on the cheek.

"You'll be great, Maggie."

"Goodie, you're a real boy again!" I put my arms around him and hold on tight. "How is it possible?"

He smiles at me. "Anything's possible, you know that, don't you?" he says, smiling his hundred-watt smile.

"Maybe," I say.

"You'll be wonderful, Maggie," he whispers in my ear. "And take care of that precious cargo," he says, patting my belly.

"What precious cargo?" I say.

Goodie smiles and takes my hand and places it on my stomach, right below my waist. He covers my hand with his and looks me in the eyes. "Happy ending. Like in the fairy tales."

He kisses my cheek and then the light shifts and he's gone. Poof.

"Maggie," someone says behind me. It's Thomas. "Ready to rock and roll?" he asks.

"Yes," I say, then look back down the street. People are coming and going along the sidewalk, rushing, bustling through the evening. But there is no Goodie, full- or pint-sized—at least not that I can see.

"Goodbye, Goodie," I whisper. "Don't stay away too long."

Thomas and I go into the club and begin our preshow preparations. Billy the lighting guy comes in carrying flowers.

"These are for you," he says, handing them to me. "Someone delivered them this afternoon. They were downstairs."

"Thanks." I open the card. *Sorry I can't be there. I have to work. Break a leg—Spider. P.S. Call me tomorrow.* I can't believe he came by and brought me flowers. It was some kind of miracle meeting Spider in the park the night of the attack. Maybe miracles happen all the time and the trick is to recognize them. I will call Spider tomorrow. I *will* call him and tell him I've had one more day without a drink.

It turns out Sidney wasn't exaggerating about a full house. It's packed. He has really hooked into the hotel trade. They bring in extra chairs. As promised, Charles and Chad are sitting in the front, and Patty and Jim are to the left of them. Bob Strong is in the back, leaning against the service bar. Thomas starts the introduction to the first song. The audience quiets down. My hands are shaking, but it's more from excitement than fear. At least that's what I tell myself. Then the lights come up on me in my blue sequined dress and I sing and sing and sing. Thomas is great. We find a groove by the third song. The audience is great too. Everything is absolutely great.

For the next to last song of the set we do one we worked on yesterday, "River of Dreams." For Jack. Thomas plays the introduction, and as I start to sing I notice a man standing at the back of the room. The lights from the bar highlight the side of his face. I recognize him as much by his stillness as by his face. It's John Eremus. I miss my entrance to the song. I look at Thomas. He plays through the introduction again. I come in this time and sing it from my heart. By the end, half the audience is crying. Charles is weeping like a baby and reaches out for Chad's hand. Patty dabs at her eyes with a tissue, then hands it to Jim. Thomas begins the last song. It's up-tempo. The Bee Gees "Stayin' Alive." It's an arrangement Goodie loved and I have a flashy tambourine solo in it. Some of the audience sings along for the last chorus. Thomas and I bow and leave the stage. I'm shaking all over. I did it. We did it. I hug Thomas.

"Thanks. You were great."

"You too," he says.

Charles and Chad find me and gush and gush. And Patty and Jim gush and gush. Friends are so nice to performers, especially when the performer is also in mourning. I decline their invitations to go out. I'm too spent. And besides, according to Goodie, I'm pregnant. Oh my God. What if it's true?

"Well," Patty says. "We'll be at the Westside Diner if you change your mind. I'm starving and I love their tuna melts."

"Thanks, I'll see."

"Fantastic," a voice booms. "You sound fantastic." It's Bob Strong. He gives me a big bear hug. "Oops, careful," he says. I hear a muffled bark from the bag Bob has slung over his shoulder. "I snuck Piper in for the show." A little head pops out of the bag and licks my face. "Piper loves live music," Bob says, cooing to the dog. "Don't you. And he thought you were terrific."

"Well, thanks, Piper," I say, scratching his head. "I know poodles have very discriminating taste."

"Absolutely," Bob booms. "We've got to run. We're seeing another show downtown. You were swell, Maggie. Really swell."

"Thanks, Bob . . . and Piper." Bob zips Piper back in the bag and off they go.

I go to the dressing room to change. I pack up my things and on my way out stick my head in Sidney's office.

"Great show, this was a great warm-up for the twenty-fifth and twenty-sixth," he says. "Call me on Monday. I want to talk about a regular night for you if you're interested." He hands me an envelope with my pay.

"Thanks, Sidney," I say.

I go back in the room to thank Billy. He is resetting the lights and the sound guy is checking the microphones. The next show is at ten o'clock.

"See you soon, Billy," I say.

"You too. Great show," he calls from his ladder in the middle of the room.

"Thanks."

I walk out through the bar, which is now mobbed with the usual Friday night crowd. I push through the throng and make my way to the exit.

"Maggie," I hear someone say. I turn around. It's John Eremus. That blush starts up my neck again.

"Hello." I smile at him and he smiles back.

"You sounded great," he says.

"Thanks," I say. He is looking at me with that unsettling look again. John Eremus is a very attractive man, I realize. He is maybe fifty years old, close to my age actually. He's wearing a gray sports jacket and white shirt with an open collar. His greenish brown eyes are deep pools of warm water I could easily step into and that is what is so unsettling. "Can I buy you dinner?" he asks.

"Sure. I guess," I say.

"All right."

"Yeah, that would be nice." We walk out into the warm evening. "There's a nice place on Forty-eighth Street. It's Italian, excellent pesto," I suggest.

"Sounds good," John says.

We get to the restaurant and are shown to a table in the back. It's an old favorite of mine, nice place, not too noisy, not too crowded.

I order the pesto rigatoni and John gets the linguini with clam sauce and a beer. I stick with Diet Coke.

"How are you doing?" I ask.

"All right," he says. "It's tough. I talked to the doctor who treated Jack in the emergency room. He said probably nothing could have saved him. He was dead in less than two minutes. He could have been in the hospital and they still couldn't have saved him. It was a massive hemorrhage. Congenital. A time bomb."

"Did they say what caused it at that particular moment?"

"Not really. They say it could have happened at any moment. At a certain point, when the artery walls are that compromised, it can be the next cup of coffee or the next belly laugh or the next intake of breath. It's a crapshoot, Maggie."

"It's amazing anyone makes it out alive," I say.

"No one makes it out alive, Maggie, that's the point," John says.

"Oh, right." I blush slightly and take a big sip of the Diet Coke the waiter has placed in front of me. I wish it were something with a stronger bite.

"Have you always sung?" John changes the subject.

"Yes, I guess. My mother had a lovely voice and I would sing with her when I was small," I say, remembering my mother sitting on my bed singing "Twinkle, Twinkle, Little Star" with me. "Then, when I was about ten years old this acting company came to our church and performed a musical version of *St. Joan of Arc*. It was wonderful. And the two actresses stayed at our house that night. My mother let me stay up late and we all sat at the kitchen table. The actresses drank scotch and smoked cigarettes and talked in these wonderful throaty voices. They told stories and my parents laughed and I laughed and I knew right then that my dream was to be onstage and to sing."

"Here's to dreams," John says picking up his glass of beer.

"Here's to a whole river of them," I say picking up my Diet Coke, tears filling my eyes. And suddenly I remember the man in my recurring dream the last time I dreamed it, when Jack was sleeping beside me. It wasn't more than a couple of weeks ago. I was standing at the edge of the abyss and from nowhere came the man who reached out his hand. It was an older version of Jack. My God, I think, it was John Eremus. Every hair on my head begins to tingle. Oh, my God.

"What is it?" John asks.

"What is what?" I ask back.

"You look a little shaken," he says.

"I am shaken," I say. "These are shaky times."

"Yes." John drops his eyes. "Yes they are." He moves his food around on the plate for a minute. "The Yankees are really kicking ass this year." He launches into the safe world of sports talk.

"I know," I say. "Did you see the game last night?" And just like that we are in the lifeboat of small talk and managing our way safely through the meal.

John insists on driving me home. Before I get out of the car I say, "I sat across from you at the monastery, in the meditation hall. Did you know that?"

"You're kidding?" he says. "At the last retreat?"

"Yes."

"I didn't see you, but then I don't look around much during those things. I try to stay focused."

"It was my first time," I say. "All I did was look around."

"That's strange that we were there together," John says. "You know I got a call the last day about Jack."

"I figured that. I didn't find out until I got back to New York."

"Of course," he says, looking at me and then dropping his eyes to study his hands.

"Odd, isn't it?" I say in barely a whisper. "I couldn't believe it when I saw you at the funeral. I thought it was you, and then when I noticed your limp, I was sure."

"That's right," he says. "I wasn't wearing my leg at the mon-astery."

"Well, not while you were sitting zazen. You were so still, so serene."

"Oh, God," John says. "If I could go back to that week before this nightmare happened. If I could have been with Jack when it happened maybe I could have . . ."

"Saved him," I say. "I know. But you couldn't have." I put my arm around John and he moves into it.

"Spend the night with me," I say quietly into his ear. We park the car and go up to my apartment without a word. When we get inside I don't even turn on a light. I walk to the bedroom and turn down the sheets. We lie down together fully clothed and pass the night in each other's arms. And at some point we sleep.

The next morning I get up first. John is turned on his side. His artificial leg is leaning against the bed. He must have removed it during the night.

"Nifty isn't it?" John asks. He is leaning on his elbow watching my reaction.

"Yeah, looks like a pretty high-end model," I say. "Do you want coffee?"

"Please," he answers. "What's the eye patch?" he asks, nodding toward my glittered eye patch that's lying on the bed stand.

"Oh, that," I say. "I hurt my eye and had to wear it."

"I like the glitter," he says.

"Well, I was playing Snow White at the time."

"In a dark time the eye begins to see," he says, gazing out the window, and I can see his face has clouded over. A dark time indeed.

"It's a line from a poem. Theodore Roethke," he says, his voice a whisper. I walk over and sit next to him. We don't talk. We just gaze out the window onto the garden in the courtyard.

"I'll put the water on," I say and John nods.

I go the kitchen and to the bathroom. I splash water on my face and brush my teeth. By the time I come out, John is in the living room and has reattached his leg. I make the coffee while he uses the facilities. Mr. Ed looks at me with his cocked head.

"What in the world is going on?" he arfs.

"I don't know," I say in a hushed a tone. "Don't judge until you've walked in my paws."

John comes out of the bathroom and we drink our coffee.

"I have to get back to Queens. I'm having brunch with my sister's family. Would you want to join me?"

"No, but thanks," I say, feeling awkward.

"What do you say we go to a Yankees game sometime?" John asks.

"Sure," I say. "Maybe . . . I don't know. It feels so . . ."

"Look, Maggie," he says. "I know this is awkward."

"Let's not say anything right now, okay? Let's not talk about this for a while. I need to . . ." I don't finish the thought. I can't because I don't know what I need, or maybe I'm afraid of what I need.

"All right," John says. He puts on his jacket and moves to the door. "But I'm going to call you. And we are going to talk at some point."

"Okay. At some point."

"Goodbye, Maggie," John says and kisses me on the cheek.

"Goodbye," I say and put my arms around him and we hug for a long moment, and then part.

"I'll be seeing you," he says, going down the stairs and looking up at me.

"Not if I see you first," I say and smile, and John smiles back. Then I turn quickly and walk back into my apartment. Damn. I bite the inside of my cheek and close the door gently.

I drink another cup of coffee and look out my window. Old Mrs. Vianey is sitting on one of the benches, feeding the pigeons. I take Mr. Ed out to the park. We walk over to the Great Lawn and plant ourselves on a bench.

"Life is funny, isn't it Ed?" I say. "Life is damn funny." Mr. Ed curls into my lap, and I think about what Dorothy says at the end of *The Wizard of Oz* movie—something about backyards and finding your heart's desire.

"Anything is possible, Mr. Ed," I say, looking across the ball fields and down to the Central Park South skyline. "It's an awfully big backyard." Mr. Ed cocks his head and nods in doggie agreement and then smiles his Westie smile. I breathe in and out and think about nothing, nothing at all, except this moment right here, right now.

Acknowledgments

Heartfelt thanks to *The Wizards:* Judy Hansen, Chuck Adams, Bob Jones, Algonquin Books, Marly Rusoff & Associates, Inc. *The Scarecrows:* Bruce Ackland, Peter Cabot, Robert Cary, Chuck Young. *The Good Witches:* Kathleen Frazier, Patty Kraft, Nancy O'Hara, Clare Veniot, Holly Webber. *The Flying Monkeys:* Lesley Burby, Celeste Carlucci and Jeffrey Klitz (xox to Bella, Sophia, and Juliette), Beth Chiarelli, Carol Coates, Toby Cox, Terri Eoff, Julie Halston, Sharon Hershey, Nancy Johnston, Lianne Kressin, Jane Michener, Rob Newton, Brian O'Neill, John Rowell, Sandy Winner. *The People of Oz:* Kay Rockefeller and the Traveling Playhouse, Rumble in the Redroomers, Thursday Writer's Group, Boogieland and the Gang, Suter's Marching Band, the Ladies in Kids and all the folks at the Eighty-second Street Barnes & Noble. And to Douglas Anderson, *The King of the Forest,* may you rest in peace.